THE FINAL BATTLE

"So this is the end. One way or another." Julia's words fell like stones into still water, sending ripples of doom in ever-increasing circles.

Laurent broke the silence. "Then even if Ferragamo's plan *is* insane, it's the only one which has any change of stopping Ark from coming under Alzedo's domination."

"You don't know what you're saying," Cai said. "The Rite can destroy the entire world."

Servants of Ark

BOOK THREE

The
Mage-Born
Child

JONATHAN
WYLIE

BANTAM BOOKS
TORONTO • NEW YORK • LONDON • SYDNEY • AUCKLAND

THE MAGE-BORN CHILD
A Bantam Spectra Book / July 1988

ISBN 0-553-27270-5

Bantam Books are published by Bantam Books, a division of Bantam Doubleday Dell Publishing Group, Inc. Its trademark, consisting of the words "Bantam Books" and the portrayal of a rooster, is Registered in U.S. Patent and Trademark Office and in other countries. Marca Registrada, Bantam Books, 666 Fifth Avenue, New York, New York 10103

PRINTED IN THE UNITED STATES OF AMERICA

O   0 9 8 7 6 5 4 3 2 1

For
Teri, Ross, Lyn, Ross,
Iris, Ted, Gail, and Miles
for their love and encouragement.
And especially for
Yvette, Rebecca, Luke, and Gemma,
for reasons which will become obvious.

The
Mage-Born
Child

Prologue

*T*he stones were silent, watching. At the center of their ancient circle stood a man— or what had once been a man.

He too was quiet, but invisible currents of arcane power swirled about him, making his silver and black cape billow and snap about massive shoulders. Huge fists were clenched at his sides; arm muscles twitched and knotted.

The man stood still, his feet planted firmly upon the ground which seemed almost to shiver beneath his weight. He faced eastward, colorless eyes intent upon some faraway target. The malice shining from those eyes was reflected in the expression on his gnarled and ugly face. Hate and pain were mixed with suppressed fury, giving the impression that, despite his silence, he was screaming with a rage that if released would raze great cities to the ground, sweep mountains aside, destroy whole islands.

His thoughts were plain in the whole aspect of his being and the stones about him shuddered at their impact.

So close! How can you have failed me now? Do you forget who I am? How I fathered you? Created you? Do not withdraw! Come back! I can destroy you, my pretties, remember that. Do not withdraw! No! No . . .

Very well. You choose to leave me alone. That is not wise. Already I feel you tremble. You are right to do so. I will not

forget such treachery. Yet perhaps you are not wholly to blame,
my daughters. These intruders . . .

Far to the east the gloomy sky began to grow bright. The
watcher's colorless eyes narrowed suspiciously, then shut re-
flexively as a blazing light leapt into view. Clear, golden ra-
diance flooded the night, revealing the gray mass of fog which
blanketed the whole vista, and which seemed to cover the
whole world except the mountaintop ringed by standing stones.

In the stones' midst the man now fell to his knees, his arms
thrust up as if to protect his eyes from the splendor that rose
ever higher in the sky. His whole attitude spoke of defeat. His
cape hung limply about his bent form.

He was still there several hours later when light came again
to the east, this time in more conventional manner. The sun
rose to disperse the last faint vestiges of the malevolent vapor.
The sea glittered serenely, leagues below the mountaintop.
Still the man did not move, and now a second creature appeared within the stone circle. The hideous bird moved awkwardly, as if existence alone caused it pain. Its shape suggested
an eagle—the cruel, curved beak, powerful wings and razor
talons—but it was deformed, enormous, twisted subtly so
that it could not possibly be mistaken for a natural bird. Neck
and head were bare of feathers and its eyes were the color
of blood. Fear shone nakedly from those crimson orbs as it
shuffled tentatively toward the man and timidly pecked at his
unmoving cape.

At first there was no reaction, and the bird fidgeted nervously. Then, slowly, Alzedo rose. He towered above the bird,
even though it would have stood shoulder to shoulder with a
normal man. Red eyes looked upward and the sorcerer stared
back at his familiar.

So you do not desert me, Sivadla. But then you wouldn't,
would you? I am such a kind and tolerant master. Do not flinch
from me, you sniveling creature! Look about you. Do you not
see the blackness, the decay, the stench of my island? Is it not
beautiful, my lovely one? Brogar is mine, to do with as I will.
Everything on it answers to my whim, Sivadla—including
you. Remember that. It should have been so on all the islands,
but for . . .

So close! My victory was only moments away!

Yet it is only a temporary setback. I must curb my impa-
tience. I see now that it was a mistake to move upon all the
islands at once. Do not look so shocked. Even the greatest of

all wizards may learn from his mistakes. Now I will move more slowly, but even more surely. My daughters proved too weak in the final conflict but they may still serve a purpose. I will help them complete their tasks one by one. That is simple enough. All the other islands have already been weakened. Except . . .

Ha! Soon Ark will cower as you are doing now, my splendid bird. That accursed island will feel the full weight of my wrath. For too long now it has been the rock on which my ambitions have foundered. They will be rejoicing even now in the foolish belief that I have been vanquished.

Do you hear me, Ferragamo? Your pretty tricks will not save you, they have merely delayed your fate. How can you call yourself a wizard? I have seen your fatal weakness—you will suffer endless torments for opposing me. You and your pathetic Servants! The next time I face you, you will grovel at my feet and beg for mercy. It will be doubly sweet to refuse.

You see, Sivadla, how a night of reflection has restored my spirits? Do not worry. Look! I am smiling. I taste my revenge already.

Part 1

Yve

Chapter 1

Lugg was the southernmost of the eleven major islands that made up the known world. Beyond them, as far as anyone knew, was only the boundless ocean.

Even though Yve did not relish the prospect of her trip, she nonetheless felt considerable relief when the *Alesia* finally set sail and left the shelter of Carrhaven harbor. It was hot, even for late summer, but at least there was a cooling breeze on the open sea, and the noisome odors of the docks were replaced by a keen salt tang. Yve remained on deck, staying in the prow in order to keep out of the way of the crew.

The *Alesia* was not the sleekest of vessels, but the sea was calm and she moved smoothly enough. At first they traveled westward, tacking in wide sweeps in the face of the prevailing winds. This kept Bram and his crew fully occupied—as they coaxed every advantage from sail and rigging—and left Yve in peace to contemplate and strengthen her resolve for the task that lay ahead. She was glad of the respite. The sailors showed scant respect for her position, and she felt that on this voyage she was somehow on trial. She knew they would soon turn southward to sail along Lugg's western coast and thence southeast toward their destination. That would leave the crew with greater leisure to discuss their passenger and she would have to face their scepticism once again.

Yve had long since grown accustomed to the fact that, as

the only female wizard in memory, she was the subject of much comment—most of it derogatory. It was only the undeniable fact that she *did* have considerable magical talent that kept the remarks from becoming downright insulting. Men and women alike considered her to be an anomaly and this attitude of suspicion was reinforced by the fact that she had still to find her first familiar. Most apprentice wizards had succeeded in doing so well before they reached Yve's age of some twenty-eight summers. The linking of minds between wizard and animal had long been synonymous with magical stature, and indeed, some said that Yve had no right to call herself a wizard while she was so obviously lacking.

This criticism hurt Yve far more than any jibes about her sex, and she resented it to such an extent that the search for a familiar had become the central core of her being. Until she could experience that unique and silent communion, so familiar to her in theory, yet so frustratingly remote in practice, she would feel incomplete. What was more, she could never face her detractors with the confidence that she knew her talent deserved. After all, if Drogo, the incredibly ancient wizard who was her master, accepted her ability, then there was no reason why others should not do so.

If only it could be that simple, Yve thought as she watched the sparkling bow wave of the *Alesia*.

She longed for the day when her familiar would present itself, and speculated on which creature it might be. A cat perhaps? Or a falcon? Even a dolphin or something more exotic? Drogo's current companion was, of all things, a hedgehog —a fact which secretly amused many. Yve knew that her master was completely indifferent to what people thought of him, and he regarded the hedgehog with great affection. Yve was aware that each wizard's relationship with his familiar was like that. She had seen the master wizard's reaction to the death, some years ago, of his last familiar. The eagle had grown immensely old for one of his kind and his end had not been unexpected, but Drogo had still been deeply affected. He had hidden his feelings from those about him but even in her younger days Yve had been able to gauge the old man's mood. When the hedgehog had appeared, the pompous and crotchety old wizard had recovered, and welcomed his new familiar gladly, despite its comic appearance and sleepy disposition.

Drogo had had many familiars, for he was centuries old, and although the animals' lives were extended well beyond their natural span, they could not match the longevity of a wizard, especially one as skilled and powerful as Drogo.

Will I ever grow to be that old? Yve wondered. *It seems inconceivable.*

She laughed aloud at the unintentional double meaning of her thoughts, and was reminded of the price that wizards paid for the extension of their lives. None of them was capable of begetting a child. That was something else that set Yve apart and which she occasionally regretted. However, being united with her familiar—she knew it existed, it was just a matter of finding it—would more than make up for this privation.

In any case, she thought bitterly, *children are not always welcome.*

Her mind went back to her own infancy, to her earliest memories and the information gleaned from those about her.

Yve had been abandoned as a tiny baby on the steps of Drogo's huge house, which stood beside the royal palace in the center of Carrhaven town. She had been warmly wrapped against the midwinter cold, but there had been no note or identification with her.

Such happenings, though no longer common, were not unknown on Lugg. Impoverished or reluctant mothers would sometimes abandon their offspring thus in the hope that the rich or noble families to whom they were bequeathed would care for the child. Yve could not know what had caused her own parents' decision, but the memory of their desertion still rankled.

On its discovery, the baby had been taken in by servants, still swaddled, and shown to Drogo, who at first glanced at the child with indifference. After a few moments' consideration, however, he had shown signs of unexpected interest. The wizard had taken the infant into his arms, and stared deeply into her eyes, while the servants waited patiently, knowing better than to question Drogo's actions. Eventually the wizard had returned her to his minions with the instruction that the child was to be brought up as one of his household.

"He has potential," mused Drogo. "Considerable. Look after him, and when he is capable of holding a sensible conversation, bring him to me. Until then, I don't want to see or hear anything of him. Is that clear?"

While surprised by these instructions, Drogo's staff had had the good sense not to show it, and when "he" was later discovered to be a girl, none of the maids to whom she was

entrusted dared face their master with the news. The fact that
the wizard had tested the baby by a strange method and found
her to have potential—of some kind—was enough for them.
Soon, all Drogo's household, except for its head, knew that
the foundling was female but Drogo was never informed of
the fact.

Some four years later, when the wizard's chief steward felt
that Yve—as the maids had named her—was ready to be presented to the master-wizard, there had been some speculation
as to what the old man's reaction would be. In the event Drogo
disappointed them by evincing no surprise whatsoever. Nobody knew whether he had merely forgotten the arrival of the
supposedly male baby or whether he chose to ignore Yve's
femininity in order to concentrate on what were to him more
important matters. Possibly he had guessed Yve's gender from
the start but had chosen not to reveal it for his own reasons.

That meeting was to be Yve's earliest memory. Before that
she had only vague impressions of warmth, noise, and bustle—
and the comforting presence of Hannah, her nursemaid and
adoptive mother. The steward entered Drogo's study, then
beckoned for Hannah and her charge to follow. They did so,
hand in hand. Yve was nervous. She had absorbed much of
the gossip about the wizard from her companions but had never
seen him clearly before—let alone spoken to him.

She faced him as bravely as she could, drawing strength
from Hannah's reassuring grip. What the young girl saw was
at odds with much of what she had heard of the master. Surely
this stooped old man—dressed in rags, his skin brown and
wizened, his head almost bald—surely he could not be the
wizard of whom everyone spoke in terms of awe? It was only
when Yve looked into his bright, almost colorless eyes and
found herself held by his penetrating gaze that she began to
understand. Her little heart thumping, she remembered her
manners and, at Hannah's prompting, curtseyed awkwardly.

"This is Yve, sir," said Hannah, her maternal instincts making her sound bolder than usual.

Drogo did not take his eyes from the girl's face.

"Come, child," he said. "Leave us," he added, waving an
imperious hand at his steward and Hannah. They had no choice
but to leave promptly, though Hannah cast several backward
glances. Drogo ignored their exit and beckoned Yve to approach his chair, admiring the manner in which she moved,
and the way her straight blonde hair bounced as she walked.

Despite his preoccupation with matters of the mind, Drogo was not wholly insensitive to grace and beauty.

"Hello, Yve."

"Hello," she whispered, remembering at the last moment to add, "sir." She tried to avert her eyes, but found herself unable to do so.

"Tell me," Drogo went on. "Would you like to be a wizard?"

Yve found herself quite unable to reply but the surprise and sudden hope in her face made the wizard smile, and the wrinkles in his face became even more pronounced than usual.

Many years had passed since that first encounter, and in that time Yve had spent countless hours in the wizard's study, and eventually accepted as commonplace the strange and wonderful things that filled its nooks and crannies. She met and became friends with the eagle, Drogo's familiar, and sensed the special nature of the bird's mind beneath his fierce exterior. She saw how the wizard affected the appearance of feebleness —the bent back, the walking stick, the grumbles and peevish complaints—but learnt to look beneath the facade to the inner strength that he only displayed openly in moments of high emotion or magical need. And, most important, she began to take the first tentative steps to realizing the magical potential of her own mind and of the world about her.

Her only regret about this process was that, inevitably, it distanced her from Hannah and her other childhood companions, as their experiences and perceptions of the world diverged. As she grew older, Yve began to realize that she was even more unusual than she had at first thought. She had searched through Drogo's library for reference to earlier female wizards, but found only one. What she read of *her* made Yve wish fervently that she had remained ignorant, and she tried very hard to forget her ancient predecessor.

As far as everyone about her was concerned, Yve was the first woman ever to aspire to wizardry, and she was treated by many with the ridicule traditionally reserved for genuine pioneers. To others she was an object of fear or contempt, and as a consequence, she grew up with many conflicting emotions battling for supremacy within her. She alternately cursed and cherished her talent and growing abilities and spent many hours sobbing out her troubles to Hannah who was sympathetic but could not really understand many of Yve's feelings and motivations. The process was thus frustrating for both of them. Drogo alone remained supremely indifferent to the fact that

Yve was both female and an apprentice wizard and for that Yve was more than willing to put up with the old man's eccentricities and imperious manner.

If only I could find my familiar, Yve thought now, for perhaps the millionth time. *Then perhaps it would be different.*

Drogo had been quite unworried by her lack of success in finding a familiar. When questioned, he had always replied that there was plenty of time. He had told her that one could not force such a union, it would only occur when destiny decreed, and then it would be a completely natural process, far easier than learning to talk. She would just have to be patient.

Easier said than done, she thought, recalling her master's words. *I'll wager he didn't have to wait this long!*

A shout from the stern of the ship brought Yve back to the present. Looking round, she saw a sailor talking earnestly to Bram and pointing to starboard. She looked to where he indicated but could at first see nothing amid the glare of the afternoon sun. Then, as she gazed westward, she found the source of the excitement.

Still distant, but moving toward them quickly, was a small waterspout, or sea-sprite as they were commonly called. The tiny whirlwind wavered and danced, flinging a twisted column of water into the air, creating about it a miniature rain shower. Yve had heard tales of sea-sprites—which only appeared in the southern oceans—of how they followed vessels, seemingly out of playfulness, sometimes making a ship's progress impossible. Yet she knew that they were only really dangerous if they got too close to a small boat, and, never having seen one before, Yve found the sight quite beautiful. The sea-sprite sparkled and shifted like a dream image.

She was surprised when the sailor who had first noticed the spout came the length of the ship and asked her to go to the captain. The request was couched in respectful enough terms but Yve heard the subtle stresses beneath his words. Wizards were generally welcome passengers aboard any vessel because they were usually able to control wind and waves to a certain extent—or, at the very least, diminish their potentially harmful effects. Yet the *Alesia* was surely not in any danger from the sea-sprite. Bram was certainly capable of navigating his vessel in order to avoid the whirlwind's path.

So why the summons? Yve wondered, her stomach suddenly queasy for reasons far removed from seasickness.

"What can I do for you, captain?"

Silently Bram pointed westward, but Yve kept her eyes on the seaman's face.

"The sea-sprite?" she queried.

"It's following us," Bram replied baldly.

That shook Yve a little, and she glanced quickly out to sea. Her surprise must have shown, for Bram smiled slightly, a hint of cruelty in his eyes.

"It would have been well astern by now," the captain went on, "if it were steering a normal course. It's tracking us. At this rate it'll intercept us before long."

Now Yve understood. She *was* on trial. Bram and his crew knew that this was her first off-island trip on her own and the sea-sprite had given them the ideal opportunity to test her wizardly mettle. Whether Bram's statement that the sprite was following them stemmed from superstition or malicious intent was irrelevant now. She decided to give them all something to think about.

Mustering all the authority she could, Yve said, "Furl the sails, captain, and bring your ship to as near a complete halt as possible." She had deliberately spoken loud enough so that several crew members would have heard her. To a man, these sailors now looked at their captain.

Bram hesitated, realizing that he had fallen into a trap of his own making. If he refused to concede his authority and sailed on, Yve would either prove him wrong when the sea-sprite passed harmlessly by, or would be able to claim that any other result came about because he had disobeyed her instructions. On the other hand, if he complied he would be taking a course of action that his seaman's instincts told him was foolish in the extreme. To deliberately becalm the *Alesia* and lose all way would mean relinquishing control over the ship—the only state in which the sprite could constitute a genuine danger.

Yve waited silently, watching the passage of these thoughts across Bram's face. She could not help but take a certain malicious pleasure from his predicament. At first he tried to hedge.

"If we lose all speed we'll be a long time making it up again," he said gruffly.

"That's your job, captain. You *are* a sailor, aren't you?" Yve retorted, not bothering to hide the sarcasm in her voice.

"I'll not be able to get us out of the way if I've no steerage."

"If the sprite's following us you couldn't anyway," Yve replied calmly. "And *if* it is, I want to face it head on."

She waited, hoping she hadn't needled him too much. She also wondered what she would do if the sea-sprite *did not* pass harmlessly by, as she was sure it would. Those not directly acquainted with magic had no idea how much power it took to affect the physical world—especially something so elemental and energetic as the waterspout. Yve was not clear about it herself, never having attempted to control anything so powerful. She hoped fervently that she would not get the opportunity to fill this gap in her knowledge.

Bram looked westward. The sprite was much closer now. He came to an abrupt decision.

"All right," he said. "I just hope you know what you're doing." He turned from Yve and began to shout his orders. Whatever the crew thought of the advisability of this course of action, it did not affect their movements. Sails were brought down smoothly and reverse oars applied until the *Alesia* sat without control in the gentle swell.

All eyes turned toward the wavering column of water. Yve ignored the bustle about her and kept her gaze fixed on the sprite, at the same time trying to judge the direction and strength of the wind and current so that she could predict its movement. What she discovered was reassuring. If it behaved normally the sprite would continue traveling southeast and pass well in front of the now-stationary vessel.

It seemed at first as if that would be the case, but a few moments later Yve noticed a change in the whirlwind. It was slowing in its course. Turning toward them!

She sensed rather than heard the sudden whispering among the sailors and their nervous movements. Yve gulped, and her heart began to pound.

Don't panic! she ordered herself. *Think! It's just a freak gust of wind.*

"*Charming,*" she heard someone whisper close by.

Yve knew that in an encounter such as this the first thing to do was learn all you could about the enemy. She forced herself to study the patterns of the whirlwind, now frighteningly close. She traced the underlying movements beneath the glittering swirl, tried to find the crucial points at which she could attack. *There . . . and there!* she decided, picturing the sprite falling in upon itself, collapsing impotently into the sea.

All too soon it was time to act. The sprite was only fifty paces away and appeared much larger now. The sailors muttered, and were obviously close to taking matters into their own hands. Yve took a deep breath to steady her nerves and gathered all her inner resources. She was just about to strike, willing to commit every last part of her painstakingly acquired magical power, when—of its own accord—the sea-sprite collapsed. Within moments, all that remained was a shimmering mass of raindrops, which held a miniature rainbow for a fleeting moment before it too fell back into the sea. The only effect upon the *Alesia* and her crew was a slight dampening of decks and clothing.

A stunned silence was broken only by the restless sounds of the sea.

Eventually, one old salt growled, "Well done, lass."

That opened the floodgates and soon everyone was talking, whistling, and cheering. Only Yve could not find her voice. She was torn between accepting the credit for saving the ship, and thus making her life easier, and admitting that she did not understand what had happened. Her confusion showed on her face, and Bram eyed her with a mixture of curiosity and new-found admiration.

"I congratulate you," he said, his voice less formal than his words. "That is a pretty skill."

I didn't do anything!

No, but you thought about it, replied a small unbidden voice at the back of her mind.

Maybe that was enough, Yve concluded.

"Thank you, Bram," she said at last, managing a weak smile. "You were right about it following us. I've never seen anything like it."

"There's strange things at sea . . . Yve," replied the captain.

You can say that again, thought Yve, still too astonished at recent events to notice Bram's use of her name.

"Yes," she said softly.

"There's strange things at sea."

"What?" Yve asked, unsure if she had heard the weak voice correctly.

Bram looked at her curiously but didn't speak. Yve shook her head as if to clear it, feeling odd, somehow detached from the world about her.

"You should rest," Bram stated, showing an understanding that surprised Yve. "You'd best go below, out of the sun. I'll get us underway again."

"Of course," Yve replied weakly, and allowed herself to be escorted to her cabin, where she fell asleep almost immediately.

She awoke two hours later, refreshed but still confused. Further analysis brought no greater understanding and threatened to produce a headache, so she turned her thoughts to more practical matters. In two days' time they would reach their destination, Haele, a tiny island only a few leagues across, which supported a small fishing community. Yve had never been there before but had heard stories of the place which were not encouraging. "As stupid as a Haeleman" was a common expression on Lugg, and the islanders had a reputation for being fiercely independent and difficult to deal with.

The *Alesia*'s present voyage was a courtesy visit, long neglected. As wizard of Lugg, Drogo also held theoretical jurisdiction over several small outlying isles, of which Haele was the most remote. It was an accepted practice that the wizard would visit each of these islands every few years, and tend to their various needs with skills that only magical talent could bring. Yve had accompanied Drogo on several such trips but this was the first time she had been entrusted with an outing on her own. She was not sure whether this had been prompted by Haele's reputation, or the decades-long gap since Drogo's last visit and the consequent uncertainty of her reception. It could also have been Drogo's increasing dislike of travel, or even a genuine desire on his part to allow Yve to spread her wings. Whatever the reason, she was on her own.

In theory, her duties should be simple enough—part diplomatic, part practical. As well as the formal functions and renewing of old ties which her visit represented, Yve would also be called upon to advise the island's leaders on any matter they wished to put before her. She would also be expected to use her healing skills and pass on as much knowledge in that field as possible. This was the one part of her mission about which Yve felt confident; healing was the most natural and rewarding branch of wizardry for her.

Now she began to find the small cabin stuffy and oppressive, and made her way to the ladder that led up to the deck. As she emerged from the hatch she noted the keen breeze and billowing sails that confirmed that the *Alesia* was once more making good time. A group of sailors stood beside the man at the wheel, Bram in their midst. Their conversation stopped as she came into view and they all turned to watch her progress.

Their expressions were markedly different from those she had grown used to.

From nowhere, another sailor appeared to help her up the last few steps on to the gently swaying deck. Yve smiled at the man gratefully and he grinned back.

"Thank you."

"We owe you more than a little courtesy, miss," he replied.

Yve was unable to speak. Feeling a fraud, she averted her eyes, but was unwilling to deny the good fortune which had so enhanced her status. As was obviously expected, she walked aft to join Bram and his men.

"You're rested, I hope," the captain said as she drew near.

"Yes. Thank you." She glanced at the sailors.

Bram cleared his throat.

"Wizard Yve . . ." he began. Yve's heart leapt. Such a sign of acceptance was very precious. "We owe you an apology."

She tried to speak, to brush aside his words, but Bram was clearly determined to have his say.

"I acted foolishly this afternoon and it is thanks to you that I am here to admit it. We've not . . . always given you the credit your skills deserve. We're sorry for that and you'll find us different from now on."

There was a chorus of agreement and Yve felt a lump rise in her throat. She had wanted this so much for so long and now it came as the result of a lucky accident! Or had it? She was almost beginning to believe she *had*, in some unfathomable way, been responsible for their rescue. One thing was certain: there was no way she would now admit her noninvolvement and lose the respect she had so unexpectedly gained.

"Your words mean a lot to me, captain," she admitted. "I only hope I can prove even more worthy of your regard in the future."

"How did you know what to do?" asked one of the others.

"That would be rather difficult to explain."

"Have you ever seen a sea-sprite before?" queried another.

"No," she replied, smiling. "They're rather beautiful, aren't they? At a distance!"

The sailors laughed, then looked at each other awkwardly. Clearly there were more questions they would like to ask but none was confident enough to broach them.

"*Why do you keep hiding?*"

"What?" Yve responded, puzzled. "I'm not hiding."

Silence descended upon the group. Yve looked at each man

in turn, but every face held the same blank look of incomprehension. Her head felt odd again, as if the sounds of the sea and wind were inside it rather than outside.

"I'm sorry," she said slowly. "A lot has happened. I need to be alone for a while."

"Of course," said Bram.

Yve walked carefully to her accustomed position in the prow and sat down. Several pairs of eyes watched her progress.

What is happening to me?

Resting her chin on her forearms Yve stared out to sea. The sun had begun to sink toward the western horizon and the slanting rays flashed and flickered on the waves. After a while Yve found herself hypnotized by the sparkling, ever-changing pattern of the spray. She even began to believe that she could see images within the rainbow hues; strange, disturbing images which were at the same time oddly familiar. Yet each lasted only an instant. However hard she strained her eyes, the evanescent images remained beyond her grasp. Until . . .

Yve found herself staring into a pair of glittering eyes. They sparkled and shimmered, seeming to waver in the flickering light—but they were very *real*.

For a few moments she stared into their hypnotic depths, holding her breath, her heart seeming to stop beating. Then Yve forced herself to shut her own eyes, and concentrated very hard on taking one breath after another, fighting down the nausea that threatened to overwhelm her. When she found the courage to look again, the disembodied eyes were gone. Yve was shaken.

You have been out in the sun too much, she told herself.

Though the unnatural eyes had faded from her sight, they refused to fade from her mind.

Chapter 2

*Y*ve slept badly that night, partly because of her earlier unscheduled slumber, and partly because her mind refused to rest. When she did eventually doze fitfully, her sleep was disturbed by peculiar dreams. Beautiful mermen with luminous, glittering eyes asked her meaningless questions and then flowed away like water before she could answer. Unknown voices faded in and out of her hearing. She saw stars overhead despite the solid wood above her bed, and the dark, gently swaying cabin became the lair of every fearful product of her overexcited imagination.

Several times during the night Yve asked herself, *Am I awake or is this part of the dream?* And each time she could not answer with any certainty.

It was a relief when the light filtering through the cracks about her door told her that she *was* awake, that the sun had risen, and that she could rise with it. Dressing quickly Yve made her way up on deck, finding Bram himself at the wheel. She watched for a moment, feeling a new friendliness toward him. The captain, though shorter than Yve, was stocky and well muscled. His physical presence was undeniable—one of the reasons why he made such a good commander. His ship now ran swiftly before a cool wind, heading toward the pale, newly risen sun.

Yve felt her spirits leap. The fresh air, the lovely morning, and the ship's eager movement all combined to blow the cobwebs from her brain, and cleared away the lurid images of her dreams. The sea was vast. No land was in sight in any direction. For a moment Yve felt the freedom of the ocean, knew why a dolphin leaps into the air. She drew a deep breath and savored it like wine.

"You're up bright and early," Bram remarked, watching her through lids half-closed against the sunlight.

"It's a splendid day," she replied, moving to his side.

"Don't get cold," he advised, glancing at her thin clothing. "This wind will have a nip in it for a while yet."

"I'm not cold."

After a moment's thought the captain said, "No. Of course not." Yve turned to look at him but he stared fixedly ahead.

"It's difficult sometimes to think of you as a wizard and not as a woman," Bram said at last.

Yve surprised him—and herself—by laughing. *Sometimes?* Aloud she said, "I'm *both*, captain."

"Yes," he replied, his weatherbeaten face showing as much embarrassment as it ever would. "I know that. But I forget that you can keep yourself warm—whatever you're dressed in."

"Even if I'm naked," she agreed, enjoying his discomfiture.

Startled, Bram glanced toward her but laughed on seeing her mischievous grin.

"No doubt," he conceded. "But I don't think it would be a good idea for you to demonstrate your ability on board."

"I can take care of myself!"

"I know *that*! It's my men I'm worried about!"

They laughed together and Yve felt an easing of her spirit that she had not known for years.

The rest of the day passed uneventfully. No more sea-sprites or impossible eyes made their appearance and Yve found herself at leisure. She spent much of the time talking to the crew, who now all seemed eager to follow their captain's lead in making her acquaintance. By evening she had learned a lot about seamanship and about Haele, and almost convinced herself that she *had* been the *Alesia's* savior the day before. The sailors seemed so keen to credit her with the deed and to ask how it was done—a question she grew adept at evading—that it was easy to step into the role.

Only one aspect of her day left Yve less than content. It was clear, from anecdotes that the men told about Haele and its inhabitants, that the crew were prejudiced in no small

measure against the southerners. True, much of it was couched
in the form of jests, but their underlying feeling was clear. Yve
did not look forward to spending even a few days acting as go-
between to the sailors and the islanders. The problem loomed
a little larger when, at dusk, Bram said, "We're making good
time. If this breeze keeps up, we'll be there early tomorrow
morning."

Later that night, soon after she had settled into bed and
extinguished her lamp, Yve began to feel strange. A rushing,
crackling noise invaded her head; plugging her ears diminished
it not at all. In fact, that action only made matters worse, for
then she was cut off from the reassuring sounds of the ship
and its crew. She tried to relax, to think about nothing, but
did not succeed. Her mind went round in circles, and the noise
in her head threatened to drive her crazy.

She was afraid of the prospect of unpleasant dreams, and
so forced herself to stay awake. She stared into the darkness
until tiny flashes of light appeared in front of her eyes. She
watched them in desperation, until fatigue won its inevitable
victory and her lids drooped.

From far away Yve heard laughter; strange, childish laughter that faded and rippled. *No more mermen,* she pleaded
silently. Then the hairs on the back of her neck began to rise.
Her eyes snapped open and she sat up abruptly, suddenly very
afraid.

In the gloom within her cabin *something* was moving.

As Yve sat petrified, faint words drifted unbidden through
her mind.

Pardon . . . afraid . . . strange here . . .

"Stop it!" Yve screamed and frantically scrabbled to relight
her lamp.

Something moved beside the cabin door. She turned to
face it—and found herself looking into the same glittering eyes
that had so disturbed her the previous day. Unable to turn
away, she met their gaze, while her heart thumped, adding
its frenzied rhythm to the rushing in her ears.

"Who . . . are . . . you?" she whispered hoarsely.

There was no reply.

"Who are you?" she yelled, fear making her words shrill.

Still there was no reply. The iridescent eyes blinked slowly.
Yve screamed.

Her cabin door was flung open, crashing with shocking

suddenness into the bulkhead. Bram stood in the entrance, lamp in one hand, dagger in the other. His face was a mixture of anger and fear.

Yve blinked rapidly in the flood of light as the captain's eyes swept round the cabin. Even before he spoke Yve knew that her room was empty. Bram sheathed his dagger and hung his lamp on a hook, then knelt beside her bed.

"Are you all right?" he asked softly. "I thought . . . I heard . . ." His voice trailed off. Yve stared at the place where she had last seen the fantastic eyes.

"I am sorry to intrude," Bram tried again nervously. "I heard you scream, and thought perhaps one of the men . . ."

Yve turned slowly to look at the sailor's worried face. His evident concern brought her back to earth, and she shut her eyes, feeling utterly weary.

"No, no," she muttered. "It was a nightmare. I'm sorry."

Yve felt strong hands take her gently by the shoulders. Her head felt *so* heavy; it seemed only natural to rest it on a man's chest, his heartbeat reassuringly steady. Safe within her savior's arms, she slept.

Chapter 3

Υ ve awoke the next morning alone, with no memory of dreams, and did not know how long she had rested in the captain's embrace. Her door had been tied open; daylight filtered in from above and after a few moments she heard sounds of movement in the corridor. Bram appeared in the doorway, the uncertainty in his face bringing back the events of the night with a rush. Yve found it difficult not to let the discomfort she felt show in her expression.

"Good morning. No more nightmares?"

Yve managed to smile, and shook her head.

"Better get up soon," the captain went on. "Haele's in sight. I'll shut your door now." His smile mirrored her own.

"Thank you," Yve said, unaccountably embarrassed. Alone again, she sat for a few moments trying to gather her wits. *Am I going mad?* she wondered briefly, then shook her head and dismissed the question. She rose and began to dress.

From a distance Haele appeared to be a floating mass of foliage, its greenness startling to those used to the golden-brown color of Lugg's autumnal landscape. Yve did not know what peculiarity of soil or climate had produced the lush growth, but realized instinctively that the island was as unusual as its people. Haele's striking aspect was emphasized by the bare rock of a mountain which towered above the forest to the southeast, the far side of the isle. The mountain was conical in shape and appeared flat-topped. It was in fact an extinct volcano and, far from being flat, its highest part formed the rim of a crater almost half a league across.

The only major settlement on Haele, known simply as the Town, was set beside a sheltered bay in the northwest corner of the isle. Two wooden jetties stretched out into the sea but the water was too shallow for the *Alesia* to navigate safely. Bram planned to anchor in the middle of the bay and ferry people from there.

As the *Alesia* approached the island, the captain called Yve to his side.

"I'll go ashore first," he said, "then send the boat back for you."

"I'd rather go ashore straight away," Yve replied firmly, preferring to face her new charges with no delay.

"The old man—Drogo, I mean—liked to keep them waiting," Bram said, his face serious. "To make sure there was a good crowd."

Yve suppressed a grin. *Just like him!* she thought. Aloud she said, "I haven't got time for that nonsense. I'll meet whoever's there."

"As you wish," Bram replied, his voice without inflection. "Will they be expecting us?"

"If they have eyes." Bram gestured toward the pennants that fluttered from the *Alesia*'s mast-head. Underneath the blue and yellow colors of Lugg, the red and gold insignia of Drogo flew proudly in the early morning breeze.

Yve nodded. "I'll go on the first boat," she said.

There was quite a crowd waiting at the jetties by the time the *Alesia* was securely anchored, and Yve watched them apprehensively, noting that the main group by the water's edge consisted entirely of men. The women held back, clustered in the doorways of the nearest drab wooden houses. Children and dogs ran about; Yve heard their excited voices clearly over the calm water of the bay. The men merely stood and stared.

Bram's crew lowered the skiff and handed down oars to the sailors within. When all was ready the captain nodded to Yve, who resolutely clambered down the rope ladder, cursing the awkwardness of her wizard's cape.

Drogo would have made quite a performance of this, she mused as she was handed into the skiff.

"You climb better than your master," one of the oarsmen remarked, echoing her thoughts.

"I *am* just a bit younger," she replied, smiling.

Bram and two of his crew joined Yve and the oarsmen. Jarlath and Krow were the burliest of the sailors and both bore the marks of past encounters. They were not men to pick an argument with, and Yve wondered whether they had been chosen deliberately.

Sitting beside Bram in the bow, she whispered, "Are you expecting trouble?" and nodded to the big men in the stern.

The captain feigned surprise, then grinned.

"Those two are merely for decoration," he said quietly. "Your page boys."

Yve laughed, and Krow turned to look at her curiously. She saw that, though his face was scarred, his expression was tranquil and somehow reassuring.

When they reached the larger of the two jetties, Jarlath climbed out quickly and secured the mooring ropes. With the skiff held steady, Yve was helped onto the jetty. Bram and Krow joined her, then, at the captain's signal, the oarsmen set off back to the *Alesia*.

While this was happening none of the islanders had moved to help, but stood silently on the land beyond the end of the jetty. In the background a child began to cry and was quickly hushed. At the end of the pier the men seemed to have closed ranks, presenting a solid mass.

"Who's in charge?" Yve whispered to Bram.

"Just look for the biggest man," he replied. "Their elective processes aren't very subtle."

"Right. Let's go."

As boldly as she was able, Yve strode toward the land. Bram followed at her shoulder, and the two "page boys" flanked them both. The boards creaked beneath their feet. As she walked toward the reception committee Yve studied the faces before her, and her heart sank. Their features were narrow, with small, close-set eyes. For a moment they seemed to merge into one, then she came closer, and noted several small deformities—a harelip, bent limbs, a sloping forehead.

Stars! Yve thought. *Their reputation is well deserved.* And then, *What are their children like?* She shuddered involuntarily.

One of the men stepped forward. True to Bram's prediction he was the largest of them. Despite his curving spine, which made him look as if he were leaning forward permanently, his

tiny eyes and massive shoulders made Yve think of a bull. She
and her companions halted. A few moments passed in silence
before the islander spoke.

"I am Damek. Head islander." His voice was loud and
harsh.

"I . . ." Yve began, but Damek interrupted.

"Where is wizard?" he demanded, jabbing a finger toward
the anchored ship.

You're not going to like this, Yve thought.

"I am the wizard," she said in a voice loud enough to carry
to all the onlookers. Though she was aware of several amazed
whispers, Yve kept her attention focused on the head-man.
Damek regarded her contemptuously, disbelief written plain
on his face.

"This is no time for jest," he said angrily. He now pointed
at Bram. "You! Where is wizard?"

"Before you," the captain replied. "As she said."

"Don't you listen?" Krow asked, his deep, slow voice heavy
with menace. Bram gestured to him for silence.

"I am Wizard Yve. I bring the greetings of Drogo and
my home-isle to Damek and his people. Grant us the peace
of your island and we will repay you with the skills at our
command."

Yve's formal speech clearly left Damek at a loss. He turned
his head and spat into the dust, then returned his gaze to
Yve. He was silent for so long that the other islanders started
muttering.

"Why not a proper wizard?" he said at last. "Old man?"

Yve was stung by the words and by Damek's tone of insulted
pride. She had at last begun to command respect from the
sailors; now she would have to prove herself all over again.
She knew that she was dangerously close to losing her temper
and was grateful when Bram spoke.

"Wizard Yve is Wizard Drogo's foremost colleague," he
said calmly. "During our voyage here she saved my ship from
a malevolent sea-sprite. Your welcome of her does your island
little credit."

More muttering greeted this statement. The reference to
the sea-sprite had clearly had an effect on the islanders. Though
Yve was too preoccupied at the time, she would later remember the captain's words and treasure them—even if they were
a slight embellishment of the truth.

The head-man spoke again. "You are a woman!" he said to

Yve, as if he had just made an earth-shattering discovery.

"As you see," replied Yve, smiling. Behind her Krow grunted scornfully. "*And* a wizard," she added firmly.

Abruptly Damek came to a decision. His face broke into a wide grin and he stepped forward, his right hand outstretched. Surprised, Yve responded happily and found her slender hand enfolded in the head-man's calloused fingers. Too late she saw the malicious glint in his porcine eyes, his innate certainty of superiority over any mere woman. She winced as he began to crush her hand, felt her joints protest at the unnatural pressures.

Then instinct—and something more—took over. The anger that had built up in her over all the years of being regarded as a freak, as something *wrong*, rose to the surface. Resentment at not being judged on her own merits flamed within her.

Calmly, and in spite of the pain, she took just a fraction of the power she had been prepared to loose upon the sea-sprite and channeled it into her hand. Never before had she used her magical talents to harm another human being. The idea was anathema to her. Yet now, coming so soon after the sailors had provided her with a measure of respect, Damek's ignorant attitude was too much to bear.

The bull-like man found the situation reversed. His hand was entwined in Yve's slim fingers, which seemed so delicate yet which now held him within a grip of steel. His grin became an agonized rictus and the gloating in his eyes turned to pleading as Yve tightened her hold, smiling sweetly as she did so. Beads of sweat stood out on Damek's forehead.

Those about them, aware of the tension of the central encounter, did not move, and Yve was able to pitch her voice so that no one but Damek could hear her.

"Damek, you should know that it does not pay to underestimate a wizard, whatever his—or her—outward appearance."

The head-man nodded eagerly, his eyes fixed on his tormented hand.

"If you wish to retain the use of your hand," Yve went on, "might I make a few suggestions?"

"Anything," Damek whispered hoarsely. After that, events moved rapidly. Guest quarters were found for Yve and the *Alesia*'s crew, and arrangements were made for the wizard to discharge her traditional duties: healing, providing advice and quasi-legal judgments, and exchanging island news.

It transpired that Damek, having conveniently found a

place in his philosophy to accommodate female wizards, had
particular reason to be glad of Yve's arrival. As she unpacked
her few belongings in the clean but austere room provided
for her, there was a timid knock at the door. At Yve's invitation
one of the island women entered. Yve judged her to be only
a few years older than herself, yet the woman's face and hands
showed signs of unremitting toil, and her clothes were drab
and faded. She had once been pretty, but the light in her
eyes had long since gone out. She stood silently, every line
of her body implying subservience, and Yve's heart went out
to her.

You don't deserve this, she thought. *It's easy to see what
life on Haele has done to you.*

"What's your name?"

The woman seemed surprised by the question. *Me?* her
eyes said. *I am of no account.*

"Ciana."

"What a lovely name! What can I do for you, Ciana?"

"Oh, it's n-not for me," she stammered, looking flustered.
"In the women's house . . ." She pointed briefly. "Please, I'll
show you."

Yve followed her into the street and along a twisting path
to a small windowless cabin set apart from the other buildings.
Damek stood alone outside the door. As they approached,
Ciana fell back, almost cowering behind Yve.

"You go," Damek commanded and Ciana turned to leave.

"No. Stay," Yve said firmly. "I may need your help."

"She cannot help," the head-man said. "She fails before.
Many times."

Ciana waited, uncertain.

"I'll be the judge of that," Yve said. "What have you brought
me here for?"

"My son," Damek said, indicating the cabin behind him.

"Is he sick?"

"Maybe. He will come soon. You make him all right." There
was a pleading note in his voice. "A man must have a son."

Yve began to understand. "In there?" Damek nodded.

"I'll do what I can. Ciana, come with me, please."

The woman, her eyes fixed warily on Damek, moved round
Yve and pushed open the cabin door. Yve followed her inside,
and was immediately assailed by the stench of blood and sweat
and pain. She fought down nausea as her eyes adjusted to the

dim lamplight. A young woman lay, moaning quietly, on a rumpled cot. She was heavily pregnant, very near to giving birth. It was clear that all was far from well with mother and child.

The pain and fear in the woman's eyes were palpable. Yve knelt quickly beside the bed and placed a hand on the perspiring forehead. She noted the woman's blue lips, swollen legs, and straining belly, and extended her wizardly awareness so that she could trace and, in part, share the woman's distress. Ciana appeared at Yve's side unasked, carrying water and cloths and began to bathe the patient. After a few moments she looked at Yve questioningly.

By then the wizard had realized that she could probably save the mother, but knew with dreadful certainty that the baby was already dead.

When Yve returned to her room that evening, she was exhausted. She had insisted that the young woman—little more than a girl, really—be moved to more comfortable surroundings. She was confident that the girl, Zana, would soon recover, with the help of Ciana and other women. She would never bear another child; perhaps that was a blessing in disguise.

The news of Yve's daylong struggle had evidently spread throughout the community, and she was the object of many curious glances on the way back to her room. Nobody had questioned her, discouraged perhaps by the expressions of her escorts, Bram and Jarlath. Damek had come to the guest house but Yve had not wanted to see him; she had sent him a message via Bram.

Alone in her room she threw herself onto the bed and slept.

She was awakened by a quiet knock on her door. It was dark outside and there were wet patches on her pillow.

"Come in," she called, sitting up and stretching.

Ciana entered with a steaming, aromatic drink. She gave the bowl to Yve, then lit the room's two lamps.

"It is for your strength," she told Yve timidly, sounding as though she expected her offering to be refused.

"Thank you. It smells wonderful." Yve sipped, and Ciana hovered over her. The hot liquid was sweet but not cloying, and was obviously infused with several herbs, some of which

Yve could not identify. She made a mental note to ask about them later.

"Just what I needed," she said, smiling up at Ciana. "Why don't you sit down?"

The island woman looked doubtful, but then smiled briefly and perched on the edge of a chair.

She looks ready to spring to attention, Yve thought, finishing her drink. Putting down the bowl, she said, "That was perfect—almost as good as moonberry wine!" Then her smile faded rapidly as she saw the expression on Ciana's face.

"But moonberries are poisonous!"

"No. They're just very powerful, and will only harm you if used carelessly. In small quantities, their magic is beneficial."

Ciana nodded meekly. "I forgot you are a wizard," she said.

"That has nothing to do with it," Yve replied. "Anyone can benefit. The berries were made specifically to protect people from any evil use of wizardry, and that wouldn't be much use if only wizards could eat them!"

"Do *you* eat them?" her companion whispered.

"A little. Everyone at court does. It's been a tradition since the War of the Wizards."

"But that was centuries ago." Ciana was awestruck.

Centuries in which we've lost so much knowledge, Yve thought, *that people think the world's greatest treasure is poisonous!*

The two women regarded each other in silence for a while. Then Ciana cleared her throat.

"Do . . . do you really think I have a lovely name?" she asked quietly, her eyes downcast.

"Yes. Don't you?" Yve replied.

"I'd never thought of it before."

There was another silence.

"I'd better go now," Ciana said eventually. "It's not long to the feast. You *will* come, won't you? It's in your honor."

"Of course. I'll be ready soon. But stay and talk to me for a while. Tell me about yourself."

"I'm Damek's first-woman," she replied after a moment, as if this were the be-all and end-all of her existence. She looked at Yve. "I've given him children," she added defensively.

"But no boys?" Yve asked quietly.

"Two—but they died."

"Girls?"

"Four. Zana is the eldest."

As the implication of Ciana's words sank in, Yve was re-volted.

"He did that . . . to his own daughter?"

Ciana would not look at her.

"Something will have to be done about that man," Yve went on, her voice ice-cold and furious. "And soon."

Chapter 4

*T*he feast that night was—with the exception of Yve—an all-male affair, a fact which irked but did not surprise the wizard. Long wooden tables had been set up in the open air, and were illuminated by lamps hung on the nearest houses, and by several cooking fires. Damek sat at the head of the central table with Yve and Bram, as guests of honor, on either side. He seemed to have dismissed the loss of his heir, and was now intent on impressing them with his hospitality. A bottle stood before him on the table and as soon as his chief guests were seated, Damek poured them a small glass each and one for himself.

"Yarglat," he explained. "Very special."

Bram sniffed the cloudy liquid, sipped it cautiously, then shot Yve a warning glance. She ignored him and, without a word, tossed back the entire contents of her glass. Damek grinned delightedly and copied her action. He poured again.

"Good, yes?"

Yve nodded and swallowed her yarglat once more. As Damek tipped his head back to follow suit, Yve winked at Bram, who promptly mouthed, "I hope you know what you're doing."

"Don't worry," came the silent reply.

As soon as all the men were seated, women appeared from the darkness bearing large wooden plates of fish, roast goat and fowl, vegetables and fruit. Bram switched to the unusual-tasting but relatively palatable ale which the other men were drinking, while Yve and Damek continued to exchange drafts of yarglat. The head-man was soon showing considerable signs of drunkenness; the wizard appeared as cool as ever. Eventually, the food was finished and the tables cleared by the same silent women, who paused only long enough to replenish supplies of drink before fading into the shadows again.

Damek made a short, slurred speech of welcome, then sat down abruptly and called for more yarglat. The noise level rose and singing began, developing into a reasonably friendly contest between the islanders and Bram's crew. Damek did not join in, preferring to concentrate his attention on Yve. His conversation was somewhat limited; Yve found him repetitious and crude but remained calm, apparently enjoying his company.

They were now well into their third bottle, but the wizard still showed no sign of losing her taste for the fiery spirit. Damek, on the other hand, was clearly intoxicated and bemused by Yve's sobriety. As a matter of honor, he continued to match her glass for glass, and their drinking contest became the subject of some comment from the other diners. When a fourth bottle was opened, the interest turned to outright encouragement, with each group urging on its own champion.

After a few more rounds, Damek rose to his feet and looked about him, desperation in his unfocused eyes. Shouts and eager faces greeted him as he picked up his refilled glass. However, before it reached his lips, he fell, crashing over backward and taking his chair with him. The head-man lay as if poleaxed, his eyes glassy and his face shining with a pallid, unhealthy sheen.

Yve stood slowly, and drained her glass with a flourish. As cheers resounded, she picked up the half-empty bottle and flung it into the air. In a dramatic—and quite unnecessary—gesture she stabbed out a finger. The bottle exploded in midair, the liquor inside igniting into a brilliant orange flare which illuminated the astonished, upturned faces of the whole company. After a moment's stunned silence, there was an enormous roar of approval from Haelemen and sailors alike. Yve sat down again, suddenly feeling quite exhausted.

That event marked the end of the festivities and the men drifted away, some of them clumsily carrying their inert leader. Soon only Yve and Bram were left in the starlight and silence.

"Are you all right?" the captain asked.

"Yes. Just tired."

"How . . . ? That stuff is lethal."

"Compared to healing others, making a few changes to my own metabolism is quite simple," Yve replied. "I've been drinking coconut juice all evening."

Bram laughed. "Remind me never to challenge a wizard to a drinking contest," he said. "You were very impressive. And the finale was quite spectacular!"

Yve looked sheepish. "That was stupid of me, a waste of energy."

"It didn't do your reputation any harm."

"It was just sheer frustration. That man's stupidity, the dreadful situation here. What am I supposed to do with this awful island?"

"Don't take the weight of the world upon your shoulders," Bram replied gravely. "You won't change them overnight."

"They've been too long alone. After all these years, I doubt if they'd *ever* listen," Yve said bitterly. "But there's so much that's wrong here. They're so ignorant they can't see the harm done by the inbreeding, and the women are no better than slaves!"

"My men could inject a bit of new blood," Bram put in. "It was a joke!" he added hurriedly, seeing Yve's expression.

Yve smiled wearily. "I'm sorry. *You* don't deserve my anger . . . and it's not such a bad idea!"

"Damek and his lot wouldn't think so."

"Well, at least none of the women will be troubled by him tonight," Yve commented with grim satisfaction. "A small victory."

"He won't be troubling anyone for several nights at my guess," the sailor replied. "Which gives us time to think of a more permanent solution."

"Yes, but I don't see what we can do. Their way of thinking is so ingrained that it will be next to impossible to change it. They just aren't open to reason."

"Can't you *make* them see sense?"

Yve glanced up at Bram, shock registering in her eyes. "With magic?" she said, aghast, then realized that his question had been innocent. "You don't know much about wizardry, do you?"

"I'll not deny it."

"Interfering with another person's mind is the most heinous thing a wizard can do. It's unthinkable. There have been wars fought over it—literally. It almost happened again a few years ago." Yve shuddered, remembering some of the appalling things she had overheard at that time, while in the company of a strange little boy. *Luke will be almost a man by now*, she mused.

"I heard about it," said Bram.

"I went to Ark with Drogo afterward, to the wizard's conclave," Yve went on.

"That's all blown over now though, hasn't it?"

"I hope so."

They were both silent for a while, Yve recalling memories of the conclave. She had not thought about it for a long time and was now invaded by forgotten emotions. Pictures of the massive granite bastions of Greyrock Harbor and of the teeming city of Starhill came into her mind. She had warmed to her hosts on Ark, especially the two-year-old prince in whose company she had eavesdropped on the conclave. Yve had been convinced—and terrified—by the arguments put forward by Ferragamo, Ark's wizard, and appalled at the ferocity with which the others, including Drogo, had opposed him. She and her master had left the very next day. Drogo had been in a foul temper, not improved by their long journey home.

Looking back now it seemed that Drogo had been right. The intervening years had been peaceful enough and Yve, now a grown woman and long since past the apprentice stage, had problems of her own.

"So what do we do?" asked Bram at last. "It seems a pity that you can't use your magic. Surely this island's state demands drastic action. No one's going to start a war here."

"No." Yve was steadfast. "If I even *consider* it, *I* will be the cause of the war, not Haele. There must be other ways."

"We could kill Damek. That would be a start," Bram suggested. "He deserves it," he added defensively. "He's not even ashamed of what he did to Zana!"

"You have a direct approach to problems."

"I'm a simple sailor," Bram replied, grinning. "You can't wait for the *sea* to be reasonable."

"Perhaps not, but killing Damek wouldn't solve anything. He would just be replaced by some other brute. We need to change their whole attitude."

"A few more demonstrations like tonight and they'll listen to you soon enough."

"You think so? They'll forget all about it before long. Anyway, the whole thing was pointless. I let my emotions dictate my actions."

"Is that so bad?" Bram asked curiously.

Yve thought for a moment. "For a wizard—yes." She did not sound wholly convinced but Bram chose not to contest the point.

"Well, we won't set the world to rights by staying up all night," Bram said. "You need some rest."

They walked slowly to Yve's cabin.

"I can protect people, perhaps change things a little while I'm here," Yve said, "but we can't stay forever. And after we leave . . ." She shrugged. "Goodnight Bram."

"Goodnight. Yve, whether tonight achieved anything or not, it was a pleasure to watch you. Sleep well."

He turned and walked away. Yve watched him go, wondering why his words awoke in her an empty ache.

The next few days passed quickly as Yve found herself fully occupied with the duties of a visiting wizard. At times it seemed as though the entire population of Haele wanted to take advantage of her healing skills. She did her best, but had to disillusion some by declaring that their ailments, mostly long-term effects of the island's unhealthily limited population, were beyond her power to remedy. This was not strictly true but Yve knew that each such patient would use so much of her strength that she would soon become incapable of dealing with their many other problems. She was already in danger of exhausting herself.

The wizard also spent a good deal of time passing on information about plants and medicines, suggestions for improved diet and so on, which could be used effectively by those not gifted with magical talents. In turn, she was told about the herbs, spices, and fruit that grew only on Haele. She absorbed the new information gladly, knowing that such knowledge, however obscure, was never wasted.

Whenever she could, Yve extended the range of her teaching to include the basic necessities for healthy and safe childbearing and, more obliquely, spoke of her beliefs about the role of women within the island community. She talked to as many of the women as possible and to any men who would listen. All were quiet and attentive when she spoke and many of the women muttered and nodded in agreement, but Yve had no great faith in the permanence of her teachings. She could present all her arguments persuasively and receive no challenge, but as soon as she was out of earshot the old ideas and prejudices would reassert themselves. It was hopeless.

Bram was right, she thought dismally. *I'm expecting the sea to be reasonable.*

After a particularly frustrating morning, spent in her other official capacity as adjudicator of the island's petty but acrimonious personal disputes, Yve decided she had had enough. She walked to the temporary village of tents where the sailors spent most of their time, and found their captain.

"Keep an eye on things for me this afternoon please, Bram. I want to spend some time on my own."

"Good," he replied. "You've been working far too hard. These people don't deserve you."

"Don't judge them all by Damek's standards," Yve replied, surprising herself. "Most of them are as decent as you or I."

"That's as may be, but you still need a break. The lads tell me there's a fine beach on the western shore. It's not far. I'll get one of them to walk you there."

"Thanks for the offer but I'd rather find it by myself. It's a good day to swim and sit in the sun."

"I'll see you're not disturbed," Bram said. "Take care."

Now that the idea had taken hold, Yve's desire for peace and solitude grew rapidly, and she set off immediately, avoiding the town and following the shoreline. It was not long before the midday sun made her regret her hastiness. She had not eaten since early morning and carried no water. This, combined with the heat, made her feel quite light-headed.

You're a wizard, she told herself sternly. *Control yourself!* Perversely, she chose not to moderate her body temperature but waited until she reached the beach, by which time her head was buzzing. Throwing off her clothes she plunged into the sea, reveling in its cold shock, and in the surge and crash of the waves that had traveled vast distances to meet her.

Cooler, refreshed but still thirsty, she splashed out of the sea and walked along the beach, admiring the fine sand which varied in color from silver gray to black, a legacy of Haele's volcanic origin. The warm breeze dried her skin but failed to clear her head. Yve felt detached and remote from her own body, almost as if she were watching herself walk down the beach.

She suddenly felt that she *was* being watched and spun round, ready to unleash her anger on the man who would dare spy on her. There was nobody in sight. Yet the sensation persisted, so she returned to her clothes and donned her undertunic.

The noise in her head was still there and she decided that she must find something to quench her thirst. If necessary she could convert seawater into something drinkable but the thought of the effort involved made her reject the idea. She could not remember having seen any freshwater streams.

There must be something, she decided, forcing herself to think rationally. *Fruit?*

Yve immediately knew that there was a fully laden tree only a little further south, behind a big sand dune. She set off and found the tree without difficulty. The fruit were unlike any she had seen before, green and star-shaped. Their skins were smooth and waxy but the flesh inside was sharp and tangy, and deliciously full of juice.

Yve had disposed of two and was starting on a third when the noise in her head, far from abating, increased to a roar, and she began to feel dizzy. She sat down abruptly. *There's nothing wrong with this fruit,* she thought. *What's happening to me?*

After a while, the feeling passed and it was only then that it occurred to Yve to wonder *how* she had known where to find the fruit tree.

She got gingerly to her feet and walked slowly back to her clothes. For a moment she thought of returning to the town and her room, but that idea soon lost its appeal. Instead she stretched out in the sun, determined to relax.

Slowly, the noise of the surf, the sun's warm rays and her own stillness combined to ease her into a state of quiescence and she dozed. The day's heat was welcome now, and seemed to squeeze out the cares of the day. *Like a sponge.* Yve giggled.

A new sound entered her consciousness, something that, unlike the earlier noises, was entirely identifiable. Close by, someone—or something—was panting heavily.

Yve sat up quickly and looked round in fright, her heart thudding. There was nothing but sand for a hundred paces. She lay down again, cursing the tricks her mind was playing, but relaxation did not come so easily now.

Eventually, half-asleep, she found herself dreaming. She was flying, soaring through the air, then diving steeply from a great height toward the sea. With a huge splash she hit the water, went below, then swam back to the surface, feeling joyful and cool. *Nice!*

Yve woke, and immediately felt hot and sweaty. *That's a good idea,* she thought and set off toward the waves, only to stop abruptly. She stood quite still, hardly daring to breathe.

Before her, at the edge of the surf, was *something.* A shimmering pattern of lights, transparent yet very real. She had seen the eyes before, but never the whole shape. It was an outline she recognized but which her mind rejected automatically; a shape from ancient tales, myths, something to frighten children with. And yet it *was* before her now, of that she was convinced.

"Who are you?"

The reply came immediately, in a faint and distorted voice that she found vaguely familiar, and which sounded *inside* her head.

You may find it more agreeable to talk like this . . . while it's so hot. Aren't you going for a swim?

"Did *you* suggest that?" Yve asked, knowing the answer as she spoke.

You don't need to talk aloud.

"What? But . . ." Yve checked herself. *But you're not here!* she ventured.

Where am I then? Don't be so silly. You're *the one who keeps fading!*

Me? Yve paused as an idea, at once exciting and disturbing, occurred to her. *I thought only wizards and their familiars could talk this way.*

What's a familiar? asked the dragon.

Chapter 5

Yve was stunned. Her mind reeled, as part of her rejoiced in the experience of mind-talk, something she had dreamed of for so long. Even if it *was* with a semi-invisible dragon! She was also busily speculating on the nature of the vision before her. If it was magical, it was a form she had never encountered before. Yet it could not be a phantasm; by its own peculiar standards the image was far too stable. And yet another part of her brain was tracing the course of recent events in the light of her new knowledge. Further back there was a nagging voice in her head which could not be ignored: *There haven't been any dragons for thousands of years!*

She saw the mythical animal fidget and caught the look of discomfort in its shining eyes.

You're confusing me, it said plaintively. *Weren't you going to swim?*

I have to think, Yve replied.

But it's so hot.

The wizard smiled inwardly at the dragon's petulant tone and said, *All right, if it will make you happy. But don't go away, I'd like to talk to you.*

She walked carefully around the dragon, catching the flashes of blue-green light from the scales on its head and body. It turned to follow her progress and she could make out a few

details of its appearance. The dragon's pointed head was like
that of a giant lizard, with slanting nostrils and a long curved
mouth.

Dragon's teeth, thought Yve. *Harder than diamonds.*

In response the beast's jaws opened and the wizard saw
the shining rows.

This is ridiculous! I'm not even frightened.

Yve waded into the surf, then dived under and swam out
beyond the breakers. She floated for a while, eyes closed,
trying to compose herself, but her curiosity soon drove her
back to the beach.

The dragon had followed her a few paces into the sea.

Is that better? she asked.

The dragon nodded, a surprisingly human gesture for a
creature with webbed wings and a tapering tail perhaps six
paces in length. The wings, like those of a gigantic bat, were
now folded neatly at its sides. The dragon's knee joints all
pointed backward, giving the impression that it was always
ready to leap forward. Yve noted all this, aware at the same
time that she could see right through every part of the creature,
and that its taloned feet disturbed neither surf nor sand.

"Are you a dream?" she asked aloud.

I don't know. Would you like me to be?

Yve laughed. *Can we talk?*

Questions? the dragon asked suspiciously.

Why not? Yve replied, sitting down on the sand.

Couldn't we just play? I know some very good games.

Another idea formed in Yve's brain.

You're young, she said, making it a statement rather than
a question.

Yes, but I'm not a baby! the dragon replied vehemently,
its eyes glittering brightly.

What's your name? Yve asked.

You see! it replied. *You do think I'm a baby.*

Yve was nonplussed.

Just because I haven't got my teeth-name yet, the dragon
went on, furious, *you think I'm a baby. It's not fair.*

What name do you have? Yve asked gently.

My fire-name, of course.

Yve waited, but the dragon gave no sign of continuing.

Aren't you going to tell me what your fire-name is? she
asked eventually.

You haven't told me yours, it retorted.

I only have one name. It's Yve.

Only one name? For fire, teeth, and wing?

Yve nodded, wondering what she was talking about, then went on, *What's your fire-name?*

You won't laugh?

Of course not.

Just because a dragon has a . . . certain type of name it doesn't mean it isn't brave and fierce.

I'm sure you are brave and . . .

And fierce, the dragon put in.

And fierce, Yve continued. *And from the size of you, you certainly aren't a baby.*

I'll get much bigger than this, it said confidently. Then doubt returned to its voice. *I'll get my teeth-name soon.*

I'm sure you will. But until then, what shall I call you? It's very difficult talking to someone without a name.

The dragon shuffled a little closer, lowering its head as if peering at her. It blinked slowly.

Sweetness, said a tiny voice in Yve's mind.

Yve fought down the giggle that threatened to rise up inside her. Under the dragon's intense scrutiny she kept a straight face. *That's a fine name*, she commented, grateful for the composure that her training had given her.

Do you think so? the dragon asked hopefully. *Yve is nice too. Though it's a bit short*, it added thoughtfully.

Are we friends, Sweetness?

The dragon pondered for a moment. *I suppose so. Do you want to be?*

Yes.

Then we are.

Can I ask you some questions now?

I suppose so.

So many things crowded into Yve's mind then that she found it difficult to know where to begin. Sweetness obviously sensed her confusion but did not offer any suggestions. As they faced each other in silence Yve became aware that the rushing sound in her head was returning. She had not noticed it since the dragon first spoke to her. At the same time, the creature seemed to flicker and grow even less solid.

Don't go, Yve said quickly.

I'm not, came the faint reply. *You are. Sometimes I can't see you at all.*

This noise, she asked. *Do you hear it too?*
Yes. It's like the passage. But different.

Yve had no chance to ask about these mysterious words, because Sweetness's voice faded from her mind just as its image disappeared from her sight. The rushing noise was gone too.

Alone again, the wizard sat on the beach for some time, feeling an indefinable but very sharp sense of loss.

When Yve returned to the town several hours later, her head was still full of questions. An afternoon of thought had produced several possible theories but no answers. Feeling tired, but knowing that she would be unable to rest, Yve did not go to her cabin but headed for Bram's tent. The captain was not there but a sailor directed her to a rock spit to the north of the camp.

Bram sat looking out to sea, playing a small flutelike instrument. Yve listened for a few moments, feeling as if she were intruding on a very private world. Lovely, melancholy notes mingled with the sound of the waves as they surged and fell between the dark boulders.

Only a few days ago, Yve mused, *there was little except prejudice and mistrust between us. Now I seek him out as a friend! Besides, I've got to talk to someone!*

The music died away and, after a moment, Yve called out softly. Bram turned, startled, then smiled and beckoned for her to join him. She stepped carefully over the barnacle-encrusted rock and sat down.

"I didn't know you were a musician."

"It's not something I advertise," he replied, "but even a simple sailor can appreciate the finer things."

There was a slightly bitter note in his voice, and Yve wondered what secret ambitions the younger Bram might have harbored.

"The more I learn of you the less 'simple' you become," she said. "I'm glad . . ."

"That we understand each other better now?" Bram completed the sentence for her. "I'm glad too. You've already taught me a lot."

"And you me."

They looked at each other for a moment, their expressions serious. Then the seaman grinned and said, "I'm sure you didn't come out here just to indulge in this mutual admiration. Was there something . . . ?" He paused on seeing the faraway look that had come into the wizard's eyes.

"Bram . . . ?" Yve stopped, unsure of herself. "Was everything quiet this afternoon?" she asked eventually.

"That's not what you wanted to say."

"No, but . . ."

Bram waited.

"What would you say," Yve went on, her words coming out in a rush, "if I told you that I'd spent the afternoon talking silently to an invisible dragon called Sweetness. It met me on the beach." Then she giggled.

"You haven't been at the yarglat again, have you?" Bram asked, smiling.

"This isn't a joke, Bram!"

"I know," he said, his expression becoming serious again. "But you can't expect me to know what you're talking about just like that. You'd better explain."

It was nearly dark when they finished talking. Bram's calmness and patient questioning had helped ease the turmoil in Yve's mind. At least now she would know what to ask Sweetness when—if—he returned.

She found herself wishing desperately that the dragon would come back.

───────────────

Yve's wish was granted sooner than she expected, though in a manner hardly conducive to clear and informative conversation. After leaving Bram she went directly to her cabin and, after eating a little of the food that had been left for her, she went to bed. The night was quiet and she slept deeply until, at the darkest hour, a commotion arose outside her cabin.

As she struggled into wakefulness, screams and laughter sounded in her ears. With an urgent flicker of her mind she lit a lamp, then jumped out of bed and threw open the cabin door. Ciana lay on the floor immediately outside, her body curled up defensively and her arms protectively covering her head. There was no one else in sight.

Yve knelt and touched the woman's shoulder. Ciana flinched, then slowly uncurled as the wizard lifted her up. She was shaking when Yve led her inside and sat her on the bed.

"It's all right. You're safe now."

Slowly, Ciana's shivering subsided and her eyes lost the look of a cornered animal.

"You're safe now," Yve repeated. "What was it that frightened you so?"

"Wraith-lights," whispered Ciana. "From the sea."

"What?"

"They say . . . they come from sailors drowned at sea. They say . . ."

"Wait," Yve interrupted. "Tell me what happened, exactly what you saw."

Ciana paused, concentrating hard.

"I had a bad dream," she said eventually. "It woke me up. Then I was so hot that I went outside for a while. That's when I saw them."

"What did you see?"

"Lights. Blue and green. By the jetty."

"And that's what scared you?"

"No." Ciana swallowed and went on. "The lights moved. I could see they were coming here."

"To this cabin?"

"Yes. So I came to warn you, but then . . ." She shut her eyes and Yve held her hands, kneeling before her and murmuring words of reassurance.

"I ran but they ran faster. They went through the walls of Adara's cabin and out the other side. I could hear things, too."

"What things?"

"I . . . I can't remember. Then the lights were all around me, spinning round, so fast. When they stopped, I saw . . ." She swallowed. "That's all I remember."

A movement in the window behind Ciana caught Yve's attention. *I know what you saw*, the wizard thought, caught between laughter and fury.

Beyond the open window two glittering eyes blinked slowly.

"Ciana, do you trust me?"

The woman nodded slowly.

"I'm going to show you something. Please believe me, there's nothing to be afraid of."

Another nod.

May I come in? asked a now familiar voice.

Not yet. Wait there, Yve flashed back. Aloud she said, "Turn round and look out of the window."

Ciana obeyed. Her body stiffened as she did so and her grip on Yve's hand tightened. "The eyes," she whispered.

So I'm not the only one, Yve thought.

"Is it a wraith?" Ciana was trembling again.

"No," Yve replied calmly. "As a matter of fact I'm not sure *what* it is, but it *is* my friend. I can talk to it."

Ciana glanced back at the wizard, her eyes wide in astonishment, then stared again at the dragon.

Can I come in now?

There isn't room for you in here, Yve replied.

Part of me then?

What? Oh. All right, but slowly. I don't want you to scare this lady again.

"Are you talking to it?" Ciana asked softly.

"Yes. Don't be frightened. It won't hurt you."

A blue-green snout appeared in the window, then one taloned foot came *through* the wall. Yve's head filled with the sound of childish laughter and Ciana gave a little scream.

"That's the noise," she exclaimed. "That's what I heard!"

Sweetness advanced until his head and most of the front half of his body were inside. *It tickles*, he remarked, amid fits of giggling.

What does? Going through the wall?

Yes, the dragon replied, as it wriggled into a comfortable position on the floor.

Can you move through anything?

Only the things that aren't solid.

Yve let that pass for the moment. If she were to believe that her cabin was *not* solid, she would begin to doubt the existence of everything. By comparison, half-seen dragons were easy to deal with.

"What's happening?" whispered Ciana. Her whole body was rigid but she no longer trembled. "Are you still talking to it?"

"Yes. Can you hear us?"

"No, but . . . there's something . . . like a baby laughing . . ."

I'm not a baby!

Be quiet, Yve snapped mentally. "Ciana, you are a very special person. I'll talk to you about this later, but now I have to ask this creature some questions. Do you want to stay?"

Ciana nodded. "I'll be quiet," she said meekly.

"Thank you," Yve replied, smiling, and turned her attention back to Sweetness.

You certainly like making grand entrances, she remarked.

I have to be true to my nature, the dragon replied. *Brave and fierce.*

So you said. But try to stop giggling so much. It spoils the effect, Yve said, adding that it also scared Ciana.

Sweetness looked downcast.

And did you have to come in the middle of the night? I was asleep.

For a while there was no reply and Yve wondered whether the dragon was sulking.

I can't always choose when I come, it said at last in a subdued tone, then brightened and added, *You say strange things when your eyes are shut.*

Yve did not like the idea of her dreams being spied upon. *We won't go into that just now.*

Do you sleep every night?

Yes.

Why?

Because I get tired and irritable if I don't.

Sweetness ignored the warning tone of Yve's words and said smugly, *I never sleep but I never get tired.*

Yve composed herself. *I've been thinking about you a lot,* she began.

That's only natural, the dragon interrupted.

And there are some questions . . .

Sweetness looked glum.

You faded away last time, Yve went on, *before I could talk to you. Where did you go?*

Nowhere! You were the one that faded.

But we ended up apart.

Yes.

Our worlds are in the same place—but different?

Your world doesn't burn.

What?

I'll show you, Sweetness said. The dragon turned its head to one side, and brilliant orange flame flickered from its nostrils. Before Yve could react, this grew to a fierce stream of fire which enveloped a wooden chair. Ciana gasped and Yve was held spellbound. After a few moments the flames stopped abruptly. The chair—which should have been reduced to charred embers—was not even scorched.

You see?

Sweetness, would you please warn me before you do anything like that again?

All right, the dragon replied, its tone implying that it didn't know what it had done wrong.

Yve pressed on, anxious to confirm her theories before they parted company again. *When you're here, in my world I mean, you do see my world, don't you? You told me where the fruit was.*

Yes. I thought you were asking, it answered, adding, *I can see through some things, though.*

The ones that aren't solid?

Sweetness nodded.

You can hear us, too?

Yes.

Can you talk to anyone else as you can talk to me?

No.

Yve was aware that the dragon was becoming restless, bored with the conversation, but she persisted.

When we first met—on the beach—you wanted me to go for a swim. Why?

You were hot.

And that affected you?

Sweetness avoided her gaze, as if bashful—a quality noticeably lacking until now. The thoughts the dragon was projecting became muddled, and for a moment Yve thought that they were losing contact again. She fought to clear her mind and asked *What's the matter?*

The dragon's confusion subsided.

I feel . . . it said slowly, *your body . . . inside.*

Yve felt the color rise in her cheeks and hurriedly quelled it, wondering what on earth Ciana was making of their silent encounter.

Is nothing private? she wondered. *My thoughts, dreams, emotions? My body?* Her own confusion now began to affect Sweetness. The dragon blinked several times with uncharacteristic quickness and fidgeted nervously.

Let's start again, Yve suggested after a pause. *When you first found me on the ship, did you see the sea-sprite?*

I did that, Sweetness responded brightly.

What!

That happens when we fly over the sea. I don't know why. It was fun, wasn't it?

That's a matter of opinion. You could have wrecked the ship.

I stopped it in time, Sweetness replied, sounding hurt. *You wanted me to, so I did.*

So you can affect my world sometimes, Yve said thoughtfully, *even if it doesn't burn.*

The dragon was quiet, obviously considering this idea. *I suppose so*, it admitted at last.

What made you come to the ship? Were you looking for me?

I knew you were there. The dream winds showed me the way.

Yve's heart leapt. The dream winds were the mysterious force that familiars often quoted when asked how they found their wizards. Perhaps Sweetness really was her familiar.

But this is ridiculous, she thought. *How can it be? Sweetness is in another world!*

And then the dragon was gone. It did not fade slowly as had happened earlier, and there was no telltale buzzing in Yve's head. One moment Sweetness was looking at her, the next she was alone with Ciana. So abrupt was the end of their contact that there was no time for farewells, let alone any more questions.

Yve felt cheated. "It's not supposed to be like that," she whispered to the empty space below the window.

"What?" Ciana asked timidly.

The wizard had almost forgotten the woman's presence and turned sharply at her quiet word. Ciana looked scared, and Yve forced herself to appear reassuring. She smiled weakly and once more held the woman's hand.

"I'm sorry, Ciana. I didn't mean to frighten you."

"Where did it go?"

"To another world. It's only a visitor here."

"I don't understand."

"Neither do I," Yve replied softly.

They were silent for a few heartbeats, each lost in speculation.

"It was a dragon, wasn't it?" Ciana said. "Like in Adara's old stories?"

Yve nodded, noting that her companion's eyes were uncommonly bright.

"Did you see it clearly?"

"It . . . it sparkled. Especially the eyes, and the flames." Ciana glanced at the unscathed chair. Her words tumbled out eagerly, and she no longer seemed afraid. "But I could see what it looked like, even though I could see right through it too. Was it magic?"

Yve had never seen her so animated. The germ of an idea began to grow in the wizard's mind.

"Yes, it was magic," she answered slowly, adding silently, *Of a sort.* "And we were part of it."

"We?" Ciana whispered, her eyes growing wider still.

"Not everyone would have been able to see the dragon. You're exceptional, Ciana. Remember that."

The islander shook her head in disbelief, then stopped and said, "I heard something too. Strange noises."

"That was the dragon laughing," Yve replied, smiling at the effect of her words. Ciana was awestruck.

"I've heard a dragon laugh," she whispered.

The next few days passed slowly for Yve. She was in an agony of indecision. Sweetness did not reappear and, though she knew that the *Alesia*'s departure from Haele was now overdue, she was loath to go in case she lost the chance of seeing the dragon again. Yve had talked about her experiences to Bram, but even his calm reassurances left her anxious and unsatisfied. She constantly looked over her shoulder, thinking she had seen those longed-for glittering eyes. Soon, everybody on the island knew that the wizard was troubled, though only two of them knew why.

At Yve's request Ciana told no one of what she had seen. She would probably have remained silent in any case, for fear of ridicule, but the wizard's plans required that Sweetness remain a secret. All would come to naught, however, if the dragon did not reappear.

Yve continued to perform her wizardly duties but found it increasingly difficult to concentrate and spent more and more time alone. She returned to the beach several times but to no avail, and it was on one of these visits that she finally made up her mind to return to Lugg. She was beginning to doubt the dragon's existence—on this world or any other. And even if it *was* real, the idea that the dragon might be her long wished-for familiar now seemed laughable and absurd.

She had done all she could—little though it was—for the blighted community of Haele, and their continued presence on the island was beginning to cause trouble. Already there was considerable tension between the sailors and the men of Haele, though, thanks to Bram's good sense and the awe which

Yve inspired, there had been no actual fighting. The situation showed signs of worsening, however, especially as the *Alesia*'s crew represented quite a drain on Haele's food resources.

It's hopeless! It's all hopeless, Yve concluded bitterly. *Let's go home.*

She attempted in her final actions on Haele to perpetuate what little good she had achieved in her stay. She spoke to many of the island's population, and most of the women were reminded of earlier lessons. Ciana was dismayed at the wizard's impending departure but bravely tried to hide her feelings. The two women had become close in their short time together and Yve hoped fervently that her attempts at bolstering her friend's self-confidence would have a permanent effect. As the wizard's constant companion, Ciana had already received much attention previously denied to her, and Yve left no one in any doubt that she wanted Ciana's new role as the island's advisor on medical matters to continue after her departure. Whether her wish would be heeded for any appreciable length of time was another matter entirely. Damek and his ilk paid her lip-service, but she had little faith in the permanence of her influence.

If only . . . Yve thought for the hundredth time, then stopped in self-disgust. *You should have done more,* she berated herself. *Now all you can do is go home and hope!*

The *Alesia* sailed north-northeast. Bram intended to take the longer route back to Carrhaven. By rounding the east coast of Lugg, he would be able to take advantage of the prevailing winds for the long northward haul.

Though the crew were in buoyant mood, happy to be at sea again and looking forward to getting back to a civilized island, Yve was thoroughly depressed and spent much of her time in the bows watching the spray. Bram's concern for her was etched into his weatherbeaten face, but, like the rest of the crew, he soon learned to leave the wizard to her thoughts.

At dawn on the second day at sea, the captain was taking his customary watch at the wheel. The sky was clear, promising another hot day and a steady breeze allowed smooth progress for the ship. As always, Bram took pleasure in the way the *Alesia* handled and felt the familiar certainty that, whatever his adolescent dreams had been, he had chosen his profession well. For a few moments he was a man completely at peace with the world—and with himself.

His tranquillity was soon shattered by two events which occurred in quick succession. Firstly, Yve—dressed only in her nightgown—burst from the hatch onto the deck. She staggered as the ship yawed slightly, holding her hands to the sides of her head. Her eyes were wild.

"Where?" she cried. "The noise has come back!"

At that moment, another shout claimed his attention. Krow's sharp eyes had picked out something astern. Bram and Yve turned to follow the line of the sailor's pointing finger.

Far behind them but gaining fast was a sea-sprite.

"Oh no, not again," Bram groaned.

"It's Sweetness!" Yve exclaimed. "I knew it!" She ran to the stern rail, her face rapt.

Everyone on deck was watching the wizard and the sea-sprite, knowing that *something* was going to happen. The twisting column of water rushed upon them, but they were confident that Yve could protect them again.

Sure enough, when the sprite was about twenty paces from the ship, it suddenly collapsed into the sea in a sparkling blue-green haze of raindrops. The crew whistled and cheered but Yve took no notice. She remained at the rail, staring fixedly astern.

Hello, said a familiar, impudent voice in her head.

Where have you been? she pleaded.

Home, Sweetness replied happily. *Did you miss me?*

The dragon was gliding along in the *Alesia*'s wake, its wings spread wide and legs tucked into its body.

Yes, I missed you, Yve admitted, not caring that she might well be reinforcing the dragon's not inconsiderable vanity. *Why did you leave so suddenly?*

I was called, Sweetness replied in a bored tone. *Where are you going?*

Back to Lugg, my home.

You can't, the dragon stated. *It's not there any more.*

Don't be ridiculous, she exclaimed. *Of course it's there. Islands don't just disappear for no reason—like some things I could mention.*

You'll see, Sweetness replied, aggrieved.

Are you coming with us? Yve asked eagerly, but there was no reply. Although the dragon kept pace with the ship it did not speak again and Yve concluded resignedly that Sweetness was sulking. *At least it's here!* she reminded herself joyfully.

Yve told Bram of the new arrival. He regarded her quizzically but asked no questions. She tried to point the dragon out to him but the seaman could see only a vague pattern of light, with no discernible shape or form. The effort hurt his eyes after a while, and he gave up the attempt.

"Just don't let it bring up any more waterspouts," he said, smiling at the change in the wizard's spirits.

An hour later, Sweetness was still silent, but by then everybody aboard the *Alesia* had a more pressing concern. Ahead of them, growing rapidly as they sailed north, was what appeared to be a huge bank of thick fog. It made no sense—but it was there.

As they drew close, the fog took on an even more menacing aspect. It stretched as far as the horizon, to both east and west, apparently endless, and was incredibly dense. Within its depths, darker shapes moved ponderously, ominously. In addition, the gray wall radiated an intense cold, entirely at odds with the day's natural warmth.

The crew watched with dread in their hearts as Bram ordered them to turn the ship about and sail east.

"We can't go through that stuff," he said gravely. "We'll have to go round. Any ideas, Yve?"

Yve shook her head, feeling sick. She recalled Sweetness's horrible words. *It's not there any more.*

"Then we go round," Bram said.

It's no good. The dragon's voice sounded suddenly in Yve's head. *The fog goes all around the circle.*

But my home . . . ? she pleaded.

Lugg's gone, Sweetness replied.

Chapter 6

*T*he *Alesia* sailed eastward, unable to outrun the fog which also traveled with the prevailing winds. For a time the sailors took a little comfort in that it appeared to be edging northward, allowing the ship to get a little closer to their home-isle. However, it soon became clear that they would be many leagues off their original course before any real progress was made, and the conclusion was inescapable. Lugg was lost to them, hidden behind the impenetrable gray wall.

Yve glanced up at Sweetness, a blue-green flicker in the sky.

Can you see it? she asked, knowing in her heart what the answer would be.

Yes.

Is there anything on the other side?

No. The gray goes on forever. It's cold.

You feel the cold?

Yes.

Yve's sensation of dread intensified. She knew that the fog was a manifestation of something so evil, so vast and powerful that she could not even hope to oppose it. It would be like setting a sparrow to defeat an eagle. The sparrow's only hope was to remain as inconspicuous as possible and try to escape unnoticed. Yve's self-esteem was not helped at all by this realization, but she saw no point in being hopelessly unrealistic.

Their proximity to the fog made her feel sick and feverish, and she longed for the clean warmth of the previous day. When Sweetness complained, in a pitiful tone, that she was making *him* feel ill, Yve admitted defeat and went to Bram.

"We have to go back," she said. "We can't get to Lugg—there's nothing I can do."

The captain was obviously at a loss, and for the first time since Yve had met him, he looked bewildered. She found the sight horribly unsettling.

"I was coming to the same conclusion," he said at last. "We're not supplied for a journey to any of the northern isles."

"Even if we were," Yve replied, hating herself for bearing yet more bad news, "it wouldn't do any good. We're cut off from *all* the islands. They're inside the circle."

Bram stared at the gray wall, his face blank. He did not seem to have heard her strange words. His crew were quiet, subdued by the horror of something they could not hope to understand. Despite the sounds of wind and wave, the *Alesia* was eerily silent.

Into this deathly hush came a new sound; a grinding, elemental roar; the reverberating, deep-throated crash of a collision between two massive forces. As the last grumbling echoes eventually died away, the crew were absolutely still. Then they breathed again, exchanged glances, and muttered fearfully.

Icebergs, Sweetness said.

Bram came back to life. "We return to Haele, lads!" he yelled. "I know the ladies there will be glad to see you again." For the next few minutes the *Alesia's* captain was constantly on the move, always talking, going from man to man, shouting orders. The crew responded to his reassuring return to normality and before long their ship was heading south, every moment taking them further from the horror.

Their second arrival on Haele was received with predictably mixed feelings. Yve agreed to work again with the island's sick, to teach and advise anyone who requested it. To refuse such work would have been against her nature.

Bram and his crew, though, arranged to keep themselves to themselves, as far as was possible. Their tented village was re-erected, and each man took turns at fishing and foraging deep into the forest. They would be as small a burden as

possible to the islanders. No one knew how long their enforced
stay would be, and Bram was determined to do all he could
to avoid trouble. He made sure that practical matters took up
most of the sailors' time and energy, and encouraged the belief
that their encounter had been with nothing more than freak
weather conditions. It was a belief he did not share, but speculation would only make their situation worse—and the waiting
even harder.

The islanders received the news of the fog and their consequent isolation without curiosity or fear. They had little enough
contact with the other islands, and what went on outside Haele
was a matter of indifference to most. Ciana was the only exception. She had been delighted at Yve's unlooked-for return,
though she did not show this openly. She helped the wizard
back to her cabin, and only when they were alone did she
comment on Yve's solemn countenance and enquire into the
reason for the *Alesia*'s unexpected arrival. Yve's explanation
horrified her, but after a few moments she plucked up the
courage to ask something that was obviously very much on
her mind.

"The dragon," she asked timidly, "did it come back?"

Yve nodded and smiled, glad to be able to speak of something more cheerful. Ciana's eyes lit up.

"Is it here?" she whispered eagerly, glancing about her as
if she expected Sweetness to walk through the walls that very
instant.

"Somewhere close," Yve replied, and hoped she was right.
"It's been flying with us for two days. I don't think it will come
to the town—and I don't want it to scare anybody. But," she
went on, seeing Ciana's disappointment, "I'm sure you'll see
it again. If I know Sweetness, your problem may be keeping
the creature away!"

Yve rose early the next morning, wanting to go for a walk.
Ciana had evidently been waiting for her and joined the wizard
as she left the town. The two women strolled in companionable
silence along the path between the rocky shoreline and Haele's
only sizable area of farmable land.

When they were well out of sight of the town, they sat on
the rocks among the tide pools and watched the restless sea.
Ciana leaned over the nearest pool and studied her reflection

for a while, then looked back at Yve and said, "I wish my hair was lovely and straight like yours."

"But yours is no worse for being curly."

"It's so ugly!"

"Nonsense."

They both leaned forward to look into the sea water mirror.

"You're beautiful," Yve said firmly, then gasped as a third reflection appeared.

Yes, I am rather, Sweetness agreed.

Ciana screamed, and both women spun round. The dragon stood behind them, still leaning over and admiring its own image.

Greatly daring, Ciana reached out to touch the scaly hide but her fingers passed right through and she shuddered. Sweetness giggled.

That tickles, it said. *Stop it.*

She can't hear you, Yve replied, as the dragon backed away a little.

"*He's* the one that's beautiful," Ciana said breathlessly.

"Don't encourage him," Yve responded.

"It *is* a he?" Ciana asked. Yve thought about it for a moment, her own curiosity aroused. None of the old stories spoke of dragons as either male or female.

Ciana wants to know, she began, aware that Sweetness had probably followed their words, *whether you're a boy or a girl.*

I'm a dragon! came the affronted reply.

Yes, but are you a male or female dragon? Yve continued, rather enjoying herself. *Will you have babies?*

Babies? After several moments' confused thought, Sweetness replied, *I will not hatch eggs. That is soft work. I am brave and fierce.*

"It's a he," Yve said resignedly to Ciana. *Eggs!* she added to herself. *Of course.*

Will we stay here long? the dragon asked. *It is a small island.*

For as long as the fog lasts. We'll wait a few days and then try again. For all I know, it may have gone by now, she added.

Shall I find out? Sweetness asked.

What? How? Yve began, then stopped as the dragon disappeared. He returned in an instant, and carefully folded his wings.

The fog remains, he reported.

You've been *there?* she asked, astonished.

Of course.

But how did you get all that way—and back—so quickly?

All what way?

Yve gave up the attempt to understand and decided to accept Sweetness's word.

Will you check for me each day?

A pleasure, my lady, he replied formally, obviously pleased with himself.

Thank you, Yve said. *I see that someone is teaching you manners.*

You are *a lady, aren't you?* Sweetness asked anxiously.

Yve laughed, not knowing whether she was being teased or not.

Some people think so, she said.

Yve's early morning walks with Ciana became a daily ritual. Every day Sweetness greeted them, reported that the fog was still there, then demanded to know what they were going to do that day.

By a series of cautious experiments Yve established that nobody but Ciana—who was by now quite used to Sweetness's presence—could see the dragon clearly. Some people blinked and looked puzzled, others rubbed their eyes or shook their heads as if to clear them, but most were totally unaware of his existence. As a consequence, Yve began to allow him to accompany her even when others were about, though she still did not take him into the town.

This arrangement worked perfectly well until the occasion when the dragon's boundless curiosity got the better of him.

One morning Ciana roused Yve earlier than usual.

"Robyn's time has come," she said. "She's asking for you."

"Is she all right?" Yve asked as she hurriedly pulled on some clothes.

"I think so, but it's her first—and she's not strong."

They hurried to the pregnant islander's hut in the half-light that heralds dawn. As they arrived, a familiar shape materialized beside them.

It's still there, Sweetness reported. *Can we play?*

Not now. I have work to do, Yve replied.

Can I help?

No.

The aggrieved dragon silently watched the two women enter the hut, his expression baleful.

Robyn was a slender girl, whose thin limbs contrasted starkly with her swollen stomach. Her contractions were coming quickly now but the baby showed no signs of making an appearance. Robyn's forehead was slick with perspiration as Yve laid a gentle hand upon it.

After a few moments the wizard smiled and said, "It's healthy and whole, Robyn. Your baby will be here soon."

"But it hurts!" the girl replied through gritted teeth. "They didn't tell me how much it would hurt."

Yve knew how much pain was involved, for she was at that moment becoming part of the birth experience, working to shield the mother from the worst effects of the suffering which she herself now shared.

"I know," she said softly. *It's the closest I'll ever get.* "But it will be worth it. Be brave."

Two hours later, both wizard and patient were close to exhaustion but knew there could be no rest yet. It was a bond between them. At last Ciana reported, "It's coming!"

"One last effort," Yve said, talking as much to herself as to Robyn.

The baby's head was visible. *Not long now.*

Suddenly, Yve felt desperately sick. So abruptly did the nausea envelop her that her concentration lapsed and her protection of the mother faltered.

"It's stuck!" Robyn screamed, hysterical with fear and pain.

Yve's confusion mounted as she found the scene before her repulsive. She felt faint, and turned her head away. As she did so, she saw Sweetness.

The dragon was partly within the hut, staring with horrified fascination at the girl on the bed.

Get out! Yve ordered emphatically. "Get out!"

Robyn screamed, the dragon disappeared and Yve's composure returned as the last echoes of her shouted command died away. Before long, Ciana tenderly laid a tiny newborn girl in her mother's arms. The wizard, after assuring herself that Robyn would be well, despite her long effort and loss of blood, left the hut and returned to her own bed.

She awoke shortly before noon, still angry with Sweetness. His ill-timed entrance could easily have had disastrous consequences. Yve had not realized that the transference of physical and emotional reactions could work from the dragon to

herself, as well as the other way round. It made the link between them even stronger and if, as she surmised, Sweetness
was still somewhat immature, it was a little hard to blame him
for the blunder.

By the time they next met her anger had softened and the
dragon, who was nervous and contrite, got away with a lecture
and the stern instruction to stay away from Yve when she was
involved in medical work. He agreed readily, shuddering at
his stomach-turning memory of the human egg, which had
obviously broken too soon.

After that, the wizard saw little of Sweetness unless she
was alone. She began to go for long exploratory walks, and
he took great pleasure in showing off his superior knowledge
of the island. He had obviously filled his solitary hours by
visiting every part of Haele, and now recounted tales of his
exploits. Though obviously embroidered, they were nonetheless entertaining.

Yve began to appreciate Sweetness as a personality, as opposed to just thinking of him as a strange and fascinating phenomenon, and delighted in his eagerness to please, his boundless
energy and naive sense of humor. The dragon was still vain,
despite her attempts to tone down his self-congratulatory ex-
cesses, but he was undeniably enjoyable company. And that
was something Yve needed very much. For a time she could
forget that her world seemed to have ended.

For several days Yve's preoccupation with the fog and its im-
plications filled her mind. Eventually, however, the thought
that Haele might be her home for some time—possibly
forever—made her remember earlier plans. Sweetness now
seemed to be a permanent part of her world—in as much as
he was ever actually *in* it—and that provided another spur to
her thoughts. She began to test her theories, making a game
of it for the dragon, who enjoyed himself immensely.

This is great fun, he remarked after one successful exper-
iment. *I thought you didn't want me to do things like that.*

A note of doubt had crept into his voice but he was reassured when Yve laughed happily. *You were very good,* she
said, *but you must only do it when I tell you to. That's very
important, Sweetness,* she concluded seriously.

The dragon nodded solemnly and then, with a characteristically swift change of mood, remarked, *Did you know the volcano is starting to burn again? It's very pretty—all yellow smoke and little red spots.*

It doesn't sound very pretty to me, she replied, sure that this was one of his more colorful tales. *Besides, the volcano's been dormant for thousands of years.*

Well, it's waking up now, the dragon said. *Shall I show you?*

It would take me too long to climb all the way up there.

If you came into my world, he suggested hopefully, *I could carry you up there in no time.*

Yve shivered. She knew that even to attempt such a thing would be a big mistake.

I don't think I can, Sweetness, she responded carefully. *Though I would like to ride on your back. Flying must be wonderful.*

No one rides us any more, the dragon said in a voice filled with ancient sadness.

Yve looked at him in astonishment. His tone was so out of character and the implication of his words so amazing that she was intrigued.

Did men ride dragons in earlier times? she asked.

But Sweetness would say no more.

Chapter 7

*H*aele's oldest inhabitant was Adara, the island's storyteller. She was a wizened old crone with wispy gray hair and filmy eyes. She rarely ventured outside her hut, preferring to spend her time with three possessive cats, whose sleek coats indicated that they ate rather better than their tiny mistress.

"Women are only good for three things: cooking, bearing children, and telling stories," was a line of argument often heard on Haele. Adara cared little for the first, her needs being tended to by others, was long past the second, but was a true mistress of the third. All but the most belligerent men gathered to hear her tales when the mood was upon her. On these occasions, her voice gained a sonorous quality, and became incredibly versatile. She was able to speak in the tones of a tiny child or a heroic warrior, and could even mimic the calls of animal or bird with stunning accuracy. This talent, together with her great age, had granted her a kind of reverential treatment unique among the women of Haele.

She was the only woman who could speak her mind to Damek and not suffer for it. Yve had tried to involve her in the process of change that the wizard was working for, but Adara professed herself uninterested in the future—or the present—and indeed seemed to come truly alive only when telling stories of the past. In the course of their conversations, however, the wizard came to respect and like the cantankerous old lady. When she heard that Adara was to be telling tales one particular evening, Yve made sure she was there.

Sweetness begged to be allowed to attend, and his pleas were so piteous that Yve, against her better judgment, agreed —as long as he promised to remain in the background and stay as inconspicuous as possible. So anxious was the dragon to hear the stories that he agreed readily to Yve's conditions and, in the event, proved to be as good as his word. In fact, Sweetness was so well hidden that had she not been specifically looking for him, the wizard would not have seen him herself. The dragon lay *inside* a stack of logs which had been stockpiled for winter firewood. Only his head and forepaws protruded, and even these seemed more transparent than usual. As Yve approached Adara's hut Sweetness watched her progress and, when she noticed his position, gave her a long, slow wink. She smiled briefly, then looked away.

Ciana had been warned to expect the dragon's presence and when she eventually saw him, carefully looked in another direction. Nobody else paid the log-pile any attention.

The news of the event had obviously traveled fast, for when Adara emerged and took her seat on the porch, there was a large gathering of children and women seated on the ground and, a little further back in the shadows, several groups of men. As guest of honor, Yve was provided with a cushion, and sat just below the storyteller's chair.

The evening began, as the wizard had learnt was traditional, with Adara surveying the eager faces before her and asking what stories they wished to hear. At each suggestion, she slowly shook her head and gave the reason why that tale would not be heard.

"That is only for silly girls."

"That's for even sillier boys."

"I'm tired of that one. My tongue dries up at the thought of it."

"Am I to disgrace my ancestors by telling such a morbid tale before so lively an audience?"

"Our guest would not appreciate such a false and boastful account."

And so on, until the audience ran out of ideas and, the game complete, Adara began to relate exactly the story that she had chosen earlier. On this occasion it was a long, in-

volved tale about the lifelong search of a young man for the
cave where the sun slept at night. His journey took him
to strange lands, across vast oceans to places stranger than
the imagination could conceive. He braved whirlwinds, giant
whirlpools, volcanoes, and forest fires; fought with savage giants,
wild wolves, and evil brigands; and was helped—and sometimes hindered—by the girl he loved, "who popped up in
the most unexpected places," by assorted kings, queens, and
heroes—"none of whom could help him beyond passing on
quite useless advice"—and even by a dragon—"who was very
shortsighted and therefore not much of a fighter, but who knew
many interesting things."

Yve glanced quickly at Sweetness at this point, fearing the
worst, but he remained motionless, transfixed by the power
of the old woman's magical tongue. Reassured, the wizard
returned her attention to the storyteller and once again became
lost in the flow of words.

It was dark when the story ended. "The young man grew
very old before succeeding in his quest. And by the time he
found the cave he was so tired that he could go no further.
He lay down to sleep—at noon, while the sun was out—and
there he stayed. To this day he sleeps in that cave, which
no one else has ever found, and at night he flies among
the stars."

Like the rest of the silent, spellbound audience, Yve found
herself gazing up into the clear night sky, searching for the
man who flew so high. When she lowered her eyes again, Adara
was gone.

As the others quietly dispersed, Yve softly approached Adara's
door. She knocked and a hoarse voice bade her enter. The old
woman lay in her bed, her wrinkled face pale and drawn in
the lamplight. She looked exhausted and Yve felt a momentary
pang of guilt for disturbing her.

"Come in, girl. Don't stand there gawking," Adara rasped.

Yve sat on a chair at the old woman's bedside. As she did
so, Sweetness appeared through the cabin wall, his expression
still rapt and without his usual fit of giggling. Yve was about
to shoo him out, but he was quiet and Adara gave no sign of
having noticed him, so she let him stay.

"You have a wonderful gift," she said quietly. "I've never
heard anyone speak like that."

Adara shrugged. "Thank you. It's a little thing, and not
much appreciated. By tomorrow morning most of them will

have forgotten every word." Her voice was weak after the rigors of her performance.

"I'll leave you to sleep," Yve said, and made as if to rise.

"No, don't go," the old woman said quickly. "Stay and talk a while. It's not often I have the chance to hear how the world goes."

"Thank you. Adara, the story tonight was new to me. Is it of your own inventing?"

The old woman smiled. "Partly. The tale itself is very old, but I embellish it a little. It would be very boring otherwise."

"Do you have books?"

"On Haele?" Adara was incredulous. "Books are for civilized islands! Here, the only place where stories are recorded is in *this*." A bony forefinger tapped her temple. "When I go most of them will go with me."

"I'm sure you're good for many years yet."

"Do you speak as a wizard, or as someone who would comfort a silly old woman?" Adara's face creased into a smile.

"As a friend, I hope," Yve replied.

"Good. As a friend, I disagree. I've been here too long already."

"Is there something wrong? Do you want me to . . ."

"No, no, child. Nothing's wrong. Don't worry yourself."

A few moments passed in silence.

"The dragon," Adara asked then. "Is it yours?"

Yve's surprise showed on her face and the storyteller cackled weakly. Sweetness blinked slowly as the wizard glanced at him.

"I didn't think you could see him."

"I may be old but I'm not blind yet. Did he like the story?"

Sweetness nodded. *Can we have another one?* he asked silently.

No, Yve shot back. *Don't be so greedy!* But aloud she said, "He liked it so much that he wants you to tell him another!"

Adara smiled. "It's a fitting end," she whispered. "Telling stories to a wizard and a dragon."

Yve looked at the old woman anxiously and rapidly changed the subject.

"The old tales," she asked, "are they all handed down by word of mouth?"

Adara nodded, and her eyes held a faraway look. "From generation to generation, always in my family. The oldest of

the stories were first told many centuries ago. No one cares
for them now."

"Surely not," Yve said, recalling the rapt interest of the
audience.

"No one understands the old tales. They can't be bothered
remembering them. I'm the last."

Yve felt a tremor of resentment that such a wealth should
be allowed to fade away and die.

"What's the oldest story that you know?" she asked.

"The oldest?" Adara lay thinking for so long that Yve thought
she had fallen asleep, but then she roused herself and spoke
again. "The oldest isn't really a story. More a sort of verse. It's
quite short. Would you like to hear it?"

Yes please, Sweetness immediately put in.

Yve nodded. "And then you must sleep."

"I will," Adara replied, then cleared her throat and began
to speak in a voice that had lost its hoarse weakness and was
resonant and crystal clear.

It's her final performance. The thought came unbidden to
Yve. Then the flow of words held her attention completely.
Sweetness too was transfixed, lost in the new magic of another
story, but as the verse came to a close, the dragon glanced
round suddenly. Yve could see nothing, but heard him say,
Go away! Leave me alone! Then he disappeared in an instant,
leaving the wizard with the unpleasant feeling that Sweetness's
departure had not been voluntary.

Yve looked back at Adara. She was asleep, breathing shal-
lowly but regularly. The wizard quietly tucked the sheets about
her, put out the lamp and left the hut. She stood on the porch
for some time before returning to her own room, and all the
time the words from Adara's oldest tale ran through her mind.
She did not think she would ever forget them.

> From the sea, peril.
> From the sea, safety.
>
> From the past, the future.
> From the future, faith.
>
> Unseen wings shall find the source,
> And stand against the dread one's march.
> The final act shall be the first.
> Beyond the hour, two isles are one.

A child, mage-born, and marked for flight,
Shall add her voice but utter naught.
Daughter of time, her fate foretold,
Must heed the words of ages past.
Gather the kindred tied by love,
Bid welcome, and thus . . . awake.

Chapter 8

"*Y*ve! Yve, come quickly!"

The wizard struggled to shake off the webs of sleep that coiled about her, and daylight flooded the room as Ciana rushed in.

"Please hurry," she gasped, breathing hard. "It's Adara."

The words propelled Yve from her bed and, throwing a cape about her shoulders, she ran out into the chill morning.

Several people were gathered outside Adara's hut but they quickly made way for Yve. Inside everything was quite still. Even the cats were gone. The old woman was dead, lying where Yve had left her the night before. Tears welled up in the wizard's eyes.

She knew, Yve thought, her heart heavy. *I knew, but I wouldn't admit it. Oh, why didn't I do something last night when I had the chance?*

She looked down at the old woman's face. Her eyes were closed and a faint smile played across the cold, fragile features. *I would have sworn she was healthy enough last night,* Yve thought ruefully. *At least she didn't suffer.*

"Can you do anything?" Ciana asked timidly.

Yve sadly shook her head. "No. Adara's gone, and even wizards can't bring the dead back to life."

Ciana nodded, as if she had expected this answer.

"You'd better tell her family," Yve went on.

"She had none," Ciana replied. "She was the last."

Adara was buried that afternoon with the island's entire population in attendance. The same evening it appeared that they were not alone in mourning her passing. The heavens themselves paid tribute, as a new star rose in the sky to the northwest, so bright that at first it seemed like a false dawn. Though it lost some brilliance as it continued to rise, the star shone like a beacon throughout the night. All those who watched it were awed by the strange phenomenon, and more than one thought it a great shame that Adara had not lived to see the star and relate the story of its birth.

"Strange times," Bram remarked as he gazed into the sky.

"Indeed," Yve murmured, wondering if inhabitants of other islands had been able to see the new sky-traveler.

"At night he flies among the stars," she whispered to herself.

The next morning Sweetness broke his self-imposed curfew and came to meet Yve in the town. The dragon entered her hut in his usual unorthodox manner, filling Yve's head with the sound of his childlike laughter. He was obviously excited; his eyes were flashing and his thoughts racing so that Yve, who had been awakened prematurely for the second day running, had to tell him firmly to calm down. When he finally became intelligible Sweetness brought the best news possible.

It's going, he exclaimed. *Blowing away and breaking up. Thinning out and burning away.* The dragon made a sort of song of the words, his happiness obvious.

The fog? Yve queried, not quite able to believe in such a good turn of events. *You're sure?*

Of course, Sweetness responded, sounding hurt. *Aren't you pleased?*

Yes, of course. It's just so unexpected. Yve smiled at last. *Thank you, Sweetness. It's wonderful news. I'd hug you if I could!*

The dragon regarded her solemnly. *I'd like that,* he said softly, in a tone so different to his earlier exuberance that it stopped Yve in her tracks. They looked at each other in silence for a few moments.

We'll be leaving Haele soon, Yve said eventually. *You will come with us, won't you?*

If I can.

The uncertainty of his answer gave the wizard further pause for thought.

Sweetness, what happened to you in Adara's hut the other night?

Nothing, the dragon replied defensively. *I had to go, that's all.*

Yve knew from his voice that she wouldn't learn any more by persisting, so she changed the subject.

I'll go and tell Bram and the others, she said, *but before I do there's something I need to arrange with you, something very important.*

Sweetness was eager once more. *What?* he demanded.

You remember those games we've been playing on our walks?

His eyes lit up. *They're fun.*

They certainly are. Now listen closely . . .

———————

Bram and his crew were delighted at Yve's news. The captain agreed to set sail at sunrise the next day and he and his crew promptly set about dismantling their camp and getting the *Alesia* back into ocean trim. All were eager to be on their way home—to whatever awaited them there—and to escape the confines of Haele. As Jarlath put it, "A change from fish, fish, and more fish would be welcome."

The islanders were also relieved at the impending departure, as it would mean an end to the depletion of their supplies and to the tension caused by the presence of so many men. Damek especially was glad that Yve would be going, as he had noticed a slight waning in his authority. The wizard was sowing unrest among the women; even some of the men, who in Damek's opinion should have known better, were being influenced by her pretty words. So it was that everyone on Haele was in an excellent mood and Yve found it easy to persuade Damek to arrange a farewell feast for that evening. So benevolent was the head-man's mood that he even agreed to the women of the island joining the celebration, though not at the same tables, of course.

It was exactly what Yve wanted.

The wizard spent her last day on Haele visiting as many

people as possible and ensuring that her medical skills were used to their greatest effect. She also devoted a good deal of time to talking with Ciana, who was perhaps the one person badly affected by the news of the departure. Together they planned the next stage of Yve's scheme. By the time evening approached, Yve was tired but eager to start.

The feast was similar to the earlier one except for the extra, smaller tables which had been set up flanking the others. At these the women of the island sat, their eyes forever straying to their menfolk, their conversation silenced by the novelty of their position. Every so often some would hurry to attend to food or drink but they always returned to their places, aware that the night was to be very special to them all.

As before, Yve sat beside Damek at the head of the central table but this time there was no suggestion of a drinking contest. She ate and drank cheerfully and even listened patiently to Damek's after-dinner speech. When she was invited to reply she accepted graciously and rose to her feet, having chosen with some care the spot from which she would speak. She would be visible in the firelight to all the diners, both men and women, but behind her was only the blackness of the island.

Yve waited for the company to quiet and then began to speak, her voice pitched so that all could hear.

"We leave you tomorrow. I thank you for your hospitality, and in return would like to leave you a gift."

There was an expectant hush. Yve paused, letting her words hang in the air. *Adara would be proud of me*, she thought.

"My gift is one that gold cannot buy. Some would call it knowledge, but it is more than that. Some would call it philosophy, but it is more than that. Some would call it magic. As a wizard, I tell you it is more than even that."

Her eyes swept the assembled company. They all faced her, waiting.

"You all know me. I have talked with most of you as a wizard and as a woman, and it is as both that I speak to you now. There are some ills on your island that I have not been able to cure. I have tried to explain their cause to you, and will not dwell on that now.

"You men are strong. That is as it should be. That you should provide food and homes for your families is also right; but do not underestimate your women just because their bodies may be less strong than yours. They have powers beyond

your imagining—as I will show you!" Yve proclaimed amid a
sudden outbreak of muttering.

Damek had risen to his feet, his face mottled and ugly with
anger. "This is not the place—" he began, but Yve cut him
short in a voice that brooked no argument.

"Sit down!" she ordered, stabbing out an accusing finger.
Remembering what he had heard about the flying bottle of
yarglat, Damek sank back into his chair. Yve took up her argument again, her voice reasonable once more.

"Women know many secrets of hearth and home, of children and of cooking fires." The murmurs of discontent were
quieted. There were even a few nods of agreement. This was
more familiar territory.

"In short, we women stand close to the secrets of the Earth.
You create life, but we bear it, nurture it—and understand it.
You bring fish and meat but we add to them from the fruits
of the Earth. You fell the trees for kindling but we use the fire
for warmth and nourishment. We are the masters of fire and
can kindle flame from the Earth itself!"

At her last words Yve was suddenly engulfed in a mass of
brilliant orange fire. The flames licked hungrily about her,
enveloping her clothes, her hair, her hands, and face. And yet
she smiled and did not move.

Many of the onlookers shrieked in horror, and leapt to their
feet, ready either to run to Yve's aid or to flee, according to
their temperament. When it became clear that the wizard was
not harmed, nobody moved.

"You see," Yve said, and the flames died away.

"As a wizard I command the Earth-fire but as a woman I
withstand it. It does not burn me. It will not burn any woman."

Fresh exclamations greeted this statement and Yve held
up her hands for silence, then continued.

"You would have proof?"

There were several shouts of approval. Yve looked over to
the women's tables.

"Ciana," she called, and everyone turned to look at the
head-man's wife. With a grace and determination that made
Yve proud of her, Ciana rose and walked to the wizard's side.

"What do you think you're doing, woman?" Damek was on
his feet, his loud voice thick with anger.

"Who better to be the first than your leader's wife?" Yve
asked coolly. "Behold the Earth-fire!"

This time the flames sprang up in a thin, searing column,

rising vertically to the height of a man. Yve placed her fist within the fire, unclenched her fingers, letting the flames play between them, and then withdrew. She motioned to Ciana to do the same. After a moment's theatrical hesitation, which Yve admired greatly, Ciana plunged her hand into the flame.

"No!" Damek bellowed, and several other men shouted, but Ciana remained silent. As the onlookers saw her face, pale but unconcerned, everything became very still. Some moments later she unhurriedly removed her hand and held it up for all to see. It was unscathed, provoking more gasps and sudden conversations. Yve turned again to the women's tables.

"Are any of you willing to match Ciana's bravery?"

At first nobody moved, then slowly, as if she were moving in a trance, Zana got to her feet and joined her mother.

"Don't be afraid," Yve said quietly.

"I'm not scared of the Earth-fire," the girl replied softly. "Only of what you're doing." Her eyes glistened in the wavering light and Yve was moved by the hope and trust that shone within. Abruptly Zana pushed both hands into the flame. When she withdrew them she was smiling and tears were running down her cheeks. Her hands were unharmed.

After that, despite the protests of several men, more and more women made their way forward and took their turn. Everyone else watched in astonished silence until Damek roared, "Enough! This trickery proves nothing. It is merely some illusion of the wizard's. The flame does not burn!"

"Then come and put *your* hand to the test, Damek. *If* you dare," Yve retorted in a voice that carried to every person present.

The big man hesitated, took several paces forward, then stopped. Except for Ciana, the women had all melted away into the background. At Yve's gesture the flame doubled in intensity, its orange glare casting flickering shadows and Ciana placed her hand within the inferno once more.

"Come then," Yve said. "An illusion cannot harm you. Surely anything your *woman* can do is not beyond you?"

Damek said nothing, the sweat glistening on his face. At last he moved forward until he was within reach of the stream of fire. Yve steeled herself for what she had to do. She would hate herself for doing it but would feel worse if she failed at this late stage. If Damek placed his hand within the flame . . .

The head-man stretched out his hand, then stopped. He glanced at Yve, and she saw the fear within his eyes. She

returned his gaze impassively and the fire regained his attention. He stood as if paralyzed, then he wavered and withdrew.

"I can't," he whispered hoarsely, hanging his head.

"But it's an *illusion!*" Yve responded sarcastically. "Shall I
call up the Earth-fire all about you? So that you can feel the
full effects of my *trickery?*" she added.

Damek looked at her in horror, then fell to his knees and
hid his face.

"No. Please!"

Yve glanced at Ciana, and saw the pity and sadness in her
face. Taking Damek by the hand, she lifted him up and said
quietly, "Go back to your seat." He obeyed meekly, without
a word. The flame went out again and in the sudden gloom
Yve's voice rang out.

"I go from Haele tomorrow, but I do not leave you. Ciana
shall stand in my stead. Her voice will be my voice in matters
of health, children, and their rearing. She is the first but she
will not be alone. There are many other women on Haele whose
voices deserve to be heard.

"You have seen tonight that we possess strengths unknown
to you before now. Your women can contribute so much to
your lives here, yet you exclude them from their rightful place
in your government, your decision-making, even—until tonight—your celebrations. Why? Are they less able to think,
to speak, to love? Would you be better off without them?

"Of course not! So why do you set them aside from so much
of your lives? Let them help you; let them share your problems
and your joys. I am a wizard. You respect me for that. But I
am also a woman. I would that you respected me for *that.*"

She paused, and surveyed the faces before her. Their
expressions varied from outright antagonism to amused tol-
erance, but here and there there were nods of agreement.
Maybe, she thought. *Just maybe . . .*

Another man spoke and his harsh voice dashed some of
Yve's optimism.

"This is nonsense. Earth does not burn, we know that," he
said, looking round for support. "Women . . ." he began, but
got no further.

In the far distance there was a massive rumbling, then a
plume of red flame leapt into the night sky. For a few moments
the outline of the volcano was clearly visible, and in the sudden
silence, someone whispered, "The earth burns!" Yve said a
silent prayer of thanks.

The dissenter showed no signs of wishing to continue his line of argument after that and Yve spoke again.

"Accept my words and the evidence of your own eyes. Accept my gift."

What happened then took the wizard by surprise. Ciana and Zana went to Damek, who still sat hunched in his chair. Together they coaxed the broken man to look up, to drink and talk. They sat either side of him on the center table, their concern evident in their faces.

Love knows no boundaries, Yve thought.

Slowly the nature of the gathering changed. The two sides began to merge. A few women joined Ciana and her daughter at the center table, some joined their men at other places, and some men even went to sit at the women's tables—a bonus that Yve would not have dared to hope for a few hours earlier. She watched the transmutation in a daze, unable to believe that she had actually succeeded. Soon, lively talk and laughter resounded all about her. Even the *Alesia*'s crew were included in the merry atmosphere, but Yve remained outside, an incredulous observer. She started when a voice spoke close to her ear.

"Congratulations. I don't know how you did it, but . . ."

Bram's grin brought her back down to earth.

"It's too good to be true," she breathed. "Something's bound to go wrong."

"It's up to them now," the captain replied. "You've given them more than they deserve."

Yve looked at him, wishing she could share his hard-nosed realism.

"You're right," she said. "They don't need me now. I'm going to my cabin."

"I'll walk you there."

"No. Thank you, but you should stay and enjoy the party. Your men—"

"I'll keep an eye on them," Bram grinned. "We've an early start tomorrow. Goodnight, Yve."

"Goodnight."

The wizard was at the door of her cabin before she realized that she was not alone after all.

Did I do all right? Sweetness asked anxiously.

You were wonderful, she replied.

Chapter 9

"Goodbye, Ciana. It's up to you now."

Farewells had been completed and all but Yve and the two oarsmen in the skiff were aboard the *Alesia*. The wizard stood with her friend at the end of the jetty, their hands clasping. It was a sad moment for them both.

"I'll do my best," Ciana said. "And I'll have help."

"Make sure they don't do anything silly with *real* fire," Yve warned, with a conspiratorial smile.

"I'll remember."

They embraced, then Yve moved toward the waiting boat. She turned back.

"I'll return when I can," she said.

"Don't make any promises," Ciana replied. "Your world is large."

And uncertain, Yve added with a quiver of anxiety.

"Say goodbye and thank you to Sweetness for me," Ciana said, a catch in her voice.

"I will. Good luck."

"Thank you for everything, Yve, and farewell. The winds favor your journey."

Even from a distance Lugg looked different, menacing, grayer somehow. Bram and his crew discussed landing on the south coast in order to make early inquiries, but in the end decided to stick to their original plan of sailing straight to Carrhaven. The capital was home to most of them, and that was where they wanted to be—whatever had happened. They had been away too long to contemplate further delays.

The final days at sea seemed to last an eternity as they battled against wind and offshore currents. They passed Lugg's northern coastline with agonizing slowness. The ominous feeling of dread that all on board felt grew steadily; when they finally arrived, their worst fears were confirmed.

Carrhaven was in chaos. The harbor was filled with debris and many ships had been sunk at the quayside, their sad skeletons lying at unnatural angles, with sometimes only the masts protruding above the water's surface. Most of the vessels looked to be beyond salvage but even those in better shape had been abandoned; except for a few scavengers, both human and animal. It was obvious that the port had been visited by mayhem of unbelievable proportions.

As the *Alesia* slipped slowly toward her usual dock, her crew keeping a keen-eyed watch for submerged obstacles, more details became clear. The few people visible seemed either to be in a daze, and wandering aimlessly, or to be acting furtively, hiding at the newcomer's approach. Several bodies lay on the quays, there were more in the water, and the stench of decay was wrapped about everything.

Although the devastation was not as obvious beyond the harbor area, even the buildings showed signs of unnatural damage, and in the distance palls of dark smoke hung over the town. However, it could be seen that fire had played no part in the destruction of the city's fleet. Whatever *had* caused it was no longer evident. Bram ordered his stunned crew to moor in their usual place. As the ropes were secured, Bram held hurried discussions with the sailors, then joined Yve who was staring at the city, as shocked and silent as any of them. She jumped as Bram tapped her shoulder.

"What's happened here?" she asked in a whisper.

"I don't know. Nobody does." He paused. "All but two of my lads have family," he said eventually, "but I can't leave the ship unguarded now. Is there anything you can do?"

Yve thought for a moment. "I'll try. Who are the two?"

"Erchan and Neil."

"Tell them I'll set a warding spell. No one will be able to get on board, but they won't be able to get off either. Do they have enough supplies for four or five days?"

Bram nodded. "Thank you. I'll tell them. I can't ask anyone else to stay until we know what's happened here." He indicated the wrecked harbor.

"What about you, Bram?"

"Me?" he replied. "I'm coming with you."

The main gates of the royal palace stood open but the approach looked far from inviting. The solid timbers lay shattered on the ground, scored and splintered as if they had been torn apart by some huge, ravening beast. Yve and Bram walked inside, their hearts full of foreboding.

Once away from the docks, Carrhaven itself had appeared relatively unscathed. The town had a frightened, unnatural air, with few people about, but damage to buildings had been slight. Though there had obviously been fighting recently, the only noticeable effects were broken windows and boarded-up doors. Here and there they had seen corpses in the street and Bram walked with his hand on the hilt of his dagger. No one had approached them, however, and Yve had been too intent on reaching the palace and Drogo's house to pursue any of the people they did see.

As they entered the courtyard two men emerged from an inner door, carrying a limp bundle wrapped in a blanket. They dumped it unceremoniously on a waiting cart, then turned to go back inside.

"Jon?" Yve called. The men spun round, hands going instinctively to the swords at their sides, and they stared at her suspiciously.

Then, "Yve?" the younger of the two said. "Is it really you?"

"You've known me from childhood. Don't you know me now?"

"But . . . we thought you were gone for good," Jon replied. "When the sea froze we gave up hope."

"The sea did what?" Bram exclaimed.

Jon motioned his companion back inside, then walked over to the newcomers.

"We have much to discuss," he said. "All of it bad. Your return is the first good news for many days."

The young man's face was pale and drawn and his right forearm was heavily bandaged.

"What has happened here?" Yve asked quietly.

"I wish I knew. Whatever manner of—*thing*—struck here is beyond my comprehension but I've seen its effects. They're not pretty. Come and sit down and I'll tell you what I know."

He led them to a small but comfortably furnished room and gave each a glass of wine. "You'll need it," he said.

The tale he told, though incomplete and sometimes confused, was indeed unpleasant. A few days after the *Alesia* had set sail, Carrhaven had been blanketed by icy fog. That in itself was unpleasant, as Lugg was unaccustomed to such cold weather, even in winter, but what followed was the stuff of nightmares.

The fog persisted and many people fell ill. A large number lost all awareness of their actions, becoming like sleepwalkers. The only people who appeared immune to the sickness were those living in or around the palace. This proved a short-lived blessing, though. After a few days the town had been invaded by soldiers who ignored the bulk of the populace—who obviously presented no threat to them—and made straight for the palace. There had been a brief but vicious and bloody battle in which Jon had been wounded and knocked unconscious. As a consequence he was more than a little hazy about the details of the fight, but related several bizarre and terrible incidents which he had been told about by other survivors. Even allowing for overripe imaginations fermented by the uncanny fog, some of these stories were difficult to dismiss.

The most persistent report was that the gray invaders had appeared lifeless—"like wraiths"—but were nonetheless ferocious fighters. Their eyes were as cold as their blades and they fought with no heed for their own safety. Jon had been told of one who had single-handedly attacked twelve defenders, cutting down four, before being killed himself. Another had apparently jumped fifty feet to a stone pavement in a suicidal bid to prevent a defender from escaping.

But the most frightening aspect had been that, although many of the invaders had been killed, there were *no bodies* left when the fog finally cleared. The butchered defenders lay where they had fallen but of the invaders, either dead or alive, there was absolutely no trace. Jon had even heard it said that their bodies melted away into a thin vapor and were then lost in the fog. He had dismissed this as hysterical nonsense but found it impossible to come up with a realistic solution.

The results of this invasion were obvious enough, however. The palace population had been decimated. Only a handful remained.

"The king?" Yve asked weakly.

"He's dead and so are his family."

"All of them?"

"Every one. There was nothing we could do." Jon's face was contorted with the memory. "We're still in the process of burying the dead, as you saw."

"And Drogo?"

"Gone. At least no one can find him. I haven't met anyone who saw him after the fog closed in, and his house is empty now."

Hannah, Yve cried silently. "I'll go and look," she said. "It was my home too."

"Hurry back," Jon said. "We have need of your skills."

Yve and Bram left the palace by one of the smaller entrances. Their route took them through the central part of the building, but they met no one. The wizard walked quickly and neither she nor her companion noticed the change in the moonberry tree as they hurried through the yard in which it grew. The slender branches now drooped sadly, the leaves were discolored and crinkled, and several of the fruit—the precious berries—had fallen to the ground. Those that remained had lost their sheen and some were split or pockmarked. For one well versed in magical lore the tree was a sorry—and ominous—sight, but Yve was so intent on discovering what had happened to her master and her adoptive mother that she marched past without a pause.

The front door of Drogo's house stood open. Inside all was quiet—and very cold. Yve knew immediately that nothing lived within its walls but she forced herself to search every room. Each was empty, and each was filled with an uncanny gloom that left her shaken. The hairs on Bram's neck stood on end. There were signs here and there of hurried departure, perhaps of a brief struggle or two, but the house had not seen any real fighting. Most of the contents were still intact. No looters had yet been brave enough to ransack the master wizard's home—even when it was clear that he was no longer there. Yve wondered how long it would be before that changed and her home was desecrated.

Finally there was only one room left—Drogo's study. Yve had instinctively left it till last, fearing what she would find there. So far there had been no clues as to her master's where-abouts or to his actions during the invasion. If any were to be found it would be in his inner sanctum.

"In here?" Bram asked, putting his left hand on the iron doorknob. Before Yve could reply, the sailor yelled in pain and wrenched his hand back, quickly comforting it beneath his other arm. Wisps of vapor coiled from the metal handle, where flecks of Bram's skin now stuck. *So cold it burns*, Yve thought. *A sealing spell! What's in there?*

"Let me see your hand."

Bram grimaced as he showed Yve his injury. She gently straightened the fingers, quickly absorbing and discarding his pain and setting the ugly, burn-like wounds on the path to healing.

"Better?" she asked presently.

Bram nodded. "Thank you." He glanced again at the study door.

"Don't touch it," Yve said quickly.

"I don't make that sort of mistake twice," Bram growled, "but we have to get in there, don't we?"

"Yes. Whoever set that seal on the door meant business. Which means there's something inside worth protecting."

"Drogo?"

Yve shrugged. They returned to the room that adjoined the study, and the wizard tested the strength of the seal.

"It's strong," she admitted as they arrived back at the only door, "but it's decaying steadily. The door is the obvious weak spot. It's the only entrance." She stopped to think, remem-bering advice from lessons long ago. *Sometimes the best course of action is to do nothing.*

"But not on this occasion!" she said aloud. "I haven't time."

Yve closed her eyes, and her face was a mask of concen-tration. The door began to glow, pulsing red and white as an invisible battle of wills was fought about it and *within* it. Bram stepped back hurriedly, knowing this contest was beyond his understanding, but willing to enter it if Yve was in danger.

Just when it seemed that a stalemate had been reached, the double doors bulged outward, then rushed back with an earsplitting crash, ending inside the study, hanging limply from ruined hinges.

Yve, her body rigid with effort, walked stiffly into the room. Bram followed closely behind, dagger in hand.

Inside the windowless room it was pitch dark. With a word,

Yve set several wall-lamps blazing, and immediately wished
she had not been so profligate. The drain on her resources had
been enormous, and in her weakened state she found the scene
before her even harder to bear.

The study had been reduced to a shambles. Broken glass
and splintered wood lay strewn about the floor. Furniture was
overturned and broken and shelves had disgorged their contents. It was as if a whirlwind had run amok within the confined
space, wreaking havoc in its attempt to break free.

Yve's first glance took all this in but she paid it little attention. Her horrified gaze was riveted on the chair at the
room's center. In it was Drogo, his limbs splayed, his head
leaning backward, open-mouthed. His eyes stared wildly at
the ceiling.

On the floor beneath one open hand was a glass in which
a few drops of liquid still lay, glinting evilly. Yve knew what
it was without having to smell the residue. Each side of the
ancient wizard's neck had been sliced open with a sharp knife
which also lay on the floor. Blood, now brown and flaking,
stained his chest and shoulders, soaked into his ceremonial
robe.

Behind her Yve heard Bram retch and barge his way out
of the evil room. For her the effect was even worse. That Drogo
was dead was bad enough, though not entirely unexpected.
That he should have chosen to die by the ritual suicide of the
old orders was even more terrible. But worst of all was the
look of abject, gibbering terror which death had frozen upon
the ancient wizard's face. Yve turned and fled.

Chapter 10

Over the next few days, some sort of order began to emerge from the chaos. People returned to the city from the inland areas where they had fled in a vain attempt to escape the fog. Carrhaven slowly began to come back to life.

The same could not be said of the palace. All that was left of the once-busy court was a handful of soldiers and servants. Drogo's house remained as cold and as quiet as a tomb.

Though the fog had gone, its effects lingered on, and many people still suffered from illnesses brought on by the unexpected cold and damp. Problems were exacerbated by the amount of time it took to bury the corpses that littered the town.

Food was scarce; crops and stores alike had suffered badly and farm animals had been left untended. Fishing had also been abandoned once the fog made navigation impossible and when, incredibly, the dockland sea froze over, it wrecked so many boats that few fishermen had gone to sea again. Those that did rarely returned to the capital, preferring safer anchorages elsewhere.

These ills, together with the fact that the castle guard, who apart from their military duties also acted as officers of the law, had been decimated, meant that Carrhaven experienced many ugly scenes. Violence and looting became commonplace until Jon and the other soldiers, who now looked to the young man for leadership, established a minimal system of patrols and appointed local watches wherever possible. Even then trouble was not eliminated and few people slept soundly.

Yve's skills were indeed much in demand. She had moved into one of the many empty apartments in the palace, unable to face Drogo's house—that she had once called home—even to collect her belongings. Bram was her constant companion and she did not think to question him on matters relating to his own kin, but accepted his presence gladly. She took his reassuring nearness for granted.

Together they traveled through the town, healing, arbitrating in disputes and encouraging a return to normality, as much as was possible. However, though many were thankful for Yve's ministrations, she found that her presence was regarded by some with suspicion, even antagonism. She worked ceaselessly, often exhausting herself in the process, but received little gratitude and was often asked in accusatory tones, "Where were you when we needed you?"

No one else she met could tell her the full story of Drogo's demise but it was clear that rumor was highly unfavorable and as a consequence both Yve and wizardry were resented. She tried patiently to counter these feelings by her work and her words and, though Bram often grew angry at the harsh treatment she received, the wizard remained calm, determined to work even harder. It was obvious that most people had little idea about what had happened during the time that the fog had ruled their world. All they knew for certain was that it had not been natural and therefore magic was a possible culprit. And they needed something on which to blame their suffering. Although Yve knew that she could protect herself if necessary —and had thus refused Jon's offer of an armed escort—she was glad that Bram's companionship often tended to defuse some potentially explosive situations before she was forced to resort to magic.

On occasion the captain was also accompanied by one or two of his scattered crew. They brought with them mixed news. Some had found their families more or less unharmed; others returned stony-faced with news of death and disease; many had so far found no trace of their kin; and the rest had not reported back at all. Erchan and Neil had been relieved, and the guarding of the *Alesia* now continued in more conventional manner.

The people returning to Carrhaven brought with them many

wild and fearful tales in which fact and fiction were irrevocably tangled. One fact did emerge, however. The fog had indeed blanketed the entire island, and there had been no escape from its gray and icy grip.

It was from one of these refugees that Yve finally learned as much as she ever would about Drogo's last hours. Lawson had been the master wizard's steward for as long as Yve could remember. He was an old man now but his mind was still keen. In his position he had witnessed many events which would have reduced others to nervous wrecks, but even *his* voice shook as he told the sorry tale. For Yve, perhaps the only person who had ever grown to love the pompous, cantankerous old wizard, Lawson's tale was horrifying.

By the time the first tendrils of mist had snaked their way into the town, Drogo had been locked in his study for more than a day. This in itself was not unusual, but when a summons came from the palace for the wizard to attend the king and give advice about the fog, the messenger received no answer. Shortly afterward, soldiers elicited a response by hammering on the door with the pommels of their swords. Drogo merely informed them irritably, "Of course I know about the fog! What do you think I'm working on in here? Go away and leave me in peace before I blast you where you stand!"

The soldiers beat a hasty retreat, recognizing the deadly intent in the old man's voice. It had then been left to Lawson to communicate with Drogo, but he learned little of any consequence, and was received with either indifference or abuse from the other side of the locked door.

For four days the wizard remained closeted, while the situation outside degenerated into panic and disorder. He took no food or drink in all that time and his steward eventually detected a change in the wizard's voice which worried him. It was not the deliberately feeble tone Drogo sometimes employed for effect, nor was it his habitual churlish sarcasm. It was something deeper, malignant, suggesting an idea so ridiculous that Lawson discarded it immediately.

Despite increasingly frantic pleas, the wizard would not emerge and when, in desperation, one soldier had tried to break down the door, he had been hurled back, with such ferocious magical force that his neck had been broken and he died instantly. After that, anger and resentment had boiled up against the old man, and his callous abandonment of Lugg became increasingly hard to swallow.

Lawson pleaded with his master, but was rewarded only with more abuse and the unsettling claim that the fog did not exist!

"Why do you bother me with these foolish prattlings of diseased minds?" Drogo bellowed. Then his voice became so weak and cracked that Lawson could hardly hear it. "There is no fog. No. No fog. It cannot be there. Nothing that big . . . over water . . . that gullible fool on Ark . . . There is no fog. It cannot be there."

A shuffling sound came from within the study and the steward lost track of the retreating voice, only to hear it once more as Drogo screamed, "I see the sun!"

Lawson had retreated rapidly, a cold more profound than any fog clutching at his heart.

The end came soon afterward. The wraithlike invaders had come, sweeping through the streets of Carrhaven and turning the palace and its surrounding buildings into places of carnage. Many of Drogo's household had already fled, but even the agonized pleas of those that remained had failed to move the wizard. He only laughed at their terror and mocked them for cowards and hallucinators.

Lawson had made his own escape at this point and, luckier than most, had reached the relatively safe outskirts of the city. His last recollection of Drogo was of the wizard yelling, "He was right. Right! The sun!" and breaking into a cackle of insane laughter which echoed horribly in Lawson's brain even now. "I never want to hear another sound like that as long as I live."

As the steward's words died away, Yve began to appreciate the depth of suspicion which surrounded her.

"Is he dead?" Lawson asked quietly.

"Yes," Yve said. "He's dead." She did not elaborate nor did the old man ask her to. "What of the others?"

"Mostly dead too," Lawson replied sadly. "Though I can't be sure of all of them. Everything was so confused when the attack came."

"Hannah?"

The steward lowered his eyes. "They killed her," he said at last. "I'm sorry, Yve. There was nothing I could do."

Since returning to Lugg, Yve had seen Sweetness only rarely. The city seemed to intimidate him, and the wizard had been so preoccupied with her own problems that she was generally too tired or too busy to pay him much attention. The dragon's attitude, however, remained optimistic and, when they did get a chance to talk, Yve found herself glad of his cheerful and innocent company. She knew now that if a "real" familiar was to appear, one in her own world, she would have distinctly mixed feelings about it. Such an event would surely mean the severing of her strange but precious link with the dragon. Sweetness had come to mean a great deal to her, and she believed the feeling to be reciprocated. She was soon to have proof that this was so.

Yve and Bram were visiting an inn on the outskirts of Carr-haven, a lonely place which rarely saw the soldier's patrols. The innkeeper's wife and two of their children were ill with chest complaints, contracted in the fog and prolonged by poor food. Yve had dealt with many similar cases and knew that, though she could bring temporary relief from their suffering, the only long-term solution lay in fresh air and good food. After relaying this advice and doing what she could, she went down-stairs with Bram and the innkeeper.

In the tap room, several drinkers huddled round the tables, in spite of the early hour. They grew quiet as Yve entered and she sensed their antagonism. A burly young man rose to his feet.

"What does the *wizard* say, father?" His contempt spilled out. The innkeeper explained briefly, as Yve and Bram stood waiting.

"They're sleeping now," he concluded, looking about nervously.

"Likely for ever!" his son retorted. "Why do you consort with those who brought the evil upon us in the first place?"

There were mutters of agreement from around the room. Yve was about to reply but Bram beat her to it.

"Only an idiot would spout such nonsense," he said in a dangerously quiet voice.

"Oh! Who is this?" his adversary exclaimed. "The pretty wizard's pet. Does she let you lick her when you're good?" He stuck out his tongue and rolled his eyes, to general laughter. Bram lunged forward, his face contorted with fury, only to be held back by Yve's outstretched arm.

"You play a dangerous game, young man," she said calmly.

"Dangerous! What right have you to tell us what's dangerous. You fled even before the fog arrived! Now you sit in the palace, all high and mighty—eating the best, I'll wager—and tell us to eat fresh fruit! When is the last time there was anything fresh at the market, lads?"

He appealed to his fellow drinkers, who, egged on by their leader's boldness and the ale in their stomachs, chorused in agreement.

"I did *not* flee . . ." Yve began but Bram's furious voice rose above hers.

"Don't defend yourself before this scum," he exclaimed. "They do not deserve you. Leave them to rot in their own slime."

Yve tried to restrain him but his pent-up anger had boiled over, like oil in a pan, and the fire that followed was inevitable. The innkeeper's son spat in Bram's direction and in a flash the seaman's dagger was outstretched before him. Then everything happened so fast that even Yve was taken by surprise.

Tables overturned, tankards clattered to the floor, and shouts rang out. The innkeeper dived for cover as Yve stood uncertain, shocked into inaction. Within moments Bram was felled and lay inert with two men standing over him. Yve's arms were grabbed by strong hands and a razor-sharp knife held to her throat.

Stars! she thought bitterly. *How did I let myself get in this mess?* She willed herself to remain calm, remembering an early lesson from her training. *A wizard can be killed by a sword or an arrow just as any other man. The art of self-protection lies in avoiding these objects in the first place!*

Having achieved their objective, the men now seemed at a loss. After the furious rush of action they were beginning to realize the enormity of what they had done. Silent, they looked to the innkeeper's son, who held the knife at Yve's neck.

"Don't move or speak," he snarled, "or I'll slit you open."

"What now?" one of his companions asked.

"Send a message to the palace. Tell them we want food, money, and horses. If we don't get them fast, these two die."

The men looked at each other uncertainly.

Another panicky voice erupted into the silence, but Yve soon realized that she alone could hear it.

What's happening? What's happening?

It's all right, Sweetness. I can deal with it, she replied as reassuringly as she could, but the dragon was not to be put off.

As one whole wall of the room burst into flames, men screamed. In their midst, Sweetness loomed large, his eyes flashing wildly and his scales glinting in the firelight. He had never looked more solid.

Yve let herself go limp and slipped from her captor's grasp. His knife clattered harmlessly to the floor beside her, as the terrified men scrambled frantically to escape from the fearsome vision. Soon only Yve and Bram remained in the room with the dragon.

What were they doing to you? Did they hurt you? he asked anxiously, his voice full of fear.

I'm all right, Yve replied, *but Bram is hurt. I have to tend to him now.* She moved to the prone figure and quickly assessed his injuries. There was nothing that wouldn't mend in a few hours but until then he would feel out of sorts.

Is there anyone outside? Yve asked.

After a moment Sweetness replied, *No. They've all run off. I scared them away.*

Yve almost responded by saying that he might just as easily have scared them into killing her, but the dragon sounded so proud of his achievement that she did not have the heart to reprimand him.

I'm glad I saved you, Sweetness added, and this time there was genuine emotion rather than boastfulness in his tone.

I'm glad too, Yve replied, smiling. *We have to get back to the palace now. Will you be our lookout?*

Oh yes! he replied eagerly, then added in more measured tones, *It will be a pleasure, my lady.*

Yve laughed and, adding the resources of her magical talent to her natural strength, lifted Bram into her arms. The seaman was still unconscious and as she followed Sweetness out into the street, Yve thought that this was just as well. His pride would not have allowed him to be carried thus otherwise.

All clear, Sweetness reported. *This way. If anyone else threatens you, I'll soon see them off.*

This is just the sort of game he likes, Yve mused, but wisely kept the thought to herself.

"No," Yve said. "This is my home!"

Bram threw up his hands in frustration. "You talk to her, Jon. Make her see sense."

The three of them sat in Yve's apartment. The wizard had been back on Lugg for a month now and had been in danger on several occasions. The incident at the inn had been only the first.

"Bram's right," the soldier said. "The atmosphere here is poisoned. Nobody knows what happened, but they're blaming magic, and what Drogo did is common knowledge now. It's no wonder people are bitter and though *we* know it's no fault of yours, a wizard is an obvious target."

Bram could contain himself no longer. "How long before you get a knife in the back or an arrow you don't see?" he asked. "You're not invulnerable—especially with a bodyguard like me," he added bitterly.

"Don't underestimate yourself," Yve said.

"I don't. I just know when I'm beaten."

"Things *are* beginning to get better," Jon put in. "In good measure due to you."

"Though you've had little thanks," Bram snorted.

"We can cope now," the soldier went on, "but I don't want to be responsible for your safety. I can't even be sure of my own men where wizardry is concerned." He paused. "I caught some of them hacking at the moonberry tree yesterday."

Yve's eyes were wide. "The tree?" she whispered. "It let them?"

"Well, it was already in a sorry state," Jon said. "As you know."

Without a word, Yve set off to inspect the tree. She returned a short while later, her face pale and expressionless. The sight of the moonberry tree, its drooping branches scarred and broken and its fruit all but destroyed, had shaken her badly. The most potent symbol of her profession was hanging in diseased tatters, and she felt sick and cold. She slumped down into a chair, staring into space.

"I can get enough of the crew together to sail in two days," Bram said quietly.

"It's only temporary," Jon added. "As soon as this has passed and memories cooled, you can return."

Yve said nothing.

"Arlon is only four days away," Bram went on. "We can

find out the news there, and it might give you some help in understanding what happened *here*."

"We could do with information from the other islands. The world has become too quiet," Jon said.

Still Yve remained silent.

"What do you say?" Bram coaxed. "Shall I gather the crew?"

Slowly, her eyes still glazed, Yve nodded. The two men glanced at each other, then stood. They left without further words but each laid a gentle hand on the wizard's shoulder as he passed. Yve did not stir until the door closed behind them, and even then her only movement was to raise a hand to brush away the tears that streamed down her face.

Chapter 11

The journey to Arlon took almost four days. Although the bitterness of her exile did not entirely leave her, Yve gradually recovered her spirits. She remembered that Arlon's wizard was Cai, a flamboyant young man, friendlier than many of his magical colleagues. Drogo had disapproved of Cai but Yve remembered him with fondness from their travels together on the voyage to Ark's fateful conclave.

I wonder what's happening on Ark, Yve mused. *Perhaps Cai will know.*

The thought of being able to discuss recent events with a fellow wizard, especially one near her own age, raised Yve's hopes, but she was destined to be disappointed. It would be many months before her path crossed with Cai's.

Yve had not seen Sweetness since leaving Lugg, yet this caused her no undue concern. The dragon's appearances were sporadic, but she did not doubt that he would return. In fact, his absence was something of a relief as it meant that there was little danger of another sea-sprite episode. Yve knew that some of the reduced crew still harbored doubts about magic, and was glad that they were spared any distraction. Bram still commanded their respect but she knew their loyalty would be severely strained if Sweetness chose to appear in one of his more visible modes.

As soon as they were in sight of land it became clear that
Arlon had fared even worse than Lugg. The harbor was chaotic,
despite the fact that a month had passed since the fog's withdrawal, and Bram decided that the *Alesia* would anchor in
open water.

"We'll go ashore in the skiff," he said. "I don't like the look
of things here, Yve. Do you still want to come?"

Yve nodded. "Of course. There's no point in my being here
otherwise."

At dusk, two of the sailors rowed their captain and Yve
ashore, arranging a signal for their return.

The town was dark and frightening. The few people that
were about went heavily armed. Yve unconsciously cloaked
their progress with as much skill as she dared use, and no one
paid them any attention as Bram led her through the back
streets. Debris and rubbish lay all about and many houses were
boarded up. By comparison, Carrhaven's recovery had been
swift.

Bram had persuaded Yve not to go straight to the king's
castle, where Cai resided, but to accompany him elsewhere
first. He knocked at a stout wooden door and waited. There
was no answer for some time, and it was only after repeated
knocking that a small peephole was opened.

"Crawn? It's me, Bram."

The hole closed and there came the sound of heavy bolts
being drawn back. The door opened and a voice said, "Inside.
Quick!"

They slipped within and waited while the door was made
secure once more. In the lamplight Yve saw a stocky man, dressed
mostly in leather. When he turned to face them she was taken
aback. Crawn bore an uncanny likeness to Bram, but the left
side of his face was marred by a long vertical scar, and his left
eye was permanently closed. *Brothers?* she wondered.

The two men regarded each other in silence for a while.

"Bad?" Bram asked eventually.

"Aye," the other replied. "The town's gone to pieces. There's
no one left to keep the law." He turned to Yve. "I'm not usually
so unwelcoming," he said. "Come in."

He urged them into an inner room, which was warm and
windowless. A blonde woman sat in the far corner, and she
shrank back timidly as they entered. Bram went to her and
said softly, "It's all right, Jenny. It's me."

A slow smile broke over her face, and Yve saw that she was beautiful.

"Bram," she whispered. "Will you play for me?"

"I can't. You know that," he replied sadly.

After a moment, the woman began to sing softly, a tune that Yve found hauntingly familiar. Then Jenny stopped abruptly and stared at the fire; when Bram turned back to the wizard, his eyes were glistening.

"This is Crawn and Jenny," he said. "My brother and his wife. This is Yve," he added.

The wizard, who had felt the awkwardness of the previous interchange, decided not to press for an explanation. Instead, she began a discussion of recent events. Jenny remained silent throughout the conversation, but Yve noticed that Bram glanced at her often.

Crawn's tale was an almost exact replica of the story they'd heard from Jon. Arlon's castle population had been decimated to an even greater extent than that of Lugg. There were only meager supplies of food; law and order was all but non-existent, and the town's atmosphere was tense and violent. As on Lugg, the fog had brought illness and confusion. It had lasted for almost exactly the same time, and had cleared on the night of the shooting star, but little progress had since been made in restoring normality.

"What of Cai?" Yve asked.

"Nobody knows," Crawn replied, his tone implying that nor did anybody care. "He was away when the fog came. He did return a while ago but no one here has much time for wizards now. He left again in a hurry."

Yve and Bram exchanged glances.

"Most people reckon we've not had a proper wizard since old Debramani died," Crawn went on. "The young one was never here when we needed him."

"Do you know where he's gone?" Yve asked.

Crawn looked at her strangely, then shook his head.

"You'll be staying?" he asked, sounding distinctly unenthusiastic.

"No," Bram replied. "I've a ship to attend to and I think we've learnt all we're going to here." He stood up. "Goodbye, Jenny," he said, but she made no response and only continued to stare into the fire. Crawn gestured for Bram and Yve to leave, a pleading look in his eyes. In the hallway he paused.

"She's not—*here*—a lot of the time," he said, then began unbolting the door. "Go carefully."

"Thank you, Crawn. Farewell," Yve replied as she went out. Bram and his brother parted silently, leaving the wizard with an almost overwhelming sense of personal tragedy.

"What did he mean?" she asked as they set off.

"Not now," her companion replied, and led her swiftly through the black streets.

They stayed on Arlon for two more days, sailing northward up the western seaboard and calling at several other towns and villages. The story was the same everywhere. At length, discussion turned to future plans, and opinion was divided. Some of the crew wanted to return to Lugg, others wanted to remain quietly on Arlon for a while, and the rest were for sailing northward to Strallen. After much debate, Bram decided on this last course and, after taking on extra supplies—for which they had to pay exorbitant prices—the *Alesia* set off north again.

It was a long haul, made more uncomfortable by the worsening weather. It grew appreciably colder, rain squalls were frequent, and it was a relief to all when, after nine days, they reached the calmer waters to the east of Strallen's southern tip. They anchored off the small port of Innis, which showed little sign of the destruction that had visited their previous ports of call. The spirits of all on board rose at the thought of shore leave and at the possibility that Strallen had somehow escaped the icy fog. Bram was still cautious, however, and sent a small party ashore before committing the *Alesia* to the docks.

The sailors returned with the news that the harbor was clear and that the locals, on being asked about the effects of the unseasonal fog had replied, "What fog?" This brought a delighted reaction from the sailors and even Yve began to harbor a tiny grain of hope that her vision—and Sweetness's—had been wrong. They took the *Alesia* into port.

That night Yve and Bram lodged at a comfortable tavern, and after their evening meal sat talking quietly in the private dining room.

"I have to go to Ahrenhold," Yve said. Strallen's capital was a large city, a day's journey from the coast.

"Of course," Bram agreed.

"What will you do?"

The seaman regarded her as if this were a foolish question. "Come with you," he said finally.

"What about the *Alesia*? And your crew?"

"They've been here before and so have I. Sailing is my business. The ship's taken care of."

"I'm sorry. I . . ."

Bram waved away her apology.

"I'd be very glad of your company," Yve concluded.

They sat for some time in silence, each lost in their own thoughts.

"Tell me about Jenny," Yve said.

Bram frowned. "Why?"

"You've been avoiding the subject for days, and it might do you good to talk to someone. Besides, I don't like mysteries. Wizards are supposed to know everything." She smiled encouragingly at the sailor, who was now deep in thought.

"There's not much to tell," he said eventually. "She doesn't live in the same world as most of us, and people call her mad. She's not, but it helps them deal with her existence."

"You loved her, didn't you?"

"We both did," Bram replied, a faraway look in his eyes. "That was the trouble."

Yve waited.

"She was a singer. She had such a beautiful voice, so high and clear . . ." Bram smiled at the memory. "She only really came alive when she was singing. I accompanied her many times but she was too good for me. Crawn was the only one who could match her." His voice faltered.

"What happened?" Yve prompted gently.

"She loved us both, and couldn't choose between us. We'd always been so close before, but this drove us wild." Bram looked at the wizard and she saw his pain. "We fought—in front of her. I nearly killed him. He never played again, and Jenny didn't even speak, let alone sing, for a whole year. She couldn't stand the sight of me and I hated myself, so I went away."

"That's when you became a sailor."

"Yes. I didn't see them again for about five years. They were married by then, of course." Bram ran out of words.

Is all the world full of sad stories? Yve wondered. Aloud she said softly, "Thank you for telling me."

Bram shrugged and looked away. They were both glad

when the landlord bustled into the room to clear their plates and ask whether they required anything else.

"Only information," Bram replied, and enquired about the hire of horses and the route to Ahrenhold. That concluded, the conversation turned to general matters.

"The summer ended so quick, it seems as though some days never happened at all," their host remarked. "Weather's been bad, too."

"Fog?" Bram asked.

"No more than usual. Cold, though, for the time of year."

"Had any trouble recently?"

"Trouble?" The innkeeper looked puzzled. "Why should there be? We're peaceable folk round here." He was offended.

"Did you see the shooting star a month or so ago?" Yve asked. "They tell me it was quite spectacular."

"Couldn't say, miss. There's been no shooting stars to my knowledge." He was beginning to regard his guests suspiciously and they decided against any further questions.

They rode out of Innis early the next morning. As soon as they were clear of the town, both horses became fretful, prancing nervously. A familiar voice sounded in Yve's head.

Why are those silly horses dancing?

Sweetness, looking smug, appeared at the side of the road.

Because you're scaring them! Yve responded.

But I won't hurt them.

They don't know that.

The horses gradually grew used to their new traveling companion and settled down, though they remained restless. Yve explained the situation to Bram, who eyed the dragon narrowly but was unable to catch more than a vague impression of the shimmering creature.

"Which may be as well," he said. "I'm still not sure I believe in dragons."

Yve glanced quickly at Sweetness. Far from showing any signs of an adverse reaction to this statement, he seemed to find it quite funny. The wizard's head echoed with his chuckles.

Shall I blow him some flames? Sweetness asked, all innocence. *He'd see that.*

No! Yve replied quickly. *I don't want to be thrown off this horse, thank you very much.*

But they're so little, Sweetness said. *Wouldn't you rather ride me?* He spread his wings and pretended to soar. *Wheee!* The horses shied at the sudden movement.

Sweetness!

Yes?

Are you sure this island was covered by the fog?

Of course. I told you. He sounded petulant. *Besides, you only have to look at the trees.*

Yve took the dragon's advice and soon realized what he meant. Many of the trees were almost bare of leaves—though winter was still some months away—and the greenery that did remain was often blighted, the leaves brown and rotting.

As they rode, she saw further evidence of the ravages of cold and damp. There were few birds and insects, unusual for the time of year, and many fields of corn were gray and sickly with mildew, the farmland looking ill-tended and forlorn. She pointed these signs out to Bram.

"Aye, something's happened here, whatever they say," he agreed.

When they stopped at a remote farmhouse, Sweetness made himself scarce without needing to be told. The farmer could only offer them water.

"We're not doing well this year," he said. "Got no food to spare." He didn't seem unduly concerned.

"Bad weather?" Bram asked.

"Can't complain," the man replied. "But there's no time to do much these days. Crops rot before you know it. Must be a blight."

"We've heard there's been a bad fog," Yve said.

"Not here, missy. By the sea, that's the place for fog. It's got cold quick though—can't think where the summer's gone."

"It's as if they *slept* through the fog," Bram commented when they were on their way again.

Yve nodded. *As though there were some days that never happened at all.* She began to feel frightened again.

They reached Ahrenhold in the late afternoon. The city had long since outgrown its ancient stone walls and now sprawled over a considerable area. After traveling through the outlying

districts, which were reassuringly busy and thronged with people, they passed into the old town through one of the huge
stone arches. Leaving Bram to make arrangements for their
horses and their lodgings, Yve went alone to visit the royal
castle. When Bram demurred, she replied that she must lose
no time in seeing Saronno, and that it would be better for her
to go alone, in her official capacity as Lugg's wizard.

As she walked to the castle—at the center of the city—she
recalled all she knew of Strallen's wizard. She had met Saronno
only once before, on Ark, and remembered him mainly for his
unhealthy-looking gray skin and his sinister familiar, a snake.
Saronno had been one of those who had sided with Drogo at
the wizard's conclave, and, if her memory was correct, he could
be almost as pompous as her ex-master. *I hope he accepts me,*
she thought as she approached the guard at the castle gates.

"I'm here to see Saronno. Could you please tell him—"

"Who?"

"Saronno. Your wizard," Yve replied in confusion.

The man turned his head and spat. "Pah! Wizards? We've
no wizards here. Don't waste my time. What's your real business?"

"You no longer have a wizard?"

"Don't you listen?" the guard said angrily. "There are no
wizards here. *There never have been.* I don't know what silly
tales you've been listening to but we don't need them here.
Now tell me what you want or clear off!"

Further argument was clearly useless. After a slight hesitation, Yve turned on her heels and left. The soldier watched
her closely for a few moments, then ducked inside the guardroom and called to one of his colleagues.

Yve walked slowly back to the inn, her mind reeling at
this latest setback. She felt frustrated, annoyed with herself
and everyone about her, but most of all she was confused.
*What is happening to the world? Drogo's dead. Cai's missing.
Now they tell me there have never been any wizards on Strallen! Has the whole world gone mad or have I?*

She gave Bram a full report, but he could make no sense
of it either, and they went early to bed, tired after their day's
travel.

In the early hours of the morning, Yve was rudely awakened

as her bedroom door crashed open. Fighting away the effects
of sleep, the bewildered wizard was aware of several soldiers
bursting into the room, trampling over the splintered wood.
By the time she was struggling to rise there was a knife at her
throat and two crossbows pointed at her chest.

Chapter 12

*B*ram awoke instantly at the sound of breaking wood, alert even in his sleep. The sound of commotion coming from Yve's room had him out of bed and into the corridor in moments. He was met by a soldier who placed a large hand on his chest to halt him.

"Not so fast, friend."

"What's going on here?" Bram demanded, then stiffened as Yve was led out of her room and marched down the stairs. He caught the quick shake of her head and did not try to follow.

"*Nothing* is going on here," the soldier replied emphatically. "And if you know what's good for you, you will have seen *nothing!*" He shoved Bram into his room so hard that the seaman stumbled and fell, and his head hit the end of the bed. The door was slammed shut. Half-stunned, he lay on the floor and listened to the retreating footsteps.

A little while later, the shock began to wear off, though his head still throbbed painfully. Bram levered himself up and dressed slowly. It was still very early and there was no one about when he ventured into the corridor and thence to Yve's room. Other than the broken door, there was nothing to show that she had ever been there. All her belongings had been removed. Bram left the inn, trying to decide what to do. Resistance earlier had been pointless. Yve had not fought, and he had been powerless. So what was he to do now?

Her abductors had been in uniform, therefore it was safe

to assume that they came from the castle, and he could confirm that easily.

Bram set off, hoping that the cold, early morning air would clear his head. The castle guard's uniforms were instantly familiar, but that was no immediate help to him. He walked about the castle, noting the number of guards and, later, when the watches were changed. His reconnaissance proved nothing except that he would be unable to enter unless on legitimate business. Even the smaller entrances were guarded and no one could enter without being checked.

He stayed near the castle all day, moving about to avoid suspicion, but saw no sign of Yve. He noted that some off-duty soldiers frequented a tavern opposite the main gates and decided to try to eavesdrop on their talk in the hope that he would learn something of value.

Two hours later all he had heard was inconsequential drinking chatter and jokes about King Illva and his new queen, who was half his age. He had been able, however, to get to know the faces and names of several people—both soldiers and servants—who lived and worked in the castle. It was a start.

Bram was tempted to present himself at the castle gates and demand to know what had happened to his friend. He had always preferred direct action, but on this occasion he decided against it. *Yve tried that yesterday*, he thought. Instead, he returned to his lodgings, checked on their horses and went to bed.

The lock on Yve's door had been repaired.

It was not until later, while on the verge of falling asleep, that Bram recalled the references to Strallen's royal family and realized that *whatever* had happened on this island was certainly far different from the disasters that had befallen Lugg and Arlon.

———————————————

The next day he resumed his vigil outside the castle.

No one at the inn had asked him about Yve's absence and he did not bring the subject up. He suspected that they too would have seen and heard "nothing."

After a fruitless morning he joined a group of castle guards at their favorite tavern and, as someone willing and able to stand a round of drinks, he was accepted into their company. His carefully phrased questions about any newcomers or unusual happenings at the castle drew no response, however, and he began to despair of this line of investigation. He took his leave as the soldiers began to drift away, then made another circuit of the castle walls.

At one of the small entrances a woman emerged, carrying a huge wicker basket. The guard on duty made a comment, and she laughed with him as she walked on, staggering slightly under the weight of her burden.

Bram quickly moved to her side.

"Can I help you with that?"

She regarded him for a moment, as though wondering what his motive was. Her young face was red and shiny from the heat of the washhouse.

"All right," she said at last and handed the basket over. They walked on.

"You're new to the city, aren't you?" she said.

"Yes. How could you tell?"

"By your accent."

"I've come up from Innis," he said, combining truth with convenience.

"What for?"

"To look for work."

The woman snorted. "Work! You can keep it. In here." She pushed open a door and led Bram into a small bare room. "Put it down over there, in the corner. What do you do?"

"I'm a musician."

"Really?" Her eyes showed interest. "Thank you for your help. Would you like something to drink?"

Bram nodded and followed her into the kitchen.

"What do you play?" she asked as she put on water to heat.

"The flute."

"I'd like to hear you play sometime."

Bram spent the afternoon walking aimlessly. He and Clara had got on well together and, though work had called her back to the castle, they had agreed to meet that evening. The sailor was looking forward to it, both for the pleasure of her company and the much-needed human contact, but also because she did not guard her words about events within the castle. She represented his best chance yet of learning Yve's whereabouts.

He arrived at the rendezvous early, then fretted until Clara arrived. He bought dinner, and they talked about themselves. Bram's version of his own history was a judicious mixture of fact and fiction. He felt guilty about deceiving Clara but knew that the truth could prove dangerous to them both.

Eventually, their conversation turned to life within the castle and Bram's diligence was rewarded. His mention of Saronno's name produced no reaction and Clara laughed at the idea of a wizard living permanently within the court.

"Why, whatever would you think that for?" she exclaimed. On the subject of the royal family she was more forthcoming.

"The old queen gave him no sons, of course, and it was a blessing in a way when she died last year. The new queen, Ula, is young—and *so* beautiful." She giggled. "It's a wonder he can keep up with her."

"Where is she from? I've not heard that name before."

Clara looked nonplussed. "Now that you mention it, I don't rightly know."

"You must hear all the gossip working where you do."

"Oh yes," she answered. "You can't stop tongues wagging in a washhouse." Bram prompted her to go on, feigning interest in various court intrigues until he saw his chance.

"And that really annoyed the jailer," Clara said, concluding one of her stories.

"You have dungeons in the castle?" Bram asked.

"Yes, though I've never seen them—and hope I never will. They're mostly empty now but even the threat of them is enough to make you watch your step. I wouldn't like to be in that poor woman's shoes."

"What woman?" Bram asked, fearing the worst.

"I didn't see her myself, mind, but I heard they threw a young woman into the cells yesterday. Poor thing." Clara shuddered. "I wonder what she'd done."

I wish I knew, Bram thought. This confirmation, though not unexpected, left him feeling alone and helpless. *What do I do now?*

Yve sat in her dark cell, feeling disconsolate. The only feeble light came though the iron bars in the door. Inside, it was cold and damp.

Although she could comfort her own body, Yve was aware that some ensorcellment prevented her from using magic beyond the confines of her cell and the iron door which sealed it. It was a spell she had not met before; this meant that whoever had imprisoned her not only knew of her abilities but also had power of his own. The obvious suspect was Saronno.

But why?

Nothing made sense. There were so many inconsistencies in what she had learnt that for the moment she could not think at all coherently.

Had she known the fate which awaited her, Yve may have tried to escape from her captors the day before—and would probably have died with an arrow in her back.

After her arrest, the soldiers had marched in silence to the castle's dungeons. Yve's questions had been either ignored or quickly silenced and she soon gave up any attempt at enlightenment.

As they went down the stairs, Yve sensed the presence of a malign magical force and instinctively began to react against it. Then alarms rang in her head. *Something* was watching over the dungeons from afar, something from which she would much rather remain hidden.

As she passed through the invisible barrier, Yve forced her wizardly potential deep into her subconscious, shrinking protectively into herself and becoming as inconspicuous as possible. Within her mind, memories rearranged themselves unbidden, some sliding into the deepest recesses so that they almost ceased to exist. The process took only moments, yet it gave Yve a comforting sense of security.

That feeling had long since faded in the lonely hours that followed, and now she was sinking even further into gloom. Had she fallen into a trap? Should she have discounted the warnings in her head and fought against her imprisonment? Why was she being ignored by her captors?

The questions multiplied. As she wondered whether she would *ever* get any answers, her mind filled with the wholly incongruous sound that accompanied Sweetness's entrance into a room. The dragon emerged slowly from the rear wall of the cell. *There you are*, he said. *I've had no end of trouble finding you. Even I can't get through some of these walls.* He sounded vexed. *And they tickle dreadfully.* His large, shining eyes blinked slowly. *Why are you here?*

I wish I knew, Yve replied. *Oh, it's so good to see you, Sweetness!*

The wizard's delight at her companion's appearance soon

diminished. Having someone to talk to was in itself a great
comfort, but the dragon's ability to reach her was of limited
use. As he had little or no physical effect on Yve's world, he
could not help her escape and, as Bram could hardly see Sweetness, let alone talk with him, he could not act as a messenger
for them. It was most frustrating.

Even so, she felt better for his cheerful company and optimistic attitude and they talked for a long time. Eventually
Sweetness left to test out a theory or two—or, as he thought
of it, to play some more games.

I wish I could do that, Yve thought ruefully, as he melted
into the wall.

Over the next few days Bram met Clara often, and heard
from her the peculiar rumors that were circulating in the
city. Objects had apparently burst into flames for no reason,
causing panic and alarm, only to appear cool and unharmed
moments later. He guessed the origin of these stories and
even fancied he saw some odd flickering lights sometimes but
could never be sure. He had no idea what Sweetness was
trying to do.

Of more immediate concern was his own attempt to gain
access to the castle. Through Clara, he eventually met some
soldiers and courtiers, each of whom introduced him to another
until, at last, he was greeted by a court musician and asked to
play. If he showed enough talent, it was implied, there was a
chance of employment for him within the castle.

Bram fought down his nervousness. He had not knowingly
played for anyone but himself for many years, and was not
sure how he would react to an audience. However, as soon as
his flute was in his hands, he felt the old magic well up inside
him. He played, as he always did, for Jenny. When he finished,
it came as something of a shock to hear the musician's reaction.

"You're good," he said approvingly. "You'll have to learn
some new songs, of course—I haven't heard that one in years
—but that shouldn't be a problem."

Clara, who had also been present, was delighted.

"You were wonderful," she enthused later. "I've never heard
anything so beautiful—or so sad. It almost made me cry."

Bram looked into her shining eyes, but saw only another
face.

"You seemed to be in a trance," she went on. "As if you weren't here at all."

"I was playing for someone," he replied before he could stop himself.

"For a woman?" Clara asked softly.

He nodded, hating himself.

"The one in the dungeons?"

"No. What makes you think that?" he asked cautiously.

"You seemed interested in her."

Careful! Bram admonished himself.

"No," he repeated. "I don't know her."

"Then who?" she whispered.

"Someone from a very long time ago. She's dead now."

"I'm sorry."

They sat in silence for a while.

"I wish someone would play like that for me," Clara said eventually.

"They will," he replied firmly. "Maybe not on the same instrument . . . but they will."

After another pause, she said, as brightly as she could, "And tomorrow you play in the castle!"

It's no use. I can scare the guards but I don't see how I can make them do what I want. And I can't make Bram see anything. Sweetness's dejected tone matched Yve's mood.

It doesn't matter, she replied. *You tried. We'll think of something.*

I've found the snake-man, the dragon said, perking up a little.

Saronno? So he is here!

Yes, Sweetness agreed. *In a room just like this one.*

In the dungeons? This news confused Yve. If the wizard himself was imprisoned, then who was responsible?

Tell me about him, she demanded.

He's in a room further down the corridor. He's asleep, but his eyes are open and he doesn't move at all.

You're sure he's alive?

Oh yes. But I don't think he's very well, Sweetness replied with unconscious understatement. *He just lies there on his back with his staff beside him. The snake moves though,* the dragon added hopefully. *It hissed at me.*

Yve tried to fit this latest piece of news into the puzzle in her head. It still made no sense.

The next morning, Bram at last entered Ahrenhold Castle. After his fellow musician had vouched for him, the guard waved them ahead and he walked inside, his heart pounding. He already knew much of the layout of the castle, thanks to his assiduous questioning, but seeing it for himself was far better. He did not learn much that first day, however. After attending the rehearsal, he was promptly escorted outside again. He surprised himself by enjoying the challenge of playing among professionals and gave a good account of himself. So when he left the castle, he fretted at his lack of progress in freeing Yve from unknown horrors, but was at least secure in the knowledge that he would be invited back.

It was only two days later that the troupe's leader offered Bram a job, and a room of his own within the castle. Both were accepted with alacrity and he soon became an accepted member of the court community. With that came the freedom he needed to explore and make plans. He proceeded cautiously, knowing that a mistake now could be fatal and would certainly leave Yve in an even worse plight. Nevertheless, he was forced to take some chances and, when he was accosted by a soldier near the entrance to the dungeons he explained that he had got lost, being a newcomer to the castle. His store of knowledge slowly grew.

A concert was planned for a few days hence as part of the festivities surrounding the first wedding anniversary of the royal couple. Many guests were expected and the castle would be full of strange faces. Bram intended to make use of that fact.

He still saw Clara occasionally, but hardened his heart and prevented the relationship from developing. No matter what she thought of him, it would be better for her in the long run if they were not connected. When the proposed escape had taken place, any knowledge of his friendship with her could prove a distinct liability. Clara was hurt by his attitude but assumed that his heart was still given to another, so accepted the situation philosophically.

By the day of the concert Bram felt that he knew the layout

of the castle well enough. He knew where the jailer kept his keys and even had an idea of which cell Yve was incarcerated in. He had mapped out their escape route, and his plans for any guards not distracted by the celebrations were simple. As always, he preferred direct action.

That evening's feast was a glittering affair. The music was received enthusiastically by the royal hosts and their guests, but was quickly forgotten as other entertainments followed. Bram slipped away unnoticed as his colleagues, their work done, prepared to indulge themselves and take a part in the festivities.

He collected the few things that he needed and walked stealthily through the almost deserted lower reaches of the castle. He reached the jailer's room without being challenged, and was astonished—and greatly encouraged—to find it unguarded. Slipping inside, he quickly took the two large keyrings, holding them carefully so that they made as little noise as possible. His dagger was in his other hand.

The key to the dungeons' outer door was already in the lock, and this saved him valuable time. He stepped within, taking the key, and closed the door behind him. After a few moments for his eyes to get used to the dim light, Bram descended the stairs as quietly as he could. At the bottom, the chill, sodden air was distinctly unpleasant. He shivered and went on.

The first three cells were empty, but the fourth contained a wretched-looking man, who stirred uneasily in his sleep as Bram peered through the grille. He could not waste time, however, and walked on. A strange, nervous tingle ran through his body and he glanced round, but could see no one. At the next door he almost cried out with relief. Yve lay within, fast asleep. Quickly he tried the various keys. The first four did not work but their noise awoke the wizard. She peered at Bram disbelievingly, then rose quickly as with a finger to his lips he signaled for quiet.

But before Bram could try another key, the door to the cell opposite was flung open and two soldiers emerged, their swords drawn. Yve screamed a warning, but was too late and could only watch helplessly as Bram was felled by a blow to the head.

"We've had our eye on you, musician," one of the soldiers said, grinning nastily. "You can join your friend in jug now."

With that they manhandled his inert body into the cell in which they had been hiding, relieved him of the keys, locked the door and left.

Yve listened to their gleeful talk until it dwindled into the distance.

"Bram," she called softly. "Bram?"

There was no answer.

Chapter 13

γve was flying. Riding on
Sweetness's neck, she was frightened and exhilarated at the
same time. Sunlit clouds flashed by, rearing over her like
mountains. She cried aloud but could not hear her voice.

The dragon changed course abruptly and she clung even
more tightly to her precarious perch. Then he began to dive;
it was only then that Yve noticed Sweetness was the wrong
color. Even her own hands were unfamiliar . . .

She was suddenly blinded. The clouds which had seemed
so white from above proved to be cold and leaden from within,
masking everything. She lost all sense of movement; only the
rushing noise of their passage remained.

They eventually emerged below the clouds, into a dark and
forbidding landscape. Far below, gray seas merged, and the
land was buffeted by tumultuous rain and hurricanes. In the
midst of all this ferment a huge volcano spewed forth flame
and ash, sulfurous smoke and fiery red lava.

The dragon hesitated, awaiting her instructions.

Down! she commanded, while part of her mind screamed
in terrified denial.

They plummeted toward the heart of the volcano.

Yve awoke gasping for air. She forced her eyes open, made

herself look at the dank, sordid cell that was now her home. Reality, however, could not dispel the dream's effect. She still felt the lurch of her stomach as she began to fall, her heart still raced, and the perspiration on her skin had lost none of its clammy chill. Even awake the dream continued, fighting with her conscious self for control of her mind.

I must be going mad, she thought desperately. *What else can it be?* Yet she knew that in questioning her sanity she denied her own assertion. *When I do go mad I won't know about it—because by then I won't even mind.* She smiled in the darkness.

She had lost all sense of how long she had been imprisoned. Day and night had no meaning here, and months had passed in stultifying monotony. The only sound she heard was the approach of the guard who pushed her meager meal through a hatch in the base of the door. He never spoke.

Bram's voice was the last human sound she had heard. After being knocked unconscious, he had been silent for so long that Yve had feared for his life. Later, though, she had heard sounds of movement and called out to him. Her would-be rescuer had answered weakly, mumbling apologies. Shortly afterward, the guards had returned and removed him from the cell, marching the stumbling figure deeper into the dungeons and thus removing all hope of contact.

In the time that followed, Yve had begun to believe that she was the forgotten victim of a ghastly mistake. Surely after all these miserable days someone would come and explain her arrest, give a reason for her imprisonment—even if it meant that she was to die for a crime she could not understand, or had not committed. But nothing happened. With Bram also incarcerated she saw no possibility of her situation changing, unless whatever authority had imprisoned her saw fit to remember her existence.

Until then, only her dreams could grant her any freedom —and they had proved a mixed blessing. Yve shivered, remembering the fearful scenes, then shook her head and spoke aloud, quoting a favorite saying of her old master. "Dreams are a distortion of reality. You can learn from them, but you cannot trust them." The words gave her little comfort, but at least the sound of her voice was real.

Paradoxically, the only thing which *had* been a real comfort in this ordeal was the aspect of her life which had no place in normal reality. Sweetness had visited her often, though she knew he found it an unpleasant place to reach, and his silent conversations gave her a measure of solace. Their relationship had changed, going beyond the initial intrigue and bemused friendship, and she now had no hesitation in believing him to be her familiar.

Many times they had gone through the frustrating process of trying to find a way in which Sweetness could help Yve escape but the dragon's inability to affect anything directly in her world always left them wallowing in a morass of helpless theorizing. The wizard had to content herself with his reports from the outside world, and it was thus that she learned that Bram was still imprisoned. Like her, he seemed to have been forgotten. She hoped that the isolation would not break his spirit. His rescue attempt had been a courageous act, but she blamed herself for his misfortune. The idea that he might end his days cooped up in the dark after a life on the sunlit, open seas was too dreadful to contemplate. He did not deserve such a fate, and Yve vowed that if she ever got the chance to leave this place, she would not go without him.

Although Sweetness found traveling inside the dungeons difficult, even painful, he did bring Yve news of the other prisoners. The gray-skinned man, who Yve thought must be Saronno, still lay in his cell, unmoving and unchanged as the months went by. Several others also languished in the widely separated cells. Sweetness reported that one or two talked to themselves, making no sense; others shouted at the unresponsive guard, demanding that their status as envoys be recognized. More than once the dragon heard some mention the name Ark, and Yve surmised from his reports that at least four of her fellow inmates were from that island. This gave her more to think about, but their imprisonment made no more sense to her than her own plight.

Little changed in the twilight world beneath Ahrenhold Castle. Sweetness told Yve of events taking place in the city, but she had lost all notion of the world outside, and his words meant little. So their talk eventually turned to other matters: the differences between their two worlds, the nature of time and space, what was solid and what was not—and so on. During these discussions, Sweetness frequently became confused and peevish, annoyed that things which he took for granted should require so much explanation, and as a consequence Yve's ideas

were only partially clarified. In an effort to help, she tried to
make a game of it, but the dragon soon recognized her tactics
and refused to play.

So it was that as the days stretched into months and winter
came to the world above the ground, the wizard and her familiar began telling each other stories to pass the time, which,
for a while at least, allowed Yve to escape from the oppressive
confinement of mildewed stone and iron bars.

At first Sweetness was a reluctant narrator, preferring to
listen, but Yve gradually persuaded him to make the effort.
Before long, he was showing an unexpected storytelling talent.
One of the wizard's favorite tales, which Sweetness claimed to
have made up himself, and which he related several times—
with minor variations—was entitled "The Wobbly Whirlpool."

*Long, long ago, in a time that all but very few have now
forgotten, there was a little boy called Belado, who lived with
a lady, mistress of a great realm. People called her the Dragon
Lady, because in her castle there were many pictures of those
fierce and brave-looking creatures.*

Yve smiled. Sweetness could not resist having dragons
somewhere in his story.

*The Dragon Lady wasn't Belado's mother, but she was very
good to him and they loved each other dearly. The boy's play-
mates were a group of children like himself—they too had no
family, and grew up in the castle of the great lady, playing
and learning. Most of all they loved the old stories of warriors,
legends of great and heroic deeds; even the girls longed to
prove themselves in battle.*

*One hot day in summer, the children were excused from
their lessons, and given permission to swim in the nearby lake.
A maid went with them to keep order, but failed in her duty.
Soon after their arrival, she fell asleep in the warm sun, leaving
the young ones to their own devices. Eight of them clambered
into a boat and set off across the water. It was great fun—if
a little crowded—and they shouted and sang merrily. After a
while, though, they grew quiet, one by one. Something was
wrong. Even with them all pulling together, they couldn't steer
the boat. But how could there be an undertow in a lake? In
spite of all their frightened efforts to get back to the shore,
the boat just went round in circles. Slowly at first, then faster
and faster, round and round they went. And then the boat
began to shake, wobbling them until they thought they would*

fall out. They cried for help, but the maid was asleep, and the other children thought they were only playing.

When, in a sickening movement, the lake disappeared from underneath them, the children in the boat went very quiet. This was awful! Something bad was happening and they didn't know what to do. They were very scared. Belado looked down over the side, and saw beneath them a whirling, twirling, roaring mass of water—they were on top of a whirlpool!

"Help!" he screamed at the very top of his voice. "Please help us!"

For a few moments, all they could hear was the sound of rushing water. But then—oh joy!—then they heard the beating of enormous wings, and a huge golden dragon appeared in the sky above them. He swooped down, dived beneath the boat, rested it firmly on his back, then headed for the shore.

The children clambered down shakily, and looked in awe at the great creature. So dragons really did exist! "Thank you," Belado said huskily, still greatly frightened. And a voice in his head replied, Don't mention it. That's what I'm for—to rescue all helpless ones from danger. A word of warning, though. Do beware of whirlpools, especially *wobbly* whirlpools.

And Belado knew that for the rest of his life, he would take great care, and would beware of wobbly whirlpools. Much chastened, the group of children set off for home. One day, they knew, their time would come and they would have a chance to prove their braveness to the Dragon Lady. But maybe not just yet!

You're getting almost as good as Adara! Yve commented as the story came to an end.

I don't think so, Sweetness replied with uncharacteristic modesty. *Not yet at least. Maybe tomorrow.*

Yve laughed and the dragon blinked rapidly, his eyes flashing. *He's growing up,* Yve thought to herself. *He can make fun of himself now.*

Outside, the guard's footsteps approached.

Shall I roast him? Sweetness asked. It was his standard question in this situation. The silent jailer had shown no sign of ever noticing the cell's extra inhabitant.

No, Yve replied. *Even if you could, I need my food, disgusting though it sometimes is.*

I'd bring you better if I could.

I know. Yve was moved to pity by the dragon's sorrowful

tone. *Besides, I'm a wizard. I can make it taste of whatever I like.*

Lobster and cabbage, Sweetness suggested.

Apricots and cream.

Wine and chocolate!

Tomatoes with chives!

Pomegranates and asparagus!

As the jailer pushed the tray though the hatch, wizard and dragon dissolved into silent laughter.

Oh well, Yve said then, resignedly. *Stale bread and cold dishwater again.*

She chewed determinedly. The guard went on his way to deliver meals to his other charges.

Is Bram still all right?

I think so. He sings a lot. The dragon's voice betrayed his uncertainty.

I wish you could talk to him, Yve said with a sigh.

So do I.

What about Saronno?

I don't know. I haven't checked lately. The dragon disappeared, then returned.

He's gone, Sweetness said.

Saronno stood within the familiar surroundings of the royal reception chamber, leaning heavily upon the staff which had once been the outward symbol of his wizardly power. His familiar, the snake Ssor, who in earlier times had adorned his arm, remained in the cell far below.

Fear showed in Saronno's eyes, but not because he was afraid for his own life. Indeed, death would have been a welcome negation of the knowledge he was being forced to accept.

"Is it not customary to kneel before one's queen?" Ula smiled coldly. Saronno made no reply, and remained standing. "I could force you, you know," she added, and made a swift gesture with her hand.

Saronno's knees buckled, and he staggered, gasping in pain until she laughingly relented. The wizard rested on his staff once more, cursing his impotence.

"What do you want with me?" he asked feebly.

"Why, Saronno, are you *so* impatient to return to your cell?"

"At least there I am free of your mocking tongue."

"And of all others, including your own," Ula remarked. "You sleep without dreams. You may sleep forever—and forever you will be at my beck and call. Does that please you, wizard?"

Saronno said nothing.

"Tell me, what do you know of the Rite of Yzalba?"

The question took him by surprise. For a moment he contemplated lying, then realized that he could not fool her, and decided that it was better to give her what she wanted than to have it torn from his mind by force.

"It is the awakening of the Earth-mind," he said. "The rite forms a direct link to the power within the world, the power that built the Earth and rules it still. It releases energies that are so great that they cannot be controlled. Using the Rite could destroy everything."

"How is the link formed?"

"There are doors. One merely has to knock in the right manner. If you are a wizard—and you have the urge to die— it is very easy."

"Can any wizard perform it?"

Saronno looked at her contemptuously. "The wizards of all the isles together could not do it. It would be madness."

"Then the rite has never been used?"

"Only once. It ended the so-called War of the Wizards, but the price was mass destruction. It will never be repeated."

Ula smiled. "You may go now," she said and turned away, dismissing him. Two soldiers entered and prepared to escort the stooping wizard back to the dungeons. The queen paused, as something else occurred to her.

"Wait! I have a riddle for you. A wizard's rhyme." She smiled at Saronno's expression of disgust. "Tell me what this means:

> A child, mage-born, and marked for flight,
> Shall add her voice but utter naught."

After a moment's consideration, the old man shrugged his shoulders.

"It's nonsense," he said. "No wizard can father a child. You know that as well as I. It follows that the rest must be meaningless."

"Thank you, oh great sage," she mocked. "Sleep well—

until I send for you again." She smiled nastily. "Take him
away."

Saronno walked slowly down into the darkness. Within
him, hate seethed impotently.

Give me one chance! he thought. *Just one!*

Chapter 14

*T*he gray man's back, Sweetness said, and Yve's hope that something might at last be happening in her unchanging world died.

"Do not even *try* to deceive me, daughter!" The image in the stone wavered as Alzedo's face contorted with anger. Fixing Ula with his cruel, colorless eyes, he spoke again. "You presume too much, and that is not wise. You knew what my wishes were concerning the wizard, and yet you chose to disobey me."

"But he is in thrall to me, father!" Ula cried.

"To *you*? Better say, to *me*! And I do not wish it. That is the end of the matter."

"But it would be such a waste."

"No excuses, Ula. What power you have is mine to command. I see I shall have to teach you a lesson."

His image disappeared, and the glass sphere in the queen's hands became once more opaque and white, featureless. Shaking with anger, she put it down. Ula did not agree with her "father," but knew that he was enormously powerful, and could indeed stop her pursuing her own course. It irked her that he had found out about Saronno. Someone would pay for that.

What had he meant by "teaching her a lesson"?

The seeing-stone changed color suddenly, but instead of

producing the usual image it began to glow a deep, threatening red. Ripples of power ran through the air. Ula's violet eyes were wide in disbelief.

How can he act from so far away? What is he doing?

———————————

In his cell far below, Saronno stirred. *What now?* he thought dismally, then realized that this was no ordinary summons. About him the world was changing. The sorcery that created dungeon walls even more impenetrable than stone was crumbling—he felt a little of his old power returning!

Quickly, he rose from his stony bed. Ssor watched him with eyes that were alert once more. The wizard did not know the reason for the change, nor did he care. If this was to be his one chance of freedom—through death if necessary—he would grasp it eagerly.

He scanned the cell, probing its barriers with his mind as well as his eyes. Iron bars and lock made the door impregnable, and the stone walls were thick. *I have not power enough yet,* he thought, but was aware that he grew stronger every moment. Turning to Ssor, he gave instructions to his familiar; the snake slithered rapidly through the food hatch in the door and away along the corridor.

Yve and Sweetness also felt the difference. They shivered involuntarily and looked questioningly at each other.

What's happening? the dragon asked, sounding very young.

I don't know.

Shall I go and find out?

Yve nodded and he began to slide through the wall into the corridor.

There's a snake out here, he commented.

Go and see the gray man, Yve said. *Hurry!*

As Sweetness retreated, the wizard looked through the grille in the door, and saw the snake pass by, heading for the stairs. *At least someone's escaping,* she thought.

———————————

"Father, what are you doing?"

The stone remained red as it transmitted the answer.

"Unless I am greatly mistaken, you have a viper in your

nest. I have set it free. I believe you will find it advisable to do my bidding now." Alzedo sounded amused.

"The dungeons!" Ula screamed. "You madman, what have you done?"

"Fight well, daughter. Use this experience to learn to handle your own talent wisely, instead of squandering borrowed power. You have an easy solution, of course—one you should have used long ago."

"Guards!" the queen yelled.

Sweetness poked his head through the closed door of Saronno's cell. The wizard regarded him without surprise.

"Interesting," he said, as the dragon blinked slowly. "Whose illusion are you? The queen's? You do not frighten me."

Sweetness shook his head in confusion.

"So you hear me, do you? Then tell your mistress this. She will degrade me no more. Let her face me—if she dares!"

The wizard struck a dramatic pose, one quivering finger pointing at the dragon's head. Energy crackled in the gloomy air. Sweetness was not affected, but the stone doorway about him began to crack and crumble. He withdrew in consternation and returned to Yve.

He's awake—and angry, he reported. *He told me to tell you . . . I think . . .* Sweetness repeated Saronno's message.

Yve was puzzled. Something was happening though, that much was clear.

What's an illusion? the dragon asked.

The jailer was enjoying himself. He sat with his feet up on the table, watching his visitor's face.

"What makes you think he's in here?" he asked, cracking another nut between jagged teeth.

"Rumors," Clara replied. "Besides, he can't have just vanished. He played here with the musicians on the feast-night, and nobody's seen him since then."

"He probably got drunk, fell over, and drowned in a puddle."

"If something like that *had* happened, he'd have been found. I'd have heard by now."

"But why should a nice boy like that end up here?"

"I don't know," Clara retorted, "but you do. *Is* he inside?"
The jailer leered. "What's it worth?"

"You're a cruel man . . ." Clara paused, her attention caught by a movement in the doorway. She almost screamed, but the snake raised its head and looked directly at her with such piercing clarity and uncanny calm that she could not make a sound.

"It's the job," the jailer answered, unaware of his visitor's distraction. "It makes you cruel. I know how to be kind to a woman, though."

Clara looked quickly back at him. Though she was sickened by his oily tone and false smile, she forced herself to respond. "Is that so?"

The man nodded. Behind him, Ssor moved with silent intent toward the hooks where the key-rings hung. Clara watched his progress out of the corner of her eye. The snake seemed familiar to her, but of course that made no sense. She was fascinated.

The jailer lowered his feet and stood up.

"I think we should be kind to each other," he said, his voice husky. "Then—perhaps—I might give you news of your boyfriend. I have a comfortable room below." He began to turn.

"No," Clara said quickly, then smiled as best she could. "Why not here?"

The jailer grinned. "You're a saucy one," he said, advancing on her. As he approached, she dodged behind the table. "So you want to play, do you?" His words dissolved into a bubbling scream as Ssor's fangs sank into his calf muscle. He staggered, flailing wildly, eyes bulging, then fell to the floor. His body twitched feebly. Clara looked on in horror. *Am I next?* she wondered, but the snake ignored her. Reaching up with its tapered, prehensile tail, it deftly flicked one of the two large key-rings off its hook, then left, dragging the keys behind it. Clara watched in astonishment as Ssor descended the stairs to the dungeons. Acting on impulse, she snatched up the other set of keys and set off after him.

Her pace slowed as the light faded and her footing became uncertain. There was no sign of the snake.

"Bram?" she called timidly. There was no answer. "Bram!" Other voices came back to her with the echoes of her shout, among them the one she sought. She walked on.

"Clara?"

It was him.

"How did you get here?"

Before she could answer, a man with horrible gray skin loomed out of the dark passage, the snake coiled about his arm. Clara was frozen with fear, but Saronno merely presented her with the other set of keys, indicating one of them.

"That's the master-key," he said. "It opens all the doors. Let everyone out—and do it quickly. It will be a diversion if nothing else. I have other things to do." He strode on, leaving Clara shocked and scared.

"Try it!" Bram urged.

Her hands felt nerveless. Slowly, clumsily, she fitted the key to the lock. It would not turn at first but she persevered and was rewarded with a dull grating sound. The door opened, and they were in each other's arms. Bram took the keys from her.

"Where's Yve?"

"Who?"

"The blonde woman."

"Oh . . . I don't know . . ." She hesitated.

"You must get out of here," Bram said. "There'll be fighting soon. Go on! Run!" He kissed her. "Thank you, Clara."

She fled, and Bram moved from door to door, unlocking each as he went. Six men emerged, watching him suspiciously but not questioning their good fortune. The inhabitants of other cells either could not move or chose not to, but Bram had no time to spare to worry about them. He began to despair of finding Yve, but then heard her voice. Running now, he came to her door, unlocked it, and hugged her quickly. Back out in the corridor, the eight prisoners looked at each other.

"What's going on?" one asked.

"I don't know," Bram replied, "but I'm not hanging around to find out."

"Up?"

"Up," the seaman agreed. "Can you help us, Yve?"

The wizard shrugged. "My powers don't seem to work down here. Maybe Sweetness can."

The others looked mystified.

"Let's go," Bram said, and led the way.

Near the top of the stairs they halted. Above stood Saronno, his back toward them, arms outstretched. All about him waves of power roiled like liquid lightning, flashing myriad hues. This was a battle only Yve could understand, and even she felt her hopes fall. The others hung back as she approached the wizard. He sensed her presence and said, "She's re-establishing the shield. I can't hold out much longer. Get out while you can." His voice told of the strain he was under.

Yve beckoned to the others and slipped past Saronno. Sweetness followed. The older wizard saw him and looked at Yve with renewed interest.

"So it's *your* dragon," he croaked. "Good. Avenge me if you can." His legs buckled as the last of the prisoners passed him. Two men went into the guardroom, emerging with three swords, a stave, and four knives. These were quickly shared among the escapers. Yve watched Saronno and the magical battle that raged about him. *It was to keep* him *in*, she thought. *Nothing to do with me at all.* His face was contorted with pain and rage—and a stubborn defiance.

"Go!" he said urgently. "Now! She doesn't know—"

Then soldiers burst into the outer corridor, running with swords in their hands, and in a moment battle was joined. The prisoners were outnumbered, but had no wish to return to their dungeons and fought determinedly. Nevertheless, five of their number fell before the first wave of guards was defeated.

As a second band of soldiers appeared, Yve instinctively threw a screen about herself, Bram, and their remaining companion. She only recalled her previous lack of power when, to her surprise, their attackers became uncertain, striking out at random.

"Go!" Saronno insisted.

With one last despairing backward glance, Yve urged her friends into flight. As they pelted down a small passageway, they left behind several bemused guards who, having been robbed of one set of victims, turned on the only target left.

With his power otherwise occupied, Saronno was unable to defend himself. His last defiant gesture was to release Ssor, whose virulent poison accounted for two opponents before a sword robbed the snake of his life. Moments later, his master met the same bloody fate, dying with a grim smile of satisfaction on his face.

The three fugitives crouched in a dark alcove, listening for sounds of pursuit. Sweetness had vanished.

"Come on," Yve whispered. "We have to get out of here before we have more than soldiers looking for us."

"Sorcery?" her new companion asked. "How do you know?"

"I'm a wizard," she replied shortly. "Let's go. This way."

By dint of natural stealth and wizardly instinct, they escaped from the castle, and emerged to find it was the dead of night. They slipped away into the maze of city streets and soon felt reasonably confident that they were not pursued.

"It won't be long before they sound the alarm, though," Bram said. "I'd feel happier if we were out of the city before dawn."

"Agreed," the other man said. "Thank you for your help —I never thought I'd see the stars again. My name is Gale. I am in your debt."

"Bram and Yve," the wizard replied. "What will you do now, Gale?"

"Try to find a ship and return to Ark."

"Ark?"

"I was an envoy to this accursed isle. That I came from Ark was crime enough for me to be imprisoned. Three of the men who died in the fight were my colleagues," he added grimly. "Where will you go?"

Yve and Bram looked at each other, and Gale noted their expressions.

"Then come with me," he said.

———————————————

As their stolen horses steadily increased their distance from Ahrenhold, Yve began to feel weaker and weaker. She slumped in her saddle, barely able to hold the reins, shaking and sick. Eventually, Bram insisted that they halt and made the wizard rest and drink icy water from a stream. She felt no better, however, and they soon continued.

They rode north, having no hope that the *Alesia* and her crew might still be at Innis. There was more possibility of finding a ship bound for Ark at one of the northern ports. They reached the coastal town of Lecom in the early evening, and found a dingy tavern near the docks.

Yve still felt ill and was unable to find a remedy. Her mind was plagued with the suspicion that her weakness was greater than could be explained by mere fatigue. She ate with the others but took no pleasure from the food, wholesome though it was.

A few discreet inquiries revealed a total lack of interest in any sailings, especially to the islands to the northwest—Heald and Ark. Eventually, Bram and Gale decided to move on and try again elsewhere. As they rose, helped Yve to stand, and walked out to the stables, two pairs of eyes watched their progress closely. As the door closed behind Gale, two drinkers got to their feet and left quickly by another door.

Bram and Gale settled the wizard, who was by now close to unconsciousness, on one of the horses and then led all three mounts out into the street. They set off in search of a tavern with rooms for rent—and perhaps a more forthcoming clientele.

Before long, Gale said, "We're being followed."

Bram glanced back and saw two men in the shadowy light. As he watched, they broke into a run.

Oh no! This is all we need, he thought, and drew his sword.

Chapter 15

Knowing escape to be impossible—Yve was in no fit state to flee—Bram watched their would-be assailants approach. In the poor light, their black clothing gave them a sinister appearance. One man limped as he ran toward them, but that made him seem no less threatening. As they drew nearer, Bram and Gale tensed themselves, ready to fight, then noted that neither of the newcomers had drawn their weapons. One was shouting.

"Wait for us! We'll find a cave of light!"

Gale stiffened at these words, but kept his knife at the ready. The darkly clad men halted a few paces away.

The envoy spoke quietly. "Where the wind chills the bones."

Bram, puzzled, looked at his companion.

"Shall I shut up now?" the other replied, then laughed.

"Durc?" Gale asked.

"Aye, the same," the dark man replied, "and Zunic." He indicated his companion. "It's good to see you again, Gale."

"It's all right. They're friends," Gale quickly told the bemused Bram. "With luck they'll know where we can find a ship."

"We do," Durc replied. "And from the look of you, we'd better get there soon." He glanced at Yve.

"They need to come with us. She's ill."

The other man now spoke for the first time. "What of the others?" he asked.

"They're dead," Gale said. "I'll tell you about it later. Right now, I'd rather be at sea."

"Let's go," Durc agreed.

Though still wary, Bram had no choice but to follow the others as they set off leading the horses.

"What was all that about?" he quietly asked Gale.

"Codewords. They're from Ark."

"And you trust them?"

"Oh yes. They're ex-outlaws and great favorites at court."

Bram gave the envoy a sharp look, but Gale only grinned happily.

Lecom harbor was dark and almost deserted, and the horses' footsteps echoed loudly amid the softer sounds of sea and ships.

"Leave the horses here," Durc said. "Someone will appreciate the gift. Can she walk?"

"I'll carry her," Bram said quickly.

Zunic led the way, warning the others of obstacles in their path as they walked quietly along the quayside and out onto one of the stone-built piers. After what seemed like an age, they approached a ship on which several lamps burnt low. Hushed words were exchanged with those on board, then Zunic ushered them along the gangplank. As he walked carefully across the slightly swaying bridge, Bram felt Yve stir within his arms. Once on deck, she opened her eyes and stared in surprise.

"Feeling any better?" he asked as behind him sailors drew in the gangplank and prepared to cast off.

"I feel fine," Yve said. "Why are you carrying me?" Looking around, she added, "Where are we?"

"You're on board the *Fontaine*," Durc replied as Bram set her down, "though you'll not see that name on the ship at the moment. In the present situation we could hardly sail to Strallen in a vessel named after the queen of Ark, could we?"

"Fontaine?" Yve said, recalling her brief meeting with Luke's mother. "Ark?"

"There are some explanations to be made," Gale remarked. He introduced Yve and Bram and later, once they were all installed in Durc's cabin, he told of his imprisonment and of the extraordinary events that had enabled him to escape. Then Yve and Bram joined in, telling their story together. The three men from Ark listened attentively, their expressions often grim. As Bram finished, Durc said, "It's not over then."

"I thought it was too good to be true," Zunic added.

"What do you mean?" Yve looked anxiously at their stern faces.

Gale answered her. "The southern islands were not the only ones enveloped by the fog."

"Everywhere suffered," Durc went on, "but Ark was at the center. That was where the final battle took place—where the fog and whatever controlled it were at length defeated. Or so we thought." He told of the years of peace which had followed the wizards' conclave, years which had left them ill-prepared for the assault that eventually came. Protected by the banks of fog, armies of wraiths had invaded the islands, killing anyone not immediately reduced to mindlessness. Many refugees had fled to Ark, which was at the center of the ever-decreasing circle within the vile gray spiral. It was at Starhill that the magic of wizardry and the ancient Servants had combined—in spectacular style—to avert the threat of annihilation.

That Luke had played a leading role in these events did not surprise Yve. She had always known that the young prince carried the weight of destiny on his shoulders. But the arrival of the girl Julia from the tiny island of Strock—on the opposite side of the known world—was unexpected and confusing. She too, it seemed, was a Servant, and kin to the legendary warriors of long ago.

"I don't pretend to understand it all," Durc concluded. "You'll have to ask Ferragamo for the full story. I don't think anyone else would be capable of telling you everything."

The wizard's name was another which resounded in Yve's memory. So much in Durc's tale had been familiar, and her experiences in Lugg, Arlon, and Strallen now made much more sense, but the whole left her chilled and afraid. That such an awesome power was alive in the world was bad enough. The fact that its defeat had been—at best—only temporary, was much worse.

They sat in silence for a while, each lost in their own thoughts. Later, Yve and Bram accompanied Durc up on deck. Strallen was by now lost to sight, the *Fontaine* sailing swiftly in a north-west direction. The night was cold, but Yve knew she would not sleep, and so welcomed the fresh air and the freedom it implied.

"Our next port of call is Greyrock," Durc said, "and I for

one will be glad to see Ark again. Traveling is no longer the pleasure it once was."

"Did you come to Strallen especially to look for Gale and the others?" Yve asked.

"Yes. Our first two envoys just disappeared. No message or anything. Gale and his partner were sent to replace them and to try to find out what had happened. When they too sent no word, Mark decided to send us." Durc grinned. "Zunic and I have certain talents which enable us to travel inconspicuously."

"Who's Mark?" Bram asked.

"The king of Ark, Luke's father," Yve replied.

"You were lucky," Durc went on. "We'd already been in Lecom for three days, and would have moved on the next morning."

"I'm glad you spotted Gale," Bram said. "We weren't making much progress on our own."

"I wasn't much help," Yve added. "I'm still not sure what was wrong with me."

"But you're all right now?" Bram asked anxiously.

"Fine. I'm just happy to be on my way to Ark. If there are any answers to be found, that's where I'll find them."

Yve looked about her, listening to the sounds of sea and wind, trying to make sense of the world. To the east, where the first faint signs of dawn were beginning to glow, she spotted a sea-sprite matching the *Fontaine*'s pace. She smiled. Ark was not the only place to have witnessed strange and wonderful events.

"How long will it take us to get there?" she asked.

"Seven days. Eight, maybe. We'll make good time if this weather holds—and navigation is easy these days."

"Why?" Bram asked.

Durc pointed to the sky.

"Wherever you are," he said, "point your bows at that star and you'll be heading straight for Starhill."

Yve and Bram looked upward in wonder.

Part 2

Heald

Chapter 16

*A*few days after Yve's second departure from Haele, the fog's clearance allowed another journey to begin, far to the north. The refugees from Heald left Ark in high spirits, preparing to return to the home-isle they had been forced to leave many weary days before. This was a voyage destined to end in tragedy, however, and one that would change the history of their island in ways that no one could have foreseen.

After the realization that their military skills were useless in the magical struggle that had driven them to Ark, Pabalan, Heald's king, and his son Ansar were glad now of the opportunity for some positive action. As soon as they were convinced that it was safe to do so, they gathered their kin and, after the traditional round of farewells, left Starhill and returned to Greyrock Harbor. There they found their ships in good order. Because of its central position, Ark had not suffered the bitter cold for very long, and thus damage to the fleet and harbor was minimal. Though the town was naturally in some confusion following the recent dramatic events, the Healdean party made swift progress in readying their vessels and getting their people aboard.

Pabalan and Ansar worked ceaselessly, with the wizard Moroski always on hand to aid them, and it was a tribute to their energy that they set sail for Heald within two days of arriving at the port. Even as they did so, father and son were already

looking forward to setting Heald to rights. That they had been
driven from it by forces beyond their understanding was no
shame, but both had felt the bitterness of exile, and longed to
begin the arduous task of reconstruction.

They traveled aboard the largest of the ships, the Healdean
flagship *Ram*, and with them were their wives, Queen Adesina
and Princess Rivera, together with her seven-year-old daughter Gemma. Moroski was also in the *Ram*'s complement, accompanied as always by Atlanta, his falcon familiar, whose
fierce aspect mirrored the wizard's imposing appearance. He
was tall and dark-skinned, his eyes almost black. With the
falcon perched upon his padded shoulder, he was a striking
figure.

As the convoy left Greyrock Harbor, Moroski stood in the
raised stern of the ship. He gazed up at the massive granite
bastions which rose on either side of "The Shoot," the narrow
strait which was the only entrance to the natural harbor. Adesina came up quietly behind him.

"Impressive, isn't it," she said.

The wizard turned quickly, causing Atlanta to flap her wings
and swoop down to a more stable perch on the railing. Moroski
smiled when he saw who had joined him. The queen's company
was always a pleasure. Her slim figure, clear green eyes, and
blonde hair belied her age, and her natural elegance was aug-
mented by a calm intelligence, which had proved invaluable
to both husband and son on occasion.

"I've been here many times," the wizard replied, "but this
place is always special."

"It's difficult to imagine the forces that could have created
something like that," Adesina said, indicating the gray cliffs
that dwarfed their passage.

"Yes," he agreed, smiling at the way the queen's thoughts
so often matched his own. "If the islands were indeed formed
during the War of the Wizards, then this place is proof that it
was a mighty struggle. I find it almost inconceivable."

"Almost?"

Moroski frowned. "Magic has lost much over the centuries,
but we've just witnessed a conflict beyond my powers. After
that, all things seem possible."

Their contemplation was interrupted by an urgent cry.
"Grandma, Grandma! Look!"

Gemma came running toward them, unperturbed by the
gently swaying deck. Adesina saw in the little girl a miniature

version of her own daughter, Fontaine. The same red hair and fiery temper to match—the same restless spirit and inquiring mind. That the two also shared a certain aggressive quality and a degree of selfishness did not worry Gemma's grandmother. Fontaine had matured into a firm but gentle woman who was both well loved and widely respected. Adesina had no doubt that Gemma would do the same—and she was secretly pleased that the girl took after her aunt rather than Rivera, her mother, who was rather too demure.

"What is it, little one?"

"I'm not little any more!" Gemma stated defiantly. She held up a small fist, then uncurled her fingers dramatically. On her palm lay a shiny red jewel, its deep color glowing in the sunlight.

"Captain Brice gave it to me. He said it would bring me luck."

"I'm sure it will, my sweet," Adesina replied.

"May I?" Moroski asked, taking the stone when Gemma nodded.

"Brice said it was polished by the sea."

"So it was. It's lovely, Gemma. See that you keep it safe." The wizard handed the stone back, and the girl skipped away to show her new treasure to more admirers. Moroski and Adesina watched her fondly.

"They grow so fast," she mused.

"You're thinking of Fontaine at the same age, aren't you."

"Yes. How did you know?"

Moroski just smiled.

Once they were on the open sea, the ships turned south to sail along the eastern coast of Ark and thence across the straits which divided the two islands. Everyone was glad to be on their way home, knowing that, whatever damage had been done by the invasion, it was now up to them to put it right. The mere fact that they were returning under a clear sky was enough to give them all a feeling of hope and happiness.

"If Laurent survived, he'll have got things moving already," Pabalan said confidently. He was sitting in his cabin with Ansar. Though it was still before noon on their third day at sea, there was an open wine bottle beside the king. He poured himself another glass as his son replied.

"Let's hope he did. We'll need all the men like him we can get. Too many were lost."

Pabalan grimaced at the memory. His gnarled and red-bearded face creased in disgust. The king was a soldier, but still could not bring himself to remember their defeat at the hands of enemies who could not be killed. Even when cut down, the invaders had melted away into nothing, only to reform and renew their attack moments later. Pabalan believed that if you were killed in battle, it was only decent to remain dead. He took another mouthful of wine.

The next morning, the sailor in the crow's nest high above the *Ram*'s main deck reported the first sighting of Heald. The news was greeted with relief, everyone knowing that in only two more days they would reach Ramsport, the island's capital — and their home. Shortly after the sighting, Rivera realized that she had not seen Gemma for some time. A preliminary search failed to reveal the child's whereabouts, and Ansar was alerted It was in response to his shouts that Gemma announced her latest adventure. A small voice floated down from the rigging.

"I'm up here! In the crow's nest."

"Come down at once!" her father yelled angrily. "No! Wait there. I'll come and get you."

By now most of those on board were aware of the situation, and peered aloft, searching for the girl amid the ropes and canvas. Pabalan muttered darkly about the lookout who had allowed his granddaughter to climb up, but, as the sailor had returned to the deck immediately on sighting Heald, he was blameless.

As Ansar began his ascent, Rivera and Adesina looked on, their faces strained with worry. Behind them, Moroski stared intently upward, his feet planted firmly on the swaying boards.

Gemma called out again. "It's all right, Daddy. I can climb down." Before anyone could reply, she began to clamber over the wooden side of the nest. She had one foot on the spar outside and one in midair when her new possession, the garnet, slipped from her pocket and fell toward the deck. Without thinking, she released her hold of the rigging with one hand and made a grab for it.

Rivera screamed and several others cried out as Gemma lost her footing and toppled over. At the last moment, she managed to stop herself from falling, but ended hanging from the spar with her feet dangling helplessly in thin air.

Ansar and two sailors immediately scrambled up the rigging as fast as they could, but it was obvious that Gemma's small hands would not be able to hold on for very long. Her rescuers would be too late.

"Help! Daddy!" The girl's voice was taut with fear and tore at the hearts of all below. Adesina quickly saw that there was only one hope, and turned to Moroski. She had no need to speak, however, for the wizard was already acting. His dark eyes blazed as he recited an unintelligible incantation, his arms outstretched as if in supplication.

"Help! Daddy!"

As Gemma's agonized cry once more rang in their ears, the horrified onlookers saw one of the upper sails' running ropes break free from the belaying ring and—by itself—snake out toward the desperate girl. All eyes were riveted on its progress as it coiled about Gemma's body beneath the arms, lashing her to the spar. Her hands fell limply to her sides, but—though she had obviously fainted—she did not fall. The rope cradled her securely until Ansar and the sailors reached her and carefully transferred her to the rigging, where she came to, safe in her father's embrace.

Amidst the drama, nobody noticed Pabalan stoop down to pick something from the deck and then clutch at his chest. He grunted and sat down on the floor, leaning heavily on the bulwark. He remained there, hunched up, his head on his knees. It was only after Gemma and Ansar had completed their slow and careful descent that anyone caught sight of him.

"What's the matter with Granddad?" Gemma asked in a voice which, while still shaky, was rapidly regaining its natural confidence.

Adesina looked round quickly. So too did Moroski, who had himself sunk to the deck when Gemma was safe once more. He looked tired and unusually pale, and his hands shook. The effort of moving the rope from so far away had clearly exhausted him, but now he roused himself and followed Adesina to Pabalan's side.

"Oh no," he heard her say quietly. "Oh no." Her face when she turned to him was stricken, white with fear and grief.

The wizard reached them as others gathered round. He lifted the king's head and probed the side of his neck with gentle fingers, but knew that they were too late.

"Granddad!" Gemma said in a horrified whisper.

The wizard looked up at Adesina. Both sets of eyes were dry but each knew how intensely the other felt their loss.

"I'm sorry," Moroski said. "He's gone." His throat closed and he could say nothing more. About them the silence deepened.

Adesina knelt, reaching out to hold her husband's clenched fist. Gently, she opened his hand.

Inside was a deep red garnet.

Chapter 17

$\mathcal{T}$ime passed, dragging its heels. The sun sank and rose again. The refugees drew ever nearer to their homes, but now their mood was colored with sadness.

"It's ironic, isn't it," Adesina said. "After all we've been through, all the dangers, the fighting . . . that his heart should choose to stop now, when we're on our way home in peace."

She looked across the cabin at Moroski, questions brimming in her clear green eyes, but the wizard had no answers, so remained silent.

"I loved him so much."

"I know," he replied softly.

"He wasn't perfect. I saw his faults as clearly as any," Adesina went on, her eyes shining with memories. "But . . . I just can't believe he's not here any more."

"I wish—" Moroski began but the queen interrupted him.

"Don't blame yourself. His time had come. Anyway, you couldn't have saved them both, and Pabalan would gladly have given up his life for Gemma." She smiled sadly at the wizard who could not hide his surprise at the way she knew what he felt even before he had time to put it into words. "Don't look so worried, Moroski. It's easy to see how you're feeling."

Their eyes met.

Is it? he asked silently. *Do you know* all *of my mind?*

The returning fleet had obviously been sighted from Heald's northern coast, and there were a large number of people waiting to greet them when the ships sailed into Ramsport. Foremost among them was Laurent, a thin, intelligent-looking man whose escape from the invaders was as pleasing as it was surprising. It was he who told the new king and his companions what had occurred while they were away.

After the dreadful battle in which so many of the palace community had died, the fog had claimed the city. An eerie stillness had descended and those few people with any wits left either went to ground or fled the city. No one knew how long the gray invasion had lasted—time had ceased to have any meaning—but by comparing accounts they decided that it had ended soon after the fog had cleared from Ark. Certainly many people remembered the shooting star that night.

Since then, rumors had been rife. With the royal family gone, the palace deserted, and most of the guards dead, there had inevitably been trouble. However, little permanent damage had been done to the city and, though the vicious cold had affected some crops, food supplies were quickly re-established. As trade built up again and the remaining soldiers returned to the palace, life began to return to normal. The necessities of everyday living took precedence over the inexplicable events of the previous days.

Laurent had arranged for messengers to go to Ark and bring back news of any who had escaped there but, before they returned, the *Ram* and her sister vessels had been sighted.

"That was the best news I'd had in days," Laurent said. "I can't tell you how glad I am to see you again. In spite of your sad tidings."

"It's good that you're here to greet us," Ansar replied. "You've obviously been working hard. Father would have been proud of you."

"I only wish he could tell me so himself, my lord."

"How did *you* escape the wraiths, Laurent?" Adesina asked quickly.

"I don't know. I remember the fighting and the retreat, but after that everything is hazy. At some point I passed out.

I must have been helped away because the next thing I can recall was riding a horse—I don't know where I was or who was with me. When the fog cleared, I was alone in a woodsman's abandoned cottage." He frowned. "There are so many gaps in the story, I'm sure I'll never fill them all."

"Never mind. All that matters is that you're here now," the queen replied.

Pabalan's burial took place fourteen days later. As he had requested, a mound had been built on top of a hill overlooking Ramsport. Even in death he would watch over his city.

The barrow was unmarked and Pabalan was interred in his tomb with a minimum of ceremony, but there were hundreds of people in the procession which slowly wound its way up the hillside to pay their last respects. Among them were several of the old king's family from the neighboring island of Ark: Pabalan's daughter Fontaine, her husband Mark, Ark's king, and their children, Luke and Beca. Luke's betrothed, Julia, was also present. They had left for Heald immediately on receiving word of Pabalan's death but could only stay a few days. They too had many pressing concerns on their home-isle.

From the hilltop the city was spread beneath them, the smoke from many chimneys mingling with the autumnal haze. Inland, green hills marched into the distance, blending into the faraway outlines of the mountains. Other far more ancient burial mounds were visible, and Pabalan took his place among them, becoming part of the island and its history. As those left behind walked back down the hill, a gentle rain began to fall.

"Ferragamo is back to his old self," Mark said. "It's good to know that I can leave Ark in his care when I have to come away."

The families were gathered together in the palace dining hall. The visitors would be leaving the next morning.

"I hope you'll do the same for me," Ansar said, smiling at Moroski. "Before this awful business started you were hardly ever here!"

"I'll be around a lot more from now on," the wizard replied, glancing at Adesina. "If you want me, that is. Your father didn't have much time for magic."

"Times change," Ansar said ruefully. "I need all the help I can get." The responsibilities of kingship were already sitting heavily on his shoulders. Beneath the table Rivera took his hand in hers and squeezed it. He smiled at her gratefully.

"When do you two intend to get married?" Heald's new queen asked, looking at Luke and Julia.

"In about a month—if we can prepare everything in time," the prince replied, glancing at his parents. His expression implied that the wedding would have been much sooner if it had been up to him.

"We'll come if we can," said Ansar, "but there is so much I have to do here—or so everyone keeps telling me—that I may not be able to get away."

"You thrive on hard work," Mark put in. "You know you'd be bored otherwise."

These words proved prophetic as Ansar threw himself heart and soul into the task of reconstruction. While he sometimes became impatient with the finer detail of administration, his dynamism and decisive character were appreciated by many. Laurent especially grew to like and respect the king who in his younger days had tried the courtier's patience sorely. He became Ansar's right-hand man and, with Rivera, was responsible for most of the advice the king received. For a while, Adesina was also prominent in the running of the court and the island it controlled, but it was not long before she began to slip gently into the background, leaving almost everything to the younger generation. Hard work had proved to be an effective antidote to grief for many, not least the widow-queen, but as she gradually came to terms with Pabalan's absence, Adesina began to be aware of another emotion growing within her. When she identified it as relief, she knew she ought to feel guilty, but could not. Every time she saw Moroski—and the two of them were together often—it felt more and more as if the world was now arranged properly, as it always should have been.

The strength of her feelings surprised her, and at first she did not know how to deal with them. The wizard had always been a true friend, his sympathetic mind much closer to her own than her husband's. His company had always been a pleasure, and she had felt the palace to be a less interesting, *smaller* place whenever he was away. Yet for all that, Adesina had been a queen and her position—and loyalty—forbade her from even *thinking* of any man other than the king, as anything except an acquaintance.

Her new circumstances had changed that. She found herself with the ability to choose her own course without constant public scrutiny. In accepting her freedom and deciding to withdraw from the limelight she also declared her intention to order her life as she wished, regardless of considerations of state. In short, she was free to choose as her heart decreed, and not as her court-trained mind might advise.

Once she had accepted that, her certainty grew rapidly. It was obvious, even before she was able to declare it openly, that she loved Moroski. Perhaps she always had.

And having made that admission to herself, it became just as obvious that he felt exactly the same about her. The only strange thing about *that* was that she had never realized it before.

"I have an announcement to make," Ansar said as he stood and looked around the dinner table at his family and friends. "Rivera and I are expecting our second child."

A round of hearty congratulations followed as the young queen blushed prettily. Moroski found himself looking at Adesina, but she would not meet his gaze.

"That's wonderful!" she said. "When is it due?"

"In about six and a half months. It was conceived on Ark," Rivera added, saving them a mental calculation.

"So that's what you were up to over there!" Laurent remarked. He was possibly the only man from whom Ansar would accept such a comment. For a moment the king appeared uncertain about how to react, but then joined in the laughter.

"I'm going to have a baby brother, Grandma," Gemma exclaimed proudly.

"But it might be a sister," Adesina replied.

"*Daddy* says it'll be a boy."

"Does he now?" She looked at her son, who grinned somewhat sheepishly.

"It was a secret until now," Gemma went on. "I wasn't to tell anyone, and I didn't, Grandma. Not even you."

"I'm glad you can keep a secret, little one."

"I won't be the littlest one soon," the princess said firmly. "You won't call me that then, will you."

"Perhaps not."

Apparently satisfied with this answer, Gemma went on. "We didn't go to cousin Luke's wedding because of the baby."

"That was only one of the reasons, Gemma," Ansar said. "There were others."

"A toast!" Laurent announced. "To the love of Rivera and Ansar and to the children that their love produces."

Everyone—even Gemma—rose and repeated his words before sipping their wine.

"That means the baby, doesn't it?" Gemma asked solemnly.

"Yes, dear. And you," Adesina replied, but as she lowered her glass she knew that Moroski's eyes were on her once more, and that his thoughts—like her own—were elsewhere.

———————

A few days later Moroski and Adesina were walking in the palace grounds at dusk. The trees were bare and the onset of winter gave the air a definite chill, but they did not notice. They were wrapped snugly in each other's company.

"I love you," the wizard said insistently. "You know that, don't you."

"Yes."

"And you love me."

"Yes."

"Then why . . . ?"

"I am old—" Adesina began.

"I am far older than you!"

"That's not what I mean. Your body . . ."

He reached out and took her shoulders, and for a moment she was frightened by the vehemence in his expression. Then he spoke, and his voice was firm, yet so gentle that she knew herself to be cherished.

"Love does not end when the body's form loses the first bloom of youth. What are you afraid of? If I tell you that you are attractive to me as a woman as well as a friend—and you are!—do you think I am lying?"

She shook her head slowly, her eyes fixed on his.

"Then why deny the expression of our love? You have

said yourself for the first time in your life you are free to do as you choose. Then choose what you know in your heart is right!"

"But Pabalan has been dead little more than two months," Adesina said, while inside she wondered, *Why am I doing this? What am I trying to prove?*

"Do you think he would wish to deny you—or me—any happiness? He loved us both. What we do now cannot hurt him. I even felt sometimes that he encouraged our friendship so that I would be here to care for you when he'd gone."

Adesina thought about this for a while. It was a plausible and attractive idea. She grinned suddenly.

"Perhaps, but I doubt if he thought of you looking after me in quite the way you're suggesting!"

Moroski's answering smile was warm. "He would understand," he said, then watched as her face became serious once more. "What is it?"

Adesina hesitated. The wizard had never seen her look so lost for words. *She's embarrassed!* he thought incredulously, and then had to stop himself from laughing when he guessed the cause of her discomfiture.

"But . . . you're—"

"A wizard," he finished for her.

"Yes," she whispered.

"And I'm also a man. Wizards are made of flesh and blood too. We don't marry because we cannot have children. That is our blessing and our curse. But it does not mean we cannot know desire. For proof of that you have only to look at Ferragamo and Koria."

"And Cai," Adesina put in.

Moroski nodded. "He's young and still looking for love. Please don't compare his conquests with *my* love. My example is better. Ferragamo and Koria found enough reasons to stay together and accept the nature of their relationship. They do not hide it from anybody. Their bedroom is a place of joy. Ferragamo found the woman he was looking for . . . and so have I."

"How long have you known?" she asked softly.

"Years," he replied. "Though I hid it even from myself for a very long time."

"Poor you."

Throughout the conversation they had been drawing

gradually closer. Now their bodies met and they clung together fiercely. When their kiss finally ended, their eyes were moist. Their decision had been made.

Still cradled in the wizard's arms, Adesina asked, "A blessing *and* a curse? What did you mean by that?"

"You'll know if you think about it."

"Tell me anyway."

"I've already lived longer than any man has a right to expect. Any children I might have had when I was Cai's age would be long dead by now. I am spared that heartache. Yet I can never know the joy of creating life, of watching it grow. Immortality can take different forms." The wizard's voice was melancholy.

"Children can be a trial too," she replied, smiling.

"But would you wish yours away?"

"No." *What would they think if they saw me now?* Adesina wondered, then realized that she had unconsciously been considering the attitudes of others toward her love for the wizard. That appeared ridiculous now and she pulled him toward her for another kiss.

She shivered as they separated once more.

"It's cold," Moroski said. "Come inside."

"It's been so long," she murmured, then thought, *This is for me!* Aloud she said, "Stay with me tonight."

———————————

Almost a month had passed since Ansar's announcement of Rivera's pregnancy, yet the thoughts that had sprung unbidden into Moroski's mind then still preyed on him, and he eventually decided to share them with Adesina. They had become lovers a few days after the king's announcement, and in the intervening time had experienced a depth of passion and happiness which neither had previously been able to envision.

Their behavior had at first been circumspect, but the idea of secrecy had become ridiculous and repugnant. Many people in court circles knew about—or guessed at—their relationship, and before long it would be common knowledge. They did not care. All that mattered was their burgeoning love, and that they should be together. Everything else was secondary.

Yet in the midst of his delirious joy, Moroski felt a nagging sense of incompleteness, an emptiness that Adesina's love alone could not fill. He knew the remedy, but even to consider it made him afraid. He was not sure that it was possible, but knew he had to try. First he had to convince Adesina.

"You'd do *that*? For me?" Her eyes were wide with shock. He nodded.

"You can't be serious!"

"I've never been more serious in my life," he replied.

"But it's been everything to you, your whole world, all those years . . ."

"My world is nothing without you, and as it is there is so much we cannot share. However close we become, we are still worlds apart!"

"Don't say that!"

"Listen, my love. I want to have a child with you. I want to grow old with you. I don't want to live as Ferragamo does, with the knowledge that I will outlive you. I want those things more than I have ever wanted anything—and I can't have them while I remain a wizard."

"But—"

Moroski held a finger to her lips.

"No buts. My mind is made up. I need you to help me."

For a while, they looked at each other in silence. Adesina's mind was racing. Moroski merely waited.

"Can you do it?" she asked at last.

"I wasn't born a wizard. What I have acquired I can lose again." He smiled, hoping it would prove to be that simple.

"How?"

"The power I have, the magic within me if you like, has to be transferred to something—or someone—else. But I can't do it on my own."

"Cai?"

Moroski nodded. "He'll understand. He'll help." As the wizard spoke, he wondered briefly whether this was wishful thinking.

"It'll be dangerous, won't it," Adesina said.

"Perhaps."

"Am I worth all that?"

"More," he replied. "Much more."

"Perhaps I should learn when to give in gracefully," she said then, smiling weakly.

"I'll send a message to Arlon right away." Now that they

were agreed, he could not bear to wait any longer and went to fetch pen and paper. Adesina smiled at his eagerness.

As the wizard began writing, a thought struck her. "I wonder what Ansar will say about this!"

Moroski looked up from his letter.

"Do you really care?" he asked.

Chapter 18

$\mathcal{A}$fter sending his message to Cai, Moroski spent the next days fretting, asking constantly for news of arrivals in the port, and gazing out to sea. He spent much time in Adesina's company, and when they were forced apart by circumstance, the wizard locked himself away in the palace libraries, searching for any reference to the voluntary discarding of a wizard's power. The little that he learned was not reassuring. There had been so few recorded instances of such a thing in the ages-old history of wizardry that the details were sketchy and incomplete. However, by diligent research he eventually pieced together the necessary elements. He discussed his findings with Adesina but, despite her quick mind, she soon found herself unable to follow his arguments. Moroski, desperate to put his theories to someone who would understand, wished fervently for Cai's arrival. He watched and waited impatiently.

On a bitterly cold midwinter day—the sixteenth after the message had been sent—his vigil was rewarded. The ropes that moored the Arlon vessel had hardly been secured before Moroski strode across the gangplank and hugged his astonished fellow wizard.

"Thank the stars you've arrived! It's been a strain waiting."

"I came as soon as I could," Cai replied, the expression on his youthful face a mixture of amusement and surprise. "And

your messenger was lucky to find me as quickly as he did, but
then . . . well, I don't need much of an excuse to get away
from Arlon these days."

Too preoccupied with his own plans to note the significance
of Cai's words, Moroski merely urged him to make haste to
the palace.

"Where is the swarm?" he asked, as an afterthought.

"They get excited when I travel," Cai replied. "And that
causes trouble I could do without, so I keep them in this."
He bent to pick up a wooden box. Several holes had been
bored in the sides and the lid, and a muted buzzing came from
within.

"Come on then," Moroski said, and set off at a brisk pace.

"What's all this about?" Cai asked, as he hurried to catch
up with his friend.

"Not here," the elder wizard replied shortly, leaving Cai
even more mystified.

Many heads turned to follow the wizards' progress as they
hurried from the harbor to the palace. Moroski was a familiar
figure in Ramsport, but had been noticeably more reclusive
recently. His single-minded progress through the town was
watched with interest. Those who greeted the wizard received
no reply, and Cai found himself the object of several suspicious
looks, as if the citizens believed him to be the reason for
Moroski's distraction. It was an odd sensation for the young
wizard—he had been accustomed to attracting attention for
other, more pleasant reasons. His slight but athletic build,
long brown hair, and green eyes all added to the good looks
which so many ladies found to their liking. And then there
were the bees. As a wizard, Cai was unique in that his familiar
was not a single animal but a swarm, each tiny mind linked
by instinct and ancestry into a complete entity. It was the
swarm that Cai communicated with, rather than any particular
bee. When, as now, they were housed within their mobile
hive, they caused little comment, but if allowed to fly free it
was a different story. They usually formed a small black cloud
above and behind their master's head, and the noise they made
was enough to frighten most people.

They were getting restless now, disturbed by their unaccustomed confinement and the hive's bouncing as Cai walked
rapidly along. He sent them a soothing message, and promised
them freedom as soon as they reached the palace.

Moroski had not spoken since they left the docks. *He's changed*, Cai thought. *What's got into him?*

———————————

Moroski's study was the top room in the tallest tower of the palace. Although nowhere near as high as the massive Starbright Tower in Ark's capital, one could look down from it on the entire city. The view was impressive. Cai had often wondered at the predilection wizards had for high places. He could only think that it was intended to emphasize their supposed superiority over ordinary men.

As they entered the room, Cai was surprised to see Adesina there. The study was usually Moroski's private preserve.

"Hello, Cai. Thank you for coming so soon." Though her smile was welcoming, her voice betrayed her nervousness.

"Hello, Adesina. It's always a pleasure to visit Heald, even when I am summoned in such a mysterious way."

"He hasn't told you?"

"No, nothing," Cai replied. He set the hive down on the floor. "May I?" he asked. Moroski nodded and the younger wizard began to unfasten the catches on the box's lid, adding as he did so, "I was rushed here in almost total silence. If somebody doesn't tell me what this is all about soon, I shall go quite mad."

Any answer was delayed by the emergence of the swarm. After a few passes around the room to investigate their new surroundings, the bees settled on a section of wall-hanging. Atlanta, who was perched upon a window-sill, watched them closely. The swarm's buzzing subsided to a gentle hum.

"Well?" Cai asked, looking from one of his hosts to the other.

"I'm sorry, Cai," Moroski said. "I've been so wrapped up in myself that I couldn't even welcome you properly. I'll make amends later but I have to get this off my chest." He paused. "There's no easy way to say this. I've decided to forswear wizardry."

Cai was stunned. "What!" he exclaimed. "Why?" No sooner had the question been asked than he looked at Adesina, and realized what the answer must be. He stood speechless, looking at the two lovers. Adesina would not meet his eyes, but Cai had no doubt whose decision this had been.

"You're serious, aren't you," he said.

"Yes I am," Moroski replied, then explained their situation and the reasons for his decision as succinctly as he could. He had been thinking of little else for days now, and the words came easily. Cai still found them difficult to swallow.

"Will you help me?" Moroski ended. The only sound for the next few moments was the restless drone of the swarm, their agitation reflecting their master's troubled state of mind.

"I honestly don't know what to say," Cai said at last.

" 'Yes' will do." Moroski smiled.

"You know what you're—?" The young wizard checked himself, shaking his head in disbelief. "Of course you do!" he exclaimed. "Stars! And I thought *I* was the irresponsible wizard around here."

Moroski grinned but Adesina said gravely, "Is that what you think we're being?"

"Yes. No. I don't know." The level of noise from the bees rose. Some of them took to the air in short, hopping flights.

Cai sat down in the nearest available chair. "Let me think," he said. Adesina brought him a drink without being asked and he sipped it absentmindedly. Moroski waited impatiently, unable to keep from fidgeting.

"All right," Cai said finally. "If I *am* going to help, there are a few questions I must ask."

"Go ahead," Moroski replied eagerly.

"Some will not be pleasant, Adesina. Are you sure you want to stay?"

"There are no secrets between us," she said with certainty.

"Please don't think I am attacking you personally," Cai went on. "I have the greatest respect for you . . . but I must be sure."

"Of course." The widow-queen faced him calmly.

The bees were tranquil again now.

"If this can be done—" Cai began.

"It can!" Moroski interrupted. "I've found—"

"I'll take your word for it. Leave that aside for now. Are you sure you have considered *everything* you'll be giving up?"

"I think so."

"Your long life—"

"But that's the whole point."

"Yes, but with that comes aging. Growing old is not an abstract idea. It changes your body, sometimes your mind.

There are things you won't be able to do before many years are out."

"It's those years that count."

"And then there's your health. As a wizard, you have control. You heal yourself and prevent illness starting without even realizing you're doing it. There is much of a man's life that you haven't experienced. You will be vulnerable once you lose the power of control. Nor will you be able to heal or protect anyone else. Could you bear to watch Adesina suffer, and know yourself to be helpless?"

The lovers were silent. Cai steeled himself to continue, knowing full well the hurtful visions his words were producing. He turned to Adesina.

"Forgive me for this. You are no longer a girl."

She nodded.

"It's a long time since Fontaine was born. If you bear another child now, you may be at risk."

"I'm not afraid."

"Moroski would not be able to help you should anything go wrong."

"He would help me by just being there."

"Are you sure?"

She stared at him, fire in her eyes. Cai swallowed and went on.

"You fell in love with a wizard. Will you still love him as a man? His power, his magic is part of him. What is left will be less than the whole."

"I fell in love with the man, not the wizard, and that will remain." Adesina looked over at Moroski and smiled. "I have no doubts."

Cai turned back to his fellow wizard. "I know Adesina did not ask you to do this. You are the one who must make the decision but before you do, I have one more point. You've relied on magic for countless years. You react to things in a way which takes your wizardry for granted. All your instincts are formed on that basis. If you lose that power, obeying those instincts may be hazardous, even fatal. You'll be a danger to yourself and everyone about you."

Moroski paused, recalling Gemma's peril on the *Ram. What would I have done?* He shut his eyes as the obvious answer presented itself. *I would have watched her die.* He pushed the image away and opened his eyes to find Adesina watching him anxiously.

"You're overstating the case," he said. "I will have to learn. I'll be like a child for a while perhaps, but that is a small price to pay."

"You're certain then?"

"Yes," they replied in unison.

Cai let out his breath slowly. "All right," he said. "How is it to be done?"

He got no answer because the lovers had leapt to their feet and were now joined in a long and passionate embrace. Cai learned more from watching that kiss than from all their preceding words.

That evening they went to tell Ansar of their plans. He and Rivera were in their private chambers and showed little surprise when Adesina and Moroski came in together.

"We have something to tell you," the widow-queen began.

"It's about time," her son replied. "The whole palace has been full of rumors—which I have no doubt I am the last to learn."

Moroski came straight to the point.

"My lord, I intend to be a proper husband for Adesina. I cannot take those vows as a wizard, and I am therefore set on renouncing wizardry."

Ansar's jaw dropped. He had been expecting the first part of Moroski's statement, but the second left him speechless.

"Heald will be temporarily without a wizard, but that can be rectified," Moroski went on. "I request your permission to go ahead."

"And I your blessing to marry again," Adesina said, smiling at the absurdity of her position. She became serious again as she saw the expression on her son's face.

"And if I refuse?" the king asked. He received no answer, but their defiance was clear in both faces. "Is this how you honor my father's memory?" Shock and bitterness made his voice loud and harsh.

"I honored him more than you will ever know," Adesina replied quietly. "And still do. He would be happy if he knew of our intentions. He recognized the power of love."

"Love?" Ansar exclaimed.

"Is it so unimportant?" his mother asked.

In the silence that followed, sounds of movement came

from behind the bedroom door, but nobody paid them any attention. Rivera spoke for the first time.

"Is it possible to stop being a wizard?"

"I think so," Moroski replied. "The process is not without risks, but we accept those."

"In other words, you'll do this *whatever* I say," Ansar challenged. The wizard did not reply, and the king turned to his wife. "What do you make of all this?" he asked, hoping for guidance.

"It's not for me to say," she replied coolly and Ansar, frustrated, had to make his own decision. He thought for some time but was unable to make sense of all the complications. In the face of the lovers' determination, he knew that to deny them would be useless, and gave in with as good a grace as he could muster. He embraced his mother, saying, "You have my blessing. I don't pretend to understand, but it's your happiness that matters most. I just hope you both know what you're doing."

"Thank you." Adesina's voice was choked with emotion.

Ansar turned to Moroski. "When . . . ?"

"Soon," the wizard replied.

Cai and Moroski shut themselves away in the study for the whole of the next day, and together pored over the various references that Moroski had found.

"Some things are clear enough and others are a matter of common sense, but there are a few gaps that I've had to fill in with my own theory."

"Guesswork, you mean," Cai said.

"Precisely." Moroski grinned.

"How can you be so cheerful? This could kill you! Or *worse!*"

"I know, I know. We've been through all that. Let's not start again."

"All right." Cai pointed to a passage in one of the books spread before them. "What does this mean?"

"That's the key. Until then it's straightforward enough. Storing power externally is something we do all the time, after all. What this refers to is the transfer of the basic elements of magic—those that enable us to gather power in the first place. Do you remember your first lessons from Debramani?"

"The ones about potential and balance?" Cai smiled. "Of course. He had to repeat them often enough."

"I have to forget all that, lose it from my mind. Then I can dispose of all remaining power easily." Moroski paused. "The problem is, those elements are so fundamental that they protect themselves beyond any normal instinctive level. I can be willing to give them up—in fact I *have* to be—but I can't do it alone."

"This is where I come in?"

"You have to take control of my mind." Moroski held up his hands to silence Cai's immediate protest. "It's not like that. Don't worry! All you do is provide the channel and open the sluice gate. And accept the greatest secrets of the world."

"Oh, is that all?" Cai remarked.

"You'd better be careful, though," Moroski advised.

"Why?"

"I'll probably try to kill you."

The wizards left the tower later that evening, Moroski going straight to Adesina's rooms while Cai went in search of food. He had hardly had a chance to greet his hosts, and so went to call on Ansar first. There he met Gemma, who volunteered to take him to the kitchens for a meal. She liked the young wizard immensely, having got to know him on his frequent earlier visits to Heald. He was funny and was always willing to invent new games. Even his bees were a source of fascination, and she was disappointed to learn that they had been left in the study. Hand in hand, they walked along the passageway.

"Are you staying long?" she asked hopefully.

"I don't know."

"Will you play with me tomorrow?"

"If I have time."

This was not a sufficiently enthusiastic answer. Gemma looked up at him, but Cai was staring ahead, paying little attention to her.

"Wake up!" she said, pulling at his arm.

"What?" Cai looked confused. "I'm sorry, Gemma. I must be tired." He smiled. "I need something to eat."

A moment later, Gemma asked, "What were Grandma and Daddy arguing about last night?"

"I don't know." *Though I can guess.* "You'd better ask your Grandma," he replied.

"She's going to marry Moroski, isn't she? Everyone says so."

Cai looked at her in surprise. Gemma obviously missed little that went on in the palace.

"It's good news, isn't it," she added. "Will you marry me when I'm older, Cai?"

"That's a very attractive proposition," he replied, "and I'm flattered. I'm afraid wizards don't get married though."

"But Moroski is!"

"He won't be a wizard for much longer," Cai said, wondering how much to tell her.

Gemma's face was creased into a frown.

"Does that mean he won't be able to take away my toothache?" she asked solemnly.

————————————

Moroski and Adesina woke at the same moment. They lay in silence in each other's arms for some time, then Moroski stirred himself.

"Cai will be waiting. I'd better get ready."

"No second thoughts?" she asked.

"None."

They rose, dressed, and made their way outside. Now that the day had at last arrived, there seemed little need for haste. Moroski sent a message to Cai, then led Adesina up onto the battlements. For an hour they walked together under a cold blue winter sky, seeing everything about them as if it were new. They spoke little, too full of emotion for words.

"Go in now," the wizard said at last. "Tell Cai I'll be with him shortly. There's someone I have to say goodbye to first." Adesina kissed him lightly and obeyed. As she left, she saw Atlanta swoop down and land on the battlements beside her master. Adesina understood how precious the link between a wizard and his familiar was. That Moroski was prepared, along with all the rest, to give this up for her was at once a wonderful confirmation of his love and a terrible responsibility. She looked away and walked slowly to the tower, leaving her love in a conversation she could not share.

You know what I am going to do?

Yes, the falcon replied, her eyes fixed upon the wizard's.

You will make yourself silent. Like all the others. There was sadness in her voice but no resentment.

If there was any other way . . . Moroski began.

You wish for a fledgling so much?

A child, yes.

I do not understand why we must no longer fly together. I am lost to my own kind now.

Torn between his own needs and the feeling that he betrayed Atlanta, Moroski could not find the words to explain. Instead he said only, *I'm sorry. What will you do?*

Atlanta surprised him by answering immediately.

I will go to the white wizard in the mountains.

Shalli? Moroski had never met the hermit or visited his wondrous cave in Ark's Windchill Mountains, but had heard many strange things from those who had. Among the stories, it was reported that he had an uncanny affinity with all animals. Atlanta herself had been to his home, many years before.

Can he talk to you? the wizard asked hopefully.

Not as you do, the falcon replied, *but he understands me.*

This made Moroski feel slightly better about leaving his familiar. With Shalli, if anywhere, she would find a measure of peace and happiness.

When will you leave?

After you have gone, she replied. *I will stay until the end. It may be that I can help.*

There was a lump in the wizard's throat. He could not speak aloud; even in mind-talk he could not hide his emotions.

Come then, he said brokenly. For the last time, Atlanta settled in her accustomed position on her master's shoulder and together they walked toward the tower where they were to part forever.

Adesina and Cai looked up anxiously as Moroski entered the study. Atlanta left her perch and flew to a windowsill. Three pairs of eyes watched her settle, then turned to the matter in hand.

"Ready?" Cai asked.

"Yes. Are you?"

"As ready as I'll ever be." His cheerful tone sounded hollow.

"You'd better leave us now," Moroski told Adesina.

"I want to stay."

"Let her," Cai put in. "When we're finished, we may need someone to hold our hands for a while. As long as she keeps out of the way . . ."

"I can see you two have been scheming. All right. It may not be very pleasant, though," Moroski added, taking Adesina in his arms. "A kiss for good luck," he said, smiling. She obliged.

"Me too!" said Cai. "I've never done this either."

Adesina kissed his cheek.

"Shall we begin?" he asked.

"Shouldn't I lie down or something?" Moroski said.

"Good idea. Then there won't be so far to fall," Cai replied. "I think I will too."

All three laughed nervously. Adesina retreated to the side of the room and the wizards compromised by seating themselves in armchairs.

"I've told the swarm what's going on," Cai told Adesina, "but I'm not sure how they'll react. Keep an eye on them for me."

He got up again and collected several items from the table. "The first part is easy," he remarked, placing them within Moroski's reach. "We'll have to take care with these afterward. They could be dangerous in the wrong hands."

The older wizard surveyed the curious collection.

"Hand-picked by myself," Cai added. "Good set, aren't they?"

"If you like incongruities," Moroski replied, picking up the largest object, a plain wooden staff shod with brass.

"Traditionalist," Cai accused, grinning at his friend.

"I have to start somewhere!"

"Don't overload anything," Cai advised. "We don't want them walking out on their own."

"Will you be serious!"

"Sorry."

They grinned nervously at each other, then composed themselves. As Moroski began releasing his power, feeding it slowly into the staff, his face became a mask of concentration. Adesina watched anxiously but Cai seemed comparatively relaxed. He knew the real test was still to come.

Moroski finished with the staff and passed it to Cai, who stored it carefully on the far side of the room. Adesina could not see any change in the wood's appearance but knew that it was now a talisman of power. Moroski picked up a gold vase, closed his eyes, and continued.

An hour later there were only a few objects left on the table but the process had slowed considerably. Moroski appeared dazed, his eyes out of focus. He swayed as he reached for a glass paperweight.

"Gently," Cai advised. "Don't force it."

"I . . . I think that's enough," Moroski whispered hoarsely. "I'll be too weak otherwise." He looked at Cai, seeking guidance, and Adesina saw the trust in his eyes. *He's defenseless*, she thought, but was soon forced to revise her opinion.

"What next?" Moroski asked.

"It's time now," Cai replied, swallowing hard. "I'll try to make contact. Are you ready to open the channel?"

"What?" The elder wizard seemed bemused. He glanced at his familiar, then back at Cai. "Yes. Atlanta says she will help if she can." His voice was stronger, but weary still.

Cai looked at the falcon, sensing the silent farewells between her and his friend. A measure of their sadness tore at his heart but he put it aside and concentrated on the enormous task ahead of him. Instinctively he reached out and clasped Moroski's hands. Slowly, he began to recite the words of power that neither had ever thought to hear.

About them the very air seemed to tremble, as if they were no longer part of the world of men. Adesina watched in terrified fascination as the grip of their hands became a contortion of unheeded pain and their expressions slowly changed. While Moroski's face became a mask of agony, Cai began to smile— but there was nothing pleasant about the curve of his lips or the sparkle in his eyes. He seemed to be burning with intense emotion, teetering on the brink of madness. The bees buzzed angrily, and Atlanta flapped her wings, shaking her head from side to side. *What's going on?* Adesina wondered helplessly. A glowing aura formed about the two wizards, enclosing them in a shield of flickering power.

"No!" Moroski yelled suddenly, trying to rise to his feet.

"Be calm," Cai commanded, but his eyes shone demoni-acally, gloating. Adesina cried out, her heart pounding.

Moroski lurched from his chair, pulled his hand from Cai's and grabbed wildly at the younger wizard's throat. "Thief! Murderer!" he screamed as they struggled.

Adesina overcame the horror which had held her mes-merized and tried to reach her lover. But the strange force which surrounded them threw her back. She staggered and fell painfully. Flashes of light shot about the room as the struggle continued.

Moroski now had his hands clamped around his opponent's neck but Cai did not seem concerned. Indeed, he appeared to be laughing silently, careless of the attempt to strangle him. Adesina realized, with a jolt that spread an icy cold throughout her body, that Cai was quite insane. Something terrible was happening—and she was powerless to intervene. She wanted to look away, to hide from this horror, but knew that she could not. She had to be there to the end.

The swarm took to the air. Seeing their master in peril, they swooped toward his attacker, but the shield that had repelled Adesina threw them back. The room was soon full of an angry, swirling mass. They surged repeatedly toward the wizards, only to be repulsed in flashes of livid, purple light. They raged in turmoil, the normal ordered structure of the swarm destroyed. It was a living picture of what was happening inside Cai's mind and Adesina knew that until the bees were sane again, there was little hope for their master.

Eventually, as if unable to remain within the confines of their collective lunacy, the bees streamed out of the window one by one until a sudden silence descended on the room. The wizards were still locked together, almost unmoving now, their faces red and contorted. Moroski was in a murderous rage but Cai took no measures to defend himself.

He's invulnerable, Adesina thought. *He's waiting for Moroski to wear himself out, and then he'll strike!* She screamed, breaking her lover's concentration. He looked at her in bewilderment. Pain, betrayal, and remorse showed briefly in his face.

"Now!" Cai said, knocking his adversary's hands away.

Moroski's eyes rolled upward until they showed only white, and he fell backward, collapsing into his chair in a dead faint.

As Cai struggled to rise, gasping for breath but grimacing triumphantly, Adesina and Atlanta looked at each other briefly, aware now that they might both lose Moroski.

"I'm sorry," Adesina whispered.

Atlanta stared back, her eyes unblinking.

Chapter 19

Once outside, the bees regrouped and the swarm once more became the black cloud that those who knew Cai were familiar with. It was only a partial return to normality, however, as the terrible, angry noise continued, rising and falling dramatically. Even in the open air the wild droning could be heard from a distance and when, as happened later, it was confined to one of the palace's rooms or corridors, the noise was horrifyingly loud.

Few people remarked on the swarm's spiral descent from the tower but there was pandemonium shortly afterward as the bees invaded the lower palace, causing all who saw the writhing, shrieking mass to flee in terror. Soon all who could had escaped from the palace into the city beyond, and those left inside cowered behind closed doors. Several unfortunates were caught by the swarm and disappeared beneath a wriggling throng of black and yellow. Most of the victims fainted from shock. Although it was later found that none had been stung, many of their faces and arms were swollen as if they had.

Several hazardous attempts were made to trap the bees, but whenever it was felt that the swarm was at last secure, the noise rose to more frenzied levels, as the bees found some hitherto unsuspected exit. Each time this happened they emerged angrier than before, and were soon left to roam as they wished.

Ansar and Laurent had been among those trying to snare

the bees, but as soon as it became obvious that their attempts were useless, they retreated to the relative safety of Gemma's bedroom, the smallest and most secure of the royal apartments. There they joined Rivera, who was in a state close to panic, and Gemma, who was excited and not at all afraid. She regarded the whole affair as something of an adventure.

"Are the bees coming, Daddy?" she asked hopefully.

"No, my pet. They won't reach you here," Ansar replied, mistaking the tone of her voice. He sat down on the bed and pulled his shivering queen close. Gemma turned to Laurent.

"What's happening to Cai?" she asked.

"I wish I knew," he replied. "We'll go and find out later, shall we? When things have quietened down a bit." He and Ansar exchanged glances.

"Why don't we go now?" the girl asked. "Maybe Cai's got lost and the bees can't find him."

"The bees have gone wild, Gemma. They'll hurt you," Rivera said, her voice shrill with anxiety. She had heard the screams of earlier victims. Gemma regarded her mother sceptically, then accepted her confinement. After all, it was not often that she had so many visitors in her room.

"I'll read you all a story," she said in such a businesslike tone that Laurent was forced to smile. "You sit here," Gemma instructed, indicating a space on the end of the bed. The courtier obeyed as she went to find a suitable book.

Ansar and Laurent grinned at each other over Rivera's head, then became serious once more.

"I could try to slip by, and get to the tower," Laurent said quietly.

"No," the king replied. "Even if you could, I doubt if either of us would be of any help in whatever's going on up there." He spoke from bitter experience of the ways of wizards. "We're better off staying here." Within his embrace, his wife nodded in silent, heartfelt agreement.

Gemma returned with her choice of reading matter and surveyed her audience critically.

"This is a very good story, but you have to pay attention," she announced firmly. "I'll get a chair."

Putting the book down, she went to fetch the small stool which stood by the door. As she bent to pick it up, something outside caught her attention and she listened for a few moments.

"Here come the bees," she whispered, and, with a quick sidelong glance back at her parents, she reached up to the door handle. Ansar was the first to react as the door opened and the angry buzzing reached their ears. He leapt up, leaving the queen and Laurent sprawling on the bed, and sprang toward his daughter. As he did so, Rivera let out an agonized scream. Ansar hesitated, torn between them, and in that moment Gemma stepped out into the bee-infested corridor and shut the door behind her.

Cai stood over his fellow-wizard, his face contorted with power and greed. The livid red weals on his neck were ignored. A line of spittle ran from one corner of his mouth.

Adesina watched helplessly, knowing that Cai was far beyond her reach. With mounting dread she saw him lean over and gently place one fist upon Moroski's forehead. The younger wizard smiled nastily, twisted his hand, and pulled sharply away, as if uprooting a plant. Atlanta cried out raucously and Moroski's body jerked. For some time afterward, he twitched convulsively, his eyes still open but showing only white.

Adesina hid her face in her hands, feeling sick, disgusted, and terribly afraid. After a few moments of comparative stillness, she forced herself to look again.

Cai had changed. He no longer gloated in triumph but appeared bewildered, looking about him as if searching for something. His clear green eyes sparkled but there was uncertainty in their depths. He was talking to himself, but his words made no sense.

Beneath him, Moroski slumped in the chair, sprawling in an ungainly fashion. He was so still that for a dreadful moment Adesina thought he was dead. Then she saw the slight rise and fall of his chest. All around the two wizards the aura of magical power still glowed and pulsed, casting strange shadows about the room.

Cai spun round suddenly, his eyes still searching in vain. He laughed then, the sound drawing slivers of ice down Adesina's spine. He covered his temples with his hands and sank slowly to his knees. Several objects within the shield of power moved. One bowl shattered, sending splinters of glass flying across the room. Cai shrank into himself, becoming smaller as he curled up on the floor and lay quite still.

Just like a baby! Adesina thought in astonishment. The silence lengthened. *What do I do now?*

The protective shield still cut both men off from Adesina's world as surely as if it were made of iron. She knew instinctively that only Cai could remove it, but he had withdrawn to a hidden place within himself and was unable or unwilling to leave it.

Adesina picked herself up carefully and walked gingerly about the room, steeling herself to break the profound silence that had fallen. Atlanta watched her closely.

"Cai," she called softly. "Cai. Wake up."

There was no response.

Rivera fell sobbing onto the bed as Ansar, closely followed by Laurent, went out into the corridor. At the sight that greeted them, the king cried out and his advisor's stomach lurched.

Gemma stood a few paces away, enveloped by a swirling black cloud. The noise the bees made was ferocious and, despite the princess's obvious peril, the men hesitated to approach. Eventually, Ansar started forward, only to be restrained by Laurent.

"Wait!" he urged above the noise. "They're not harming her! Look!"

Ansar saw that although Gemma was in the midst of the swarm, she gave no sign of discomfort. Her head was tilted back, and she spun round in her attempts to follow the dizzy progress of the bees. She did not appear in the least bit afraid. In fact, she seemed to be talking, though it was impossible to hear what she said. King and courtier looked on in amazement as the swarm gathered into a tight, black formation and sped off down the corridor. Before either of them could react, Gemma followed, running as fast as her little legs would carry her.

"Naughty bees!" they heard her call. "Come back." Glancing at each other, they set off in rapid pursuit, only to turn a corner and find a repeat of the earlier scene. Gemma was once again in the midst of the swarm. The buzzing seemed a little less agitated now but when Ansar moved closer, several bees made sweeping, angry passes at him. He heeded the clear warning, leaving his daughter to it. She was smiling happily, still quite unharmed, and talking nonstop.

"Go and tell Rivera she's all right," Ansar whispered urgently. "I'll follow them." Laurent slipped away, leaving the king listening to the one-sided conversation.

"He won't hurt you, silly bees! Come here. Come with me. Back to Uncle Cai."

The shape of the swarm shifted and twisted but they calmed gradually, and Gemma's words became easier to follow.

"He's in the tower, isn't he? Come on, I'll lead you there now. Naughty bees." Gemma took a couple of steps down the corridor, then turned to look back at the swarm, which still hovered uncertainly. The princess stamped her foot angrily. "Come *on!*" she exclaimed, and set off with a determined stride.

Ansar watched in astonishment as the bees meekly formed up and followed his daughter. He had always known her to be at ease with Cai's unusual familiar, but this development was quite beyond him. He followed at a safe distance.

Their progress was marked at intervals by the appearance of other palace inhabitants, most of whom fled in horror at the approach of the princess's strange entourage. A few made as if to attempt a rescue—only to be waved away by Ansar who still trailed behind, watching closely. He had no time for explanations, and his subjects received little response to their whispered questions.

At last Gemma reached the tower and began the ascent to the wizard's study. That was an anxious time for Ansar, as he lost sight of the swarm at each turn, but his daughter's voice kept up its reassuring chatter.

"Nearly there now. I'm sure Uncle Cai will be pleased to have you back again."

Gemma reached the door to Moroski's room just as Adesina decided that she must go for help. She had been reluctant to leave, but neither wizard had moved for some time, and she knew it was time for her to act. As a consequence, the door was opened without the princess having to knock. She made a suitably regal entrance, as if she had expected no less, and Adesina could only gaze open-mouthed at this latest development.

"Hello, Grandma. I've brought the bees." Gemma looked curiously at the two wizards as they slumped within the flickering dome of light. "Are they asleep?"

"Yes," Adesina replied, hoping it was true.

"They don't look very comfortable. Why don't you give them a pillow?"

"You can't . . ." the older woman began but stopped short as Gemma picked up a cushion and gently maneuvered it beneath Cai's head. The magical barrier that had repelled Adesina so violently had allowed the little girl to pass freely through. She seemed quite at ease with the arcane power that flickered about her, and sat down on the floor between the two wizards, watching over them protectively.

Ansar, appearing in the doorway, took his mother in his arms. He was just in time to see the swarm, much quieter now, begin a slow, smooth circling around their master. After some time, Cai's eyelids flickered and he began to follow the swarm's progress. Slowly, painfully, he smiled.

"Hello, Uncle Cai. I brought your bees back," Gemma said brightly. "They were being ever so naughty."

"Thank you," the wizard replied, sitting up anxiously and shaking his head as if to clear it.

Adesina could contain herself no longer. "Is he all right?" she asked. "What happened, Cai?"

He looked up at her, blinking rapidly. "I'm not sure. Give me a moment." His eyes went back to the swarm, as if seeking reassurance. Then he muttered a few incomprehensible words and the shield of power began to fade. As it did so, Moroski's eyes closed and he stirred as if in a dream.

"He's all right," Cai said wearily. "Let him sleep."

"Did it . . . did it work?"

Cai nodded. "Yes. It worked." There was a significance to his words far deeper than their surface meaning but Adesina knew better than to pursue that now. The shield disappeared completely, and she went to her lover and gently held his hand. As Ansar helped Cai to rise and then settle back into his chair, Adesina looked over and simply said, "Thank you."

Cai merely shook his head, and closed his eyes. One by one the bees landed on the chair about their master. Soon they too were asleep.

Chapter 20

*E*vening shadows were gathering when Cai at last opened his eyes. He looked over at Adesina, still sitting close by her sleeping lover. Ansar and Gemma, the latter under protest, had left the tower.

"How are you?" the widow-queen asked quietly.

"Tired—and rather too powerful for my own good," he replied thoughtfully. "I never knew that employing the magic arts could get you drunk."

"Are you hungover?"

"What?" Cai looked confused. "No. It's not like that. Besides," he grinned, "I can get drunk if I want to, but I've never seen the point of suffering for it. Being a wizard has its advantages." His voice trailed off as Adesina looked down at Moroski. "Has he woken yet?" he asked, more serious now. Adesina shook her head. "He'll likely be confused when he does," Cai went on. "We'll just have to wait and see."

Adesina smiled up at him gratefully. They sat in silence for a while.

"It almost went wrong, didn't it," she said eventually.

"Yes. He warned me, but I didn't realize just how powerful the enchantment would be," Cai replied in an awestruck voice. A moment later he added, "If Gemma hadn't brought the swarm back, I might not have had the strength to refuse it."

"Refuse what?"

"The chance to have Moroski as my helpless puppet, totally

in my thrall, with all his power and abilities at my command."
The young wizard frowned at his own words. "There's more
to it than that, but it's difficult to explain."

"That's more than enough." She shuddered. "It seems that
my granddaughter has hidden talents."

"It certainly does," Cai agreed thoughtfully, looking at the
sleepy bees about him.

"Is that why Moroski attacked you?" Adesina asked after a
pause. "Because you could have dominated him?"

"No. That was just a wizard's instinctive defense mecha-
nism," he replied, gingerly touching the weals on his neck.
"However much he wanted to lose his fundamental powers
and skills—the things that *made* him a wizard—he couldn't
accept their going. He couldn't see what I was doing as anything but evil—even though he *wanted* me to do it! Reactions
like that go far deeper than ordinary thought."

"But the two of you knew all that before you started, didn't
you?" Her tone was accusatory.

"We didn't know it would be so strong," Cai replied defensively. He stood up, steadying himself with a hand as he
swayed slightly. "I suppose I'll get used to this eventually,"
he muttered, "but until then . . ." Picking up one of the unused
objects from the table he used the same process as Moroski
had, and stored some of his excess power. Then he seemed
steadier. "Hangover cure," he said to himself, and grinned.

It was another two hours before Moroski finally awoke. The
lamps were lit and Cai, after having left briefly to talk to Ansar,
was back in his chair. It was the young wizard that Moroski
saw first when he opened his eyes, and his face rapidly went
through a series of expressions. Fear, hate, and envy all flickered briefly in his eyes but the supreme emotion was obviously
confusion. His gaze swept the room, taking in the bees, and
the cluttered paraphernalia of his study, lingering on the still
form of Atlanta, who remained perched on the windowsill. It
was only when he reached Adesina and found himself looking
into her love-filled eyes, that a measure of composure returned
to the former wizard's face.

"Welcome back, my love," she said, smiling gently. Her
relief showed in her voice.

"Over?" he asked, barely audible.

"Over," Cai confirmed.

"What happened?"

"Don't worry about that now. Just rest and get used to the

idea of your new life," Cai advised. Moroski looked at him for a few moments as if working out the import of these words, then nodded slowly. A rustle of wing-feathers caught his attention and he struggled to his feet, Adesina supporting his arm. Atlanta bobbed her head then turned and swiftly launched herself from the window.

"Goodbye," Moroski whispered as the falcon flew away. When he turned back, he was surprised to see tears running silently down Adesina's cheeks. She felt the sadness of the parting, and wanted so much to ask for his reassurance that he was still glad of the sacrifice, but the lump in her throat made speech impossible. Moroski sensed her need and took her in his arms.

"By comparison with us, it doesn't matter at all," he said, and the love and certainty in his voice were stronger than any magic.

"Gemma!" Cai shouted. "I need to talk to you."

The girl detached herself from her group of friends and joined the wizard. Together they walked to Cai's chambers.

"Your grandmother told me what you did yesterday," he began. "I wanted to thank you."

"That's all right," she said brightly. "It was fun."

"I've always known that you got on well with the swarm, but how did you get them to come back to the tower?"

"I just told them to," Gemma replied.

"How?"

The princess considered this question. "They weren't happy," she said at last, evidently in some confusion.

"Did you *make* them happy?"

She nodded slowly. "Then I brought them back to you. Wasn't that right?"

"Oh yes!" Cai replied emphatically. "If you hadn't . . ." He paused. "But how did you get through the shield?"

"What shield?"

Cai regarded her thoughtfully. "You know, Gemma, I wouldn't be at all surprised if you didn't become a wizard yourself one day."

"Would you marry me then?" she returned instantly.

There was soon tangible evidence of Moroski's conviction about the future. When Rivera gave birth to Ansar's son and heir, Keran, five months later, Adesina's own pregnancy was well advanced. She felt somewhat ridiculous supervising the labor of a woman half her age.

By now the palace community—and the rest of Heald for that matter—were reconciled to the widow-queen's remarriage and expectant state. If any thought her foolish or unwise, it was in the face of the evidence of her obvious happiness. Despite her increasing heaviness, she remained active, and positively radiated good health and contentment. However, this did not stop Moroski fussing over her at every opportunity. He was frustrated because he could no longer use any healing skills to check on her progress, and was forever badgering Cai to confirm Adesina's reassurances that both she and the baby were well.

The younger man had, by unspoken agreement, taken on the mantle of Heald's wizard and was now treated as such by everybody. Even those who had suffered at the hands of the swarm accepted him and his familiar's presence without question.

For some time, many people wondered why Cai had not returned to his home-isle. He showed no inclination to do so, and when, finally, Ansar asked him about his future plans, his reasons became clear.

"I remained on Ark a few days after you," the wizard said. "I don't know why, but I had a bad feeling about going back to Arlon. Still, duty called and I set off, with some of Mark's envoys as escort. I might as well have stayed in Starhill." There was bitterness as well as sadness in his voice.

"Why?" Ansar asked, blunt as ever.

"Arlon was in chaos. The palace community had been blown to the four winds. I think most of them were dead, but I never got the chance to find out. The city was in total disorder— senseless violence, illness, no food, no one to even try to establish any order. We didn't get the friendliest of welcomes," he added. "Any outsiders were regarded as a threat, and my presence was greatly resented. They felt that I should have been there when they'd needed me. Since I wasn't, they could now do without me, thank you very much.

"I tried, but the men I was with faced constant danger, and eventually it came to fighting. Some of Ark's people were killed and I fled with the remainder. We sailed to Tiarlon—

the small island just to the east—and stayed there a month and a half. The people there had also suffered, but weren't so antagonistic. We licked our wounds, repaired the ship, and I did what I could to repair the damage caused by the fog. But it was obvious that I wasn't trusted.

"In the end, Mark's envoys had to leave for home so they dropped me back on Arlon. I was on my own this time. That had both advantages and disadvantages, but nothing had really changed. I traveled round the island for a month—a good part of the time in secret—then returned to the city and found Moroski's message waiting for me. I didn't need asking twice."

"I can understand that," Ansar said, then paused before asking, "What did you make of Moroski's request?"

"He didn't tell me what it was then, just asked me to come as soon as possible. He was very mysterious."

"And now? Do you approve?"

"When I see the two of them together," the wizard replied, "I can do nothing else."

Ansar looked relieved. "Will you stay with us on Heald?" he asked, smiling. "We seem to have a vacancy at court."

"I thought you'd never ask," the wizard replied, his grin matching the king's. "Besides, if I didn't stay to see Rivera and Adesina through their pregnancies, I would be failing an important trust."

Ansar was taken aback. "My mother is pregnant *already*?" he exclaimed.

"Count on it," Cai laughed.

That had been a mere three weeks after Moroski had given up his wizardry, but it was soon clear that Cai was right. At first, many people—Rivera included—felt Adesina's pregnancy to be unwise, even unnatural. But by the time Keran was born, the two royal mothers-to-be had spent so much time together, comparing experiences, that it seemed a perfectly natural occurence. And no one could deny that Adesina was thriving and happy.

Though it was seven years since Rivera had given birth, she had a relatively easy labor, and with Adesina's calm supervision, all went smoothly.

"Thank goodness it's a boy!" was Rivera's immediate reaction. Before long, Ansar showed them why her relief had been so profound. He was insufferably proud of his new son, and his face was rarely seen without a smirk of satisfaction, though he always remained tender and considerate toward his wife. Adesina became concerned that Gemma might take her father's preoccupation with his heir amiss, but the little girl showed no signs of envy and was openly curious about her new brother, cuddling him and talking to him seriously at every opportunity.

While these happy events were occurring in Ramsport, the news they received from other islands was less pleasant. Cai's tale of Arlon's plight was reinforced by several reports which came in either direct or via Ark.

After Alzedo had been beaten back and the fog dispersed, Mark had sent envoys to all the major islands except Brogar, which had been cut off from the outside world for years. Some had returned with descriptions which tallied closely with that received later from Cai, and it became clear that the outer islands had suffered even more than Ark or Heald, though it had been there that the conflict reached its climax. Other reports were confusing and contradictory, with some islanders claiming no knowledge of the fog at all. It was hard to impose any sense on the overall picture.

A few emissaries had not returned at all, including three of the four sent to Strallen. The fourth had been rescued from a lengthy imprisonment there, and had arrived safely back on Ark in the company of a young wizard called Yve. She came from Lugg and Cai remembered her as Drogo's apprentice. The tale they brought with them was both horrible and inexplicable. Drogo and Saronno, Strallen's wizard, were dead, but while Lugg and Arlon languished in leaderless confusion, the people of Strallen were blissfully unaware of the world-shaking events which had enveloped them. Cai was determined to meet Yve, who now resided in Starhill—and her strange familiar—as soon as possible. They had already created quite a stir on Ark—as a female wizard and a semi-invisible dragon were bound to do—and some of the tales reaching Heald were no doubt somewhat exaggerated. Cai would have preferred to verify them himself but for the moment it was not feasible.

Ansar and Cai exchanged many messages with Mark and Ferragamo, discussing what could be done about the diverse reports, but no decision was reached. Though Ferragamo muttered darkly about the evil that was rising again, he knew no better than anyone what could be done to oppose it. He had in any case withdrawn more and more from the debate in recent months, because Koria, his love and partner of many years, had fallen ill, victim to a mysterious wasting disease. It seemed that even the wizard's considerable powers could do nothing to counteract it. The illness progressed slowly, but those who knew and loved Koria—and there were many—felt its wrongness. She had always been a calming influence on Ferragamo and retained her composure even now, despite her discomfort and slowly ebbing supplies of energy. In spite of this, the wizard had spells of dark depression and unreasoning fury at his inability to help the person who meant more to him than the whole world.

Cai and Moroski felt his agony, but could do nothing from afar; their immediate concerns were with the royal ladies of their own island.

So it was that Keran was born into a world whose future was far from certain. On the night of his birth, Adesina wondered what his fate would be. No one could have foreseen then that his inheritance would be stranger than their wildest imaginings.

Cradled in his grandmother's arms, Keran looked up at her with innocent brown eyes.

Four months later his aunt was born.

Chapter 21

Fontaine arrived in Ramsport during the last month of Adesina's pregnancy. Like everyone else, she had been amazed by the news of her mother's remarriage and Moroski's renunciation of wizardry. However, she quickly understood and appreciated their motives, and was characteristically fierce in their defense when anyone presumed to criticize.

The disturbing events on Ark and elsewhere had prevented her from returning to her former home-isle earlier, but nothing could have kept her from her mother's side now that her time was due. Despite the reports of Adesina's excellent health, Fontaine was naturally concerned that the rigors of childbirth would prove hard for a woman of her mother's age. These fears were soon dispelled on their reunion, as Adesina seemed to have grown younger since their last meeting. Any awkwardness that they might have felt at their unusual situation was rapidly forgotten as they talked.

"How could I be anything but healthy?" Adesina said in answer to her daughter's inquiry. "I'm being fussed over by one wizard, one ex-wizard, one granddaughter, and what seems like three hundred other people."

"Add one daughter to that list," Fontaine said, basking in the glow of her mother's large contentment. "You look wonderful."

"I feel wonderful—though I do get tired rather quickly these days." They smiled at each other fondly.

"How's the expectant father?"

"Nervous."

"He has no need to be, by the look of you."

"Of meeting you again," Adesina corrected.

"Me?" Fontaine looked momentarily nonplussed but soon realized what her mother's words implied.

"He did replace your father rather quickly," Adesina went on. "And if you don't mind me saying so, your tongue can be rather sharp at times."

"Oh, that's silly!" Fontaine exclaimed. "I must put him right at once. It was a surprise at first of course, but . . . anyway, I put it all in my letters."

"I told him that, but—"

"I've always been sure you were right and now that I've seen you, there can be no doubt at all!"

"Tell him that when you see him."

Fontaine nodded. "Men!" she said with exasperation, then laughed. "Is he really scared of me? He's always been such an imposing figure." She became serious. "Has he changed?"

"Only the things you know about. He's still the same person I fell in love with. He gets frustrated sometimes when he can't do something, especially when it concerns my health, and drives Cai crazy with all his questions! But apart from that, no, he hasn't changed. Maybe he's not as fierce. Atlanta's gone, of course." There was a touch of regret in her voice.

"He's happy?"

"I think so," Adesina replied, in a tone which implied far more certainty than her words.

With the innate sense of timing common to so many newborn children, Adesina's baby chose to make her entrance into the world in those gray hours before dawn known throughout the islands as "the wolfing hours." In spite of this, there were several people on hand to help, and eventually Fontaine had to send various of them away to ease the congestion. She remained, with Cai and, of course, Moroski.

Moroski was so nervous that he found it difficult to keep still. His body shuddered with sympathetic contractions and it was Adesina, by whose head he sat, who had the task of keeping him calm, rather than the other way round. She teased and joked with him until the final moments, when she had no time for anything but the wonder and agony of bringing a new life into the world.

Fontaine also tried to keep the mood light during her mother's confinement. She made the most of the reversal of usual roles and masked her concern beneath a smiling face. Cai too contributed to the happy atmosphere. Apart from those times when he was monitoring the internal progress of the unborn child and its mother, he talked almost nonstop and proved, when necessary, to be a most efficient midwife. Despite his relative youthfulness Cai, by reason of his wizardly training, was familiar with most matters of health and had attended several births. When Fontaine complimented him on his expertise he replied offhandedly, "It's just a matter of understanding."

"Perhaps, but I doubt if you could drag Ansar within a league of here at the moment. He couldn't bear to watch Keran's arrival—for all his proud doting now."

"Well, there's blood and there's blood," Cai replied.

"Leave my eldest out of this," Adesina commented drily. Although her voice was strained, there was humor beneath the surface. "My youngest is now definitely on its way."

The baby's cries of outrage at being forced to leave her warm haven soon confirmed the truth of Adesina's words.

Once Moroski was sure that both wife and child were healthy and comfortable, the tension drained out of his gaunt face in a rush. His smile was tinged with wonder as he tenderly picked up the baby girl. His daughter, quiet now, stared back at him through half-closed eyes and he laid her gently in her mother's arms. As he did so, he noticed a small birthmark on the baby's left shoulder but soon forgot it as he leaned over to kiss the mother of his child, his eyes moist with emotion.

Adesina was exhausted but totally relaxed and very, very happy. It had been so many years since Fontaine's birth that the experience had overwhelmed her as if it were quite new. Now, as she held the baby in her arms and looked into Moroski's glowing eyes, she felt invincible, as if their love could overcome anything. There was nothing in the world that could threaten their happiness or that of their child.

Cai and Fontaine left the three of them in a blissful and silent contemplation, soon to become the peace of well-earned sleep.

Chapter 22

*T*he girl was named Tzigane, an ancient name which held a special significance for her parents, but which they refused to divulge to anyone.

She was a demanding child from the first, requiring constant attention and an inordinate supply of food, but this posed no problem. Her parents were perfectly willing to devote every moment of their time to her and when they were temporarily called away, there were several others more than willing to take their place. Ten days after the birth, Fontaine received a disturbing message from Ark which told her, among other things, that Koria's illness had taken a turn for the worse. This was despite all Ferragamo's ministrations, and the wizard was now so preoccupied that he paid little attention to the increasingly urgent matters of state. Lacking the wizard's advice, and aware of his agitation, Mark was obviously becoming seriously worried. Fontaine knew that her place was by his side.

Even when she left, Tzigane did not lack for alternative nursemaids. Cai took enormous pride in the fact that he had been the one to bring her into this world, and needed little excuse to spend time with the infant. Gemma too was a persistent visitor, dividing her time between Keran and Tzigane, both of whom she found absolutely fascinating.

"Why doesn't she talk, Grandma?" the princess asked on an occasion when Tzigane was crying intermittently.

"She can't yet, little one," Adesina replied. "Babies have

to learn how to speak by listening to us. That's why you should always talk to them, even when they don't talk back."

Gemma considered this. "Is she listening to us now?" she asked, watching the baby closely.

"Of course she is."

"She doesn't seem to be," Gemma noted critically. "Perhaps we're not talking loud enough."

"Oh, I think we are!" Adesina replied quickly. "She just has so much to hear and see and touch. Everything is new to her, so she doesn't pay attention just to one thing."

After further thought, Gemma went off on a private mission. Soon after she had marched purposefully from the room, Moroski and Cai came in together.

"What have you been telling Gemma?" Moroski asked as he sat down beside his wife, accepting Tzigane with pleasure. "We've had very strict instructions to talk properly to the baby."

"Yes," Cai added. "I got the distinct impression that we'll be on trial from now on. Hello, gorgeous," he added, kneeling so that he was on a level with Tzigane's face. The baby watched the young wizard closely and stretched out one tiny hand toward his long, brown locks.

"There isn't a girl who can resist you, is there?" Adesina said, smiling.

"Can I help that?" Cai replied in wide-eyed innocence, as he gently shook his head to allow his hair to play over Tzigane's hand. "It's not my fault that I'm handsome, charming, and intelligent. It just comes naturally."

Adesina gave him a playful shove and he fell to the floor in theatrical manner, laughing until the baby started crying loudly. He got up again and, from his knees, faced the tearful child.

"It's all right. I'm not hurt," he said.

Tzigane quietened immediately, her screams replaced by a quizzical frown. The infant's expression was mirrored by her father's. There was something between Tzigane and Cai that he didn't understand, and it caused him a moment's disquiet. Adesina saw nothing of this, and laughed at Cai's antics.

"You're just a child yourself," she said. "Gemma will have something to say if she catches you acting like that!"

A little while later, Gemma returned, carrying her favorite storybook. This, she had decided, was the way to enable Tzigane to learn to talk quickly. The tales were so exciting that she was bound to pay attention to them rather than all the

other things about her. She proceeded to read one herself, the
three adults making up the rest of the audience and then, as
a favor, allowed Cai to read them all another. True to expec-
tation, and much to Gemma's satisfaction, the flow of words
held Tzigane spellbound. As the story came to an end Gemma
looked at the baby and asked, "Can she speak now?"

It was Cai who first noticed that the birthmark on Tzigane's
tiny shoulder was changing shape.

"It's getting bigger, I'm sure it is," he said, pointing it out
to her parents.

"It's nothing serious, is it?" Moroski asked, desperately
seeking reassurance.

"Of course not!" Adesina replied.

Nevertheless, they watched the mark closely from that day
on and found that, although at first imperceptible, the outline
clearly changed. A few days later, it had reverted to its original
shape. But then it began the whole remarkable process again,
repeating the cycle every six days or so. It was curious and
disturbing, and was not mentioned to anyone else within the
palace.

At first neither Tzigane's parents nor Cai could make any
sense of the transformation, but gradually the repeatedly assumed shapes became familiar, until one night Moroski knew
what they reminded him of. He slipped out of bed, and crept
over to the baby's cot to make sure. It was obvious! He knew
precisely how the outline of the small brown birthmark would
change, and the realization sent a tingle of excitement mixed
with fear though his entire body. What could it mean? For the
moment, he had no idea, but it was clear that Tzigane was no
ordinary child.

What does the future hold for you? he wondered, gazing
at the sleeping face of his child. The quiet room provided no
answer and eventually he went back to bed. He could not sleep
for some time, as his brain tried to work out why his daughter
had been marked with the tiny and ever-changing silhouette
of a falcon in flight.

Moroski shared his discovery with Adesina and later, inexplicably reluctant, with Cai. They both saw the falcon immediately but had no more idea than he about what it could mean.

"Perhaps Atlanta is with you still," Adesina suggested quietly, one evening when the lovers were alone together.

"Perhaps," he replied, but was not convinced and, in the event, nobody had time to conceive a plausible theory for the bird's appearance.

When Tzigane was barely three months old, news came of events which would shatter forever her young world, and the world of all about her.

Chapter 23

 T he herald of war was a huge, grotesquely deformed eagle which circled the city as though on a reconnaissance mission. Its baleful red eyes missed no detail and those unfortunate enough to be caught and held by its malevolent glare shuddered. When it flew back out to sea, the inhabitants of Ramsport were relieved, but wondered what the bird's appearance presaged; it did not take a wizard's intuition to see that it was a sign of ill-omen.

When the eagle returned two days later it was accompanied by an army of formidable size. Rumors had preceded their arrival and the dire warnings had not been inaccurate. So large was the fleet that carried them that it was forced to make landfall at several different sites along the coast, on either side of the city.

Ansar had done what he could to increase the size of Heald's army in the limited time available to him since returning to his home-isle. The world had obviously become a dangerous and unpredictable place, and such precautions were necessary. However, as soon as he saw the extent of the invading forces, it was immediately clear that his own would be woefully inadequate. Calmly and steadily, he prepared to do what little he could to salvage the honor of his island, at the same time making hasty plans to get his family away from the holocaust that was coming.

The first battle was fierce. The invaders poured ashore, heedless of the midwinter cold and the rough seas that capsized many of their smaller boats and soaked them with icy spray. They were met in force wherever possible and, as the Healdean soldiers had considerable positional advantages, all went well for the defenders for a time. Inevitably, though, the sheer weight of numbers soon began to tell and the increasingly weary Healdean army was stretched beyond breaking point. They began to lose ground, and before long there was a real danger of a massacre as the invaders continued to surge ashore. Reluctantly, Ansar called a retreat, conceding the enemy the landing in order to give his soldiers a chance to regroup and reorganize.

The king's mood was grim, and was made worse by the fact that he could not be in the thick of the combat. Generalship was something which did not come naturally to Ansar and he had to fight against his own instincts as well as against the enemy. Although he knew he would soon have the chance to use the strength of his own sword-arm, this gave him little satisfaction. He was aware that by then his island would be all but lost.

There was only one glimmer of hope in the events of that terrible day. The invaders they fought were men like themselves; they bled and died, and had done so in their hundreds. Ansar had been dreading the possibility that his men would face the invulnerable wraiths who had driven him from his home a year and a half ago, and he took a dark satisfaction in the grisly slaughter of the violators of his land.

The first retreat of Ansar's army was the beginning of the end, as he had known it would be. Many of the people of Ramsport had tried to flee into the surrounding countryside, but the invaders soon had the city surrounded and wreaked havoc among the panic-stricken citizens. Ansar's forces were pushed further and further back, until the only stronghold left was the high-walled palace. Grim-faced, he gathered his remaining allies about him and prepared for their final stand.

The king and his men watched in agony as smoke began to rise from the city. The victorious invaders ran amok, looting and killing, delighting in wanton destruction. The sights and sounds of that morning became an unbearable torture for the last remnants of Heald's army.

Laurent found Ansar crouching on the battlements,

keeping low to avoid arrows. The courtier was begrimed and bloody and looked near to exhaustion. He slumped down beside his king.

"I can't take much more of this," Ansar grated. "What are they waiting for? They could have overrun us several times by now!"

"It's as if they've been set loose to play," Laurent replied. "They're like ravening beasts out there."

"Are the women away?" the king asked bleakly.

"No. There's been no chance. The secret routes are still free but the city is in chaos."

Ansar seemed about to explode. "There *must* be ways," he exclaimed. "Are they insane?"

"They want to leave no more than you do," the courtier replied. "And the men you charged with their safety are only human."

Ansar's expression became steady and calm. He grasped Laurent by his shoulders and spoke gravely.

"Old friend, I am going to lay a heavy burden on you. Don't interrupt, just listen. You've done your share of fighting. There'll be more to come for you, no doubt of that, but let it be in the cause of my choosing. This is the last thing I will ask of you."

The king's voice was so serious and so full of determined authority that Laurent could only wait in silence for him to continue.

"Get them away. Rivera, Keran, and Gemma. My mother too, if she will go. I can face a soldier's death, but I *cannot* face the thought of the ones I love in the hands of those barbarians. You know this city and Heald better than anyone. You escaped against all the odds last time. Save them for me, Laurent."

The courtier could only nod. Nothing he could have said would have conveyed his feelings at that moment.

"Good man," Ansar said.

They parted without further words, with only a fierce handclasp. Then Laurent moved off quickly, bent low to keep out of sight of the archers below. Ansar watched him until he was out of sight then shut his eyes in silent anguish. When he opened them again it was to the realization that the city beyond the palace walls had become suddenly quiet.

Cautiously, he peered over the battlements. Several of the enemy were in view but they no longer seemed intent on mayhem. In fact, to Ansar's amazement, they were strolling about as if on a carefree summer outing, and as he watched, an even more remarkable transformation began to take place.

From many of the houses, previously shuttered and barricaded, the people of Ramsport began to emerge. They walked out, blinking in the pale winter sunshine, as if there was no danger at all. And indeed, there seemed to be none! Very soon, Healdeans and enemy soldiers were mingling peaceably in an ever-increasing throng, filling the streets and squares surrounding the palace.

What's going on? This is madness! Ansar thought, totally bemused. Below him the crowd grew but still an eerie silence lay over the whole inexplicable scene. This unnatural lull was somehow more ominous than the carnage that had preceded it. Ansar's skin began to crawl in anticipation and it was not long before his worst fears were realized.

He noticed a huge, gray ship in the harbor. It dwarfed all the other vessels, and Ansar assumed that it was the flagship of the invasion fleet. Then there was a stir in the crowd on the far side of the main square, and, together with his comrades on the battlements, Ansar saw the people draw back to allow a platoon of soldiers to march into their midst. As the new force came into view, the king's stomach turned to ice. He had seen those gray faces and soulless eyes before. He knew, without requiring any proof, that these arrivals were wraiths, cruel and utterly invincible. *Why had they not been used in the invasion?* Ansar's last hopes for even an honorable death faded away into a numb and hopeless dread. He prayed silently and desperately that Laurent would succeed in his mission. The wraiths halted in formation, cleared a large area in the center of the square, and rolled a cart into the space. Then they became still and waited with everyone else.

What now? Why are they taunting me? Ansar was near breaking point; the next arrival pushed him even closer.

A giant of a man strode into view. Even shrouded in his flowing cape of silver and black he appeared massively strong, and his colorless eyes glinted evilly in a gnarled and ugly face. Behind him, limping awkwardly, came the red-eyed eagle. The people in the square watched his approach with rapt expressions of pleasurable subservience. Ansar felt sick.

It's him! he thought in despair.

Alzedo halted beside the cart and looked up at the palace, his gaze directed straight at Ansar. The king rose to his full height, aware that arrows were now the least of the dangers he faced. Alzedo smiled. It was a horrible sight. When he spoke, his voice shook the palace foundations. No one could miss his ominous words.

"Greetings, Ansar. We meet again—at last. I trust that your appearance means you wish to surrender."

Ansar stood trembling, unable to find his voice. The sorcerer went on, his tone reasonable.

"I have no quarrel with you, and am quite prepared to forgive your past foolishness. The other islands have already yielded. Soon Ark will stand alone—and then the world will be mine. You can choose either to be a part of that new world, or to sacrifice everything pointlessly. You cannot stop me—so why suffer for it?"

A small, rebellious thought stirred in Ansar's quaking mind. *I've heard his arguments before! Don't trust him.* Still he could not speak. The mighty, persuasive voice went on.

"Surrender and you—and those about you—will not be harmed."

No, Ansar thought, *they will become mindless zombies to fuel your monstrous evil!*

Alzedo's massive right hand emerged from beneath his cape and swept wide, indicating the passive crowd about him.

"Your people are in your hands. Give me what I want and they will live. If not . . ."

A woman detached herself from the throng and walked into the open space. She clambered on to the cart and stood there facing her king. Her face was placid, her eyes empty. Alzedo's left hand came into view. The middle finger was grotesquely extended in a long, razor-sharp talon which glinted like steel. Casually, he raked the claw upward, slitting the woman open from thigh to throat. Blood and entrails cascaded down as her body fell to the wooden boards, where it twitched feebly for a few moments before becoming still. Alzedo smiled.

Ansar felt the bile rise in his throat, and his face was white with anger and disgust. Retching sounds came from the other soldiers on the battlements. The crowd below merely watched and listened as incuriously as before.

"You have only to place your palace and its people in my hands, and peace will return to your island."

I will not live to see your peace, Ansar thought defiantly. *One way or another . . .*

"Your people will be safe, free to continue their lives as

my subjects." Alzedo paused. "But, by necessity, I make one exception to this. All so-called wizards are an abomination, and must be destroyed, together with those their blood pollutes. The wizard's child must die."

How does he know about Tzigane? Ansar wondered frantically. Then he became aware of many pairs of eyes upon him. Those within the palace were looking to him for their lead—perhaps they had not yet realized that whichever course he chose would condemn them. Although it was clear that some expected him to give in to the sorcerer's demands, he knew in his heart that he could not.

"Your hesitation is unwise," Alzedo boomed. Another citizen had mounted the cart, heedless of the bloody mess that defiled it, and was callously gutted.

"No!" Ansar yelled. His mind had finally snapped. It was suicidal, but he was at last acting instinctively, doing the one thing which came naturally.

Sword in hand, he tore down the steps from the battlements, heading for the main gates. As he ran he rallied his men, who reacted with surprising speed. It did not occur to Ansar to wonder why those within the palace community were immune to the mass hypnosis which had afflicted the general populace. He yelled his orders, racing ahead of his men out into the city square where chaos reigned as the enemy soldiers renewed their butchery.

Ansar rushed heedlessly toward his detested enemy and the wraiths that surrounded him.

Alzedo's mocking laughter echoed over them all.

All movement in the palace had been stilled by the first sound of Alzedo's voice. Everyone was held frozen by his words, and though they were spared the sight of his brutality, the sorcerer's presence was enough to awaken every secret fear.

Laurent had found Rivera and her children moments earlier. He was still breathing hard, but knew that if they were to attempt to escape it must be soon. When the sorcerer's voice resounded about them he feared that it might already be too late, yet found himself unable to move or even think coherently. He listened helplessly to the message of doom.

In a nearby chamber Moroski and Adesina also stood

transfixed. Their thoughts were already of Tzigane, and at the dreadful words, "The wizard's child must die," their eyes went wide with shock and they turned involuntarily to the sleeping girl.

The spell broke when Ansar made his decision to attack, though those inside did not know it then. Freed from the malign enchantment, Adesina immediately gathered the baby into her arms.

"Why?" she asked softly. "What has she done?"

Moroski had no answers. He felt doubly and frustratingly impotent. Even as a wizard he had been helpless before Alzedo. Now he could not even begin to think of a way to protect those who were dearer to him than his own life. Taking them both in his arms, he could only cavil against fate. *She wasn't born just for this!*

They started violently as the door of their room was flung open, and Cai came in.

"Laurent's going to try to get Rivera and the children away," he said breathlessly. "If you hurry, you can go with them. It's a slim chance, but the only one."

The lovers looked into each other's eyes. Within moments each knew what their decision must be, but Cai was impatient. "What are you waiting for? Come on!"

"I ran away before," Moroski replied, "but not this time. This is my home-isle."

"Mine too," Adesina said.

"But Tzigane!" Cai exclaimed in horror. "You heard what he said."

"He thinks she's important," Moroski agreed. "I don't know why, but she has to get away." He was very calm now, and continued, overriding Cai's attempted interruption. "I gave up much to father this child, but I cannot help her now. You're the only one who can. Take her with you. Go with Laurent and the others."

"Please," Adesina added.

"But Ansar—" Cai began.

"You can do nothing for him," Moroski said. "Salvage what little you can from this appalling mess."

"Save her, and Heald's sacrifice will not be totally in vain," Adesina said. "Please, Cai. For us."

The young wizard stood for a few moments, perplexed. Then, with time pressing, he asked, "Why don't you come too?"

"We'd hinder you," Adesina said, "and we *must* stay, so

that Alzedo will think Tzigane is still here. While he's looking for us, you'll have a better chance of getting away."

"Take her and go," Moroski pleaded.

Laurent's shout sounded from the corridor. Reluctantly Cai said, "All right."

Adesina almost balked at handing the baby over but at an even more urgent shout from outside, she kissed Tzigane tenderly and gave her into Cai's care. For a moment the wizard hesitated, his eyes full of all the words there was no time to say.

"Go," Adesina prompted in a voice choked with emotion.

"Farewell," Cai said and, without waiting for a reply, he turned and fled, Tzigane cradled contentedly in his arms.

The tears came then, but neither wished to make their decision over again. They clung to each other desperately, until their weeping lessened and they could push back the wrench of separation with thoughts of action. A few moments might make all the difference. They would give Cai and Laurent all the help they could, so that their own end would not be meaningless.

"Wrap a pillow in her shawl," Moroski said. "We'll show ourselves. It might fool him for a while."

Adesina did as she was instructed, and together they walked out into the battle. The fighting was already within the palace, and the wraiths were in the forefront now.

One of the steely-eyed enemy caught sight of the couple and shouted, pointing at them with his sword. His distraction led to his downfall as a defender leapt forward and ran him through. However, within a short time the body had disappeared, dissolving into a swirl of gray matter which then became a soldier once more.

Even before this unnatural transformation had occurred, the wraith's companions had taken up his cry and several of them set off in pursuit of Moroski and Adesina.

"To the tower," the former wizard said, taking the burden from his wife. They set off at a run, knowing that their enemies were only a short distance behind them. The wraiths were reckless in their chase and many were cut down by the remaining palace guards. This gave the couple a brief respite, but they were still barely able to get within the basement of the tower and bar the entrance before their assailants were battering on the iron-shod door.

The lowest room of the tower was cold and dark, bare of

any furnishings beyond a few forgotten items left there to moulder.

Adesina slid down to the floor, sitting against the bare stone wall. She was gasping for breath.

"Do you think . . ." she began.

"I don't know." Moroski shrugged. He put down the pillow and sat beside his love. "Do you want to climb up?" he asked, indicating the stairs. "We could see what's happening."

"I don't think I can," she replied, white-faced and still breathing hard. "I've hurt my ankle."

They sat in silence, listening to the sounds of fighting outside. The wraiths had stopped beating on the door and now heavy footsteps approached.

Alzedo stood before the tower, heedless of the skirmishes about him. Behind him, the hideous eagle limped to a halt. The sorcerer smiled as the wraiths withdrew to a safe distance.

"This will be a pleasure for me," he said. "A suitable end for these petty enemies." He turned to his familiar. "You see, Sivadla, how the obstacles in my path are being swept aside. Watch and learn."

He raised both massive arms and spoke. His words clashed and grated in the cold air, and the grinding sound of tortured stone rose up, assaulting the ears of all around with ever-increasing violence.

"So much for prophecy!" Alzedo roared, then threw back his head and laughed his triumph to the skies.

Within the tower, Adesina and Moroski lay in each other's arms, wondering when the final assault would come. They had found a sort of peace deep within themselves and knew that whatever horrors were still to come would be made easier because they faced them together.

"Was it worth it?" he asked softly.

"Oh, yes," Adesina replied at once, her heart in her words.

They were the last she uttered. At Alzedo's command, the wood, stone, and mortar of the wizard's tower imploded and fell earthward in a colossal deluge.

The lovers' last embrace was entombed by the jumbled mass of rock which would forever be their monument.

Part 3

Ark

Chapter 24

*F*ontaine had been away from Starhill for little more than a month, but much had changed —for the worse—since she had left to attend Tzigane's birth. Mark's letter had sounded almost desperate, and it did not take Ark's queen long to see why.

It had become increasingly clear that the islands were heading toward a crisis. Since the time when Alzedo, aided by his evil fog, had so nearly achieved total control over their world, Mark had made strenuous efforts to re-establish cordial relations with all the other islands except Brogar. He had met with little success. The hostile attitude Gale and his colleagues had found on Strallen was far from unique. Over a year had passed now, and Ark's rulers still stood alone. They saw the need for unified action to confront the inevitable evil uprising, but even their closest allies on Heald were preoccupied with other matters.

To make things worse, it seemed that some islands were fighting amongst themselves, blaming each other for recent misfortunes. Even though the reports Mark's envoys did manage to bring back lacked detail, the rumors of war were too persistent to discount. Ferragamo suspected the hand of Brogar's renegade sorcerer. However, he was so bad-tempered that few could stand his tirades for long, and many suspected his theories to be based on paranoia. When Koria had fallen victim to the wasting disease which afflicted her still, the

wizard's moods had become more and more abrasive and vol-
atile. Mark's letter to Fontaine hinted that Ferragamo had now
reached the point where he was incapable of rational speech
for more than a few sentences. The despairing wizard was so
preoccupied with his lover's illness that everything else paled
into insignificance.

"He's living in the past," Mark told Fontaine as soon as
they were alone together. "Talking about when I was a child
and so on, but mostly about his early days with Koria. He loves
her so much he can't bear not being able to help her, so he's
living in the time when she was well. I feel so sorry for them."

"It's almost as if something were trying to hurt him on
purpose," Fontaine said, but Mark was too immersed in his
own problems to hear the implication in her words.

"The worst of it is, I *need* him now more than ever," he
said ruefully. "Events are building up to something awful—
and he's just not here to help me!"

Mark's relationship with Ferragamo had gone through many
variations since the time when the young prince had been an
enthusiastic—if dreamy—pupil of the wizard. There had been
periods of distrust and even antagonism over the years, but
these were vastly outweighed by the mutual love and respect
that they still felt for each other. Mark's own father had been
a remote and sometimes alien figure, and, after Ather's untimely death, Ferragamo had been, for a time, even more of
a paternal figure for the youngest of Ark's princes. Ever since
then, the wizard's advice—and mere presence—had lent stability to Mark's life and their loss was keenly felt.

"You have other advisors," Fontaine said. "Me, for one!"
Mark smiled, as she had intended he would.
"I'm glad you're back," he said softly.

———————————

Ferragamo sat in the bedchamber he and Koria had shared for
so long. His right hand rested on the bed in which his lady
slept. The left was constantly moving; tapping the arm of his
chair, running fingers through his short white hair, fingering
the buttons on his disheveled clothing. His green eyes stared
at the opposite wall, where his familiar, Owl, perched, but
Ferragamo saw a different scene.

Koria was rarely out of bed for more than a few hours each
day now, but even when she slept the wizard was never more

than a few paces away. His inexplicable inability to heal—or even diagnose—her illness had left Ferragamo in a state of shock. His mind, once a sharp and formidable force, had retained its power but lost its anchor, and now drifted at the mercy of winds and tides no man could fathom.

Robbed of the company of the only woman to have captured his heart in the two and a half centuries of his life, his only resource was to fall back upon memories of happier times. The past was his haven. Once there, he could taste again the heady wine of their early love, when each had been intoxicated by the other, drinking greedily of passion in spite of the disapproval of the unheeded outside world. There he could walk again at Koria's side, exploring the coastline and countryside around their cottage retreat in the southern village called Home. And there too they could lie, warm and satiated in each other's arms, after their love had proved itself yet again in the most incontrovertible of ways.

Theirs was a match that would not be denied, and they accepted the nature of their life together without qualms. Both knew that Ferragamo would remain almost unchanged with the years—he had the physique of a man in his thirties even now—while she would age and finally leave him to carry on alone. But all this had been far in the future. Koria had not yet completed her first half century of life and until now had not known an illness requiring more than a common remedy or, at most, a moment of the wizard's healing touch. That she should have been struck down now—and in such a diabolical way—seemed an act of senseless cruelty.

She had always been slim and physically active, but now her body was shrunken and weak, and she tired very easily. Though gaunt, her face retained the appeal that Ferragamo found so much more attractive than mere beauty, but now pain showed in her brown eyes for most of her waking hours.

Predictably, Koria had borne her illness with great fortitude, her innate good sense allowing her to remain optimistic and calm. She was mystified and a little frightened by her lover's inability to understand the disease but, she reasoned, wizardry was not the sum total of all the knowledge in the world. If this was beyond Ferragamo's skill, then she would meet it with all the other weapons at her command. In fact, despite her discomfort, she worried more about her lover's deteriorating mental state than about herself, and spent much of her energy in remaining cheerful and calm for his benefit.

However, the effort was becoming more of a strain and she slept great portions of the days away, lost in dreams that alternated between unease and moments of bliss in which she joined the wizard in the past.

She slept now, and beside her Ferragamo sat as though in a trance. Owl watched over them both with large sad eyes, sharing his master's bewilderment, and seeing with him the scenes of happiness which, it seemed, were gone forever.

Chapter 25

Luke and Julia were not in Starhill when the prince's mother returned from Heald. They had been visiting the small northern port of Coro and were now riding slowly back toward the capital, making the most of the mild autumnal weather. About them, the rolling green hills presented a placid picture, with the highlands almost lost in the mist to the west. Yet despite the peaceful setting and their leisurely pace, their thoughts were ominous, full of foreboding.

In Coro they had heard rumors of violence and unrest in the northern isles, and this had only served to confirm their feeling of impending crisis. Several people had expressed surprise that the royal couple traveled without an escort. Ark had been free of strife since the day these two had combined their powers to defeat the spiral of malevolence that had engulfed all the islands. The possibility that he and Julia might need protection had never even occurred to Luke, but as they returned to Starhill, he wondered aloud if it might become necessary.

"That will be a sad day for Ark," his young wife replied.

A silent voice sounded in their minds. *I'm glad to see you are both being idiotic about this. You're well matched, as ever.*

These sarcastic words came from the cat who rode on the front of Luke's saddle. Muscles was black and white, except

for four muddy brown paws, and, like his sire, Longfur, he
had a caustic turn of phrase. He went on:

*If the unrest we've been told about comes here, it will be
as an invasion from outside. Then everybody will need an
escort—not just you. If it doesn't, then the only people you
have to fear are your own citizens—the only islanders who
haven't been causing trouble.*

Luke and Julia looked in surprise at Muscles, who gave all
the signs of sleeping peacefully, so that his voice had come as
a shock. They were both used to mind-talk with the cat, though
not with each other. That the three of them could communicate
in this way had once been a source of amazement, but was
now an accepted part of their lives. Mark and Longfur had a
similar facility, conversing directly in thoughts just as wizards
did with their familiars.

"All right, clever claws," Luke said, speaking aloud so that
Julia could hear both sides of the conversation. "If everything
is fine, why do I feel so uneasy?"

"Me too," Julia added.

Because you would have to be addle-headed not to, the cat
retorted. *Everyone does.*

"It's more than that—" Luke began.

*Of course it is. You're Servants, both of you. Or had you
forgotten?* Muscles yawned insolently. *The very fact that I can
talk to you is proof of that, and because of it you're sensitive.*

"But the *real* Servants lived centuries ago," Luke persisted.

Maybe you are addle-headed, Muscles commented acidly
and Luke became silent, wondering for the hundredth time
about his ancient predecessors. The first Servants had been
heroes, men who aided the wizards of their time to defeat a
tyrannical and dangerously powerful sorcerer. They had named
themselves for their dedication to the cause they served. The
War of the Wizards, as it had come to be known, had been
fought with unimaginable forces of magic as well as men, and
had changed the face of the world. Could the threat looming
over them now really be as serious as that which the Servants
had pledged themselves to fight? There were many points of
similarity, but even so, Luke's brain refused to admit that he
could be a leading player in such events. And yet . . . he had
so often been guided by instincts he had not known he'd pos-
sessed, and his magical abilities—unlike those of a wizard—
were unpredictable and often beyond his control. It was as if

he were being used as the tool of a higher purpose, a destiny that not even his strange childhood had prepared him for.

Julia too was lost in contemplation. Her own origins were shrouded in horror but she had overcome her evil heritage. However, though she was now free of Alzedo's influence, the memory of it haunted her still and she dreaded the next trial of strength. She knew it was coming soon.

They were both interrupted by Muscles, who resumed his commentary.

Besides, he said. *You two are in little danger. One look at you and most ruffians would run a league.*

Husband and wife glanced at each other and grinned.

"Why?" Julia asked. "We're not that ugly!"

You have the eyes of enchanters, the cat replied in tremulous tones, mocking the reactions of some of Ark's more incredulous inhabitants. *It's enough to make strong men wet themselves. Strike me dead if I say a word of a lie.*

Luke and Julia laughed, but they knew that there was a grain of truth in the cat's exaggerations. They were indeed a striking young couple. Luke's blond hair and tall, muscular frame gave him an imposing presence that belied his seventeen summers. Julia's build was slim and athletic, and her lovely face was framed by black hair streaked with silver, though she was only a few months older than her husband. Yet their eyes, as Muscles had indicated, provoked the most attention. Luke's were a golden amber, which glowed at times of excitement, and at others were capable of mesmerizing anyone who looked into their liquid depths. They had been thus ever since he had eaten a whole moonberry at the age of two, but even before that his stare had held many with its intensity. Julia's eyes, on the other hand, were a delicate shade of violet which captivated many while at the same time communicated a subtle thrill of danger. Their color still caused Mark an occasional involuntary shudder, reminding him of an earlier conflict with Alzedo's evil.

"Well, we can't help *that!*" Julia said.

That's what they all say, Muscles concluded.

They rode on in silence. After a while, Luke said aloud, "I wonder how Koria is."

You may not find out today at this pace, his feline companion replied. *Do these great lumps have to go so slowly? We'll miss dinner at this rate.*

"You know perfectly well that you complain about the bumping if we go any faster," Luke retorted, but nevertheless they spurred their mounts on, anxious to be back in the city before the chill of evening.

They entered Starhill through Star Gate, one of five entrances evenly spaced about the city's circular walls. After exchanging greetings with the soldiers in the guardroom, they rode up the paved thoroughfare which led directly to the center, where the castle lay. Such a road led inward from each of the gates, like the spokes of a wheel, dividing the city into five sectors. These were known, perversely, as "quarters."

As they neared their journey's end, Julia returned to their earlier concern.

"We'll go and find Yve," she said. "If anyone has any news of Koria, she will."

Luke nodded gravely. The young wizard from Lugg was the only person who still retained Ferragamo's confidence. While all his old friends were unable to help, and were treated with varying degrees of indifference—or worse—the newcomer Yve was always welcome in the elder wizard's chambers. She alone was allowed to assist him with looking after Koria, and therefore acted as intermediary for the rest of the court.

"Yes," Luke agreed sadly. "I don't seem to be able to talk to Ferragamo any more. Yve is our best bet."

Yve had been on Ark for seven months now, and had become an accepted part of the castle community as soon as the double shock of a female wizard and her unconventional familiar had worn off. Understandably, she had been the subject of considerable interest and, with the help of Durc, Gale, and Bram, she had had to relate her story several times to various audiences. The ghastly tales of Lugg, Arlon, and Strallen made unpleasant listening, but similar accounts had been sent back from other islands, and so they were received with no great surprise.

After that, attention had switched to the wizard herself and thence to Sweetness. Yve's personal history was novel, and caused many people to reassess their ideas of the world. Julia especially had been filled with admiration for the wizard's lonely struggle for acceptance and the two young women became close friends, exchanging stories from lives which had been spent at opposite ends of the known world.

Koria had been ill for some time when Yve arrived on Ark, but even so, she had welcomed the newcomer as soon as Ferragamo introduced them. He had obviously hoped that another wizard would be able to solve the mystery of the disease, but Yve proved as helpless as himself, much to their joint disappointment and distress. Nevertheless, Yve grew close to her taciturn older colleague and his patient lover. It filled her with sadness and impotent anger that, like Ferragamo, she could only watch Koria slide ever deeper into the darkness of pain and, as a consequence, she did all she could to help her in other ways. Her efforts were appreciated and Yve marveled at the way Koria remained cheerful and calm in spite of her suffering.

Many others at the court had grown to know and like Yve and she was now an accepted figure within the castle. The same could not be said of her familiar.

Sweetness was a mystery to most people, and that was probably a blessing. Many could not see the dragon at all, except for an occasional blurring of their vision, and those that could had learned to treat him as a mirage, of importance only to Yve. Few took him seriously. This had irked Sweetness for a while, and he had caused panic with a few fire-blowing demonstrations. Yve put a stop to that, and now the dragon spent much of his time outside the city walls, finding the atmosphere there more congenial. Apart from causing a few minor problems for one or two shepherds and cowherds, this arrangement suited everybody. Mark, especially, was glad that Sweetness was rarely in view. Even though he could barely make out the creature's outline and only glimpse his glittering eyes, that was more than enough to bring back unwanted memories of his own youthful struggle with one of dragon-kind.

Beca, on the other hand, found Sweetness fascinating and was able to see him more clearly than most. She often accompanied Yve to her meetings with her familiar, and watched with awe as Sweetness preened and paraded for her benefit.

"He's so beautiful!" the princess exclaimed in admiration on one occasion.

"Don't encourage him," Yve replied, smiling. Silently she admonished the dragon. *Has anyone told you you're a dreadful show-off?*

But I have so much to show off!

"Can you ride him?" Beca asked breathlessly.

"No. I'm afraid not," Yve said regretfully. "Sweetness is not entirely in our world. Touch him, you'll see what I mean."

Gingerly, Beca extended a hand toward the dragon's obediently still snout. As her fingers passed through him she gave a little squeal of surprise and Sweetness drew back quickly, sneezing violently.

"Did I hurt him?" the princess asked anxiously.

"No," Yve laughed. "But you see now why I can't ride him."

You've never tried, Sweetness said unexpectedly. *You could always come to my world,* he added. *Oga said he could show us how.*

Yve felt confused and unhappy, sure that something was wrong. Sweetness sounded eager, but his words rang false.

Who's Oga? she asked.

A friend. The dragon was defensive and suddenly unsure of himself.

In your world?

Sweetness looked as if he did not understand the question. Then he nodded, but refused to say any more.

"What's happening?" Beca asked, aware of the unheard conversation.

"Nothing," Yve replied. "We'd better go back."

No one, not even Ferragamo, had been able to shed any light on Sweetness's strange half-existence and Yve no longer questioned it. She had accepted her unconventional familiar and it was only on occasions such as this that he caused her any great concern.

"It would be good to ride on him, wouldn't it?" Beca said, as they walked toward the castle. "Soaring up into the sky like a bird."

"Yes," Yve replied. "Yes, it would." *I wish it were that simple.*

Chapter 26

$\mathcal{M}$ ark sat on a stone bench in the tree yard, thinking of the earlier conflicts the place had witnessed. He was sure now that another would be upon them soon. Luke and Julia had returned from Coro the previous evening, with yet more tidings of unrest and Mark, like them, felt a rising unease. He had hoped after the trials and adventures of his youth that his life would be one of peace and contentment, but it had not been so. He had known much happiness, but there had also been times of horror and despair.

I wish it were over, he thought longingly, then shuddered at the idea that perhaps the age-old promise of the Servants might never be fulfilled. Endless centuries of vigilance stretched before his mind's eye. No time to rest, to relax, to live an ordinary, uneventful life. *I wish it were over!*

His gaze fell upon the moonberry tree in the center of the courtyard. Its slender trunk stood no taller than a man, and the gracefully curved boughs were still decked with pale green leaves, despite the imminence of winter. The precious fruit looked innocuous enough, silver-gray in color and the size of a thumbnail, but Mark knew better. Their potency had been demonstrated many times.

From his seat, the king began counting the berries, wondering as he did so whether there were any left in the other islands. If Yve's tale was typical, it was possible there was none, or at best very few. It was not a comforting thought.

Nineteen. Koria must have taken one recently for the regular meal. The thought came automatically, but then Mark realized that someone else must be supervising the careful use of the moonberries in preparing food for everyone within the castle. This process had once been only a tradition, but more recently had literally become a matter of life and death. Even with Koria's absence, the kitchen staff had not been forgetful, and Mark made a mental note to commend them for it. The tree produced fruit at the necessary rate and a new berry would soon take the place of the one that had been picked. That at least could be relied on. Mark's reverie was interrupted by the arrival of Jani, who stepped from the doorway at the base of the Wizard's Tower. The king was surprised. Since Ferragamo hardly left his apartments now, the tower was rarely entered. It had been the wizard's special preserve and though Luke, Julia, and others had often visited, they rarely did so now. Mark could not remember the last time he had climbed the winding staircase to the wizard's study.

Jani smiled, seemingly at ease, but Mark knew that he would receive no explanation of the big man's presence. Jani was deaf and dumb. His well-muscled body was covered only in thin shirt and trousers, and, despite the cold, his feet and bald head were bare. As ever, he appeared calm and dignified, his gentle nature belying his imposing size. It was hard to believe that he had once lived as cook for a band of outlaws.

Mark smiled awkwardly, wondering what Jani had been doing inside the tower. He received the answer from a most unexpected source.

He was helping me, said a familiar voice in the king's head. *Unfortunately, opening doors is not among my many talents.*

Longfur Mousebane emerged from the tower, his tail erect and his black and white coat arranged as eccentrically as ever. The cat shared an understanding with Jani which, though falling short of his two-way communication with Mark, allowed him to share the man's thoughts and feelings when necessary. Luke and Muscles also had a similar empathy with the ex-outlaw.

What were you doing? Mark asked.

I wanted to see the conclave room again, Longfur replied. *Why?*

To remember my dreams, the cat said enigmatically. *For the next time.*

Mark was puzzled. *But there'll never be another conclave*, he said with certainty.

Not here, perhaps.

Longfur, what are you talking about?

The next challenge is coming, the cat retorted impatiently. *Some of us are trying to prepare for it, instead of just sitting about moping.*

Mark was stung by the accusation in his friend's tone. *What am I supposed to do?* he asked.

Longfur did not answer at once. He slid around Jani's ankle, rubbing his foot as if to thank him. The giant stooped to stroke the cat's head briefly then strode out of the yard, waving farewell to Mark as he went. Longfur moved over to the king.

I thought it was better that he went, the cat said. *I wouldn't like you to get embarrassed.*

Thank you for your concern, Mark replied ironically, ignoring Longfur's sarcastic tone.

You could at least be positive. Lemon juice would be sweeter than you look.

I can be miserable if I want to, Ark's ruler replied with irritation, unable to remain calm in the face of Longfur's criticism.

No! the cat retorted. *Too many people are looking to you for a lead. If you give up now . . .*

I'm not giving up, Mark put in. *I just don't know what to do!*

So you do nothing, Longfur sneered.

What would you suggest?

Think, came the instant response. *I know the process is alien to you but it wouldn't take you too long to come to several avenues worth pursuing.*

Mark waited.

Dreams, for a start.

Dreams?

The last two confrontations were preceded by symbolic dreams, Longfur explained patiently. *You with the Mirage Warrior, then Luke with the whirlpool. They guided you.*

Uninvited memories filled Mark's head. Pushing them aside, he asked, *But how can that help us now?*

Who has been having strange dreams recently? Longfur exclaimed. *Ask!*

Who?

Everyone.

That's crazy, Longfur.

More crazy than losing Ark? the cat shot back. *And another thing—the Servants must come into this. First it was you, then Luke and Julia—all Servants. Perhaps there's someone else.*

Mark considered this. *I don't think so. Only the three of us can use mind-talk, except for the wizards, of course. There isn't anyone else. This is pointless.* Dejected, he looked away.

I haven't finished yet, Longfur snapped, his fur bristling in all directions. *The most obvious link hasn't been mentioned yet: the prophecies. The old parchment you found and the inscription Julia brought from Strock. Somewhere, there must be a third. All we have to do is find it.*

All? Mark exclaimed, close to losing his temper at the constant needling. *You don't just* find *these things!* he said heatedly. *We have no idea where to look. It could be anywhere—even on another island.*

The trouble with you, Longfur commented, *is that you've had things too easy. The prophecies just fell into your lap.*

The slight element of truth which colored these unjust remarks left Mark silent and simmering. Longfur went on relentlessly.

You keep protesting your impotence—that way you have an excuse for doing nothing. If we found a prophecy, then we would all have something to work toward. Even if it's not the real thing!

Mark was astounded and his face showed it. Longfur's eyes now sparkled with feline amusement.

It would give us a purpose. Build up morale.

You can't just make one up! Mark said, aghast.

Easiest thing in the world, the unrepentant cat replied.

Longfur then struck a theatrical pose, legs planted four-square, tail upright.

From the sea, peril. From the sea, safety, he intoned lugubriously. *Isn't that how they start?*

Stop it! Mark warned, but Longfur took no notice. The king tried to close his mind but the cat would not be put off. He held the king's eyes with a stubborn stare, and began to recite solemnly.

> *Arkon's cat, Long Fur the Brave,*
> *Sat by his king and made him rave.*
> *Servants shall dream and battle once more,*
> *Guided by a noble paw.*

Mark didn't know whether to laugh or cry—or lose his temper. The monologue continued.

> *Using his great dramatic art,*
> *Noble Mousebane, paw on heart . . .*

At this point Longfur matched action to his words and stiffly raised his right forepaw in front of his chest. As he did so, an absurd look of consternation came over his face and slowly, ridiculously, he toppled over, making no attempt to right himself. His expression of mock surprise was so perfectly realized that, despite himself, Mark found that he was laughing. It felt good.

Longfur picked himself up, feigning injured dignity.

You may laugh, he said, delicately straightening his whiskers. *But this is serious!*

His affronted tone only made Mark laugh all the more and, though he had realized by now that he was being manipulated, he was grateful to his small friend. The cat's performance had provided a bright moment in a bleak day and Mark felt better for it. Nothing had changed but now he felt that he could face the world with a lighter heart.

All right, the king said. *I'll go along with your mad ideas. How do you always manage to talk me into these things?*

Elementary psychology, Longfur replied smugly. *You fall for it every time.*

Chapter 27

"*L*uke and Julia were asking after you last night," Yve said. "Would you like them to visit you?"

"You shouldn't tire yourself," Ferragamo put in quickly.

Koria smiled at him wanly.

"Having the people I love about me won't do me any harm," she said. "Exactly the reverse in fact." To Yve she added, "Ask them to come tomorrow, will you?"

The two wizards sat at Koria's bedside. From habit rather than from any conviction that it would help, they had already tested the boundaries of her illness with their special skills. As always, they came up against an impenetrable barrier within her. As always, they probed for weaknesses but there was none. Whatever held them back was immensely strong, and within, Koria's strength ebbed away.

"Would you get me something to drink?" she asked.

Ferragamo stood, leaned over and kissed her lightly, then went off to the kitchen. Koria watched him go, then sighed and sank back into her pillows.

"Did you ever think of marrying?" she asked.

"No." Yve was slightly taken aback. "It's never been a real possibility for me." She paused, then added, "I can't have children either."

"Of course," Koria replied.

They sat in silence for a few moments, each thinking about what might have been.

"Magic can only do so much. I've always known that," Koria said eventually. "He'll need someone to look after him when I've gone."

"What are you saying? You're going to get better," Yve insisted.

"Of course," Koria smiled, but her voice betrayed her feelings. "But if—when—I do, it will only be a matter of time. I'm not a wizard."

Yve had no answer to this and so remained quiet, remembering what she had heard about Moroski. Her thoughts were brought abruptly back to the present by Koria's next statement.

"He likes you, doesn't he? And you will live as long as he does."

The words hung in the air between them.

"I'll do what I can to help him . . ." Yve said at last.

"Thank you."

". . . as a friend. He'll never take another lover." The wizard knew that she spoke the truth, and felt sure that Koria knew it too.

The subject of their conversation returned bearing a tray with three steaming cups. On seeing their solemn expressions, he spoke with forced cheerfulness.

"My special brew all round. To keep out the winter's cold." He passed the drinks out, then settled back into his chair. "What have you been talking about?" he asked.

Time passed, yet little changed. The air of impending doom intensified; every new vessel that came to port brought fresh rumors of strife, but life on Ark went on. The everyday necessities of court, city, and island continued. No direct threat had been made to Ark and, even if an invasion were to happen tomorrow, people needed to eat today.

However, when a few confused reports came in from the northern isles of Rek and Tirek of a massive outbreak of war—reports that were followed by an ominous silence— the efforts already being made to reinforce Ark's defenses were increased. Army captains had been traveling the length and breadth of the island for some months, recruiting men, inspecting armories and fortifications, and commissioning smiths. A network of communication throughout Ark was devised so that news could travel swiftly to the capital and forces quickly deployed. Mark was convinced that such action was beneficial even if, in the end, it proved insufficient or inappropriate. As Longfur had decreed, it was better than doing nothing.

Longfur's other suggestions had produced little result. None of Starhill's court had had any dreams that could be interpreted as prophetic. The king had been told of an amazing variety of nocturnal imagery, some of it highly colorful, but this had achieved nothing. His subjects had reacted with varying degrees of embarrassment and Mark eventually delegated the task of inquiry to others. He learned a lot about his court—including much he would have preferred not to know—but none of the disjointed and nonsensical dreams was even remotely like the one he had experienced so many years ago.

Nor did anyone show signs of displaying the talents shared by himself, Luke, and Julia, and thus inheriting the mantle of the ancient Servants. If help *were* to come from that direction, it would obviously arrive unannounced.

The search for a prophecy which might guide their course had seemed at first the most promising area. Here at least there were plenty of avenues to be explored. Every library in the island had men and women assigned to study the texts for anything that resembled the earlier verses. Rewards were offered for the relaying of ancient inscriptions or carvings. This was prompted by the prophecy that had been recorded thus on Strock, where it had been found by Julia's old mentor, the wizard Ashula. The inducement had produced a flood of offerings—most of which were not remotely ancient—and which varied from the comic to the incomprehensible, from the illiterate to the obscene. Needless to say, none was of any use.

Ferragamo did not participate in any of this, and as a consequence, Yve was often asked for her advice. She gave it freely but often felt strangely inhibited, almost as if there were something on the tip of her tongue, waiting to be said. This was aggravating, but she had many others concerns to occupy her mind. By the time she realized what her subconscious had been trying to tell her, it was too late to change Ark's course—or her own.

In the three months following Fontaine's return from Heald, Koria's condition had deteriorated consistently, and Ferragamo withdrew even more from the outside world. He hardly ever left his lover's bedside now that she was unable to get up. The wizard's moods varied wildly between dark depression, manic self-directed anger, and long periods of mental absence when he wandered in another, happier place.

Yve watched him almost as closely as she looked after Koria and became anxious that, in his increasingly unstable state, he would do something desperate. An insane wizard was not a pleasant prospect.

As a consequence, she spent much of her time with the couple, hoping against hope for a miracle that could save them both. Her respect and growing love for Koria were reinforced by that lady's fortitude, and, for all his quirks and awkwardness, she recognized in Ferragamo a humanity worthy of his love. Yve witnessed their joint decline with a heavy heart, and knew that many others shared her dismay.

Ark was gripped in midwinter's iron glove. A thin covering of snow and ice glittered on the cobbles and roofs in the early evening moonlight as Yve hurried across the courtyard, heading for the haven of the food hall. She had left Koria asleep, with Ferragamo continuing his silent bedside vigil. It had not been an easy day and she was looking forward to food, warmth, and cheerful company. The flow of fire- and lamplight from the high windows of the hall was inviting.

Once inside, she was welcomed and rapidly installed in a chair near the roaring open fire. She was asked few questions—everyone knew where she spent most of her time—and her answers to the inevitable inquiries about Koria were brief. Food appeared and she ate automatically, then sat back and began to drowse.

Before her, the fire crackled and roared, sweeping upward in a sheet of red and orange. Yve's eyes closed and her head tipped slowly forward. When she suddenly nodded, the action woke her and she felt momentarily dizzy. Her whole being seemed to fall toward the glowing embers, which shifted and sparked before her. For a moment she was desperately, inexplicably afraid. This must have shown on her face, as several people looked at her with concern.

"You're tired, Yve. Why don't you get an early night?"

A face appeared before her. She had to make an effort to bring it into focus, but then she smiled. It was Bram.

"I think I will," she said, and took the hand that was offered. They walked to the wizard's room in silence. At the door they paused.

"You'll do no one any good if you exhaust yourself," Bram said quietly. "They may be beyond your help."

"I have to try."

"Yes, I know," he admitted. "Everyone here is grateful for what you're doing. But you must rest sometimes."

Yve nodded wearily.

"Good night Bram—and thank you."

"Sleep well," he said, and strode away.

Yve watched him go, thinking how little she had seen of him recently. She had no idea how he spent his days now. Pangs of regret and guilt assailed her and she was about to call him back, but was suddenly overcome with weariness. She turned and entered her room, and shortly afterward was snugly wrapped in her quilt.

The nightmare took her like a wild thing, tearing her from her safe cocoon and flinging her into the cold sunlight above the clouds.

Once again she felt her stomach lurch as the dragon beneath her began to dive. The clouds enveloped them in a clammy embrace, then released them into the turmoil of the world below. Their flight leveled out and, amazed, she watched the incredible scenes beneath the dragon's wings. Even from their great height the sheer scale of the violence was awesome. The land was ravaged by hurricanes and thunder-driven rain. Tsunami raced across the seas, adding to the terror of the white-water oceans which hurled themselves against the coastlines, wrenching great boulders from the cliffs and flattening the feeble homes of men. Avalanches of rock and snow left behind trails of destruction as mountains shuddered and the earth cracked.

A huge volcano was erupting, adding to the darkness with clouds of smoke and ash, and coloring the scene a lurid red as flames leapt up and lava flowed in bubbling streams. The immense furnace threatened to tear the world apart, to destroy all that was left.

Yve knew what would happen next. Like so much that

had been suppressed during the long days in the dungeons of Ahrenhold, it was still in her head, buried deep. The horror came back now, but she was powerless to stop it. She could not even control her own actions.

Down! she ordered.

They plunged toward the heart of the volcano.

As they fell, their world contracted. The red furnace grew, and dominated all about them. The air grew hot, acrid with the stink of sulfur. Closer and closer they came. Now the wizard could make out the individual fissures through which the molten rock spewed forth. She could see the details of its flow, the boulders *melting* in the unbelievable heat.

At the center of this vast conflagration was a massive geyser of lava. Rivers of red ran in all directions, carrying away the fiery debris of the explosive eruptions which shot hundreds of paces into the air.

It was toward this maelstrom that the dragon and rider flung themselves. Screaming, they were engulfed in a world of fire and pain. All her senses fled and Yve experienced a moment of nothingness before she was born again into a world so alien that her mind could not comprehend it.

She and Sweetness—if indeed it was him—were still flying, yet were no longer in the air, no longer subject to the pull of gravity or of the winds. They flew, or perhaps swam, *within* the elements of the earth. Coils of energy, glowing red, orange and white, snaked past the wizard. She sensed rather than saw them, because sight and the other normal senses had no meaning here.

She began to test nascent powers within her, playing with the forces about her, knowing that this was somehow important. All pain had gone, all sense of time or place had disappeared. The dragon wheeled joyfully within his new element, but inside the wizard a small, cold numbness was growing within what had once been her heart. The coldness blossomed into a mass of uncertainty and dread which *became* the being that was Yve and left her without meaning.

Yve awoke, shaking and soaked with perspiration, her mouth open in a soundless scream. She lay listening to a harsh, ugly sound and for several moments did not realize that it was her own ragged breathing. Eyes open now, staring at the canopy above her bed, she saw nothing but the images of her dream. Even awake it would not leave her and she experienced, over and over again, the terrible disorientation of the nightmare's final moments.

For she had somehow been *beneath* the earth, sharing its inner secrets, but at the same time she had been *beyond* the earth.

Out of reach.

Chapter 28

L ike Yve, Ferragamo dreamed. Unlike her, he was awake.

He sat like stone beside Koria's bed, her limp hand clasped between his own. The only movement in the room came from Owl, who ruffled his feathers as if uncomfortable in the warm air.

In his dream, the wizard talked. Perhaps Owl heard him; perhaps no one did; but Ferragamo required no audience except the one who could not hear him now. His voice was little more than a whisper, sometimes rising to an anguished howl or breaking into laughter, but throughout the long night his words tumbled on, conjuring up scenes of joy and bitterness, fondness and regret. Memories multiplied before his unseeing eyes, layer upon layer of experience, until the patterns of his existence became meaningless and he could impose no rational order to the images. He spoke to Koria as the calm and level-headed woman whose love and reassurance had helped him through the time of Ather's overthrow. Then he spoke to the girl who was a newcomer to the court and in awe of Starhill and its teeming populace. At the same time she was the frail, pain-ridden lady who had grown old so cruelly and so fast, betrayed by forces beyond her understanding. And yet again he spoke to the Koria he had never known except from her stories, the village girl whose childhood had been happy until her parents' untimely deaths, and who had journeyed alone to the city in search of her future.

There were other Korias: She had never had a child of her own, but had been a mother to several. Mark especially had benefited from her kind, warm presence after the death of his own mother when he was still an infant. Koria knew better than most what that must feel like.

She had been a lover, too; at first hesitant, unable to believe in what was happening and yet incapable of denying it; then fierce and single-minded in her determination to do what she wanted, what was *right*. She was passionate, but there was no cruelty in her passion. She was sensual, yet few could match her common sense and her advice was sought often, not least by Ferragamo.

There were other Korias: the cook, adept at preparing a superb meal from the most meager ingredients—a skill her lover often found more amazing than his mundane magic; the woman equally at home—and welcome—among royalty or village fishermen; the wise-woman steeped in the lore of herbs and the fruits of nature; the spirit that no peril could break.

There were many Korias, and all were in the room with Ferragamo.

In his dream, the wizard talked.

"Do you remember the pig?" A slight smile lit up his eyes. "The one my searching spell brought to the cottage? It nearly flattened Mark before we got it under control. And my hat. You found my old hat and put it on my head, cobwebs, onion-skins, and all!" Ferragamo laughed softly, his thoughts going to other, earlier scenes, and his words flowed on, an unstoppable torrent.

"The sea gulls wheeling on the beach, white against black, the night we danced around our campfire. We were the only people in the world. It was warm, midsummer, but the wine was cool from being left in the edge of the surf. And when the embers had died down, we lay on our backs in the sand and watched the shooting stars."

His thoughts jumped again, forward this time to another, more spectacular shooting star. The wizard's face changed, grew haunted, and his eyes were bleak with the memory.

"I almost lost you then. I couldn't bear it—couldn't move. That vile gray stuff reaching out to take you away from me. I won't let *anyone* do that. Never! What would be left?"

Ferragamo's hands tightened their grip as another thought crossed his mind, and his expression was knotted with hate.

"It's him!" he hissed. "Him! *He's* doing this. He couldn't take you then, so he's striking back now, like this." The wizard's voice had risen to a shriek but now it became quieter, urgent, and desperate. "You must wait, don't let him win. Fight. Now I know it's him, I can save you. If only I had more time." He paused.

"I'll kill him!" he screamed, then his face contorted with rage. "Kill!"

He quietened abruptly, and the rigid muscles in his neck and shoulders relaxed a little. He muttered a few unrecognizable syllables as his head sank down onto his chest, then looked up, smiling. When he spoke again it was as though nothing had interrupted his flow of memories.

"I'm glad I took you to the mountains. I should have done it long before, but it never occurred to me, fool that I am. Everyone should meet Shalli. Who am I to keep his company to myself? You remember the cave? It's amazing, isn't it, a wonderful place. Do you remember bathing together in the hot spring water, the rock-light flashing and laughing at our softness? We'll go there again soon. It will be good for both of us."

The wizard's high spirits disappeared as he looked down at Koria's head on the pillow.

"You're cold," he said softly. With one hand he tenderly pulled the covers up about her, still holding her hand in the other. "I'll warm the room up again."

A few sounds came from his throat, and the temperature in the room rose dramatically. Owl shuffled on his perch and blinked slowly.

In his dream, the wizard talked. Hours passed and still he sat, his lover's hand in his, the words pouring out. He spoke of all the times, all the places they had known, and the people in their lives. He spoke of events, both great and small, momentous and trivial, from the magical conflicts of recent years to their discovery of a shared craving for hazelnuts. He recalled their lovemaking in such tender and complete detail that it roused his flesh even as he spoke. He told Koria of his pride in her and in others' love for her.

Hoarse now, but still too full of words, he talked until the wolfing hour.

"There's something I have to do," he said at the last. "Before I go."

He stood and tucked her arm beneath the bedclothes, releasing her hand with evident reluctance. Leaning over, he kissed her gently.

"I love you," he whispered in anguish. "I will always love you."

As he straightened up, his face was bleak but expressionless. Spinning on his heels, he pointed dramatically at the door of the chamber.

The door exploded.

It exploded slowly, silently. Splinters of wood drifted across the room, turning end over end in lazy circles. Tiny shards of metal from the lock and hinges dispersed in all directions, like dandelion seeds blown by a gentle but mercurial breeze. The lamplight wavered as the silent concussion shook the room. One larger piece of debris, charred on one side from the power unleashed upon it, spiraled languidly toward the wizard, changing from black to white, white to black, as it spun. Ferragamo knocked it aside automatically, and surveyed the results of his action.

It had been an act of wilfulness from a man who knew he had the power to conjure demons or move mountains, yet could not turn his strength to the simple task that was more important than anything in the world. It was the act of a man beyond the end of his tether, an act of frustration and impotent anger.

The ragged, empty doorway mocked the wizard. About him, the room became still once more.

Ferragamo looked back at the woman's head on the pillow. For a reason he did not understand, the wizard had a vision of a swan, white and elegant, with long neck and clear eyes, gliding on silvered water.

"Goodbye, my swan," he said softly, then turned and walked out into the gray hour before dawn.

Chapter 29

$\mathcal{W}$hen Yve rose the next morning the sun had been up for some time. The pale light that came through her window held little warmth, and she shivered as she dressed, rejecting the use of magic for her personal comfort.

She felt exhausted and her mouth was dry and gritty, as if she had been breathing smoke all night. Forcing herself to put the images of the dream behind her, Yve splashed her face with icy water, then drank deeply from the ewer.

She had lain awake for what seemed like hours after coming out of the nightmare, but fatigue had eventually overcome her mental agitation. Sleep had come but she felt now that it had been of little benefit. Filled with a sense of foreboding, of restless confusion, she left her room and walked swiftly to Koria's apartment.

It was obvious that something was very wrong even before she saw the shattered remains of the bedroom door. The corridor nearby was filled with strange emanations, echoes of mental turmoil, and the air itself was tainted. Dust motes danced on gusts of wind which were far too warm to be natural.

Yve stopped in the deserted outer chamber and looked in horror at the carnage produced by Ferragamo's torment. The bedroom door was simply not there. It had been blown to smithereens, leaving only a jagged, gaping hole. Splinters of debris littered the room about her, yet nothing else was damaged or displaced. Yve was appalled at the thought of power used with such ferocity, yet under exquisite control. And to what purpose?

Steeling herself to face whatever lay beyond the empty doorway, Yve walked slowly forward, her feet leaden.

Inside the bedchamber, more charred and twisted remains of the door were strewn about, yet the room was strangely peaceful, and nothing had been damaged—the bedclothes were not even ruffled. The air was very warm. A tiny feather gently floated down from the ceiling.

Koria's eyes were closed, her face calm and pale, her hair spread upon the pillow. She did not stir as the wizard approached, and Yve knew that the older woman would never wake from the sleep that held her now.

A tiny measure of the destructive madness which had gripped Ferragamo touched Yve. She felt his enormous frustration, and could also feel the lingering signs of his love. Koria had been dead for several hours, yet her body was still warm, protected by her lover's last act of kindness. Ferragamo had stayed, wanting to help her with her first steps into the unknown, and she had appreciated his companionship, the final part of a lifelong gift. Her expression was serene and unafraid, the lines of pain smoothed away. Her courage, as well as her love, had stayed with her to the end.

Looking at her now, Yve found it hard to believe that Koria would not soon awake, and talk and laugh in her usual manner. It was incredible, impossible to comprehend, yet it was true.

Koria was gone. And so, after his own fashion, was Ferragamo.

"All of them?" Mark exclaimed, his face a picture of dismay.

"Yes. Come and see," Luke replied grimly.

They left the royal quarters together, walking round the castle's inner wall to the entrance to the treeyard. They climbed the steps and entered, joining Julia, who stood transfixed, staring at the moonberry tree at the center of the courtyard. As Mark walked slowly forward to inspect the tree, Luke went to her side and put an arm round her shoulders.

At first glance, the tree appeared little changed. The slender branches stooped no more than usual; the slim leaves were their normal shade of pale green. But then the anomalies became apparent. Where were the fruit? The small silver-gray berries had disappeared—every one had been plucked from its stem. Mark searched frantically for one—just one—that might have been overlooked, but in vain. They were all gone, had been torn away roughly, as though in haste, and with no thought for the health of the tree. A little sap congealed beneath several of the gashes where shoots had been ripped from the branches.

On closer examination, Mark saw that this was not all that was wrong. Several leaves now curled at the ends, as if cut off from the life of the earth.

Gingerly, Mark reached out to touch the foliage. At the contact with his fingers, the leaf seemed to draw back, then it crumpled and dust fell to the floor. As Ark's king looked on in horror, the whole tree drooped, lost its hold on existence, and began its journey back to the earth whence it came. Autumn had finally come to the moonberry tree.

Mark turned to Luke and Julia. His face showed no anger, only bewilderment.

"Who did this?" he asked quietly.

"We don't know," Luke replied. "What amazes me is that the tree made no attempt to defend itself. I'm sure it could have done."

Julia nodded, unable to speak. The power of the moon-berries had been instrumental in saving her from a life of unimaginable vileness, and the loss of the security supplied by the tree left her shaken and afraid.

"Get Ferragamo," Mark said with sudden decisiveness.

"But—" Luke began.

"I don't care," his father retorted. "He's the *only* one who can help us find an explanation for this."

"He hasn't been out of their apartments for days," Luke said.

"Didn't you hear what . . . oh, never mind. I'll get him myself." Mark strode off, but halted as Yve appeared in the doorway.

"You can't," she said shortly. "He's gone. Koria's dead."

With that terse announcement, the dam inside the wizard burst, and the flood that she had held back broke free. Julia went to comfort her, tears brimming in her own eyes, leaving Luke and his father to stare dumbly at each other. Both faces mirrored the shock of this second devastating blow.

Mark's final reserves of confidence drained away and he slumped down on the low stone wall that surrounded the dying tree. Burying his head in his hands, he wept.

Their trials that day were not yet over. They had only a few hours in which to mourn Koria's death and to puzzle over Ferragamo's presumed theft of the berries before a rider galloped into the castle on an exhausted and sweating horse. The messenger, the last in a chain of riders linking Starhill to the south of the island, brought dire news. Heald had been overrun by a massive invading force and Ark itself would soon be under attack. The soldier also reported that a small group from Heald had escaped the onslaught and had made their way to Home. They were now traveling toward Starhill, and would, with luck, arrive at the capital later that afternoon.

"Who is in the party?" Fontaine asked, desperate for reassurance. But the messenger did not know, and the queen was left in an agony of fear, hope and dread. As Mark and his captains made emergency arrangements to cope with the coming invasion as best they could, Fontaine could only watch and wait for the approach of horses from the south.

They arrived in the late afternoon, entering a city in turmoil. Preparations for war were now in full swing, with supplies being stockpiled in case of a long siege, animals being herded to safety, and defenses reinforced. The soldiers escorting the Healdeans led them straight to the castle, where they were met by Fontaine.

She quickly scanned the faces of the new arrivals. While she was happy to see several that she knew, it was the lack of so many more that had the greater impact. *At least the children got away,* she thought, and pushed aside the bleak notion that their escape might only be temporary.

The travelers were exhausted, and Rivera with her two children were soon installed in comfortable quarters. Yve took charge of Tzigane, despite Cai's protests, leaving the wizard and Laurent to talk to Fontaine. Mark joined them as they told of the overthrow of Heald and their subsequent escape.

"Ansar ordered me to get them away," Laurent said. He was slumped in a chair in the queen's quarters. "I had no choice." His tired eyes pleaded for their understanding, perhaps for forgiveness.

"You did well," Mark said firmly. "Staying would have served no purpose and only condemned those who came with you."

Cai spoke then, looking sadly at Fontaine.

"Your mother and Moroski begged me to take Tzigane. They would not leave. I couldn't refuse."

"It's all right, Cai. I understand," Fontaine said quietly.

"I should be with her now," the wizard went on. "She is in my trust." He made as if to rise.

"Hold still," Mark said. "Tzigane is in good hands, and you need your rest."

Cai paused, then nodded and sat back. "How long has Yve been here?" he asked.

"Not far short of a year," the king replied. "She has become a good friend to us all."

They sat in silence for a while, each occupied with their own thoughts and memories. The newcomers had been told of Koria's death and Ferragamo's disappearance. It seemed to all of them that this day was too full of dread and horror—they could not bear it all and remain entirely sane.

"How *did* you get away?" Fontaine asked eventually.

"We left the palace through the secret passage into the back streets," Laurent replied. "After that, we moved as quickly as we could toward the north of the town."

"I did what I could to cloak our passage," Cai added, "but we didn't seem to need it. Luck was on our side."

"Yes, almost as though a friendly presence were guiding us," Laurent agreed.

"You felt that too?" Cai asked.

Laurent nodded. "We *were* seen, yet no one took any notice, not even the enemy soldiers." He shrugged. "That side of town was pretty quiet. After the tower fell, nothing seemed to be moving.

"We stole a horse and cart and left the city. It was slow going, and we always thought we'd be caught at any moment. Then at dusk a mist came down. It was cold and made traveling even slower, but at least it hid us from prying eyes. We kept going well into the night, using the old pathways. In the end, we didn't really know where we were, just that we'd reached the northern forest. Then we found a woodman's deserted hut. It was sound enough and the children needed warmth and rest, so we stopped."

"That was a *very* strange place," Cai put in thoughtfully.

"Yes, but it welcomed us," Laurent went on. "In spite of everything, we all slept well. Even me—and I was supposed to be on watch." He smiled ruefully, then went on.

"I had a dream," he said, frowning slightly. "About the forest and an evil man who tore living branches down as though in spite. He brought fire. The trees hated him, and made him lose his way, so that he wandered round and round for days, until finally he lay down and never rose again."

Laurent stopped, aware of the curious looks his tale had provoked. Mark was about to speak but Fontaine silenced him with a gesture and the Healdean courtier continued.

"A magpie stole something from the man's pocket, and flew away with it high above the trees. Then it dropped its find, which fell down toward the earth, flashing and glittering in the sunlight. In my dream, I saw it fall toward me.

"Then I woke up, and found myself looking at a small object hanging on a nail on the cabin wall. It was rocking gently. I took it down and put it in my pocket, meaning to look at it the next morning. I'd forgotten about it until now." He reached inside his leather jerkin, fumbled about for a moment, then withdrew a gold ring. He glanced at it, then looked at Fontaine, his eyes wide with surprise.

"I think this is yours," he said, offering it to her.

The queen took the ring, knowing immediately that Laurent was right. It was tarnished now, but the seal was plain enough; the letter F inscribed over the Healdean arms.

"The ransom note," was all she said.

"Maybe somebody *was* helping us," Cai said. "There was too much of that journey which was made easy for us."

"And the mist and the forest and the firewood ready-stacked and—"

"My dream," Laurent concluded. "It happened like that before, when I escaped from the fog. I'd never understood how I got away."

Mark was the first to break the ensuing silence.

"There are so many aspects of this conflict that we will never understand," he said. "We just have to accept them. Right now you two need some sleep and I need to help my captains. We don't have much time."

Laurent agreed. "We got here quickly enough, thanks to your relay-stations, but even so, they can't be far behind."

"I'll come and help," Cai offered.

"No. Sleep now," Mark said. "We'll make our plans in the morning."

The three men went out, leaving the queen alone. She slid the ring slowly onto her finger, remembering the time, nearly eighteen years before, when it had last adorned the hand of Princess Fontaine of Heald.

Chapter 30

Ferragamo's journey had be-
gun before dawn, and he stopped for nothing. The wizard's
horse, chosen for his size and strength, flew on through mist
and powdery snow, across green hills and river fords, and up
mountain paths. The unceasing gallop would have torn the
charger's heart open had not Ferragamo diverted a portion of
his own magical energy to the horse. He had plenty to spare.

The wizard had taken nothing with him except the clothes
he wore and a small leather bag on a thong about his neck.
He sat rigidly in the saddle, guiding his mount with only a
tiny part of his mind. The countryside passed by in a blur,
unnoticed.

By nightfall, he was already deep in the Windchill Mountains, but even there his breakneck progress continued. The
horse had lost all its natural caution, aided by a horse-light
pebble which enabled him to see even when the light failed,
and was buoyed up by great surges of power from his demented
rider. The midwinter winds howled about the white peaks,
flurries of snow whirled past, but still they galloped on, defying
the logic which insisted that their course was suicidal. In truth,
Ferragamo barely noticed the appalling conditions. His mind
was already at his destination, planning the next stage in his
terrible, predetermined course.

When Ferragamo arrived at the cave, Shalli was waiting
for him. As usual, the time and manner of his friend's arrival

had come as no surprise to the ancient hermit. He stood at
the entrance to his home, oblivious to the cold, dressed in his
habitual, eccentric collection of goatskins. As Ferragamo approached, finally allowing the horse to slow to a walking pace,
two birds flew out of the cave entrance. They each landed on
one of Shalli's shoulders, lending an even more outlandish
aspect to his appearance. Ferragamo recognized the falcon—
he had known Atlanta for many years—but did not remember
the other bird. It was a sea gull, standing crookedly on its
precarious perch, its head cocked to one side.

Shalli nodded in greeting, his beard and long white hair
blowing about his face. Ferragamo silently dismounted and
followed the hermit inside the cave. The air was warm and
slightly moist and the rock itself glowed with varicolored light,
illuminating the main tunnel and its many side-chambers. The
horse entered with no fear. None of this caused the wizard
any surprise—he had been here many times before and took
the cave's wonders for granted.

After installing his horse in the "stable"—a cavern supplied
with constant fresh water, and also on this occasion with
grain—Ferragamo, moving as though in a trance, went with
Shalli to the room where the hermit slept. The two birds
flew ahead, settling into niches in the walls. As they did so, a
mournful hooting sounded from the cave's entrance and shortly
afterward, to Shalli's evident delight, Owl swooped into the
chamber, becoming the third feathered onlooker. Ferragamo
stared at his familiar, at first in surprise and then shamefacedly.
Owl had evidently followed his master's desperate, headlong
ride, but Ferragamo had not even been aware of his companion. The sea gull squawked raucously in greeting.

"Kirt," Shalli said, indicating the lopsided bird. It was the
first word spoken between the two men.

Ferragamo looked at the sea gull, and through the haze of
his raging mind, he identified the creature. *Kubiac's familiar*.

The young wizard from Julia's home-isle had been mur-
dered over a year ago. Ferragamo was sure that Moroski was
dead too. They all end up here, he thought. *Will Owl stay
with Shalli when I'm gone?*

This speculation was a moment of rare clarity in Ferragamo's fevered brain. It did not last long. As he began to fumble
with the bag about his neck, Shalli frowned and held out his
hand, wordlessly demanding to see the contents. The wizard

hesitated, then wearily handed the pouch over. The hermit loosened the strings and peered inside, showing no surprise at the presence of the moonberries. He simply said, "Later," then left the chamber, taking them with him. Ferragamo knew better than to argue and when, after a few moments, Shalli returned with a wooden bowl full of a steaming, spicy mixture, he drank gladly and surrendered to a sudden, overwhelming lethargy.

Tomorrow, he thought. *I'll do it tomorrow.*

Shalli stood and watched his sleeping friend with a mixture of concern and satisfaction on his face.

The early morning debate in Starhill showed no signs of reaching a conclusion. Mark had set up a command center in the great hall and all about him there was much coming and going. The king left most of the military organization to his captains Shill and Durc, but was very much involved in the attempts to find out where Ferragamo had gone and why. There were many theories, but none made much sense. It had been reported that a man, possibly the wizard, had left Starhill by the Mountain Gate in the early hours, but until the scouts returned, there could be no confirmation that this had indeed been Ferragamo's route.

Mark now lived on the edge of total nervous collapse. He heard everything that was spoken by those around him, but most of the words were meaningless. A feeling of total helplessness, that all hope was gone, grew within him. It took an enormous effort just to keep himself from breaking down, and it was only his waning sense of royal leadership that helped him face the outside world.

"It *must* have been Ferragamo who took the moonberries," Luke insisted. "The tree would have allowed no one else to disturb it that way."

"But why?" Fontaine asked.

"I don't know, but he must be planning something."

"Yes, and it's something drastic," Cai added, "if he needs all those berries, and has to get away from here to do it."

"Has Koria's death driven him mad?" Fontaine sighed.

Nobody had an answer to that. Not even Yve.

Longfur's voice sounded in Mark's head.

It's pretty obvious, isn't it? He's gone to Shalli.

The king had not spoken to anyone for some time, but, prompted by the cat's suggestion, now said,

"Shalli's cave? Could he have gone there?"

"Yes!" Luke and Julia said simultaneously.

"That always was his retreat," the queen agreed.

Yve spoke up now. "Can anyone tell me exactly where the cave is? I've got an idea."

"I can try," Mark replied, and with help from the others who had visited Shalli's home, he described the journey. Yve nodded, then left the room.

"What was that all about?" Shill asked.

Surprisingly, it was Beca who answered.

"She's going to send Sweetness," she exclaimed. "Perhaps she'll ride him!"

The princess slipped out after Yve, leaving those inside dumb with astonishment.

Can you find it? Yve asked.

Of course, Sweetness replied. *Shall I go right away?*

Yve nodded but Beca, who had followed her to the city walls, said quickly, "Can I come too? I've never been to the cave."

The dragon looked puzzled and angry, then his expression cleared.

Only if Yve comes too, he replied, strangely eager.

"What did he say?" Beca asked breathlessly.

"No, Beca. You can't ride him," the wizard said, her face set. "Sweetness must go alone."

"Oh."

The dragon looked momentarily sullen, glancing about him, then brightened.

Back in a moment, he said, and disappeared, flickering out of existence.

Yve felt uneasy, as she always did at moments like this.

"Could you go to his world if you wanted to?" Beca asked.

"I think so," the wizard admitted reluctantly.

"Then why—?"

"It scares me," Yve said quietly. "I'm not sure I'd be able to come back."

"Oh." Beca was obviously disappointed. She glanced at the wizard, but seeing the unhappiness and doubt written plainly on her face, wisely decided to say no more.

Sweetness was back within the hour, at pains to explain that he would have been quicker but for the fact that Ferragamo was asleep when he arrived. "The white man," who Yve knew was Shalli, had not allowed the wizard to be disturbed. However, he had woken shortly afterward, and Sweetness had been able to ask him the questions Yve had sent. Their conversation had been conducted through Shalli who, as Yve had hoped, was able to communicate with the dragon as he did with all familiars. However, Ferragamo had not been specific about his plans, and as a result, Sweetness had become confused. Yve went back to the castle, and reported her findings to Mark.

"So the facts are," she concluded, "Ferragamo *is* at the cave, he *does* have the moonberries, and he's planning something which, in his own words, is long overdue. He refused to tell Sweetness what it was, but he did say that any help from here would be welcome. Whether we choose to help him or not, he is still going ahead."

"How can we help when we don't know what he's going to do?" Mark asked, voicing the question in many minds.

Yve shrugged. "He did say one curious thing at the end," she said. "*Tell Luke to consider the precedents.*"

Everyone turned to look at the prince, but he remained silent, as bemused as the rest. It was Cai who spoke next.

"I was afraid of this," he said. The young wizard would not meet anyone's gaze and his face was uncharacteristically drawn. Many worried glances were exchanged within the group as they waited for him to continue.

"That's a reference to the failed conclave," Cai said at last. "Luke may not remember, but he interrupted the proceedings with words much like that. He was trying to persuade the wizards to agree to the Rite of Yzalba. *That* is what Ferragamo intends to do now."

"On his own?" Yve exclaimed.

"With Shalli. From what I've heard, they make a formidable pair."

"It's madness!" Yve responded, but deep within her, a frightening certainty began to grow.

"Why else would he take *all* the moonberries? That in itself indicates enormous desperation. We won't get a second chance."

Cai looked at his fellow wizard, seeing the impact of his words. She was convinced, he saw, but was even more frightened than he.

"You mean he intends to eat them all?" Fontaine asked, incredulous. "But *one* nearly killed him!"

"I don't think Ferragamo expects to survive this time," Cai replied quietly.

"He's mad!" Mark said.

"He's been mad for months," Shill muttered.

"Without the moonberries, we can't stand before Alzedo's magic for long, if at all," the king went on. "Ferragamo's taken our last and only defense."

"No," Luke said vehemently. "The moonberries couldn't help us now. If we can't defeat Alzedo with what is already in us, then we're all dead anyway. You heard what happened on Heald. What chance would we have against an army that size?"

In the silence that ensued, king and prince stared at each other, one doubting, one obstinate.

"So this is the end. One way or another." Julia's quiet words fell like stones into still water, sending ripples of doom in ever-increasing circles. When the surface was smooth again, Laurent spoke. He had been silent until now, but knew that something positive was needed.

"It's simple then," he began.

"I'm glad you think so," Durc muttered under his breath.

"We have a choice," Laurent went on, ignoring the interruption. "Either we stay here, defend Starhill and Ark as best we can and leave Ferragamo to his own devices. Or we go to him and help him with what could be our last chance. Which is it to be?" The Healdean courtier looked directly at Mark, hoping for a decisive lead, but it was Shill, as Captain of the Castle Guard, who replied first.

"How can we help Ferragamo? I'm a soldier. I was driven out of my home before, and I'll not leave again."

"Forgive me," Durc put in, "but Ferragamo's been strange for a long time. Koria's death may have unhinged him completely. Aren't we in danger of encouraging his insanity if we try to help him?" He turned to Yve. "Did your dragon say anything about how he looked?"

"Nothing that I could interpret," she replied.

"Is blowing a door to bits the act of a sane man?" Shill asked.

"Grief takes many forms," Yve said.

"Perhaps he *needs* to be mad," Cai put in thoughtfully.

Shill made a noise as though he were being strangled, but Laurent got in before he could speak, trying again for rational argument.

"Surely it's just a matter of alternatives," he said. "Can we defeat Alzedo as we are?"

Nobody answered. There was no need.

"So even if Ferragamo's plan *is* insane, it's the only one which has any chance—no matter how slim—of stopping our world coming under the domination of that monster."

"You don't know what you're saying," Cai replied bleakly. "The Rite could *destroy* the world completely. In fact, it probably will."

"Then if Ferragamo is going ahead, we may as well help him," Luke interrupted. "*That* way he has a better chance of succeeding, and if he doesn't, we're no worse off."

"Besides, you wouldn't want to live in Alzedo's world," Julia added with heartfelt sincerity.

Yve, whose mind had been going round in circles, entered the debate. Despite her inner misgivings, she was beginning to agree with the line of argument advanced by Laurent and Luke.

"The Rite *can* succeed," she said. "It frightens me terribly, but it worked once before. Perhaps it should have been performed years ago, after the conclave. Then we would have been spared all this. Julia's right. This *is* our only chance and, even if most of the wizards are dead now, we have to try."

"You seem very certain about the history of the Rite," Mark said.

"I've made a study of Yzalba, for obvious reasons," Yve replied.

"What reasons?"

"Yzalba was the only other woman ever to become a wizard," she answered. "I feel very close to her sometimes." *Too close*, she added to herself, then shuddered.

"Why don't the old stories mention that?" Luke asked.

"It wasn't considered important then," Yve replied. "And when later copies were made, most scribes assumed she was a man."

"Historical detail is all very well," Durc said. "But what are we going to *do*?"

"That's obvious, isn't it?" Luke said. "We have to go to the mountains."

"That's crazy!"

"Not all of us. Just those who might be able to help Ferragamo. The wizards, those of us who are Servants, and perhaps a few others. A small group could move that much faster."

"You expect me to abandon Starhill to the enemy? To just
walk away from my people?" Mark sounded disbelieving. "I
can't do that!"

Once again father and son faced each other. The others
watched them silently, aware that the fates of all on Ark would
be decided by the outcome of this confrontation.

"The Servants are important, father. That's been proved
time and time again, and I am sure we have a part to play in
this. If we stay here, we can only die uselessly or surrender
without honor." Luke's words sounded harsh even to himself
but he knew they were necessary.

"I *am* the ruler of this island," Mark retorted. "Is this how
you see my duty? To run away?"

"You won't be running away!" Luke replied angrily. "This
may well be the only chance to *save* your people. And if it's
being king that worries you, abdicate! Pass the crown on to
whoever you choose. Such titles don't matter now!"

Mark was dumbfounded. "You talk as if it were *just* a title,"
he said quietly.

"The world has changed, father. Whether you like it or
not. Our responsibility now is to the future, not to family
heritage."

The silence stretched agonizingly, and Mark seemed to
shrink into himself. He became *smaller*.

It's killing him, Luke thought, feeling pity tinged with pride.
But he's accepted the truth.

Mark rose slowly from his chair.

"I'll go," he said in a small but steady voice. "Decide who
else is to come and we'll leave immediately."

Unable to face them any longer, Mark turned on his heel
and walked quickly from the hall.

After a moment, Fontaine hurried after him.

Chapter 31

When Ferragamo woke, he lay with his eyes closed, collecting his thoughts. The frenzy of his journey had left him, and had been replaced by a cold, implacable determination. He knew that Shalli had deliberately made him sleep, and he was grateful. He now felt rested and prepared, calmer than he had for months.

Koria's dead. He formed the words deliberately, forcing himself to accept them as the truth. *This will be for her.*

He had decided that the desperate plan, conceived in the aftermath of his lover's death, would still be carried out. His return to normality had done nothing to weaken his resolve.

At a word from Owl, he sat up and was greeted by a sight that was strange even to wizard's eyes. Shalli and Sweetness were deep in a silent conversation, obviously fascinated by each other. Only the dragon's head was inside the sleeping chamber, but the strange rock-light reflecting from his scales made him appear more solid than ever before.

As Ferragamo moved, the dragon turned to look at him. He had obviously learnt a good deal from Shalli but there were still questions in the glittering eyes, and Sweetness fidgeted impatiently.

"Our beyond-friend wishes your future thoughts," the hermit said. He smiled as he spoke, but Ferragamo felt an inexplicable reluctance to reveal his plans to this creature, and said nothing.

Shalli turned back to the dragon and after another silent exchange, Sweetness shook his head and looked again at Ferragamo.

"What is he? Where does he come from?" the wizard asked.

"Beyond," Shalli replied in a tone which meant there was absolutely no point in Ferragamo's asking "beyond what?"

"Have you told him what we're going to do?"

"What is future?" the hermit responded, shrugging. "Who tells?"

"I'll take that as a no," Ferragamo said, thankful for once for the hermit's obscure mode of speech. He turned to Sweetness. "Tell Yve that what will happen here is long overdue. If she—or anyone else—wants to help, that's good, but there's no point trying to stop me. Us," he amended, glancing at Shalli. "Tell Luke to consider the precedents," he added after a moment's silence.

His words only confused the dragon who, after another brief consultation with the hermit, withdrew. Shalli watched him go, his ancient eyes bright with excitement, then sat down cross-legged on the floor. From the voluminous furs that covered his body he produced the pouch containing the moonberries. Opening the drawstrings, he took out one of the fruit and offered it to Ferragamo.

Just like that? the wizard thought, then, *Why not?* and took the berry and put it in his mouth. He gently split the skin with his teeth, and sucked out the juices slowly, drop by drop. As he did so, a wave of potent warmth enveloped him, and a tingling rush of power spread throughout his body. For a moment, he felt light-headed, invincible, and wildly optimistic. Then he forced himself to control the process, to store the vast supplies of energy, channel it and keep his grim purpose clear and predominant.

Koria's dead, he reminded himself, and that was all he needed to stay sober and resolute. Even though she was no longer there, his love remained his shield and strength.

Shalli watched his companion intently, then, apparently satisfied, he took out another moonberry.

Too soon, Ferragamo thought. *I'm not ready yet.*

But the hermit had other plans. In the past, he had always refused to eat anything containing the fruit, claiming that he was "too white." As far as anyone could make out, this was a reference to a time, centuries earlier, when he had ingested a substantial quantity of the moonberry's essence. The process had forever isolated him from normal human contact.

Now Shalli put the berry in his mouth and bit down upon it as if it were no more potent than a grape. As the puissant juices filled his mouth, the hermit's eyes glowed and his body trembled, but he smiled broadly as if this were the greatest pleasure of his life.

Ferragamo looked on, amazed by his friend's constant ability to surprise. Shalli laughed, throwing his head back and cackling with glee.

About them, Atlanta, Kirt, and Owl added discordant voices.

By the time Mark and the others arrived at the cave, in the afternoon of the next day, most of the moonberries had been consumed. Neither Ferragamo nor Shalli had slept that night; indeed, neither was even aware of the passage of time.

As the weary horses were led up the final steep slope, the travelers were glad of the prospect of shelter and warmth. Their hurried departure from Starhill had left them ill-prepared for a night in the snow-covered highlands of the aptly named Windchill Mountains.

Nobody came out to greet them. Luke, who had become the group's effective leader, organized their arrival, stabling the horses and storing the few things they had brought with them. Cai and Yve went in search of Ferragamo, while Mark merely slumped down in the nearest available cavern. The ex-king was deeply depressed, and nothing could raise his spirits. He could not shake off the feeling that his abdication and retreat to the cave betrayed his island, his people and himself.

I see you're preparing to make your usual vital contribution to the proceedings.

Stop nagging me, Longfur! Mark snapped. *I'm here, aren't I?*

Yes. That's something. But everyone else is occupying themselves usefully, the cat replied, indicating the bustle in the main cavern.

My part has finished. Yours too, if you'd only admit it. There's nothing we can do to help them with the Rite. Mark's voice was sad and tired. *I wish it was over.*

For once, Longfur had no answer, and illogically, Mark felt

sorry that even the indomitable feline spirit was wilting with
his own. It was the first time he had ever won an argument
with his cat, and the victory gave him no pleasure.

I'm sorry, Longfur, he added softly.

We'll sleep, the cat replied a few moments later. *We may
need our strength tomorrow*. His tone made it clear that he
did not believe it.

Looking for her husband later that evening, Fontaine found
him asleep, with Longfur curled against his chest. The sight
took her back to earlier days, and brought a lump to her throat.
She watched them sadly for a while, then left them to the short
time of peace that remained.

Fontaine and Julia had been busy preparing accommoda-
tion for Keran and Tzigane, and had tried to keep the older
children out of trouble. Beca had taken Gemma under her
wing, and the two girls had gone exploring, with squeals of
delight marking their progress.

Fontaine's task was made difficult by Rivera. Exhausted by
constant travel, and traumatized by recent events, she was on
the point of collapse. Her voice was shrill and edged with panic,
and it was some time before she could be persuaded to accept
that the cave was a safe refuge. Eventually, she settled down
to rest.

By that time, Luke, assisted by the remaining members of
the party—Laurent, Jani, and Bram—and with advice from
Muscles, had arranged quarters for them all in the deeper
recesses of the labyrinthine cave. Although there were now
sixteen people and many animals in Shalli's home, they were
not at all cramped.

"You could get half an army in here," Bram remarked in
wonder.

"Yes," Luke agreed, smiling at his companion's amazement. "With water, food, warmth, and light all supplied." Then
he was serious again.

"The entrance," he said simply.

Laurent nodded. "We should be prepared," he said as they
walked back toward the open air. "There aren't many of us,
but it is a superb defensive position. We could—"

"Let's hope it doesn't come to that," Luke put in. "I wonder
how the wizards are faring."

They're having a party by the sound of it, Muscles remarked silently.

There was indeed a great deal of noise, even laughter,

coming from the cavern into which Cai and Yve had gone. The sight that greeted the newcomers when they first entered was a mixture of nightmare and farce.

Ferragamo and Shalli sat cross-legged on the floor, facing each other, both talking nonstop. Their expressions changed constantly. They looked serene, then anguished, beatific, then grotesque; their eyes glowed and sent beams of light flashing about the cavern. Their skin too was translucent, as though their entire bodies were made of light. Even their hair, Ferragamo's short and bristly, Shalli's long and wild, shone as if lit from within.

Between them lay the pouch containing the last of the moonberries, and about them the walls of the cave were an ever-changing swirl of color, striations varying in brightness and texture with every moment. The rock appeared to move at times, but within their respective niches the birds remained stable, only occasionally making small, agitated movements and adding their voices to the wizards' babble.

It took a great effort of will for Yve to make herself step forward into that maelstrom, even with Cai at her side. Neither was entirely sure that the rock underfoot would support them. Yet they had to try.

Some time passed before Shalli noticed them. He quietened slowly, and eventually drew a shuddering breath. Ferragamo took one of the remaining berries out of the bag and offered it to the hermit, who declined and indicated Yve and Cai.

Ferragamo looked round, his eyes flashing, and laughed. Holding the fruit in the palm of his hand, he asked "Want some?" then dissolved into a fresh bout of mirth. Shalli and the birds immediately joined in, and it was some moments before their inexplicable hilarity subsided. When silence fell at last, Yve was able to shake off the trance she had fallen into. The buildup of magical forces in the cave was overwhelming her, and she began to fear for her own sanity. She already had severe doubts about Ferragamo's.

"What are you doing?" she asked, even though the answer was obvious. The sound of her own voice was reassuring though, and it seemed to help Ferragamo regain his composure.

"Koria's dead," he stated, his face serious. The darkness beneath his humorous surface showed through.

"I know," Yve replied quietly. "I'm sorry."

"Is the dragon with you?" Ferragamo asked sharply.

"No," Yve said, taken aback. "He's outside, acting as lookout."

Ferragamo nodded, satisfied, then Shalli spoke for the first time.

"You come." He pointed a finger at the floor. "Help?"

"Yes," Cai said. "If we can."

"Good," Ferragamo said. "Sit down. The Rite is difficult, and needs a lot of preparation."

"A few words first?" Yve requested. "We need to let the others know what is happening."

"Who else is here?"

Yve told him.

"The Servants may be able to assist us. Who knows?" Ferragamo said. "And the power you two bring is certainly welcome, but the rest had better keep their distance." He laughed again. "We don't want any interruptions when we're playing with the end of the world, do we!"

Chapter 32

*T*wo days after Mark and his party had left Starhill, dawn broke over a still and quiet city.

Too quiet, Durc thought as he strained his eyes, trying to pick out any movement in the distance. Shill stood by his side on the battlements of the tower between Sea and Field Gates. As they gazed eastward in the slowly lightening gloom, waiting for the sun to rise, the Captain of the Castle Guard echoed his colleague's thoughts.

"They should have been here by now," Shill said. "From the reports we got, Grayrock was overrun the night before last."

"Perhaps they enjoy keeping us in suspense," Durc replied drily. "Not bad tactics when you have all the advantages, as they do."

"We're prepared for a siege of months, if necessary. One day's not going to make any difference."

"I doubt if many of us got much sleep this night," Durc said. "Which doesn't exactly help."

"True," Shill agreed sagely. "The waiting's always the hardest."

"You think so?" Durc said. "I'm in no hurry to face those fellows."

The sun peeked over the horizon, slanting a few rays between leaden gray clouds.

"Perhaps they'll get snowed in," Shill suggested, smiling.

"Perhaps I could blow the sun out like a candle," Durc replied.

The morning light revealed no sign of the invading army: no smoke from camp fires, no light glinting on armor or blades, no movement at all.

Starhill waited. Every citizen knew that their fate hung in the balance but few were willing to discuss it. They spent their time watching, preparing the defense of their homes as best they could, and making half-hearted attempts to continue with the routines of day-to-day life.

A few people chose to blot out the ominous future by blurring the present with drink, but there was little trouble. The city was ominously quiet.

By midmorning there was still no sign of the enemy. Tiny flakes of snow had begun to fall, but even so, visibility was still good enough to convince the lookouts that no attack was imminent.

Durc and Shill remained in the eastern tower, slapping their arms and blowing on their hands to try and combat the bitter cold. One of Shill's officers joined them.

"Our riders have just returned," he said, "with nothing to report."

"Thank you, Luca. What do you make of it?"

"I don't know, sir. Perhaps they're trying to move round to the north or south and hit us from an unexpected direction."

"But why?" Shill said. "They must know we'll be watching all possible approaches. They can't hide an army that size."

"Maybe they're holding off deliberately, hoping *we'll* go out to look for *them*," Luca suggested. "They can't fancy storming these walls, and in open field they would be impossible for us to defeat."

"Stars!" Durc exclaimed suddenly.

The soldiers looked at him.

"It's obvious! We can't see them coming because they're *not* coming!" Durc's weather-beaten face was creased in self-disgust. "They're on their way to the mountains. Luke was right. *We're* no threat to them—they could take Starhill any time they wanted. What they're worried about is Ferragamo and the Rite. *That's* where they're headed!"

The conviction in his voice silenced his audience for a few moments, then Durc went on. "We've got to warn them . . . help them—"

"Wait," Shill cut in. "This may be a trap. Once outside the city, we could walk into an ambush."

Their discussion went on for some time, and ended when Durc lost his temper.

"I'm not going to be party to this madness," he concluded icily. "I am leaving *now*. The longer we wait, the less chance there is of warning Ferragamo."

He strode away, leaving Shill and his officers shaken but resolved that the defense of Starhill was still their first priority.

As it happened, Durc was not alone when he left the city. Five others rode with him—Zunic, his oldest ally, and four other soldiers who had overheard and been convinced by his arguments. They rode quickly through the biting wind, keeping a watch on all sides.

By midafternoon they were in sight of the trail that led into the foothills. The snow had stopped and they continued riding, though their pace was slower now. In the fading light, they were still able to lead their mounts up the zigzag path of packed scree which led to the lower snow-fields. At last they reached the plateau, which was bathed in orange light from the sun low on the horizon. As they did so it was obvious that they came too late.

Far ahead of them, camp fires blinked and smoke rose; the gleam of metal flashed in the rays of the dying sun. One whole mountainside seemed to be crawling with soldiers.

"Damn!" Durc said in dismay. "Their front ranks must be at the cave by now."

"Even if they're not, we'd never overtake them," Zunic agreed grimly.

"Now what happens?" one of their companions asked.

Durc did not reply. He merely sighed, a long, drawn-out breath of despair.

The sun went out like a candle, and they were plunged into shuddering darkness.

Chapter 33

"You have more power than I'd supposed," Ferragamo said, looking at Cai. "That's good."

"It's not all my own doing," Cai replied. "Ever since Moroski . . ." His voice trailed away as he saw the pain on Ferragamo's face. The elder wizard did not like to recall the only sacrifice he had been unable to make for his love.

Koria's dead, Ferragamo reminded himself, using her as a touchstone in death as he had in life. The moment passed.

Cai and Yve had returned to the chamber where the light danced, and now all four sat on the floor, watched over by the birds and Cai's swarm. Luke and Julia had returned with them, and sat near the doorway. Muscles curled at their feet, his fur bristling, eyes flickering about the room.

I've reached the conclusion that there are a considerable number of bird-brains in here, the cat remarked.

Be quiet! This is important, Luke shot back.

That's what worries me, Muscles replied.

The scene before them was indeed bizarre, and Luke began to wonder if his father had been right in refusing to join them. On being woken, Mark had declared that his destiny—if one he had—was to fight, sword in hand if necessary, and that he would play no more part in the rituals of wizardry and Servants. Luke had been shocked by his father's attitude but saw the melancholy certainty beneath the weary surface, and so had not argued.

Ferragamo was speaking again now, his voice even and calm, though it was obvious that it cost him a considerable effort to keep it so.

"The calling itself is not difficult," he said. At this, Yve's eyebrows rose in surprise but she kept silent as Ferragamo went on.

"But controlling it afterward *will* be. The Earth-mind contains more power than we could comprehend. All we can hope to do is channel it, turn it to our purpose. To destroy Alzedo!" His face broke into an ugly mask of hate, a shocking contrast to his normal countenance. Small white sparks spat from his hair and fingernails.

Shalli moved a languid arm, and with a shudder, Ferragamo regained his composure. Then, with another sudden change of mood, he was laughing.

"You two had better eat some of these," he said, indicating the remaining moonberries. "Shalli and I have had quite enough." The hermit grinned back at him and rolled his eyes ridiculously.

Luke, looking on in an agony of uncertainty, remembered Cai's words: *Perhaps he needs to be mad.*

"Go on," Ferragamo urged. "They're rather good when you get used to them. Aren't they Luke?"

The prince was saved from having to answer by Cai.

"I don't think I'll ever get used to them. I've already got as much power as I can handle—these things would probably destroy whatever usefulness I have."

"Anchor," Shalli said, and they looked at him, puzzled. When he did not elaborate, Ferragamo prompted him.

"What?"

"Cai. Anchor," replied the hermit, as if this were perfectly self-explanatory. "Not white."

Julia spoke from the edge of the cavern.

"He's saying that Cai will act as an anchor for the rest of you, so he shouldn't eat any berries. I think."

Shalli nodded happily, then threw his head back and gave a long drawn-out howl, like a midnight wolf.

Ferragamo ignored him and said, "That's ridiculous. If this thing works, any power Cai has will be totally used up. And if it doesn't, nobody will care!"

"All the same," Cai decided, "I'd rather not."

"What about you, Yve?" Ferragamo said. "You're not going to hold back too, are you?"

Indecision showed plainly on Yve's face. She suspected that she knew more about the Rite than anyone present, and the thought of the vast amount of energy that the moonberries could bequeath her was tempting. But . . .

"I've never . . ." she stammered. "I don't know if . . . I need to be clear-headed." She looked at Cai, appealing for his support. "I won't take any now," she added finally. "Perhaps later."

"There may not be any left later," Ferragamo said jovially. He looked back to Shalli. "It's you and me, then. One more for luck?"

With that, he picked up a berry, tossed it into the air and, tipping his head back, caught it neatly in his open mouth.

———————

As dawn came to the mountains, it illuminated a beautiful scene. The first rays of the sun glittered on majestic, snow-covered peaks, and the sky turned the palest blue, unblemished by cloud. Outside the cave entrance, a small plateau of verdant green, kept unfrozen by the warm waters from within, shone like a jewel set in a sea of white.

Bram and Laurent stood there, dressed warmly against the bitter mountain cold. They were not unmoved by the natural beauty before them, but their main concern was to look for any signs of pursuit. Keen eyes scanned the horizon to the east, but nothing moved in that desolate world except the wind.

"How long do you think we have?" Bram asked.

"That depends on how soon they realize where we are," the Healdean replied.

Neither was sufficiently familiar with Ark's geography to speculate further and, in any case, there was no guarantee that the enemy forces would consider their small band worth hunting down. Both fervently hoped that they would not.

At length, satisfied that there was no immediate threat, they returned to the cave, threading their way through the hastily prepared defenses at its mouth. They joined Jani who sat, apparently quite relaxed, staring out over the valley below. Longfur lay at his feet beside carefully placed weapons. The cave's defenders were few in number, but they would not be an easy conquest.

Mark and Fontaine emerged from one of the smaller

caverns, hand in hand. Mark smiled sheepishly as the guards turned to look at them.

"Any sign?" he asked, rubbing sleep from his eyes.

"All clear," Bram replied.

"Shouldn't you be with the wizards, my lord?" Laurent suggested. "They thought the Servants would be important."

"Don't you start," Mark responded. "Luke was bad enough. And while we're about it, forget the titles. I am no longer a king, nor a Servant." His voice was weary but firm. "If I am to provide any further service, it'll be with this." He touched the pommel of the sword which hung from his belt.

"With luck it won't come to that," Bram said gruffly.

"I hope so," Fontaine added.

Me too, Longfur agreed in Mark's head. *From the look of you, she's worn you out already.*

The wizards and their onlookers had not moved all night; none had even thought of sleep.

Ferragamo continued to display a wild variety of moods, but despite this had been able to instruct them all in the procedures to be followed. Shalli occasionally put in a word or two, prompting his old friend in ways he alone could understand. Somewhat to Ferragamo's surprise, Yve had also contributed valuable knowledge to the discussion, and the older wizard soon began looking to her for confirmation.

Eventually, their arrangements were almost complete, and they grew quiet and solemn. Even the rock-light, marked by crystal formations and seams of mineral ores, settled to a steady glow. Luke and Julia looked on, aware of the knife-edged moment, but they felt remote, and excluded from the esoteric ritual. They had not been given any idea about what they were supposed to do, and were reluctant to disturb the participants' concentration at such a crucial moment. Hands clasped, they could only wait.

"There are two berries left," Ferragamo said quietly. "Do you want them?"

"No," Yve said.

"No," Cai echoed.

"We're ready then. Let us begin."

"But—" Yve said, bewildered.

"There is no more," Ferragamo said.

"But—" Yve tried again, but Shalli interrupted her.

"Daughter of time. Begin." The ancient hermit's voice was *full*. Full of emotion, of authority, certainty, perhaps even love. As he smiled at Yve, his expression was as open and as free of deceit as a child's; his eyes were windows looking out over centuries of life, long ages of knowledge. Gazing into their depths, Yve felt her own personality slip away. She no longer had the freedom to choose her own path, yet at the same time she felt the weight of responsibility lifted from her shoulders. In spite of her continued doubts and uncertainty, she knew she would obey Shalli's command.

With difficulty, Yve recognized the voice that spoke the first words of the Rite of Yzalba as her own. Others joined in, and the world ceased to exist. The floor on which she sat, Luke and Julia, the animals, the cave itself, the mountains, Ark, her faraway home of old; they were all gone. Only the voices remained, becoming one. Impersonal. Universal.

Yve let the sensation take her, as she knew she must, and felt it to be overwhelmingly familiar. This was comforting at first, but soon the visions came and with them, terror.

She witnessed scenes of appalling savagery: warriors being torn limb from limb by ravening beasts; unnatural creatures preying upon defenseless women, their tentacles probing and gouging; she saw sailors sucked down beneath the roaring waves of a gigantic whirlpool, crying pitifully for a savior; a giant rose before her, crushing mens' skulls with his bare hands; and a dragon's fiery breath turned a soldier's armor into a red-hot oven of torture.

Then, abruptly, she was free, floating high above the earth, immaterial. Only the voice followed her.

In the sky far away, two tiny specks appeared. They headed for her, growing larger. As they did so, Yve became a being ruled by fear. The creatures were still unrecognizable but she knew them to be the quintessence of all her childhood nightmares and adult terrors.

They grew larger, took on form, and still Yve could not move.

Beyond them, a dragon appeared, a rider on its massive neck.

"Yzalba!" Yve shouted, but knew she was not heard. "How does it end? We don't know how it ends!"

The distant dragon wheeled around, then dived into the unseen depths.

The creatures of nightmare grew larger still.

Sweetness, Yve pleaded. *Help me!*

It was Jani who saw the first sign of the enemy's approach. Raising a heavily muscled arm he pointed at the sky, but it was a few moments before the others saw the two birds.

"Eagles," said Bram. "They don't look right, though."

"They're not," Laurent said grimly. "They're deformed. There was only one in Ramsport, but I'd recognize that horrible shape anywhere. They're Alzedo's *pets*."

They watched in silence as the two enormous eagles approached. For all their awkward flight, they moved with great speed.

The repellent creatures flew past, fixing the cave entrance with baleful red eyes, and everyone instinctively cowered, shrinking from their malevolence. Then they flew eastward again, leaving only a shadow of fear behind.

"Was I seeing things, or was one of those monsters really transparent?" Bram asked.

"You're right," Fontaine said. "I thought it must be an illusion."

"What does it mean?" Laurent asked. "One half-seen creature is bad enough!"

They did not have long to speculate; within the hour they had other things to concern them.

Alzedo's army marched into the valley. Even at a distance of two leagues or more, it was clear that its numbers were vast. Yet that was not the most frightening aspect.

In the vanguard was a mass of uniform gray. No one had any doubt about the enemy they would soon be facing.

They're here, Sweetness reported, his voice tinged with fear.

I can see that, Yve replied, still lost in her horrific vision. *Where are you?*

She was desperate. The eagles, one of them flickering translucently, were drawing ever closer. Yve could see their bald heads, their cruel, beady eyes, their huge, ragged wings and razor talons.

Where are you, Sweetness?

The dragon did not answer directly. Instead, he began to recite:

> *From the sea, peril.*
> *From the sea, safety.*

Alarm bells rang in Yve's head; she felt a wave of nausea, and reeled with dizzyness.

> *From the past, the future.*
> *From the future, faith.*

The walls within Yve's mind began to crumble. *Adara*, she thought, yet it was Sweetness's voice that continued to prompt her subconscious. *Don't stop*, she urged. The dragon's reply confused her.

What? I wasn't talking to you.

There was a pause and Yve felt his disorientation. Then the verse continued.

> *Unseen wings shall find the source,*
> *And stand against the dread one's march.*

Yve almost cried out in joy and pain. The vital memories she had locked away beyond recall while incarcerated in Strallen were rising to the surface, released by her familiar's prompting and by her own need.

She opened her eyes, and the cave materialized about her. Ferragamo, Cai, and Shalli sat like statues, yet still their fourfold voice went on. Beyond them, Luke and Julia were transfixed, unable to comprehend the scene before them. Rocklight flashed and flickered.

> *The final act shall be the first.*
> *Beyond the hour, two isles are one.*

The voice was silent.

The earth trembled. Unimaginable forces gathered, waiting for release.

As the wizards came out of their trance, their eyes held an awful knowledge.

"What's wrong?" Cai whispered. "It's there. I can feel it. Why . . . ?"

"We've finished," Ferragamo breathed.

"We haven't!" Yve exclaimed. "We don't know how it ends. I tried—"

The earth shuddered.

"What have we done?" Ferragamo groaned, burying his head in his hands.

Only the ancient hermit had remained calm. Yve found Shalli's eyes upon her; without quite knowing why, she spoke aloud.

"A child, mage-born, and marked for flight,
Shall add her voice but utter naught."

"Tzigane?" Cai said. "Tzigane!"

Through the entrance to the cavern, a small bundle floated, wriggling as it approached. A covering dropped away and Tzigane's smiling face appeared.

Delighted by her new-found mobility, the baby laughed and waved her limbs until she came to the center of the cavern. There she floated, unsupported, a full pace above the floor. All eyes were upon her, and she delighted in the attention. As Tzigane chuckled, the refrain in Yve's head continued.

Daughter of time, her fate foretold,
Must heed the words of ages past.

Yve looked at Tzigane and saw a succession of other faces, so fast they became a blur. Adara was there, and Ciana, Koria, Fontaine, and Adesina, and many, many more.

Gather the kindred tied by love.

"Julia!" Yve shouted.

Luke glanced quickly at his wife but she had not been startled by the urgent summons. Her violet eyes glowed softly and her face was set, determined and sure.

"All of them?" she asked.

"Of course," Yve replied.

Darting a quick look at her husband, Julia fled the room, leaving Luke bewildered.

In a few moments, she returned with Beca and Rivera. The older woman was sobbing and walked unsteadily, so that the other two had to support her.

"I can't find Gemma," Julia said. "Luke, go and fetch your mother. We need her here."

At that instant, a full-throated battle cry sounded from the outer entrance to the cave.

"The Servants!"

Luke recognized his father's voice and ran. At the same

time, the swarm gathered and flew out into the main corridor, following it into the depths of the mountain.

Yve and Julia looked at each other, sharing a world of hope and dread.

As they waited, Owl, Atlanta, and Kirt left their perches and dived from the chamber, following Luke toward the open air.

They had been watching the approach of the gray wraiths for nearly two hours; Mark thought it was the longest two hours of his life. When the hostile army reached the foot of the slope, the promise of action was almost a relief. From the size of the enemy, the defenders felt that it would only be a matter of time before their small group was overrun, but they intended to sell their lives dearly.

Mark and his troops took full advantage of their position during the first phase of the fighting. Each was armed with a bow and all five sent a deadly rain of arrows at the approaching mass. Though this could not kill the wraiths, it slowed them down considerably, and as time went on their morbid regeneration became slower. However, so large were their numbers, that the time soon came when the bows had to be abandoned as useless.

For the wraiths were at last upon them, and the battle was hand to hand. Even so, the defenders still had a positional advantage, and they made the most of it. As Mark's sword claimed its first victim, he was filled with battle lust.

"The Servants!" he cried, and knew that his struggle was not over. Not yet.

Moments later, Luke replaced Fontaine at her position between Mark and Jani.

"Go to the wizards!" he shouted above the clamor of battle. "They need you!"

As Fontaine turned to go, casting one backward glance at her berserk husband, the three birds flew past her and into the cold mountain air.

Mark, Luke, Jani, Bram, and Laurent fought on doggedly, without real hope, but with an unreasoning stubborness. They took heart from the massive casualties they were inflicting and from the extraordinary fact that the wraiths felled by Mark's sword *did not* come back to life, but lay still, as dead and cold as any corpse.

The assault had slowed, but did not halt its remorseless progress. When Bram took a spear in his chest, they knew that it was an end they could all expect—and soon. Yet his comrade's death spurred Mark into even more furious action. He leapt forward, abandoning the protection of the fortifications, spreading a wall of death about him.

Above them, unnoticed, another battle raged. Owl, Atlanta, and Kirt had set their tiny beaks and talons against the hideous might of Alzedo's eagles, and had quickly found that one of their foes was totally invulnerable. He simply did not exist in their world, and any attack merely passed through his transparent body. Conversely, this eagle could do nothing to harm them.

With Sivadla, it was different. He was solid, flesh and blood, and his curved beak and huge talons made his assailants look ridiculous. Yet the little birds had speed and maneuverability on their side, and were at least able to distract the eagle and prevent him from attacking the cave. Indeed, they harried Sivadla so successfully that he grew wild and did not realize that he was being lured closer and closer to the cliff-face. Meanwhile, Atlanta's razor-talons made many small cuts in the eagle's neck and wings. In themselves they could do Sivadla little harm, but the stinging pain drove him wild.

At last, the birds chose their moment. Owl and Atlanta swooped beneath the eagle's wings from opposite sides, disrupting his flying stroke, while at the same time Kirt flapped and pecked about the fearful, snapping beak. Sivadla's dive became a death plunge as his crippled wings failed to save him from a collision with the jagged, icy cliff. His neck was broken and the huge, ungainly body flapped and fell lifelessly into the depths below. With him went two of his opponents, their deaths unnoticed except by the lone survivor.

The other eagle screamed with impotent rage.

Far below, the fight was nearly over. Both Luke and Laurent were too badly wounded to continue and only Mark and Jani struggled on, waiting for the inevitable. A slight lull gave them a temporary breathing space, but then a fresh wave of gray surged forward.

This is it, Mark thought, and raised his sword. Two wraiths were upon him. One he cut down, knowing as he did so that the other would end his own life. *We've had a good run,* he decided at the last moment, as he waited for the deathblow.

It never came.

Instead, the air about him teemed with fur and feather, claws and antlers, streaks of color—red, brown, white—and an unearthly howling. The animals of the mountain, so long the providers for Shalli, had come to protect him at the last. Foxes, lynx, stags, goats, buzzards—they were all present, biting, snarling, slashing, and kicking. Through a haze of blood and fatigue, Mark saw a bear lumbering amongst the enemy, clubbing them down with its huge paws. He and Jani stared in disbelief at the scene before them. Behind the two men, Longfur and Muscles greeted their brethren with outlandish calls of their own.

Then suddenly all was quiet.

Animals and wraiths melted away.

Alzedo himself paced slowly up the slope toward them, his colorless eyes blazing with hatred and anger.

For the second time that day, and now with complete certainty, Mark prepared to die.

"Where's Gemma?" Yve pleaded frantically.

"They can't find her," Cai said, and Rivera wailed.

"Tell them to split up," Yve said.

"I have," he replied. "I'm sure she'll be here soon."

"She must be. We need all the links in the chain."

Ferragamo looked up, first at Shalli, who was smiling benignly and taking no notice of the turmoil about him, then at Tzigane. The baby still wriggled in her midair cradle and seemed quite at ease. He turned to Yve.

"What's happening?" he asked. "Why—?"

The rock about them shook; far below, the mountain roared as if preparing to uproot itself.

Over the clamor, Yve said, "The kindred are gathering. Then we can complete the Rite." Her eyes gleamed in the pulsating light.

"Riddles," he replied as the earth shuddered again. "Whatever it is you're doing, do it quickly!"

As Yve nodded, Gemma came running into the cavern, surrounded by a cloud of bees. She fell, and Rivera screamed, but it was the trembling floor and ever-changing light which had caused her daughter to stumble. The girl looked at Cai.

"What's happening? I'm scared. Why is the floor shaking?"

She got no answer. Instead, Yve rapidly began to issue instructions.

"Gather round, all of you. Now! Quickly. We need your help. That's right. Beca, help Rivera. Fontaine here. Gemma behind Cai. *Quickly.*" The wizard pointed and beckoned as the women drew closer. "Julia, with me." The two friends smiled at each other.

"Watch Tzigane!"

They all obeyed, their eyes reflecting varying degrees of fear and fascination.

"Her mark's moving!" Gemma exclaimed. "It's flying."

Tzigane's mouth opened and she cried out in the voice of a falcon. From far away another bird answered her call, and she laughed.

Bid welcome and thus . . .

"It's ready. We need only invite—"

They all felt it then, in their different ways.

To Tzigane, it was one more new sensation in her young life, which she accepted without question. She felt herself cocooned in a warm darkness that fed and nurtured her, that sang with the steady rhythm of a mother's heartbeat.

To Rivera, it was both fear and longing, balanced by a feeling of rightness that dwarfed her conception of the world. It was so vast that she surrendered completely, becoming truly free for the first time in her life.

To Fontaine, it was confirmation and security; the knowledge of her link with history and of the many other women who had carried within them the future of the Servants, continuing the ages-old task which now—if ever—was to be completed.

To Beca, the images were of home and family, confused but comforting, extending far beyond the world she had known. She sensed the mighty purpose within those about her, and knew she would play her part.

To Gemma, it was as though her father had just folded her

in his strong arms. She felt safe, protected and invulnerable—
and something more. Possibilities she could not comprehend
flowered within her. She heard Cai's voice saying, *One day*,
and the bees humming in agreement.

To Julia, it was the rebirth of life, a stone tree bursting
forth into new growth. Being part of this company at this time
was the final justification of her existence, and she embraced
the moment with a sense of wonder and joy.

To Yve, at the center of the circle, it was the culmi-
nation of all her longings, all her suppressed desires. Her
vision was complete and within her Yzalba's voice whispered,
"Welcome."

The voice spoke then; the same voice, yet subtly changed.
It was one and it was seven. It was young and old, trusting
and afraid.

Each mouth, each tongue moved but only one word emerged.
"Welcome."

. . . *awake.*

The Earth awoke. Power beyond imagining flowed forth
into the kindred's circle.

Tzigane and the wizards became pure light.

Alzedo paused in his approach and screamed.

The sun was blotted out, plunging them into utter darkness.

Am I dead? Mark wondered.

A giant voice boomed from the void.

"You fools!" Alzedo roared. "You have destroyed your world!"

Chapter 34

*T*he dream had returned. Yve was still in the cave, standing within the ring of unmoving, staring women, yet part of her was already in the sky. She stooped to pick up the two remaining moonberries, and swallowed them.

Sweetness! I want to ride you now!

No sooner had she called than he was there, resplendent in his multi-hued coat and sinuous strength.

There haven't been any dragons for thousands of years— a thought from Yve's past.

He lowered his head and Yve climbed upon his neck.

We fly? he asked.

We fly.

They rose from the cave of light, passing through the mass of rock above as if through air, and burst forth into the darkening sky.

The bald eagle pounced immediately, sweeping down to tear at Yve with venomous talons, its red eyes glistening. The wizard ducked and Sweetness swerved to avoid the attack, forcing Yve to cling to him even more tightly.

As the deformed bird returned, Sweetness cried out.

Oga! Why are you doing this? He sounded young and very frightened.

My brother fell because of you, came the snarling reply. *You betrayed us. You betrayed your world.*

It was upon them again.

No! Sweetness screamed. His breath turned to flame, searing the sky with a burst of fierce orange. The eagle tried to stop its headlong plunge but could not. Fire licked at its wings, blackening its ragged plumage and filling the air with the stench of burning feathers. Flightless, it plunged toward the black earth far below.

Sweetness flew on upward and Yve surveyed the panorama that unfolded beneath them. Already the scenes of destruction were growing familiar. She could not bear to translate them into genuine experience for the people of the islands, and so closed her mind to all speculation and concentrated on her search. She soon found what she was looking for.

Down! she ordered, this time fully in control.

The volcano reached up to welcome them and Yve dived into its heart without fear, but knowing that she carried a great responsibility.

She and Sweetness passed through the nether-region between the worlds of Air and Earth and swam once more within the elements of the Earth-Mind. Coils of energy—released by the Rite—snaked past the wizard. Sensing its pattern, Yve followed it, gaining knowledge rapidly. She recognized its strengths and weaknesses; where chaos threatened and where stability still existed; and last of all she saw the sickness in places where infection had spread a cancer through the tissues of the earth. Once again, she tested her powers.

I am a healer, she thought.

Slowly, the energy that roiled about her began to respond to her prompting. Little by little she pushed and pulled, manipulating the awe-inspiring forces now at her disposal as if they really were her own modest skills.

Slowly, the Earth-patient responded to the wizard's treatment. Though the illness did not leave willingly, it was forced out—the evil suppurations cleansed, lanced, and cauterized by Yve's healing touch.

Satisfied at last that the Earth, though seriously weakened, would now recover fully, Yve ceased her toil and rested. A contented exhaustion enveloped her.

Beneath Yve, Sweetness flew, taking her ever onward. Beyond.

Mark awoke to find that night had come to the world—true night this time. He could see a few stars away to the east. In places the sky glowed red. As he forced himself to his feet, every muscle protesting at the movement, the earth beneath him shook. A distant rumble told of an avalanche.

Nearby, Jani got up slowly. He and Mark supported each other as they climbed over the fortifications, back into the cave. As they clambered in, the rock-light reappeared, casting weak shadows. Luke and Laurent lay within. Both were unconscious but still alive. As Mark touched his son's hand, Luke came to, pain scarring his return to the world.

"What happened?" he asked hoarsely.

"Alzedo's gone," Mark replied.

"Dead?"

"I hope so. At any rate, the wraiths are nowhere to be seen."

"Did they . . . ?" Luke began, trying to look into the cave. "Julia?"

"I don't know." To Jani, Mark indicated, "Stay here with him."

"No," Luke said. "I'm coming too."

He spoke with such determination that his father could not argue. Leaving Jani to look after Laurent, he helped his son into the cave, and they stumbled to the wizards' cavern, blood-streaked and bone-weary, arms about each other's shoulders. The rock-light here had returned to normal and the scene that greeted them was to remain with them forever.

In the center of the floor, Ferragamo, Shalli, and Cai lay still, unmoving. Fontaine was kneeling beside Ferragamo. When she looked up and saw her husband and son, her drawn face dissolved into tears of relief and sorrow. In the midst of the wizards lay a small bundle. It too was still.

Beyond them, Rivera lay in a dead faint. Beca was at her side, gently chafing her aunt's hand. Nearby, Gemma stood looking about her, wide-eyed and white-faced. Closest to the two men was Julia, and it was she who was first to react to their arrival. She was trembling, but the joy with which she greeted Luke overpowered all else within her. As she took him in her arms, settling him down and beginning to tend his wounds, Mark left his son's side and went to Fontaine.

"Are you all right?" he asked softly, kneeling to embrace her.

"Yes." Her voice shook but her meaning was clear. "Now that I've seen you."

"The others?" Mark glanced around.

"Ferragamo's dead. And Tzigane." Her eyes went briefly to the tiny bundle in their midst, then she took a deep breath and went on. "Cai's alive, but barely, and I think Shalli is too. I'm not sure, though. He's a strange one."

"Yve?"

"She's gone."

"Where?"

"With Sweetness. She was like him in the end. You could see right through them both."

"She rode on him!" Beca added breathlessly. "They went straight up through the roof."

Mark glanced upward, then at Fontaine, who nodded.

"The rest of us are all right, I think. Rivera fainted. What about you?"

"Bram's dead, and Laurent's lost a lot of blood. Jani's with him now. We've all got a few bruises, but they'll mend soon enough."

"The wraiths?"

"They've gone."

Fontaine sighed with relief, then started when a new voice sounded from the corridor.

"Hello?"

Durc appeared in the doorway, Keran asleep in his arms.

"I thought there was no one here but this little one," he said. "The world's gone mad out there."

"It's not been altogether sane in here," Fontaine replied wearily.

Chapter 35

*M*uch had changed in the aftermath of that fateful day. Three years had passed, and the world had regained stability, but the effects of the disruption were still being felt. As Cai explained to Gemma some time later, forces had been unleashed that day which were too strong for them to control.

"Like the sleeping giant?" she replied, referring to one of her favorite stories.

"Yes. But much bigger."

Gemma's eyes widened, then she nodded gravely.

"Much bigger," she repeated softly.

"That's why the world is different now. Yve made sure that all the bad things were destroyed, but lots of other things had to change too."

"Where did Yve and Sweetness go?"

"I don't know, Gemma."

"Are they happy?"

"I think so," Cai replied promptly, knowing that to hesitate would leave his adopted niece uncertain and unhappy. *I hope so,* he added to himself. *Wherever they are.*

Gemma looked at him closely, but was apparently satisfied by his answer.

"The mountains didn't change," she said after a moment.

"That's because you were there!" Cai replied with a measure of truth, wondering at the child's powers of observation.

For one so young, she doesn't miss much. The most obvious changes were geographical. Earthquakes and volcanic eruptions had obliterated some islands and built new ones elsewhere. The associated tidal waves had added to the destruction, wiping many seaports from the face of the earth. The sea itself claimed some land but was pushed back elsewhere. Mountains rose as others fell, although as Gemma had noted, the Windchill range was relatively unaltered; it had been the epicenter of the disruptive force.

Rivers changed course, towns were leveled and enormous forest fires added to the plumes of volcanic smoke and ash in the sky. The sun was not seen for many days, and the islands' survivors shivered in the coldest winter they had ever known.

The cartographers were only now beginning the massive task of mapping the world anew. Their progress had been slow, not least because almost all shipping had been destroyed by the cataclysm; it had been a long time before anyone had energy or time enough to rebuild a fleet. Eventually, a few bold spirits braved the uncertainty of the now uncharted seas, and contact between the islands was slowly being re-established. So much was unfamiliar to these courageous navigators that at first no one could make sense of any of their sightings and reports. However, certain facts did become clear.

One of the most dramatic was that Brogar, the lost island which had been the breeding ground for Alzedo's hellish evil, had vanished completely, destroyed by a huge volcano. Though they had not been aware of it at the time, it was this eruption which had blotted out the setting sun as Mark and Jani stood at the entrance to the cave, waiting to die.

No trace of the foul island was left. To the west was only sea, although there were to be persistent rumors in later years of a periodic, giant whirlpool where Brogar had once stood, which was to make sailing in that area hazardous.

The second major change to be confirmed was that Ark and Heald—if they could still be called by those names—were now one island. The straits that had once divided them had vanished, and had been replaced by a strange, eerie region. Few dared venture there for many months. Although rumors of unnatural creatures, mysterious vegetation, and alien landscapes played a part in this, the main reason was that people preferred to spend their time in trying to reconstruct their lives on land which was at least slightly familiar. Exploration was a low priority when the daily requirements of shelter, warmth, and food needed such strenuous effort.

Beyond these two discoveries, much was uncertain. Many new islands had apparently sprung into existence far to the south; there were reports that several of these were joined together, forming a landmass much larger than had previously existed in the known world.

Strallen still existed—though it too had changed dramatically—but nothing had been heard of the islands to the east or north other than a few distant sightings of what might have been smoke.

The cost in human life of the catastrophe had been enormous. Thousands of people had been killed, whole communities destroyed. The towns and cities had suffered most and the survivors now lived close to the land, returning to the rural origins of their ancestors. The cold and dark which followed the earthquakes had led to the death of many, but as the skies slowly cleared and spring arrived at last, those spared found they had considerable resources. The land provided enough to support the diminished population and, amazingly, a large number of animals, both wild and domestic, had survived. The patient work of rebuilding civilization began.

Starhill had not suffered as badly as some of the other great cities. The Wizard's Tower had fallen, destroying much of the castle, but the city's massive stone walls still stood. In spite of the chaos and collapsed buildings, the fires and floods, food shortages and epidemic illnesses which had to be overcome, the populace of Old Ark's capital could count themselves lucky. They at least had not fallen under Alzedo's despoiling influence and had only natural catastrophes to deal with before a semblance of normal life could be re-established. Cities on other islands had not been so fortunate. Waking from the nightmare forced upon them by the sorcerer's malice, they found themselves in a nightmare of reality—totally unprepared for the disruption and elemental violence that now faced them.

Their main consolation came in reports, slowly spreading far and wide, about Alzedo. The first to hear this tale were Mark and his friends in Shalli's cave. The narrator was Durc.

"We'd just arrived on the plateau, and could see the army ahead of us. That's a sight I'd like to forget as quickly as possible.

"A huge black cloud came up so fast that the sun was just

blotted out. I thought I'd gone blind! We had no idea what was happening. Then our eyes adjusted to the faint starlight—by that time the ground was shaking, and we could hear the sound of an avalanche in the distance. I think it must have hit the enemy, because they were in a worse mess than we were. We could hear them panicking from where we stood. They were running in all directions, crawling all over the valley like insane termites. Our horses were fretting and almost wild, but in the end they calmed down, and ran for us."

"That was a wild ride," Zunic said. He sat beside his captain. "How we stayed on, I'll never know."

"We came down the valley at a gallop," Durc said, taking up the story again. "The few men we saw fled from us as though from avenging furies, and then at last we came in sight of the cave."

"Getting the horses to stop was harder than riding them!" Zunic commented.

"What we saw when we *did* stop almost made us ride away again," Durc went on. "We'd seen several strange lights about us as we rode but hadn't been able to tell what they were. Now we got a closer look." He frowned, looking rather pale. "They were wraiths. At first they looked much like ordinary men, except for the gray light in their eyes, but they were staggering, howling in agony. They took no notice of us.

"As we watched, one of them gave an earsplitting scream and started to *glow*. He was tearing at his face. I could see it blacken and blister like a log on a fire, then he *exploded*, bursting into a ball of flame, sizzling and spitting. He screamed all the while." Durc swallowed and shut his eyes for a moment.

"When the flames went out there was nothing left. Then it began happening with another . . . and another . . . and *then* we saw Alzedo.

"He was standing with his back to us, arms akimbo, halfway up the slope to the cave. He stood so still in that black cape of his that we could hardly make him out. It was as if he'd taken root.

"Then the last wraith was gone, and he moved. The silver on him glittered. He said something, but I couldn't make it out—sounded like 'sivaddle ogre.' Just nonsense. What he said next was pretty clear, though."

"It practically deafened me," Zunic added.

"He shouted 'No!' then started a sort of dance. Very slowly. And there was a *glow* about him. Not like the wraiths—this was blue, and it flickered as he moved. It didn't last long. It seemed to be some sort of protection, a shield, and when it was gone . . ."

Durc paused. Those about him were perfectly silent, waiting for him to continue.

"He unclenched his hand slowly, and I could see that one of his fingers had become a long blade."

Laurent, guessing what was to come, shuddered.

"Gradually, as if he were being forced to do it, he brought his hand up in front of him. Then his whole body jerked violently and the tip of the blade burst out between his shoulder-blades. He'd driven it through his own heart!"

"But he didn't fall," Zunic told them. "Just stood there with blood pumping out."

"It wasn't ordinary blood, either," Durc went on. "It was red all right, but orange, like molten rock. It spat and sputtered, and flamed when it hit the ground.

"Then he wrenched the blade upward, and down—trying to cut himself in half. He was shouting again, pleading, but we couldn't make out the words. He had blood all over him and his cape was burning, but still he kept twisting the knife and screaming. In the end all we could see was the flames. His body seemed to have *melted*. By the time it was safe for us to get close, the only thing left was a black lump of what looked like sticky rock. It was too hot to touch—not that we wanted to. You'll be able to see it for yourselves in the morning."

If there is a morning, he thought, remembering the sudden darkness of the western sky.

The others were silent after Durc finished speaking. The gruesome tale had left them stunned and sickened and, though Alzedo's demise was a cause for comfort, the world outside still reeled. No one was in the mood for conversation.

During that night, both Cai and Shalli returned—briefly— to wakefulness. Cai was very weak, unable even to talk. They hid Tzigane's tiny body from his sight, careful not to cause him further distress. Shalli seemed to be faring better, but nobody could be quite sure as his speech was, as usual, almost unintelligible. He looked around and smiled, apparently seeing nothing untoward in the scenes about him, and showed no sign of grief at Ferragamo's death.

The rest spent the night as best they could. Wounds were tended, helped by the extra supplies brought by Durc and his men. Then Durc and Zunic stood guard while the others slept.

In the morning, those with any strength went to view Alzedo's ghastly remains. The black rock was rounded and reflected nothing of the small amount of light filtering through
the gray clouds above.

"It looks smaller," Zunic commented.

The ground still shook intermittently, so no one ventured
far that day. They could hear the sounds of avalanches, and
boulders crashing from the cliffs. Retreating to the comfortable
safety of the cave, they continued the slow process of recovery.

The next day was much the same, but Zunic remarked that
the black tombstone again appeared smaller than before. This
time the others agreed with him.

"It's sinking into the earth," Julia said. She spoke with
such certainty that no one argued, and she was proved right,
with less of the black boulder showing above the grass each
day. Eventually it disappeared completely—as if it had never
existed—leaving the sward unmarked.

"The earth has claimed its own," Julia stated.

"I'm glad I don't have to pay that sort of debt!" Durc added.

It was ten days before they felt fit and daring enough to
leave the cave and venture out into the new world. The earth
was still blanketed by dark clouds and the weather was bitterly
cold, but the earthquakes had abated and everyone was anxious
to see for themselves the state of their island homes. In the
years since, more than topography had changed. Most of those
who had been party to the fateful events in Shalli's cave now
lived in the re-emerging city of Starhill, and all were engaged
in the continuing work of reconstruction.

Luke and Julia had been pressed—much to their surprise—into accepting the responsibilities of leadership, as the
city and island recovered and began to feel the need of government. They accepted the task, throwing themselves into
the work gladly, but Luke refused to be crowned king. He
said that as his father had renounced the title, therefore he,
Luke, had no claim to it. When it was discovered that Ark and
Heald were now physically united, he proposed that he and
Julia should rule as regents, acting as guardians for Keran who,
on coming of age, would rule the joint lands. This idea was
readily accepted.

Rivera, with Gemma and Keran, also settled in Starhill; no
trace of Ansar was ever found. Years later, much to her children's pleasure, Rivera remarried and lived quietly and peacefully, well away from the bustle of the new court. Gemma

became the dear and constant companion of Cai, who also made his home in the city. The wizard was disturbed by strange dreams which he discussed only with her and, as she grew older, Gemma began to understand him more and more. He now only used magic for the purposes of healing—and then only when no simpler remedy was available. Magic was unnatural, almost painful to him now, and he refused to be called a wizard.

"Magic has ended," he said on more than one occasion. "It's dead. Look at the moonberry trees."

The tree in Starhill was indeed lifeless, long since shriveled up and decayed, and a similar report had been received from what had once been Heald.

It appeared to many that Cai was now a more sober, subdued character, and for much of the time this was true. The memory of Tzigane's brief life haunted him and he blamed himself for her death, despite all that others said to try and dissuade him. He had seen the darker side of the world, and its effects on him were obvious. However, there were still times—especially when he was alone with his protégé—when the carefree spirit of old reasserted itself. He no longer toyed with the affections of countless young women, but he had not forgotten how to enjoy himself.

For Gemma's tenth birthday he presented her with a giant kite. How he had managed to keep its manufacture a secret was a mystery—for it was huge, a crazy-looking construction of metal frame, ropes, and canvas. By strapping themselves into the specially fitted harness, Cai and Gemma were able to soar from the walls of the city, gliding over the heads of the astonished shepherds as they learned to play the subtle shifts of wind and air.

Their flights invariably ended with them rolling in a heap in one field or another but, despite Rivera's dire warnings and disapproving air, they suffered no injury—and the kite was easily mended. They felt that the danger was worth it for the sheer excitement of those shared aerial journeys, and shouted and laughed as they wheeled above the land like some outrageous bird of prey.

Cai did not spend all his time in the city. Every few months, like Ferragamo before him, he felt the need to visit Shalli in the mountain cave. The hermit still showed no signs of wanting to leave. The lopsided sea gull, Kirt, was now the old man's constant companion, but little else had changed.

Cai always went alone to the mountains and was more at ease when he returned.

Beca, who was fast becoming a beautiful young woman, commiserated with Gemma during one of his absences.

"What does he see in that old hermit?" she asked. "He was bizarre!"

"The animals like him," Gemma replied thoughtfully.

"That cave was fun!"

"Yes. I wish Cai would take me with him."

"Maybe he will one day," Beca said with an encouraging smile.

"I hope so. After all, we *are* going to be married once I'm old enough."

"You're a bit young to be talking of marriage aren't you, my lady?" Laurent suggested. He had approached unnoticed while the girls had been talking.

"It's not polite to eavesdrop on private conversations," Gemma said reprovingly. "And anyway, I'm nearly eleven."

"A thousand pardons," the courtier replied, bowing formally.

"I thought you'd gone to the south," Beca said.

"That was two months ago," Laurent responded. "Did you miss me so little?" His face was stricken, but his eyes smiled.

"Stop teasing my friend," Gemma ordered, "and tell us what you've been doing."

For the next hour, Laurent told them of his journey to the ruins of Ramsport, and his survey of the land which had once been Heald. He painted a sad picture but one not without hope. There, as on Ark, life was being restored.

Laurent was not the only explorer. Durc and Zunic had returned to their itinerant ways of old. They spent little time at their nominal homes in Starhill, preferring to indulge their taste for adventure in evermore ambitious voyages. Like his father before him, Luke had reason to be thankful for the services of the two ex-outlaws, and relied on them for much information about the world beyond his realm.

"Have you heard about their latest exploit?" Luke asked Julia as they relaxed in their bedchamber after an exhausting but rewarding day. Julia shook her head.

"They sailed north, trying to find Strock."

Julia stiffened at the mention of her old home-isle and Luke went on quickly.

"They never got there—a huge reef of coral barred the way. Nearly wrecked the ship, it seems. Then they saw giant turtles walking along the reef, and spent ages trying to catch one. All they succeeded in doing was scratching themselves badly and getting half-drowned. I wish I could have seen that." He chuckled. They lay in silence for a while.

"Tired?" he asked.

"Mmm."

"Want to go to sleep?"

"No," she replied softly, snuggling closer.

Well I do! commented a voice from under the bed. *Try not to make too much noise.*

Muscles, get out of here! they returned in unison.

Some people had not returned to Starhill. Ferragamo and Tzigane had been buried in the mountains and nobody was ever able to discover where Yve had gone. The other absentees were Mark and Fontaine. He had stuck to his decision to abdicate, wanting no more of public life. He knew that the fight with the wraiths had been his last act as a Servant; the age-old promise had been kept and he was now free. He asked no more than to be with Fontaine, to see his children occasionally—provided they came to him—and to live out the remainder of his life in peace and obscurity.

Together with Jani and Longfur, they had journeyed south, making for the place that had once been called Home. They found the village eventually, though it had changed almost beyond recognition. Home had once been a fishing village, its small harbor and stone jetty providing anchorage and shelter for brightly colored boats. Now, the nearest stretch of coastline was many leagues away and the jetty, which had survived the earthquakes, ran out over dry shingle and broken rocks. The cliffs to the south had crumbled in places and now looked out over the strange landscape which had once been the sea bed. The beach to the north of the village had gone completely.

Home itself had suffered badly in the upheaval, but its position—the harbor faced southeast—had saved it from the giant waves that had devastated so much to the west.

Most of the houses had been wrecked, and there were few families who had not lost at least one member of their households, but by the time Mark and Fontaine arrived the restoration process was well underway.

The newcomers were welcomed and helped to make their

home on the foundations of the Cottage, Ferragamo's old retreat. Mark took great pleasure in the ordinary tasks of car-
pentry and simple labor, learning diligently from the people
who had once been his subjects. They were given shelter by
the villagers in various homes until their own dwelling was
habitable, and repaid this hospitality with work, though nothing was asked of them. The people of Home had of necessity
changed their way of life—fishermen no longer—and there
was always much to do.

As the years passed, contact with the outside world was re-
established, and their farming skills grew, making life easier
for the people of Home. There was occasionally time for leisure
amid their toil and Mark was finally persuaded to talk about
the past. He had been reluctant to do so, fearful of reviving
too many painful memories, but Fontaine had bullied him into
a deep happiness, not allowing him to mope. Eventually he
found himself able to talk about Starhill, Ferragamo and Koria,
Shalli and the others without bitterness or pain. His tales were
soon much in demand at the Mermaid—which had been
rebuilt—and he began to enjoy his role as storyteller. His
audience listened raptly but Mark was never quite sure whether
they believed in the events he told them about, or just saw
them as fascinating stories, as the myths of old had been to
him. But he did not care; in telling the tales of his life and of
those once about him, he was setting the past in perspective,
exorcising demons.

I'm a farmer now, he reminded himself. *What do I know
of dragons, wizards, and kings?*

He was content.

For many months no one set foot on the land that had once
been beneath the sea. It was believed to be treacherous, with
shifting sands and unknown monsters. It was generally agreed
that the salt would make it infertile, and so few attempts were
made to use the land. Yet strange plants did grow there and
eventually curiosity overcame natural caution, and explorations
were made.

It was a landscape of decay and growth, of genuine danger
and a strange alien beauty, and it fascinated Mark, who made
an increasing number of forays into that unknown territory.
He always came back with some new find: a plant, a fossil, a

piece of the skeleton of an old sea-beast. He soon became quite an expert on these peculiar objects, which were regarded with suspicion by the former fishermen of Home. Gradually, however, his enterprise began to bring positive results. The old sea-bed *could* be farmed if the right crops were planted, and wild game was plentiful. Home expanded eastward.

Only one voice continued to complain about the sea's withdrawal—Longfur's. By feline standards, Mark's familiar was now ancient. He had outlived many of his descendants, his lifespan extended by the special nature of his link with Mark, but he showed no signs of submitting to old age. He was still active and, with Mark, Fontaine, and Jani all his willing slaves, he led a good life. But one thing bothered him.

Home is not what it used to be, he remarked as he sat with Mark on the old jetty, watching the villagers at work in the new fields.

Why? Mark asked, looking up from the notes he was making.

No fish, the cat replied. *All you catch now are old bones!*

There are fish in the stream.

Tiddlers! Longfur remarked contemptuously.

You're already too fat, Mark said, grinning but not looking at his outraged companion.

I will not dignify that with a response.

Anything for a quiet life, Mark teased.

You should know, Longfur shot back.

They stared at each other for a moment, then laughed.

We've earned a quiet life, don't you think? Mark said.

Perhaps. Longfur paused. *All in all, I think Muscles and I raised the two of you rather well. Of course, in Luke Muscles had better material to work with.*

Belying his age, Longfur easily avoided the friendly cuff Mark aimed at him.

You'll have to be quicker than that, he chided. *They don't call me Lightning Longfur for nothing.*

You mean you pay *them to be admiring?* Mark asked in mock astonishment.

I assume, Longfur replied loftily, *that that was intended to be what, for you, passes as a joke.*

Smiling, Mark went back to his notes, but Longfur had not finished. *And another thing*—he began, then halted abruptly, his eyes drawn to an attractive young female cat at the end of the jetty. Longfur's whiskers twitched.

Mark followed the direction of his gaze and laughed.

Really, Longfur! At your age!

Some of us, the cat replied, *are able to combine maturity and virility. Can I help it if humans can only display one or the other?* He stalked off, tail erect. *Watch*, he added. *You might learn something!*

Epilogue

From the sea, peril.
From the sea, safety.

From the past, the future.
From the future, faith.

Unseen wings shall find the source,
And stand against the dread one's march.
The final act shall be the first.
Beyond the hour, two isles are one.

A child, mage-born, and marked for flight,
Shall add her voice but utter naught.
Daughter of time, her fate foretold,
Must heed the words of ages past.
Gather the kindred tied by love,
Bid welcome, and thus . . . awake.

"*T*hat's him," Yve said to the little girl who held her hand.

The child nodded, but her expression was thoughtful.

"They can't see us or hear us, can they?" she said.

"No. This is their world, Tzigane. Not ours. We can only come here because of the gateway."

"The gateway that we made?"

"Yes."

"I helped, didn't I?" Tzigane said proudly, looking up at Yve.

"You were the most important part!"

Just in front of them, Cai and Shalli sat on the grass, peacefully gazing over the mountain valley. Kirt, limping on his shorter leg, strutted beside the two men. The sky above was blue and cloudless, and the midsummer sun beat down.

Quite a contrast to conditions when I was here last, Yve thought. She felt again a sharp pang of remorse as she remembered the death of Bram, her faithful companion. He had been killed defending her, yet she had been unaware of his demise until much later. She fervently hoped that whichever world he now inhabited Bram had found some measure of contentment.

"The white-haired one looks funny," Tzigane commented.

"He's very special."

"Why?"

"It's because of him that the gate is still here. He keeps it open for friends. Without Shalli, I couldn't have brought you here to see Cai."

"He's nice," Tzigane said, switching her attention to the young wizard. "I knew he would be."

"You and Cai were great friends when you were in his world," Yve said.

"Then why am I here with you?"

The child's question caused her guardian some uneasy heartache.

"You couldn't stay," she replied lamely.

"Why?"

"It was time for you to go."

"But I was only little."

"Yes," Yve agreed. "Most people have to wait much longer. But you were special."

Tzigane considered this.

"Does everyone come to our world in the end?" she asked eventually.

"No. It takes a very special kind of magic," the wizard replied, hoping that this answer would prove sufficient.

There was another long pause as Tzigane watched Cai, then she returned to her questions.

"Why didn't you bring me here before?"

This time Yve was able to reply with greater comfort and certainty.

"Because you were too small. You wouldn't have been able to ride Sweetness."

"*You* couldn't ride him once."

"That was different. He wasn't real then."

I most certainly was!

You know what I mean, Sweetness.

It was you *that wasn't real*, the dragon went on, determined to make his point.

Well, we're both real now, Yve returned firmly.

Tzigane looked back and forth between dragon and wizard, her expression implying that she thought them quite mad.

"Of course you're both real," she stated. "Don't be so silly."

"We were in different worlds once," Yve replied, then wished she hadn't as Tzigane looked puzzled.

"Then how did Sweetness get to you before the gateway?" she asked after a thoughtful pause.

"I had my own gateway," Yve answered, "but only Sweetness could use it."

Now we use Shalli's, the dragon added. *He was my friend. He understood before I did.*

"What's he talking about?" Tzigane asked.

Yve took a deep breath. *Will there ever be an end to her questions?* she wondered.

"Before we came to this world," Yve told the little girl, "there was an evil man who you helped to fight, even though you were only a baby. Bad people helped him trick Sweetness into letting him know our secrets."

"That was silly!" Tzigane said, turning to the dragon, who had abruptly lost all interest in the conversation.

"Sweetness was very young then—not much older than you are now, by dragon standards."

Tzigane was not impressed by this explanation, but said nothing.

"Besides," Yve went on, "Shalli knew that the evil man's tricks wouldn't work in the end. By tricking Sweetness, he let me know the most important thing about opening the gateway. His deceitfulness brought about his own downfall."

"So Sweetness was really a hero," the little girl concluded.

"Of course."

The dragon rapidly regained his interest in Yve's story, and his large head came down to nuzzle her neck.

"He's tickling you!" Tzigane exclaimed, delighted.

We must go soon, Sweetness said.

Yes, Yve replied. She had also been feeling the pull of their own world. "Come on," she said to the girl who had become the daughter she could never have. "Time to go home."

With several backward glances at Cai and Shalli, Tzigane was led back into the cave. There, she and Yve climbed upon Sweetness's neck and he took off, flying up through the stone gateway and into the sky *beyond*.

"I felt very odd earlier today," Cai remarked. "As if I were being watched." He and Shalli were back inside the hermit's cave, at ease, their evening meal completed.

"Mountain eyes, many eyes," Shalli responded, spreading his hands. "Unseen wings."

Kirt squawked in agreement.

"I don't doubt it," Cai laughed. The young wizard was relaxed—as he always was after just a few days in the mountain air. He had come to appreciate the cave and its eccentric inhabitant in much the same way that Ferragamo had done before him. It was a place of tranquillity once more, after the traumatic events of earlier years. And yet it held so many memories. As they sat together in companionable silence, Cai remembered some of those events, and soon felt the need to talk about them. Conversations with Shalli tended to be one-sided and rather confusing, but the hermit made a good listener.

"It's strange," Cai began. "Ferragamo and Koria were as inseparable as any pair could be. I always thought they'd find a way to stay together, even given the obvious discrepancy in their aging. It's so wrong that they died apart. They're not even buried together."

Cai was leaning back, his eyes on the ceiling, and he didn't notice Shalli's change of expression. The hermit's eyes reflected puzzlement, then understanding. He mumbled something, then pointed at the deepest recesses of the cavern, urging Cai to look.

Cai looked—and gasped.

The cave wall was still there, but the sea was inside it, waves rolling in upon a beach. Trees waved in the breeze, and a couple walked along the sand, arm in arm. As they came closer, Cai recognized them. Ferragamo looked the same as ever, with white hair bristling and his green eyes shining, but Koria was young—not a girl, but a woman in her prime, black hair blowing in the breeze, her face expressive as she talked. Together they laughed, looking into each other's eyes, then kissed.

They spoke again, laughing once more, but Cai could not hear them. His heart was nearly breaking at the sight of Koria as she had been before her illness, happy and energetic. Her cruel fate struck him more forcibly than ever.

"Why?" Cai asked, trying to hold back tears. "Why are you showing me this? I already have too many memories."

"Now," the hermit said. "*Now*. The other side."

Cai's attention was fixed on the vision of his former friends and Shalli's words did not register at first. When they did, he was filled with emotion.

"Now?"

"Now."

The realization grew within him, becoming a power that was Cai's own, yet was also beyond him, reaching out, connecting. He glanced at Shalli, but the hermit's smile remained as enigmatic as ever. Tears rolled down the wizard's cheeks as he turned and looked once more at the vision.

The sound of surf filled his ears. Then voices. Ferragamo and Koria were still talking.

"You disreputable old man!" Koria exclaimed amid giggles. She struggled half-heartedly to escape from his embrace.

"Less of the old," Ferragamo replied. "I can be whatever age I choose to be. And so can you."

"So you keep telling me."

The wizard's face grew serious.

"Losing you once was bad enough," he said. "I tried . . . I hoped . . . I knew it was possible and now that you *are* here, I won't ever let you go again. *I* make the rules here. How many times did I tell you that I would always love you? Well, I intend to do just that. You will not age unless you *want* to."

"For you," Kori replied, her whole being radiating happiness, "I'll accept this gift of magic."

"Not magic," Ferragamo replied. "Choice."

Is it possible? Cai thought, his heart full.

Ferragamo turned, and across the unimaginable gulf between the two worlds, their eyes met. Ferragamo smiled. And that was enough.